The Dead That Walk

The Dead That Walk
Zombie Stories

Edited with an Introduction by
Stephen Jones

Ulysses
Press

For full copyright information see pages ix–x.

Published in the United States by
Ulysses Press
P.O. Box 3440
Berkeley, CA 94703
www.ulyssespress.com

ISBN 978-1-56975-737-6
Library of Congress Control Number 2009936107

Acquisitions Editor: Keith Riegert
Managing Editor: Claire Chun
Editorial: Lauren Harrison
Production: Judith Metzener
Cover illustration: © 2010 Les Edwards
Design: what!design @ whatweb.com

Printed in Canada by Transcontinental Printing

10 9 8 7 6 5 4 3 2 1

Distributed by Publishers Group West

For
Richard Matheson
and
George A. Romero
fathers of the modern zombie

Contents

Acknowledgments

Special thanks to Keith Riegert, Dorothy Lumley, Val and Les Edwards, and Stefan Dziemianowicz; Steve Biodrowski (*Cinefantastique*), Paul M. Riordan (Syfy Network), and Ray Routhier (*Maine Sunday Telegram*) for the quotes by George A. Romero, Richard Matheson, and Stephen King; plus all the contributors, who came through when I needed them.

Introduction
Shoot 'em in the brain

Back in the 1990s, when vampire romance novels were booming (for the first time around), a writer friend of mine declared on a panel at a convention that, "vampires are the new *Star Trek*."

For those who are not aware of the context, *Star Trek* tie-in books were the biggest publishing franchise back then, but romantic novels with vampire protagonists were quickly eclipsing them on the bookshelves. Yet in the way of things, all such trends are cyclical, and as other genre tropes rose to prominence to replace them in the balance sheets of publishing houses, the undead were eventually consigned back to their coffins and crypts until it was their time to rise again halfway through the first decade of the 21st century.

For some years now, Byronic bloodsuckers (and the occasional love-struck lycanthrope) have dominated publishers' lists, but more recently something very strange seems to have happened. In 2003, Max Brooks (the son of comedian Mel and a writer for TV's *Saturday Night Live*) published an irreverent volume entitled *A Zombie Survival Guide*, which sold surprisingly well. Three years later, the same author released *World War Z: An Oral History of the Zombie War*, a serious horror novel depicting a worldwide zombie pandemic which quickly became a bestseller and cult favorite.

Almost overnight, that most gruesome of creatures—the walking dead—were suddenly a hot literary property! (And while we are on the subject, I just want to say that, on a personal note, "the walking dead" is always the correct description for zombies—not "the undead" nor "the living dead," which more traditionally are used to refer to the vampire. Trust me, these things matter to us monster fans.)

Soon other zombie volumes were clawing their way into the bookstores: David Wellington's apocalyptic novel *Monster Island*, which started out as an online serial, became the first of a trilogy that concluded with *Monster Nation* and *Monster Planet*, and even the world's most famous horror author, Stephen King, got in on the act with *Cell*, his 2006 novel about a cell phone virus that turned most of the world's population into homicidal zombies.

However, it was the publication of *Pride and Prejudice and Zombies*, a mash-up between author Seth Grahame-Smith and Jane Austen's literary classic in which the match-making Bennet sisters came from a family of zombie-slayers, that opened the floodgates and prompted no less an institution than the venerable *Time* magazine to declare in its April 9, 2009 issue that "Zombies Are the New Vampires."

As it turns out, when it comes to the pantheon of literary monsters, the zombie has only been around for less than eighty years.

The first popular reference to these resurrected corpses appeared in William Seabrook's 1929 travel guide *The Magic Island*, in which the author colorfully described voodoo rites on the West Indian island of Haiti, where the dead were reputedly revived as soulless slaves to work in the sugar cane fields.

Throughout the 1930s and '40s, the zombie was mostly restricted to the pages of such pulp publications as *Weird Tales* and other similar cheap magazines, or else exploited as a bug-eyed bogeyman in Hollywood "B" movies.

In fact, pretty much everything we know about zombies comes from the cinema.

The first zombie movie was *White Zombie* (1932)—an independently made production supposedly suggested by Seabrook's book and a forgotten Broadway play entitled *Zombie*—that starred an already-slumming Bela Lugosi just a year after his career-defining role in *Dracula*.

The same producers followed it up four years later with the even cheaper *Revolt of the Zombies*, which featured a regiment of invulnerable French-Cambodian soldiers, and it was not long before the resuscitated dead were turning up in such low-budget fare as *King of the Zombies* (1941), *Revenge of the Zombies* (1943), *Voodoo Man* (1944), and *Zombies on Broadway* (1945).

The one exception to these poverty-row programs was *I Walked with a Zombie* (1943), a darkly romantic Gothic made by Val Lewton's "B" movie unit at R.K.O. Radio Pictures which, like Seth Grahame-Smith's packaged pastiche more than six decades later, was actually a thinly-veiled reworking of a classic book—in this case Charlotte Brontë's *Jane Eyre*.

Although filmmakers continued to feature the walking dead in such pictures as *Zombies of Mora Tau* (1957), *Voodoo Island* (1957), *The Dead One* (1960), and *The Plague of the Zombies* (1966), it was George A. Romero's revisionist *Night of the Living Dead* (1968) that changed our perception of the reanimated dead forever with its grainy black and white images of corpses chowing down on the flesh of their victims.

But if Romero's grim gorefest and it's sequels, *Dawn of the Dead* (1978) and *Day of the Dead* (1988), set the standard for zombie cinema, then it was Italian director Lucio Fulci's quickie cash-in *Zombie* (a.k.a. *Zombie Flesh-Eaters*, 1979) which was much more influential in opening up the floodgates to an entire sub-genre of low-budget, gruesome zombie movies which continues to this day.

In 1989, "Splatterpunk" authors John Skipp and Craig Spector celebrated the twentieth anniversary of Romero's original film with *Book of the Dead*, an anthology of new zombie stories nominally inspired by *Night of the Living Dead* (and even featuring a foreword by the director himself). The editors followed it up three years later with *Still Dead: Book of the Dead II*, and soon the zombie anthology briefly flourished with such titles as Byron Preiss and John Betancourt's *The Ultimate Zombie* (1993) and my own *The Mammoth Book of Zombies* the same year.

Since then, zombies have remained with us in one form or another—whether in video games (*Resident Evil* and *Left 4 Dead*); comic books (*Marvel Zombies* and *The Walking Dead*); movies (*Shaun of the Dead* and *28 Days Later*); redundant remakes (*Dawn of the Dead* and *Day of the Dead*); direct-to-DVD releases (*Zombie Strippers* and *Flight of the Living Dead: Outbreak on a Plane*); made-for-TV films (*All Souls Day* and *Dead and Deader*); children's cartoons (*Scooby-Doo on Zombie Island* and *Zombie Hotel*); stage productions (*Night of the Living Dead* and *They're Not Zombies*), or anthologies (John Skipp's *Mondo Zombie* and John Joseph Adams' *The Living Dead*).

George Romero even expanded his Living Dead trilogy with two new entries, *Land of the Dead* (2005) and *Diary of the Dead* (2008), while October 26, 2008 was designated "World Zombie Day" to commemorate the 40th anniversary of the director's *Night of the Living Dead*. People dressed up as the walking dead in cities all over the world, with many using the event to raise money for charity.

It has only taken the unexpected success of Max Brooks' *World War Z* and Graham-Smith and Jane Austen's literary fix-up to propel the humble zombie to the top of the Monster-Most-Likely-to-Be-Exploited chart. In fact, it's already started: Joe Schreiber's *Death Troopers* is a zombie novel set in the Star Wars universe; the young adult market is jumping on the bandwagon with zombie books aimed at teenagers, and although it will always remain difficult for zombies to crossover into the romance market and usurp the vampire's position as unnatural love interest, I'm sure that there are numerous pseudonymous writers out there now trying to make rotting limbs and eating brains seem sexy.

Which brings us to the new anthology you hold in your hands. When I was approached initially by the publishers, I had my doubts. After all, I had already done my zombie anthology more than fifteen years ago (and it's still in print), and I wasn't sure that there was anything as an editor that I could bring to such a project.

But then I decided to view it as a challenge. Given the way in which the zombie is already being debased as an iconic monster figure—just as happened to the vampire and werewolf before him—could I assemble a book that reinstated the reanimated dead to their proper place in the horror hierarchy?

I therefore contacted a number of writers, both established and relatively new, and started about putting together a volume that was a mixture of reprints and originals that would showcase the zombie in its many and multifarious forms.

So although you will find the popular flesh-eating variety of the walking corpse ably represented within these pages, you will also discover more traditional voodoo zombies, scientifically created zombies, and magically revived zombies. There is a zombie Richard Nixon, a zombie guardian, a zombie Christmas present, and even a person playing a zombie in a George Romero movie. In short, there are all types of zombies—from the 19th century, through the Great Depression of the 1930s, up to the modern day.

So are zombies really the new vampires? I'm not so sure. But I do hope that if this anthology proves anything, it is that—as with their much-maligned bloodsucking kin—zombies are more than just shambling, flesh-eating ghouls. As with all the iconic monsters of fiction and film, in the capable hands of talented and inventive writers it is always possible to reinvent and revitalize the walking dead in new and entertaining ways.

As anybody with half a brain will tell you.

Stephen Jones
London, England
July 2009

Where There's a Will
Richard Matheson
& Richard Christian Matheson

Richard Matheson is a master of modern fantasy and horror, and Stephen King credits him with single-handedly regenerating a stagnant genre. In 1950 he sold his story "Born of Man and Woman" to *The Magazine of Fantasy and Science Fiction* on the first attempt, and it became the title of his debut collection (a.k.a. *Third from the Sun: Tales of Science Fiction and Fantasy*).

Having moved to California, he began to blur the boundaries between horror, fantasy, and science fiction with his hugely influential treatment of vampires and zombies, the 1954 novel *I Am Legend* (filmed four times).

"For me, zombies were the slave workers in *White Zombie* with Bela Lugosi," recalls *Night of the Living Dead* director George A. Romero. "I took the idea from Richard Matheson's novel *I Am Legend*—I ripped off the siege and the central idea, which I thought was so powerful—that this particular plague involved the entire planet. I also felt that, rather than opening with a *fait accompli*, as in the book, it might be more interesting to observe the world during its collapse, to watch the disintegration of the old guard as its downfall is brought about.

"But I didn't want to do vampires because he had already done vampires. So what could I do to make it my own? I made them flesh-eaters instead of blood-drinkers. But I never thought of them as zombies; I never called them zombies in *Night*. They were 'ghouls' or 'those things.' But it was never really about them. They were just the problem driving the characters—it could have been anything, like a Hitchcock MacGuffin."

"I have no opinion about George Romero's *Night of the Living Dead*," says Matheson. "I watched it one night on television, and thought to myself, Gee, that's awfully close to *I Am Legend*. He, I guess, prefers to believe that it's just a derivation, but it seems pretty close to me."

Matheson followed his first novel with *A Stir of Echoes* and numerous short stories (collected in *The Shores of Space* and four volumes of *Shock*). He scripted his Hugo Award–winning 1956 novel *The Shrinking Man* for the movies and worked for many years adapting his own and other authors' work for film and television.

Not only did he script fourteen episodes of Rod Serling's classic *The Twilight Zone*

TV series, but his produced screenplays include *The Fall of the House of Usher*, *Pit and the Pendulum*, *Master of the World*, *Night of the Eagle* (a.k.a. *Burn, Witch, Burn*), *Tales of Terror*, *The Raven*, *The Comedy of Terrors*, *Fanatic* (a.k.a. *Die! Die! My Darling!*), *The Devil Rides Out* (a.k.a. *The Devil's Bride*), *De Sade*, *Dracula*, *Trilogy of Terror* (with William F. Nolan), *Twilight Zone: The Movie*, *Jaws 3-D* and *Trilogy of Terror II* (with William F. Nolan and Dan Curtis), along with the two "Kolchak" TV movies, *The Night Stalker* and *The Night Strangler*, and various episodes of *Thriller*, *Star Trek*, *The Girl from U.N.C.L.E.*, and *Night Gallery*.

His later novels include *Hell House*, the World Fantasy Award–winning *Bid Time Return*, and *What Dreams May Come* (all filmed), *Earthbound* (as "Logan Swanson"), *7 Steps to Midnight*, *Now You See It . . .*, *Hunted Past Reason*, and *Come Fygures Come Shadowes*. More recent collections of his short fiction include *Richard Matheson: Collected Stories*, *Nightmare at 20,000 Feet*, *Duel: Terror Stories*, *Darker Places*, and *Button Button: Uncanny Stories*. *The Richard Matheson Companion* was compiled by Stanley Wiater and Matthew R. Bradley, while *He is Legend: An Anthology Celebrating Richard Matheson* is edited by Christopher Conlon.

He has received both the World Fantasy Award and the Horror Writers Association Bram Stoker Award for Life Achievement, the World Horror Convention's Living Legend Award, the Edgar Allan Poe Award, the Golden Spur Award, and the Writer's Guild Award.

Richard Christian Matheson is the son of the famed fantasy writer. He is an acclaimed short story writer, novelist, and TV and film writer and producer.

He has scripted and produced scores of network television series, ten features (including the subversive *Three O'Clock High*), three miniseries, and twenty comedy and dramatic pilots. Matheson has worked with Steven Spielberg, Bryan Singer, Joel Silver, Ivan Reitman, and Richard Donner.

His debut novel, *Created By*, was nominated for the Horror Writers Association Bram Stoker Award, and sixty of his published stories are collected in the critically hailed *Dystopia*. Stephen King has called his work "brilliant," and he is considered a cutting-edge voice in dark fiction. For the limited TNT series *Nightmares & Dreamscapes*, his adaptation of King's short story "Battleground" was called a "minor masterpiece" by the *New York Times*.

Matheson studied drums with the legendary Cream drummer, Ginger Baker, and plays drums for the blues/rock band Smash-Cut, in which he performs along with Preston Sturges, Jr. The band recently released their eponymous first album. He has also worked as a researcher at the UCLA Parapsychology Labs and continues to consult on cases.

"The legendary agent Kirby McCauley was editing a 'landmark' horror anthology, and my dad and I were invited to submit a collaborative story," explains the younger Matheson. "We talked over some ideas, settled on a man buried alive, needed a twist, found one, handed drafts back and forth to each other until we had something we liked.

"Writing the story together was a distinctively *Matheson* father/son experience—bonding meaningfully over a man trapped in a casket."

The collaboration that follows is a perfect example of a story written by two masters of the short, sharp, shock . . .

HE AWOKE.

It was dark and cold. Silent.

I'm thirsty, he thought. He yawned and sat up; fell back with a cry of pain. He'd hit his head on something. He rubbed at the pulsing tissue of his brow, feeling the ache spread back to his hairline.

Slowly, he began to sit up again but hit his head once more. He was jammed between the mattress and something overhead. He raised his hands to feel it. It was soft and pliable, its texture yielding beneath the push of his fingers. He felt along its surface. It extended as far as he could reach. He swallowed anxiously and shivered.

What in God's name was it?

He began to roll to his left and stopped with a gasp. The surface was blocking him there, as well. He reached to his right and his heart beat faster. It was on the other side, as well. He was surrounded on four sides. His heart compressed like a smashed soft-drink can, the blood spurting a hundred times faster.

Within seconds, he sensed that he was dressed. He felt trousers, a coat, a shirt and tie, a belt. There were shoes on his feet.

He slid his right hand to his trouser pocket and reached in. He palmed a cold, metal square and pulled his hand from the pocket, bringing it to his face. Fingers trembling, he hinged the top open and spun the wheel with his thumb. A few sparks glinted but no flame. Another turn and it lit.

He looked down at the orange cast of his body and shivered again. In the light of the flame, he could see all around himself.

He wanted to scream at what he saw.

He was in a casket.

He dropped the lighter and the flame striped the air with a yellow tracer before going out. He was in total darkness, once more. He could see nothing. All he heard was his terrified breathing as it lurched forward, jumping from his throat.

How long had he been here? Minutes? Hours?

Days?

His hopes lunged at the possibility of a nightmare; that he was only dreaming, his sleeping mind caught in some kind of twisted vision. But he knew it wasn't so. He knew, horribly enough, exactly what had happened.

They had put him in the one place he was terrified of. The one place he had made the fatal mistake of speaking about to them. They couldn't have selected a better torture. Not if they'd thought about it for a hundred years.

God, did they loathe him that much? To do *this* to him?

He started shaking helplessly, then caught himself. He wouldn't let them do it. Take his life and his business all at once? No, goddamn them, *no!*

He searched hurriedly for the lighter. That was their mistake, he thought. Stupid bastards. They'd probably thought it was a final, fitting irony: A gold-engraved thank you for making the corporation what it was. On the lighter were the words:

TO CHARLIE
WHERE THERE'S A WILL . . .

"Right" he muttered. He'd beat the lousy sons of bitches. They weren't going to murder him and steal the business he owned and built. There *was* a will.

His.

He closed his fingers around the lighter and, holding it with a white-knuckled fist, lifted it above the heaving of his chest. The wheel ground against the flint as he spun it back with his thumb. The flame caught and he quieted his breathing as he surveyed what space he had in the coffin.

Only inches on all four sides.

How much air could there be in so small a space he wondered? He clicked off the lighter. Don't burn it up, he told himself. Work in the dark.

Immediately, his hands shot up and he tried to push the lid up. He pressed as hard as he could, his forearms straining. The lid remained fixed. He closed both hands into tightly balled fists and pounded them against the lid until he was coated with perspiration, his hair moist.

He reached down to his left-trouser pocket and pulled out a chain with two keys attached. They had placed those with him, too. *Stupid bastards.* Did they really think he'd be so terrified he couldn't *think?* Another amusing joke on their part. A way to lock up his life completely. He wouldn't need the keys to his car and to the office again so why not put them in the casket with him?

Wrong, he thought. He *would* use them again.

Bringing the keys above his face, he began to pick at the lining with the sharp edge of one key. He tore through the threads and began to rip apart the lining. He pulled at it with his fingers until it popped free from its fastenings. Working quickly, he pulled the downy stuffing, tugging it free and placing it at his sides. He tried not to breathe too hard. The air had to be preserved.

He flicked on the lighter and looking at the cleared area, above, knocked against it with the knuckles of his free hand. He sighed with relief. It was oak not metal. Another mistake on their part. He smiled with contempt. It was easy to see why he had always been so far ahead of them.

"Stupid bastards," he muttered, as he stared at the thick wood. Gripping the keys together firmly, he began to dig their serrated edges against the oak. The flame of the lighter shook as he watched small pieces of the lid being chewed off by the gouging of the keys. Fragment after fragment fell. The lighter kept going out and he had to spin the flint over and over, repeating each move, until his hands felt numb. Fearing that he would use up the air, he turned the lighter off again, and continued to chisel at the wood, splinters of it falling on his neck and chin.

His arm began to ache.

He was losing strength. Wood no longer coming off as steadily. He laid the keys on his chest and flicked on the lighter again. He could see only a tattered path of wood where he had dug but it was only inches long. It's not enough, he thought. It's not enough.

He slumped and took a deep breath, stopping halfway through. The air was thinning. He reached up and pounded against the lid.

"Open this thing, goddammit," he shouted, the veins in his neck rising beneath the skin, "*Open this thing and let me out!*"

I'll die if I don't do something more, he thought.

They'll win.

His face began to tighten. He had never given up before. Never. And they weren't going to win. There was no way to stop him once he made up his mind.

He'd show those bastards what willpower was.

Quickly, he took the lighter in his right hand and turned the wheel several times. The flame rose like a streamer, fluttering back and forth before his eyes. Steadying his left arm with his right, he held the flame to the casket wood and began to scorch the ripped grain.

He breathed in short, shallow breaths, smelling the butane and wood odor as it filled the casket. The lid started to speckle with tiny sparks as he ran the flame along the gouge. He held it to one spot for several moments then slid it to another spot. The wood made faint crackling sounds.

Suddenly, a flame formed on the surface of the wood. He coughed as the burning oak began to produce grey pulpy smoke. The air in the casket continued to thin and he felt his lungs working harder. What air was available tasted like gummy smoke, as if he were lying in a horizontal smokestack. He felt as though he might faint and his body began to lose feeling.

Desperately, he struggled to remove his shirt, ripping several of the buttons off. He tore away part of the shirt and wrapped it around his right hand and wrist. A section of the lid was beginning to char and had become brittle. He slammed his swathed fist and forearm against the smoking wood and it crumbled down on him, glowing embers falling on his face and neck. His arms scrambled frantically to slap them out. Several burned his chest and palms and he cried out in pain.

Now a portion of the lid had become a glowing skeleton of wood, the heat radiating downward at his face. He squirmed away from it, turning his head to avoid the falling pieces of wood. The casket was filled with smoke and he could breathe only the choking, burning smell of it. He coughed his throat hot and raw. Fine-powder ash filled his mouth and nose as he pounded at the lid with his wrapped fist. Come on, he thought. Come on.

"Come on!" he screamed.

The section of lid gave suddenly and fell around him. He slapped at his face, neck and chest but the hot particles sizzled on his skin and he had to bear the pain as he tried to smother them.

The embers began to darken, one by one and now he smelled something new and strange. He searched for the lighter at his side, found it, and flicked it on.

He shuddered at what he saw.

Moist, root-laden soil packed firmly overhead.

Reaching up, he ran his fingers across it. In the flickering light, he saw burrowing insects and the whiteness of earthworms, dangling inches from his face. He drew down as far as he could, pulling his face from their wriggling movements.

Unexpectedly, one of the larva pulled free and dropped. It fell to his face and its jelly-like casing stuck to his upper lip. His mind erupted with revulsion and he thrust both hands upward, digging at the soil. He shook his head wildly as the larva were thrown off. He continued to dig, the dirt falling in on him. It poured into his nose and he could barely breathe. It stuck to his lips and slipped into his mouth. He closed his eyes tightly but could feel it clumping on the lids. He held his breath as he pistoned his hands upward and forward like a maniacal digging machine. He eased his body up, a little at a time, letting the dirt collect under him. His lungs were laboring, hungry for air. He didn't dare open his eyes. His fingers became raw from digging, nails bent backward on several fingers, breaking off. He couldn't even feel the pain or the running blood but knew the dirt was being stained by its flow. The pain in his arms and lungs grew worse with each passing second until shearing agony filled his body. He continued to press himself upward, pulling his feet and knees closer to his chest. He began to wrestle himself into a kind of spasmed crouch, hands above his head, upper arms gathered around his face. He clawed fiercely at the dirt which gave way with each shoveling gouge of his fingers. Keep going, he told himself. *Keep going.* He refused to lose control. Refused to stop and die in the earth. He bit down hard, his teeth nearly breaking from the tension of his jaws. *Keep going,* he thought. *Keep going!* He pushed up harder and harder, dirt cascading over his body, gathering in his hair and on his shoulders. Filth surrounded him. His lungs felt ready to burst. It seemed like minutes since he'd taken a breath. He wanted to scream from his need for air but couldn't. His fingernails began to sting and throb, exposed cuticles and nerves rubbing against the granules of dirt. His mouth opened in pain and was filled with dirt, covering his tongue and gathering in his throat. His gag reflex jumped and he began retching, vomit and dirt mixing as it exploded from his mouth. His head began to empty of life as he felt himself breathing in more dirt, dying of asphyxiation. The clogging dirt began to fill his air passages, the beat of his heart doubled. *I'm losing!* he thought in anguish.

Suddenly, one finger thrust up through the crust of earth. Unthinkingly, he moved his hand like a trowel and drove it through to the surface. Now, his arms went crazy, pulling and punching at the dirt until an opening expanded. He kept thrashing at the opening, his entire system glutted with dirt. His chest felt as if it would tear down the middle.

Then his arms were poking themselves out of the grave and within several seconds he had managed to pull his upper body from the ground. He kept pulling, hooking his shredded fingers into the earth and sliding his legs from the hole. They yanked out and he lay on the ground completely, trying to fill his lungs with gulps of air. But no air could get through the dirt which had collected in his windpipe and mouth. He writhed on the ground, turning on his back and side until he'd finally raised himself to a forward kneel and began hacking phlegm-covered mud from his air passages. Black saliva ran down his chin as he continued to throw up violently, dirt falling from his mouth to the ground. When most of it was out he began to gasp, as oxygen rushed into his body, cool air filling his body with life.

I've *won,* he thought. I've beaten the bastards, *beaten* them! He began to laugh in victorious rage until his eyes pried open and he looked around, rubbing at his blood-covered lids. He heard, the sound of traffic and blinding lights glared at him. They crisscrossed on his face, rushing at him from left and right. He winced, struck dumb by their glare, then realized where he was.

The cemetery by the highway.

Cars and trucks roared back and forth, tires humming. He breathed a sigh at being near life again; near movement and people. A grunting smile raised his lips.

Looking to his right, he saw a gas-station sign high on a metal pole several hundred yards up the highway.

Struggling to his feet, he ran.

As he did, he made a plan. He would go to the station, wash up in the rest room, then borrow a dime and call for a limo from the company to come and get him. No. Better a cab. That way he could fool those sons of bitches. Catch them by surprise. They undoubtedly assumed he was long gone by now. Well, he had beat them. He knew it as he picked up the pace of his run. Nobody could stop you when you really wanted something, he told himself, glancing back in the direction of the grave he had just escaped.

He ran into the station from the back and made his way to the bathroom. He didn't want anyone to see his dirtied, bloodied state.

There was a pay phone in the bathroom and he locked the door before plowing into his pocket for change. He found two pennies and a quarter and deposited the silver coin. They'd even provided him with money, he thought; the stupid bastards.

He dialed his wife.

She answered and screamed when he told her what had happened. She screamed and screamed. What a hideous joke she said. Whoever was doing this was making a hideous joke. She hung up before he could stop her. He dropped the phone and turned to face the bathroom mirror.

He couldn't even scream. He could only stare in silence.

Staring back at him was a face that was missing sections of flesh. Its skin was grey, and withered yellow bone showed through.

Then he remembered what else his wife had said and began to weep. His shock began to turn to hopeless fatalism.

It had been over seven months, she'd said.

Seven months.

He looked at himself in the mirror again, and realized there was nowhere he could go.

And, somehow all he could think about was the engraving on his lighter.

For the Good of All

Yvonne Navarro

Yvonne Navarro lives southern Arizona, where by day she works at historic Fort Huachuca and by night she chops her time into little pieces, dividing it among writing, dogs, birds, and family (not necessarily in that order).

She has written seven solo books, including the zombie novel *deadrush*, and such film tie-ins as *Ultraviolet*, *Elektra*, *Hellboy*, and seven novels in the Buffy the Vampire Slayer universe. Her fiction has won the HWA's Bram Stoker Award, plus a number of other writing awards. She is currently working on a new novel entitled *Highborn*.

"'For the Good of All' was written in the universe I created as a setting for a previously published story called 'Feeding the Dead Inside,'" Navarro explains.

"In this lovely little world, the walking dead are just another fact of life. You know about them, you deal with them, you adapt; life goes on . . . or maybe not. And you take whatever steps you deem necessary to wage your personal battle against them."

FIDA CAN HEAR THEIR MOANS through the floor.

The boarders are restless and hungry—they're always hungry—but there isn't much she can do about that.

Broxton House doesn't do bed and breakfast anymore, doesn't even rent to new boarders. Hell, nobody needs to rent now that a good seventy percent of the city population is gone. If a person wants to move, they move; all you need to do is make sure the new place is empty of both the living and the dead.

The law now says that if you live in it, you own it, period. Squatting is okay, taking it by force isn't. People work jobs just like before, but they make less money, and there's a clear division in classes.

Fida's in the lower class, and that's fine with her. She grows most of her own food and has learned to live without the electricity she can't afford anyway. There's a weekly flea market in the parking lot of the abandoned high school two suburbs over, nice and safe within a secure eight-foot iron fence. Someone with a sense of humor dubbed it the "Lock 'n' Swap" and the name stuck.

Fida goes over and does small sewing jobs. She picked up the talent from her grandmother (who died decades before this zombie mess), and it earns her money for firewood in the winter, candles, enough gasoline to go to a different church each Sunday, and the few other things she can't make on her own.

. . . . .

Fida is ready when the priest knocks on her door at a quarter-to-twelve, even though he's fifteen minutes early. She's glad he didn't forget or decide not to come, because when that happens—and it does occasionally—it always shakes up her faith. Faith is all she has, and she mustn't let it waver. Too much depends upon it.

"Good afternoon, Miss . . ." He falters for a moment because she never told him her last name.

"Just call me Fida," she tells him. "Long *e*, rhymes with Rita." She steps to the side and motions to him. "Please, come inside."

He nods, and Fida can see the relief in his eyes as he steps over the threshold. His car, a heavy sedan that, like almost everyone's, has mesh soldered over the windows, is parked at the curb. It had probably seemed like a very long way from the sidewalk to her door. No one without an armed escort wants to be outside too long nowadays.

Fida judiciously bolts the door, then leads him into the drawing room. "Make yourself comfortable." He obliges by settling on one of the two floral-printed couches and passing a white handkerchief across his forehead. It's impossible to tell if it's the June heat or fear that makes him sweat. Some people just do.

She's made a simple lunch, homemade flat bread baked pizza-style over a grating in the fireplace of the old-fashioned kitchen, then topped with a sliced tomato and green pepper from her little greenhouse (she's privately called it the "Lock 'n' Grow" since hearing the nickname of the swap meet). She hasn't had mozzarella cheese in years, but a sprinkling of dry Parmesan before it goes over the heat works well. She serves it to him along with a glass of room-temperature water freshened by a small sprig of mint. A good man should have a good meal before he gets on about his business. A man such as Father Stane.

They eat without saying much of anything. After about ten minutes, Fida can see the priest finally relaxing. Even though she's herded the boarders to the far end of the house, they have a tendency to fight amongst themselves and now and then one of them gets loud.

Occasionally a snarl sails along the upstairs air currents and drifts through the unused heating vents. The first time this happens, Father Stane visibly twitches; when all Fida does is meet his gaze and shrug, he appears to accept that she has made her home safe. The next couple of noises make him raise an eyebrow, but his deep brown eyes are wise and he knows that the time for discussion isn't long in coming.

She can tell by his black hair and heavy bone structure that he is perhaps Slavic or Serbian. A man from the old country, where the faith is ancient and strong. Excellent.

Fida sets the dishes aside and folds her hands on her lap. "I appreciate you coming all this way," she says. "I know it's troublesome to travel alone."

Father Stane tilts his head. "Indeed. You said there was something important you wanted to discuss?"

Fida nods, then picks at the rough edges of her fingernails as she considers the phrasing of her question. "Father, do you believe in forgiveness?"

"Of course," he answers without hesitation. "Forgiveness is the core of our faith. Christ died for us, so that we would all be redeemed." He studies her. "You attended my mass last Sunday, but I won't presume you're Christian."

"I'm Catholic."

"But do you believe? These are difficult times, Fida. Even the strongest man or woman of faith can stumble."

"I do believe, very strongly."

He nods. "Then what is it you wanted to discuss?"

Fida takes a deep breath. "Do you believe in redemption? That souls can be saved?"

"Of course," he says again. He leans forward. "Do you need to make a confession? Is that why you asked me to come here—for privacy?" She shakes her head, but he continues anyway. "These are terrible times, Fida. A lot of people have done . . . questionable things, just to stay alive." He reaches over and gives her a paternal pat on the hand. "Many don't want to be public about it. They feel hypocritical. I understand."

Hypocritical . . . like Jesus and the Pharisees and scribes? No, she does not equate herself with them. "I only try to save people," she replies, and both of them look toward the ceiling at the sound of a faraway thump.

Father Stane sits back. "Ah," he says. "You have . . ." He hesitates, unsure of his terminology.

"Boarders," Fida answers for him. "They all lived here . . ." Another pause. "Before."

The priest's forehead furrows. "They came back?"

She nods. "They came *home*. I don't believe that the living dead are just monsters, creatures without thought or purpose. They have memory. They seek comfort." Her hands are squeezing tightly together now, almost in supplication. "They didn't ask for this. They want to be rescued, to be *saved*."

Father Stane rubs his chin. "Have you considered that their return might just be instinct? There have been studies—"

Fida waves away his words. "You mean the experiment labs, where they're dissected like lab rats, treated with chemicals and used as targets for the security forces to try out their latest and greatest weapons?" Heat climbs up her face. "And let's not forget that the science centers are the perfect place for people to drop off their relatives—parents, spouses, *children*, for God's sake—then walk away with a clean conscience, saying that what they're doing is for the good of all.

"You mentioned hypocrites? *Those* are the hypocrites, Father Stane. Those are the monsters. The ones who won't take responsibility for people they once loved." She crosses her arms so tightly that the muscles in her shoulders spasm. "So much for *until death do us part*. The living dead, Father Stane. The *living* dead."

He takes a drink of water and puts it back on the coffee table, carefully centering it on a coaster. "All right. Let's say they are still alive, after a fashion. Then what?"

"They need to be *saved*," she tells him firmly. "Forgiven, like Jesus forgave us all at the Last Supper. It was his body and blood—"

"Metaphorically," the priest reminds her.

"Obviously, Father. I was about to say 'via the bread and wine.'" Fida squashes her irritation, then picks up again. "That's how mankind was forgiven, through his love and sacrifice. That's how we continue to be forgiven." She rises and crosses the drawing room, lifts a photo album from a mahogany side-table next to the fireplace. She brings it back and opens it in front of Father Stane, pointing to the pictures.

"This is Patrick. A good Irish boy, first room at the top of the stairs. He's been out of work so he's a bit behind on his rent." She flips the page. "This is Manuella. She lives . . . *lived* here with her boy, Reynaldo, in the biggest room at the back. Reynaldo's gone, though. He was only six."

Father Stane nods his head sympathetically. She taps a fingernail against a picture of a sallow-skinned Asian man; his eyes are thin and mean and a gang tattoo curves around the back of his bald skull. "This is Cade. I have to admit that he tries my patience sometimes." She lifts her chin. "Still, I have hope."

"I see."

"Do you?" Her eyes burn as she flips a couple more pages, locking her voice, determined not to show too much emotion. "Jesse and Tina. They're only sixteen. She's four months pregnant and they're hiding from her father, who told her he was going to kill Jesse." Another turn of the page. "Max is a heroin addict, always trying to kick the habit and always blowing it. He's come back here four times because he knows I'll help him keep on trying. And the last one is Sylvie. She's thirteen and a runaway."

Father Stane frowns at her. "You let a thirteen-year-old runaway stay here?"

Fida's gaze doesn't waver. "Her mother turned her out as a prostitute when she was eleven."

The priest's jaw works but he says nothing as Fida puts the album back in its place. "These are my tenants, Father."

"You talk about them as if things never changed."

"I don't think they have, at least not to them. In their minds, they're just lost." She sits back down and clasps her hands again. "Don't you see? These are *my* family. My responsibility. If I don't care for them, don't keep them safe and try to save them, then *I* will be a hypocrite. No better than so many others."

Father Stane nods and, to his credit, she can see him struggling to comprehend her way of thinking. "So why did you call me here, Fida? What can I do to help you with this situation?"

He stumbles a bit on the word *situation* and Fida's stomach twists inside. Does he believe, truly? His faith must be complete. It must be pure. If it isn't, he might as well go on home now.

"Will you do something for me, Father?" On the other end of the couch is a large wicker basket covered with a simple, clean white cloth. She pulls the basket to her side and lifts the cotton; beneath is more freshly baked flatbread, five good loaves of it, and a round crystal decanter of dark red wine. "Bless this bread and wine," she says. "Consecrate it with all your faith and everything you believe in. Like you do the Eucharist at mass."

"And then what?" he asks sternly. His gaze rolls upward. "You feed it to them? There is no forgiveness without confession. You know that."

She shakes her head. "But we have to *try*. The body of Christ, the blood of Christ. Miracles *have* happened. That the dead can walk is in itself a miracle, don't you think? Who's to say that a—a *reverse* miracle can't occur?"

"And if it doesn't? Will you be the one to stop them?" He glances pointedly at the machete hanging at her belt.

Fida looks at her hands. Sometimes she feels so much sadness she can hardly speak the words. "To kill out of judgment is not my place." He doesn't reply and she turns her hands palm up. "It's a small thing that I'm asking, Father. A sacrifice of symbology. A spreading of the Word, the faith, the Sacrament."

"All right," he says after a few moments, but he sounds tired. Is he doing it because he wants to, or because he feels it's what will be necessary for him to leave and feel as if he's done his best?

He reaches for the basket but she stands and lifts it with her. "Upstairs," she says. "In Patrick's room. They're all down at the end, where Manuella stays." She doesn't add that the Mexican woman, whose skin and eyes have gone as grey as old cement and whose mouth is rimmed with the dried blood of her son, spends most of every day moaning and standing over the daybed where the boy used to sleep.

Fida can tell by the expression on Father Stane's sturdy face that he wants to protest, but he doesn't. This gives her reason to hope; a faithless man would have refused, would have asked how dangerous it was and was she sure that the creatures were safely locked away. But Father Stane is a good man. A faithful man.

.   .   .   .   .

He follows her up the stairs and she hands him the basket, then opens the door to Patrick's room. The priest pulls back but the room is empty, the door that joins it to Jesse's closed. The bed is rumpled, as if the boy has slept in it, but she knows it isn't so. She makes it up every morning, even changes the sheets once a week, but the boarders only bump against it, or sometimes fall onto the antique quilt. They never sleep, though, just get up and wander away. There are no mirrors in this room because the living dead version of Patrick doesn't like his reflection and he always breaks them.

Fida takes the basket back and walks inside, then sets it on the dresser across from the door. She lifts the cloth reverently and stares at the contents for several seconds without saying anything, then backs away and looks at the priest. "Will you bless it now?" she asks.

Father Shane clears his throat. "Yes." He takes his place in front of the dresser, bows his head and begins to pray, and Fida relaxes a little as the familiar words coat the air with promises of holiness.

"On the night he was betrayed, he took bread and gave you thanks and praise. He broke the bread, gave it to his disciples, and said, take this, all of you, and eat it: this is my body which will be given up for you." Father Shane holds up one of the loaves and breaks it into two. She smiles and nods when he glances at her, then says in a soft voice. "I'll be right back. I have to get my crucifix. Don't stop."

She feels his gaze as she slips out of the room, but when she leaves the door open, his voice resumes and she hears more confidence in it. Excellent.

"When supper was ended, he took the cup. Again he gave you thanks and praise, gave the cup to his disciples, and said, take this, all of you, and drink from it: this is the cup of my blood, the blood of the new and everlasting covenant. It will be shed for you and for all men so that sins may be forgiven. Do this in memory of me."

He has spoken only a few words by the time Fida gets to the end of the hallway and Manuella's door. She bends and sweeps aside the soiled clothing that has kept the living dead clustered there all day, then walks quickly back to Patrick's room. She knows just where to step so the floor doesn't creak—along the edges of the baseboards where the nails are strong and the old oak boards haven't sagged in the middle. As she silently reaches out, pulls the door shut and bolts it, she hears another part of the mass in her head—the words that are always said in preparation of the altar and the gifts. They are out of order, but there is nothing more appropriate.

May the Lord accept the sacrifice at your hands, for the praise and glory of his name, for our good, and the good of all . . .

It takes only about thirty seconds for her boarders, her *family*, to lurch down to Patrick's room, where the final door that separates them from Father Stane is not locked. A few seconds later, the priest begins to scream.

Fida sits on the hallway floor and stares at the crucifix she took off the wall down by Manuella's room, discouragement leaving yet another bitter taste in her mouth. She was wrong about Father Stane—his faith had *not* been strong enough, he hadn't been truly sacred and believing in the body and soul of Christ. If he had, he would have been spared, and her loved ones would have eaten the blessed bread and wine, and they would have been cured.

She'll just have to try again. There is another Catholic church, Saint Benedictine, about five miles away, and she can drive Father Shane's car there next Sunday.

After mass she will ask one of the priests to come to her home and speak to her in confidence. These days, the priests are always out in the community, ministering and spreading the word of God for the good of all.

No one thinks twice when they don't come back.

THE THINGS HE SAID
Michael Marshall Smith

Michael Marshall Smith is a novelist and screenwriter. He had already established a critically acclaimed career under this name—including more than sixty published short stories and the novels *Only Forward*, *Spares*, and *One of Us*, two of which were optioned by major Hollywood studios—before starting to write thrillers under the name Michael Marshall. These include The Straw Men series, *The Intruders*, and *Bad Things*, all of which have been international bestsellers.

He has won the Philip K. Dick and International Horror Guild awards, has been nominated for the Crime Writers Association Silver Dagger and is a five-time winner of the British Fantasy Award.

The author is currently starting work on his tenth novel and is involved in television and film adaptations of his own work for networks including the BBC and ITV.

He lives in London with his wife, Paula, their son, and two cats.

"'The Things He Said' came about from a very simple idea," Smith explains, "which is that the end of the world as we know it might not come as either a big change to some people, nor even be seen as a bad thing.

"We spend so much of our time—egged on by the media—focusing on the Next Big Thing, the Oncoming Big Disaster. But the truth of the matter is that in our heart of hearts, where we really live, the biggest and most destructive events of our lives may already have happened."

MY FATHER SAID SOMETHING to me this one time. In fact he said a lot of thing to me, over the years, and many of them weren't what you'd call helpful, or polite— or loving, come to that. But in the last couple months I've found myself thinking back over a lot of them, and often find they had a grain of truth. I consider what he said in the new light of things, and move on, and then they're done. This one thing, though, has kept coming back to me. It's not very original, but I can't help that. He was not an especially original man.

What he said was, you had to take care of yourself, first and foremost and always, because there wasn't no-one else in the world who was going to do it for you. Look after Number One, was how he put it.

About this he was absolutely right. Of that I have no doubt.

.   .   .   .   .

I start every day to a schedule. Live the whole day by it, actually. I don't know if it makes much difference in the wider scheme of things, but having a set of tasks certainly helps the day kick off more positively. It gets you over that hump.

I wake around 6:00 a.m., or a little earlier. So far that has meant the dawn has either been here, or coming. As the weeks go by it will mean a period of darkness after waking, a time spent waiting in the cabin. It will not make a great deal of difference apart from that.

I wash with the can of water I set aside the night before, and eat whatever I put next to it. The washing is not strictly necessary but, again, I have always found it a good way to greet the day. You wash after a period of work, after all, and what else is a night of sleep, if not work, or a journey at least?

You wash, and the day starts, a day marked off from what has gone before. In the meantime I have another can of water heating over a fire. The chimney is blocked up and the doors and windows are sealed overnight against the cold, so the fire must of necessity be small. That's fine—all I need is to make enough water for a cup of coffee.

I take this with me when I open the cabin and step outside, which will generally be at about 6:20 a.m. I live within an area that is in the shade of mountains, and largely forested. Though the cabin itself is obscured by trees, from my door I have a good view down over the ten or so acres between it and the next thicker stretch of woods. I tend to sit there on the stoop a couple minutes, sipping my coffee, looking around. You can't always see what you're looking for, though, which is why I do what I do next.

I leave the door open behind me and walk a distance which is about three hundred yards in length—I measured it with strides when I set it up—made of four unequal sides. This contains the cabin and my shed, and a few trees, and is bounded by wires. I call them wires, but really they're lengths of fishing line, connected between a series of trees. The fact that I'm there checking them, on schedule, means they're very likely to be in place, but I check them anyway. First, to make sure none of them need re-fixing because of wind—but also that there's no sign something came close without actually tripping them.

I walk them all slowly, looking carefully at where they're attached to the trees, and checking the ground on the other side for signs anything got that far, and then stopped—either by accident or because they saw the wires. This is a good, slow, task for that time in the morning, wakes you up nice and easy. I once met a woman who'd been in therapy—hired a vacation cottage over near Elum for half a summer, a long time ago this was—and it seemed like the big thing she'd learned was to ignore everything she thought in the first hour of the day. That's when the negative stuff will try to bring you down, she said, and she was right about that, if not much else. You come back from the night with your head and soul empty, and bad things try to fill you up. There's a lot to get exercised about, if you let it. But if you've got a task, something to fill your head and move your limbs, by the time you've finished it the day has begun and you're onto the next thing. You're over that hump, like I said.

When that job's finished, I go back to the cabin and have the second cup of coffee, which I keep kind-of warm by laying my breakfast plate over the top of the mug while I'm outside. I'll have put the fire out before checking the wires, so there's no more hot water for the moment. I used to have one of those vacuum flasks and that was great, but it got broken. I'm on the lookout for a replacement. No luck yet. The colder it gets, the more that's going to become a real priority.

I'll drink this second cup planning what I'm going to do that day. I could do this the night before, but usually I don't. It's what I do between 7:30 and 8:00 a.m. It's in the schedule.

Most days, the next thing is going into the woods. I used to have a vegetable patch behind the cabin, but the soil here isn't that great and it was always kind of hit-and-miss. After the thing, it would also be too much of a clue that someone is living here.

There's plenty to find out in the woods, if you know what to look for. Wild versions of the vegetables in stores, other plants that don't actually taste so good but give you some of the green stuff you need. Sometimes you'll even see something you can kill to eat—a rabbit or a deer, that kind of thing—but not often. With time I assume I may see more, but for now stocks are low. With winter coming on, it's going to get a little harder for all this stuff. Maybe a *lot* harder.

We'll see. No point in worrying about it now. Worry don't get nothing but worry, as my father also used to say.

·　·　·　·　·

Maybe a couple hours spent out in the woods, then I carry back what I've found and store it in the shed. I'll check on the things already waiting, see what stage they're at when it comes to eating. The hanging process is very important. While I'm there I'll check the walls and roof are still sound and the canvas I've layered around the inside is still water-tight. As close to air-tight as possible, too.

I don't know if there are bears in these parts any more—I've lived here forty years, man and boy, and I haven't seen one in a long time, nor wolves either—but you may as well be sure. One of them catches a scent of food, and they're bound to come have a look-see, blundering through the wires and screwing up all that stuff. Fixing it would throw the schedule right out. I'm joking, mainly, but you know, it really would be kind of a pain, and my stock of fishing wire is not inexhaustible.

It's important to live within your means, within what you know you can replace. A long game way of life, as my father used to say. I had someone living here with me for a while, and it was kind of nice, but she found it hard to understand the importance of these things, of playing that long game. Her name was Ramona, and she came from over Noqualmi way. The arrangement didn't last long. Less then ten days, in fact. Even so, I did miss her a little after she walked out the door. But things are simpler again now she's gone.

Time'll be about 10:30 a.m. by then, maybe 11:00, and I'm ready for a third cup of coffee. So I go back to the cabin, shut and seal up all the doors and windows again, and light the fire. Do the same as when I get up, is make two cups, cover one to keep it semi-warm for later. I'll check around the inside of the cabin while the water's heating, making sure everything's in good shape. It's a simple house. No electricity—lines don't come out this far—and no running water.

I got a septic tank under the house I put in ten years back, and I get drinking and washing water from the well. There's not much to go wrong and it doesn't need checking every day. But if something's on the schedule then it gets done, and if it gets done, then you know it's done, and it's not something you have to worry about.

I go back outside, leaving the door open behind me again, and check the exterior of the house. That does need an eye kept on it. The worse the weather gets, the more there'll be a little of this or that needs doing. That's okay. I've got tools, and I know how to use them. I was a handyman before the thing and I am, therefore, kind of handy. I'm glad about that now. Probably a lot of people thought being computer programmers or bankers or TV stars was a better deal, the real cool beans. It's likely by now they may have changed their minds. I'll check the shingles on the roof, make sure the joints between the logs are still tight. I do not mess with any of the grasses or bushes that lie in the area within the wires, or outside either. I like them the way they are.

Now, it's about mid-day. I'll fill half an hour with my sculpturing, then. There's a patch of ground about a hundred yards the other side of the wires on the eastside of the house, where I'm arranging rocks. There's a central area where they're piled up higher, and around that they're just strewn to look natural. You might think this is a weird thing to do for someone who won't have a vegetable patch in case someone sees it, but I'm very careful with the rocks. Spent a long time studying on how the natural formations look around here. Spent even longer walking back from distant points with just the right kind of rocks. I was born right on this hillside. I know the area better'n probably anyone. The way I'm working it, the central area is going to look like just another outcrop, and the stuff around, like it just fell off and has been laying there for years.

It passes the time, anyway.

. . . . .

I eat my meal around 1:00 p.m. Kind of late, but otherwise the afternoon can feel a little long. I eat what I left over from supper the night before. Saves a fire. Although leaving the door open when I'm around the property disperses most of the smoke, letting it out slowly, a portion is always going to linger in the cabin, I guess. If it's been a still day, then when I wake up the next morning my chest can feel kind of clotted. Better than having it all shoot up the chimney, but it's still not a perfect system. It could be improved. I'm thinking about it, in my spare time, which occurs between 1:30 and 2:00 p.m.

The afternoons are where the schedule becomes a tad more freeform. It depends on what my needs are. At first, after the thing, I would walk out to stock up on whatever I could find in the local towns. There's two within reasonable foot distance—Elum, which is about six miles away, and Noqualmi, a little further in the other direction. But those were both real small towns, and there's really nothing left there now. Stores, houses, they're all empty and stripped even if not actually burned down. This left me in a bit of a spot for a while, but then, when I was walking back through the woods from Noqualmi empty-handed one afternoon, I spied a little gully I didn't think I knew. Walked up it, and realized there might be other sources I hadn't yet found. Felt dumb for not thinking of it before, in fact.

So that's what I do some afternoons. This area wasn't ever home to that many vacation cabins or cottages, on account of the skiing never really took off and the winter here is really just kind of cold, instead of picturesque cold—but there are a few. I've found nine, so far. First half-dozen were ones where I'd done some handy work at some point—like for the therapy woman—so they were easier to find. Others I've come upon while out wandering. They've kept me going on tinned vegetables, extra blankets. I even had a little gas stove for a while, which was great. Got right around the whole smoke problem, and so I had hot coffee all day long. Ran out of gas after a while, of course. Finding some more is a way up my wish list, I'll tell you, just below a new vacuum flask.

Problem is, those places were never year-round dwellings, and the owners didn't leave much stuff on site, and I haven't even found a new one in a couple weeks.

But I live in hope. I'm searching in a semi-organized grid pattern. Could be more rigorous about it, but something tells me it's a good idea to leave open the possibility you might have missed a place earlier, that when you're finished you're not actually finished—that's it and it's all done and so what now?

Living in hope takes work, and thinking ahead. A schedule does no harm, either, of course.

Those lessons you learn at a parent's knee—or bent over it—have a way of coming back, even if you thought you weren't listening.

· · · · ·

What I'm concentrating on most of all right now, though, is building my stocks of food. The winter is upon us, there is no doubt, and the sky and the trees and the way the wind's coming down off the mountain says it's going to land hard and bed itself down for the duration. This area is going to be very isolated. It was that way before the thing, and sure as hell no-one's going to be going out of their way to head out here now.

There's not a whole lot you can do to increase the chance of finding stuff. At first I would go to the towns, and had some success there. It made sense that they'd come to sniff around the houses and bins. Towns were a draw, however small. But that doesn't seem to happen so much now. Stocks have got depleted in general and—like I say—it's cold and getting colder and that's not the time of year when you think hey, I'll head into the mountains.

So what I mainly do now is head out back into the woods. From the back of the cabin there's about three roads you can get to in an hour or so's walking, in various directions. One used to be the main route down to Oregon, past Yakima and such. Wasn't ever like it was a constant stream of traffic on it, but that was where I got lucky the last two times, and so you tend to get superstitious, and head back to the same place until you realize it's just not working any more.

The first time was just a single, middle-aged guy, staggering down the middle of the road. I don't even know where he'd come from, or where he thought he was going. This was not a man who knew how to forage or find stuff, and he was thin and half-delirious. Cheered right up when he met me. The last time was better. A young guy and girl, in a car. They hadn't been an item before the thing, but they were now. He believed so, anyway. He was pretty on the button, or thought he was.

They had guns and a trunk full of cans and clothes, back seat packed with plastic containers of gasoline. I stopped them by standing in the middle of the road. He was wary as hell and kept his hand on his gun the whole time, but the girl was worn out and lonely and some folks have just not yet got out of the habit of wanting to see people, to mix with other humans once in a while.

I told them Noqualmi still had some houses worth holing up in, and that there'd been no trouble there in a while on account of it had been empty in months, and so the tide had drifted on. I know he thought I was going to ask to come in the car with them, but after I'd talked with them a while I just stepped back and wished them luck. I watched them drive on up the road, then walked off in a different direction.

Middle of that evening—in a marked diversion from the usual schedule, but I judged it worth it—I went down through the woods and came into Noqualmi via a back way. Didn't take too long to find their car, parked up behind one of the houses. They weren't ever going to last that long, I'm afraid. They had a candle burning, for heaven's sake. You could see it from out in the back yard, and that is the one thing that you really *can't* do. Three nights out of five I could have got there and been too late already. I got lucky, I guess. I waited until they put the light out, and then a little longer.

The guy looked like he'd have just enough wits about him to trick the doors, so I went in by one of the windows. They were asleep. Worse things could have happened to them, to be honest, much worse. There should have been one of them keeping watch. He should have known that. He could have done better by her, I think.

Getting them back to the cabin took most of the next day, one trip for each. I left the car right where it was. I don't need a car, and they're too conspicuous. He was kind of skinny, but she has a little bulk. Right now they're the reason why the winter isn't worrying me quite as much as it probably should. Them, plus a few others I've been lucky enough to come across—and yes, I do thank my luck. Sure, there's method in what I've done, and most people wouldn't have enjoyed the success rate I've had. But in the end, like my father used to say, any time you're out looking for deer, it's luck that's driving the day. A string of chances and decisions that are out of your hands, that will put you in the right place at the right time, and brings what you're looking for rambling your way.

· · · · ·

If I don't go out hunting in the afternoon, then either I'll nap a while or go do a little more sculpting. It only occurred to me to start that project a few weeks ago, and I'd like to get some more done before it starts to snow.

At first, after the thing, it looked like everything just fell apart at once, that the change was done and dusted. Then it started to become clear it didn't work that way, that there were waves. So, if you'd started to assume maybe something wasn't going to happen, that wasn't necessarily correct. Further precautions seemed like a good idea.

Either way, by 5:00 p.m. the light's starting to go and it's time to close up the day. I'll go out to the shed and cut a portion of something down for dinner, grab something of a plant or vegetable nature to go with it, or—every third day—open a can of corn. Got a whole lot of corn still, which figures, because I don't really like it that much.

I'll cook the meat over the day's third fire, straight away, before it gets dark, next to a final can of water—I really need to find myself another of those vacuum flasks, because not having warm coffee in the evening is what gets me closest to feeling down—and have that whole process finished as quick as I can.

I've gotten used to the regime as a whole, but that portion of the day is where you can still find your heart beating, just a little. I grew up used to the idea that the dark wasn't anything to fear, that nothing was going to come and do anything bad to you—from outside your house, anyway. Night meant quietness outside and nothing but forest sounds which—if you understood what was causing them—were no real cause for alarm. It's not that way now, after the thing, and so that point in the schedule where you seal up the property and trust that your preparations, and the wires, are going to do their job, is where it all comes home. You recall the situation.

Otherwise, apart from a few things like the nature of the food I eat, it's really not so different to the way life was before. I understand the food thing might seem like a big deal, but really it isn't. Waste not, want that—and yes, he said that too. Plenty other animals do it, and now isn't the time for beggars to be choosers. That's what we're become, bottom line—animals, doing what's required to get by, and there isn't any shame in that at all. It's all we ever were, if we'd stopped to think about it. We believed we had the whole deal nailed out pretty good, were shooting up in some pre-ordained arc to the sky. Then someone, somewhere, fucked up. I never heard an explanation that made much sense to me. People talked a lot about a variety of things, but then people always talked a lot, didn't they? Either way, you go past Noqualmi cemetery now, or the one in Elum, and the ground there looks like Swiss cheese. A lot of empty holes, though there are some sites yet to burst out, later waves in waiting.

 Few of them didn't get far past the gates, of course. I took down a handful myself, in the early days.

I remember the first one I saw up here, too, a couple weeks after the thing. It came by itself, blundering slowly up the rise. It was night-time, of course, so I heard it coming rather than seeing anything. First I thought it was someone real, was even dumb enough to go outside, shine a light, try to see who it was. I soon realized my error, I can tell you that. It was warmer then, and the smell coming off up the hill was what gave it away. I went back indoors, got the gun. Only thing I use it for now, as shells are at a premium. Everything else, I use a knife.

Afterwards I had a good look, though I didn't touch it. Poked it with a stick, turned it over. It really did smell awful bad, and they're not something you're going to consider eating—even if there wasn't a possibility you could catch something off the flesh. I don't know if there's some disease *to* be caught, if that's how it even works, but it's a risk I'm not taking now or likely ever. I wrapped the body up in a sheet and dragged it a long, long way from the property. Do the same with any others that make it up here from time to time. Dump them in different directions, too, just in case. I don't know what level of intelligence is at work, but they're going to have to try harder at it if they ever hope to get to me—especially since I put in the wires.

I have never seen any of them abroad during the day, but that doesn't mean they aren't, or won't in the future. So wherever I go, I'm very careful. I don't let smoke come out of my chimney, instead dispersing it out the doors and window—and only during the day. The wires go through to trips with bells inside the cabin. Not loud bells—no sense in broadcasting to one of them that they just shambled through something significant. The biggest danger is the shed, naturally—hence trying to make it air-tight. Unlike just about everything else, however, that problem's going to get easier as it gets colder. There's going to come a point where I'll be chipping dinner off with a chisel, but at least the danger of smell leaking out the cracks will drop right down to nothing.

Once everything's secured for the night, I eat my meal in the last of the daylight, with the last hot cup of coffee of the day. I set aside a little food for the morning. I do not stay up late.

The windows are all covered with blackout material, naturally, but I still don't like to take the risk. So I sit there in the dark for a spell, thinking things over. I get some of my best ideas under those conditions, in fact—there's something about the lack of distraction that makes it like a waking dream, lets you think laterally. My latest notion is a sign. I'm considering putting one up, somewhere along one of the roads, that just says THIS WAY, and points. I'm thinking if someone came along and saw a sign like that, they'd hope maybe there was a little group of people along there, some folks getting organized, safety in numbers and that, and so they'd go along to see what's what.

And find me, waiting for them, a little way into the woods.

I'll not catch all of them—the smart guy in the car would have driven straight by, for example, though his girl might have had something to say on the subject— but a few would find my web. I have to think the idea through properly—don't know for sure that the others can't read, for example, though at night they wouldn't be able to see the sign anyway, if I carve it the right way—but I have hopes for it as a plan. We'll see.

It's hard not to listen out, when you've climbed in bed, but I've been doing that all my life. Listening for the wind, or for bears snuffling around, back when you saw them up here. Listening for the sound of footsteps coming slowly toward the door of the room I used to sleep in when I was a kid. I know the wires will warn me, though, and you can bet I've got my response to such a thing rigorously worked out.

I generally do not have much trouble getting off to sleep, and that's on account of the schedule as much as anything. It keeps me active, so the body's ready for some rest come the end of day. It also gives me a structure, stops me getting het up about the general situation.

Sure, it is not ideal. But, you know, it's not that different on the day-to-day. I don't miss the television because I never had one. Listening to the radio these days would only freak you out. Don't hanker after company because there was never much of that after my father died. Might have been nice if the Ramona thing had worked out, but she didn't understand the importance of the schedule, of thinking things through, of sticking to a set of rules that have been proven to work.

She was kind of husky and lasted a good long time, though, so it's not like there wasn't advantages to the way things panned out. I caught her halfway down the hill, making a big noise about what she found in the shed. She was not an athletic person. Wasn't any real possibility she was going to get away, or that she would have lasted long out there without me to guide her. What happened was for the best, except I broke the vacuum flask on the back of her head, which I have since come to regret.

Otherwise I'm at peace with what occurred, and most other things. The real important thing is when you wake up, you know what's what—that you've got something to do, a task to get you over the hump of remembering, yet again, what the world's come to. I'm lucky that way.

The sculpting's the one area I'd like to get ahead of. The central part is pretty much done—it's coming up for three feet high, and I believe it would be hard to get up through that. But sometimes, when I'm lying in the dark waiting for sleep to come, I wonder if I shouldn't extend that higher portion; just in case there's a degree of tunneling possible, sideways and then up. I want to be sure there's enough weight, and that it's spread widely enough over the grave.

I owe my father a lot, when I think over it. In his way, through the things he said, he taught me a great deal of what it turned out I needed to know. I am grateful to him for that, I guess.

But I still don't want to see him again.

THE LAST RESORT
Mark Samuels

Mark Samuels is the author of three short story collections: *The White Hands and Other Weird Tales* (Tartarus Press, 2003), *Black Altars* (Rainfall Books, 2003) and *Glyphotech & Other Macabre Processes* (PS Publishing, 2008), as well as the short novel *The Face of Twilight* (PS Publishing, 2006).

His tales have appeared in both *The Mammoth Book of Best New Horror* and *The Year's Best Fantasy and Horror*, and a fourth collection of Samuels's stories, *The Man Who Collected Machen & Other Stories*, is scheduled to appear from Ex Occidente Press.

"The menace of flesh-eating zombies first appeared in the countryside," recalls the author. "The setting for *Night of the Living Dead* is rural, not urban, and so too with *The Living Dead at the Manchester Morgue* and more recent movies such as *Dead Meat* and *The Zombie Diaries*.

"Even in the original *Dawn of the Dead*—in which the zombies have taken over the cities—the most effective scenes are perhaps those in which hordes of them are seen from a helicopter wandering over the vast open spaces of the United States.

"Such scenes came to the surface of my mind when I wrote 'The Last Resort' for this anthology. If you want to dig a little deeper for influences, I'd recommend you seek out 'The Shining Pyramid' by Arthur Machen. No zombies there I'm afraid, but I guarantee you'll find the territory explored just as horrifying."

THEY WERE ALL OVER Grey Hill, just like bloody tourists in the summer, wandering around vacuously looking for the Mynydd Llwyd stone circle. But Henry Davies would have been glad to have the tourists back and not these groaning things that stank to high heaven and hungered after the living. It was nightmarish to see people he recognized now amongst the ranks of the things, brain-dead, slack-jawed, their skin yellowed and dry, with only a memory of what they had been in life remaining. They still held onto the instinct that this was their land.

Davies thanked God that he had a shotgun as a last resort.

It was almost the only firearm he could legally own, being a farm small-holder, but he was better off than all the other unarmed folk. All the towns in the area had been overrun, since the living dead first appeared in populated areas. But when there was no-one living left in them, some of the zombies had wandered off into the hills in search of food, consuming whatever was in their path. They were like a horde of flesh-eating locusts, eating insects, rodents and livestock, when no human was available. All the people up from Newport, from Usk, from Abergavenny, from Caerleon, who had enjoyed tramping across the Black Mountains at weekends, keeping fit, now they were enjoying a permanent stroll, but one driven by the desire to feed.

Through his binoculars, Davies counted twelve zombies on top of the hill, milling around aimlessly. He recognized four of them, although Bryn Owen only by his ubiquitous brown tweed jacket. His face had been half-eaten away, presumably when the zombies had attacked him, and before he'd become one of them himself. All of his right cheek was gone and the exposed rows of teeth, visible all the way back to his jaw-line, made it seem as if he were grinning insanely.

Silence was the key to survival. He'd learned that the hard way. At first he'd followed the advice from the radio and boarded up his farmhouse, but the noise of all the banging had attracted them. Their eyesight was poor, but their hearing had been unaffected. In fact, the world was a much quieter place, with all the man-made sounds gone. Around twenty of the zombies had converged on the farm, dragging themselves through the woods from all directions, but luckily Davies had completed his fortifications before the first of them began mindlessly pounding at the planks covering the window.

The sound of their breathing unnerved him most of all. They gasped at air like asthmatics, although he had no idea whether this was simply a leftover instinct, or whether they required oxygen to live. They'd surrounded the farmhouse, wheezing and groaning outside, straining to tear away or break down the planks he'd nailed in place across the doors and windows, but Davies retreated upstairs into the roof-space. He'd cradled his shotgun in his lap the whole time, listening to the emergency broadcasts on the radio at a very low volume, and eventually the zombies either gave up or forgot what they meant to be doing, and wandered away. Their attention span was usually minimal.

.   .   .   .   .

Of course, at the beginning, everyone thought it was an April Fool's joke. On the morning of April 1st people were waking up to these reports of the dead having come back to life overnight. There couldn't be anyone who hasn't seen one of those zombie films, or at least heard about them. Davies himself had seen one back in the 1970s, on video, but he hadn't been much impressed. It seemed to him poorly acted and ridiculous.

And anyway, the whole thing was impossible.

Like most people when they heard the news on that April morning, he'd passed it off as an elaborate prank. Even the news services were divided on the subject. Some were calling into the radio stations to complain that the joke had gone too far, and had spotted pranksters out on the streets, groaning and pretending to be the living dead.

A lot of people had died that first day insisting the whole thing was a hoax. Apparently right up until midday it was still being regarded as being one of those mass zombie walks where people plod around in gory make-up and try to break the record for the biggest crowd of "zombies" gathered together. The same thing happened in the United States, several hours later. The whole world thought the Brits had started the jest. But in fact they'd merely been the first butt of it, the joker with the warped sense of humor being God, the Devil, Nature or maybe just Destiny. In any case, by the time folk finally began to take it seriously, the whole situation was out of control.

People have long been ready to believe even the most bizarre conspiracy theories, thought Davies; about faked moon-landings, inside 9/11 attacks and Kennedy being shot by the CIA. They just stopped believing what the media was telling them, especially when it was as outlandish as something like the dead coming back to life. In an age of information overkill, it was scarcely surprising.

Davies recalled the first time he'd realized it was for real, absolutely real without question. He'd been out repairing one of the rabbit hutches when it happened. It had been during that first morning, as the reports came in and people were still arguing about them. He'd been trying to find some music on the portable radio that he'd brought out with him to listen to while he worked, but all anyone was interested in, even the music stations, was whether or not they were being told what was happening was really happening. As he'd flicked between frequencies, dodging static, he'd heard the cracking of a twig from behind and turned to see Constable Lewis ambling towards him. Funny, Davies had thought, later on, how despite being dead, his walking gait hadn't changed.

The policeman's uniform was torn and his helmet was askew on his head. Constable Lewis had been doing the rounds of the Grey Hill homes for twenty years, and he and his cycle were a familiar sight in the area. Davies had never seen Constable Lewis in such a state and without his bicycle either at his side or underneath him. But he looked as if he'd been assaulted. His face was a mass of cuts and bruises.

Davies hailed him, but Lewis didn't reply, and instead stared more intently, like he were a complete stranger. There was something disturbing about his stare, and within moments Davies realized what it was: Lewis wasn't blinking. But although there was no response to his greeting it was not the case that Lewis was silent. On the contrary, he was groaning and gasping as if in mortal agony as he approached, and he seemed to have become brain-damaged. That was Davies's first thought of course, that Lewis had been involved in an accident and was coming to him for help. But the memory of the reports on the radio and television crowded out that possibility.

"Christ, Lewis! What's wrong with you, man?" Davies had shouted.

But Lewis had paused not one step in his advance, and appeared to be deaf as well as a bloody idiot.

Well, that was it, of course. The man was a bloody zombie. No serious doubt involved. Lucky that Constable Lewis had arrived alone, and not accompanied by a gang of fellow flesh-eaters. The things were slow-moving and, individually, could be dodged or destroyed. When they were in packs, however, it might be more difficult.

Davies backed off, turned around and jogged back into the farmhouse. His shotgun rested on the mantel above the fireplace. He didn't want to use up shells unless absolutely necessary. Last resort only.

He thought of the sledgehammer in the cupboard. It lay neglected in a back corner, covered by a mass of cobwebs and dust. Hurry up, Davies told himself. He'd left the front door open, and didn't want zombie Lewis getting inside where he'd have to deal with him in a confined space. He grabbed the weapon with both hands and darted back outside.

Lewis was already on the porch. The wooden boards creaked beneath his slow tread. His jaw was opening and closing, but only a hiss of air escaped his lips. Was he trying to say something, or was this something the zombies did in anticipation of a feast? No, his eyes were inhuman. There was nothing behind them, no sign of intelligence, only a void—a machine of dead flesh.

Davies swung the sledgehammer at Lewis's head. It smashed into his left temple, the impact taking the dead man off his feet. His policeman's helmet rolled across the porch. He had fallen in a crumpled heap, one of his hands pawing at the wound. His skull had been broken open, shattering his eye-socket and smearing his face with gore. Was he in pain? Davies had no idea, but his stomach turned over at what he'd done. He felt as sickened with himself as at the sight of the bloody carnage he'd inflicted. Bile burned the back of his mouth as he readied the sledgehammer for another blow to Lewis' head. He shut his eyes as he brought it down with all the force he could muster.

. . . . .

No more zombies turned up on that first day. He'd dragged the remains of Constable Lewis off the porch and dumped the bloodied mess in the bushes. Then he brought the radio and the sledgehammer inside, cleaning the weapon in the sink, watching the spiral of blood drain away into the plug-hole. When he'd finished he propped it up beside him at the kitchen table, bolted all the doors and windows and started tuning the radio again until he found more news.

As yet, only a few of the stations had gone off air. Those in the big cities had gone first, shortly after 4:00 p.m., but the others kept going.

Some boffin was talking about a flare of radiation from the sun being the cause of the phenomenon, and damage to the Van Allen belts, whatever they are, and Davies understood little of it. Someone else was complaining that if the majority of British troops weren't currently overseas fighting, the situation at home could have been properly contained. There were even one or two cranks insisting that it was a government plot to impose martial law, and they certainly hadn't seen any so-called "zombies" for themselves. What people were seeing, they claimed, were the walking wounded, victims of state brutality who had defied official instructions to stay off the streets. It all descended into shouting matches.

In the end, Davies switched off the radio. It seemed less important to people to know the truth than to cling to their pet-theories at all cost. But, in the silence, he was suddenly much more conscious of his isolation. The radio provided the illusion of human contact. Since his wife, Marie, had left him, he'd listened to it most of the time. Ironic how he hadn't touched a drop since she'd gone, given that his drinking had been the source of her dissatisfaction, or so she said. The last bottle of wallop he'd bought was still up there in the food cupboard, untouched, nestled amongst the tins, the jars and the packets of rice and pasta. Marie thought he drank in order to escape her, to block out the world around him. But that wasn't the reason. Booze made him feel less like an empty vessel incapable of feeling anything at all, even despair. He drank just to feel human again, and not to escape anything. Or so he thought. But she'd gone and he'd lost the taste for it. He supposed that now her absence gave him the same feeling being drunk had done.

. . . . .

The next day he'd boarded up the farmhouse, following the advice from the emergency broadcast service. The regular radio stations had gone off air overnight. All the fruitless debating was over. Sure enough the racket Davies made as he hammered boards over the windows and porch door had attracted a crowd of zombies, but luckily he'd completed the reinforcement work before all of them had shown up.

When they'd realized they couldn't break in, they lost interest. Davies came down from the roof space and peeped out through gaps in the boarded-up windows to see what was going on. Most of the dead had wandered off, having forgotten what they were doing there in the first place, but some lingered in the area, picking at the ground for grubs to eat, sitting cross-legged in the grass. One of them, a child with a broken neck and not more than five-years-old, sat staring at the sky. Her head lay twisted on her left shoulder and she leaned backwards, resting on the palms of her hands. Davies wondered what she was looking at, and followed her gaze.

She was staring directly into the sun. And like all zombies, she didn't blink. Her retinas must have burnt out after the first five minutes, but still she continued to stare. She sat there all through the day, and, long after the sun had moved on, dipping below the tree line, she was still sat there staring at the same vacated part of the sky.

.   .   .   .   .

After two more days of doing nothing but eating from cans and watching the zombies pass by outside, Davies decided to climb to the top of Grey Hill. From there he would be able to see clear across to Newport and the Severn Estuary. The emergency service had gone off air that morning, and, with its disappearance, he supposed that the chance of organized rescue was slim. It would possibly take weeks for the authorities to reach all of the farmhouses in the area, and, for all he knew, the battle against the zombies might already be lost.

Provided he kept quiet and didn't run straight into a pack of the living dead, he was sure he could avoid, outrun or dodge them. He knew the woods all around, had kept himself fit, and wasn't likely to be caught. The main danger lay in twisting an ankle on a concealed root, but even so that would only slow him down, and he had the shotgun as a last resort. He checked outside, saw it was almost clear, and stepped out onto the porch.

Only one zombie was still hanging around; the little girl who stared into the sky. The creaking noises Davies' footfalls made as he crossed the porch were, although faint, enough to alert her, and she rolled forward, clambering to her feet. She began to hiss, her arms flailing around, and tried to seek him out. Her yellow and blue flowery dress was stained with dried blood and dirt. One of her plimsolls had come undone, and she tripped over the lace as she blindly lurched forward.

He jogged away from her, looking back only once. She made no attempt to follow him, but instead had settled in her new place and gone back to blindly staring at the same point of the sky. Even had the sun been in the right position it would have been completely obscured by the thick dark clouds that had rolled in during the early morning. Davies could sense the likelihood of rainfall in the oppressive and dank air. It might make his reconnaissance more treacherous, what with wet ground underfoot, but, then again, it would probably hinder the zombies more than him. They were hardly mountain goats and found it difficult to keep their feet, even on level, dry ground.

The climb to the summit was steep, and he took the direct route that had been worn down by untold numbers of tourists. There were plenty of footholds and handholds to use and he made rapid progress. Only the most determined of zombies would have taken this route, and then only when chasing after some close-at-hand prey. Any zombies would have made their way up aimlessly on the other side, where the ascent was gradual but much longer.

Amongst the zombies spread out across the summit was Bryn "bulky" Owen, same tweed jacket, two sizes too small for him. People used to say he'd be buried in that jacket. Not quite, Davies thought, stifling a humorless laugh.

Bryn Owen had been a local historian and tourist-guide. He used to lead coach parties uphill from Forester's Oakes car park, shepherding them to the remains of Mynydd Llwyd stone circle. It wasn't altogether easy to find the megaliths, since they were located in a hollow just over a dip and the bracken obscured a clear sight of the ruins from a distance.

What had drawn Owen back? Some vestige of memory? Haunting places he'd known in life, places that were important to him?

The idea led to Davies thinking about his wife Marie. She'd gone back to Newport after they'd split up. Her parents were there, and would have been overjoyed to have her back in their clutches. They'd insisted that Davies had been too old for her from the start, and too much of an old lush. He'd thought about her over and over again since the outbreak, but from the first her mobile remained unanswered and then the signal had failed. If she were dead, and one of the things, wouldn't she make her way back to his farmhouse? Just like Bryn Owen and the summit of Grey Hill? For the first few months, most of the time, Marie had been happy to be with him, and it looked like things were going to work out. Come back to him? *What was he thinking?* If something came back, it wouldn't be Marie, *his Marie*, it'd be just as much a horror as Bryn Owen with his eaten-away face.

It had finally started raining. The zombies had noticed, and had turned their faces to the sky. They seemed mildly baffled by the downpour, as if experiencing one for the first time. Some of them pawed at the air, apparently doing so in order to try and cause the rain to stop falling.

Davies decided this would be an opportune moment for him to skirt around them towards the hollow, where he could obtain the best view over Newport and the Severn Estuary. He had no idea how long the zombies would be distracted by the cloudburst, but knowing that their attention span was so limited, he doubted it would be for very long. Nevertheless, the hollow wasn't any great distance away and he could be there and back within five minutes.

He crept from sheltered spot to sheltered spot, crouching low and making no movement whenever one of the zombies was looking his way. Given that their eyesight was poor, and the fact that the noise of the downpour covered what little sound he made, he might have been nothing more than a fugitive shadow. Even had he crossed a zombie's direct line of sight, the nearest of them was fifty yards away.

He reached the hollow, and headed for the only standing stone, since this provided the best cover. The rain had got heavier and despite the leaden clouds racing across the sky above, it was still possible to see down into the valley through the gloom. Newport was a smoking wreck. Davies would doubtless have picked up the smell of burning had the wind not been blowing from the north. He could see no sign of life.

Davies slumped down to sit with his back to the standing stone. He nestled the shotgun in his lap, took out his rolling papers and tobacco pouch, and then made a cigarette. He lit up with his zippo, checking around behind the megalith before he settled himself to have his smoke. There was no zombie within a hundred yards. He hadn't been spotted yet.

Him smoking. Another thing Marie didn't like, he thought, as he took a deep drag. Not at his age. Not when you're well into your late forties, she'd said, and the more booze you drink, the more you smoke. Well, a clean lifestyle hadn't done much good in the end for all the poor fuckers in Newport, smokers and non-smokers alike: boozers and teetotalers too. Funny that, really.

He slowly finished the cigarette, right down to the point where it nearly burned his lip, and dropped it into a puddle that had formed to his left. Just before the burning tip was extinguished with a hiss by the water, he saw a reflection on the surface. A shadow loomed to his left.

It was the Bryn Owen zombie. While Davies had been distracted, taking in the sight of Newport's smoldering ruins, he'd let his guard down. Moreover he was not alone. Seven other zombies, only twenty yards away, had trailed after him into the hollow and were shuffling towards the standing stone. Davies doubted that the others knew he was hiding there, since their advance was lethargic and silent, and he suspected they only followed Owen to the megalith because of some vestigial sense of curiosity.

Seen close up, rather than from a distance, Owen's reanimated corpse was far more terrifying. Since Davies had known Owen when he was alive, the change that had taken place since his death was especially stark and gruesome. Bryn Owen had not been a handsome man to begin with, but now he was a horror in dead flesh; a foul wreck washed back up on the shore of life. His skin was parchment-yellow and mazy with deep dry wrinkles. But it was the almost destroyed left side of his face that presented the worst of the carnage wrought upon him. Davies could see each tooth that formed his macabre grin, the spittle that oozed over the cracked enamel, and the white cheekbone that poked out through torn-away skin. He could see the ugly crater where a clump of his hair had been torn from its roots, a crater that harbored a mass of squirming maggots.

And Owen's eyes! There was no recognition of Davies in them at all, no friendliness, no disdain, no emotion, to be found in his gaze, just an inscrutable void—the black eyes of a porcelain doll or the black eyes of a shark.

Davies saw all this in a mere instant, but the image burned into his mind like acid.

The Owen zombie lunged at him and Davies rolled over on his side to avoid the attack. He scrambled to his feet, the shotgun firm in his grasp, raised the barrel and aimed it directly at the middle of Owen's forehead. One pull of the trigger would blast the ghoul's brains all over Grey Hill. But no, he'd only brought the weapon with him as a very last resort, and he could just as easily dodge Owen as he could bring him down for good. And the noise of the shot would echo, drawing the attention not only of the zombies close by, but also of all the zombies in the wider area.

He took off at a sprint, easily outdistancing Owen, who let out a wailing groan of frustration. Whether the other zombies were alerted by the noise Owen made or by the sight of himself breaking cover, Davies could not know for sure, but he strongly suspected the former. He need not have worried about firing the shotgun in that case, since Owen had done enough on his own to attract the attention of the other zombies.

They were now all in pursuit of Davies.

But he had been correct in his earlier assessment. The slow-moving ghouls were too spread out to present him with a major difficulty. He weaved between them with ten yards to spare at the least, and reached the steep, half-hidden pathway that led towards his own farmhouse without any great difficulty.

But the zombies, rather than losing interest, were following, with Owen leading the way, guiding the party as he had done in life.

The rain had not only increased but was accompanied by bursts of thunder and lightning. The deafening cracks, and the sheet flashes illuminating the terrain in vivid silver monochrome, did not serve to distract the zombies as Davies expected they might have done. They seemed to have adopted Owen as their leader, and were willing to follow him despite any other claims on their attention. Perhaps he had recently led the group to a particularly successful kill, and the memory still lived in their dead brains. Maybe this kill had got mixed up in their minds with his role as a tourist guide. Certainly, Davies found it difficult to believe it was only the sightseeing aspect that made the zombies such devotees of Owen in death.

Davies had little choice but to head back the way he came and attempt to lose his pursuers in the tangle of woodland further along, zigzagging towards the farm-house, in order to put them off his trail.

Although he had realized it was a possibility given a heavy downpour, he had not anticipated quite how rapidly the steep and narrow track on the side of Grey Hill would take on the appearance of a fast-running stream. Rainwater was pouring from the lip above him, making it almost impossible to keep one's footing in what was now slippery mud. He was already soaked through to the skin. He set the safety catch on his shotgun and awkwardly jammed the weapon between his belt, but he was fearful he might lose or damage it during the descent.

There was something else to contend with, too. Davies looked up above him, half-blinded by the driving rain, and saw, silhouetted in a lightning flash, one of the living dead leap off the top of the track. The zombie had decided that this was the fastest way down the slope. Davies watched it flying through the air, and then crash into a large rock some forty yards below, its back broken by the force of the impact. It wriggled like some half-squashed insect, the limbs twitching, but it was no longer a threat to Davies. Two more zombies made the jump, and through luck rather than design, avoided the same fate. After rolling through brambles and exposed roots, they came to a halt, and were awaiting Davies's arrival.

Meanwhile, Owen and the more cautious zombies were doing their best to follow Davies by taking the slower route down the side of Grey Hill. They were hopelessly inept and uncoordinated, and Davies feared that, at any moment, one of them would lose his foothold and plummet directly on top of him.

But his luck held, in that one respect at least, and Davies made it to the level below without a collision coming from above. But now he faced the two zombies who were waiting for him. One of them had a useless right arm, having fractured his humerus upon impact. A shard of jagged bone poked out through its dead yellow flesh, just below the sleeve of his rain-soaked Manic Preachers T-shirt. Davies jumped to the zombie's right side, easily avoiding his awkward lunge.

The other zombie blocked the narrow path ahead, and there was nothing else for it but to go straight through the obstacle. This zombie was a huge pig of a corpse, bald and with a massive paunch, its horn-rimmed eyeglasses lopsided on its broken nose. Davies gripped his shotgun, turned it around, and charged the zombie. He drove the butt into the center of its face, crushing its forehead and driving the plastic lenses deep into its pulped eyes. The thing clutched at its face, spun around, and began screaming. Davies had not heard a zombie scream before, and had no idea that they did so. The noise was unearthly, quite unlike the scream of something living and suffering terror or pain.

He wished he had the time to finish it off, and smash the screaming zombie's head in, but Owen and his followers had reached the lower level, and were scarcely twenty yards away. He had to press on, get some distance between them, and then try and lose them in the labyrinthine confines of the woods.

．　．　．　．　．

Davies recalled the times he and Marie had wandered through the woods together, at the start of their marriage. Then, they had been a source of wonder. And now, alone, in the oppressive heart of the storm, and with zombies infesting them like grubs in a carcass, they were a source of horror.

He had not expected so many. He could hear their groans and their rasping breaths almost everywhere. They seemed to have arisen from the soil itself, but he knew this notion was nonsense. The fires in Newport must have driven hordes of them out, sending them on a quest for human flesh elsewhere, and, since the Severn Estuary was at their backs, the hills and the woods to the north were the only places they could go.

Once or twice he saw Bryn Owen through the trees, his hair plastered by the rain over the ruined side of his face, wandering around aimlessly. He had lost his followers in the maze of the woods and seemed to be trying to find his way back up to the summit of Grey Hill.

Finally, sure that he had thrown all the pursuing zombies off the scent, Davies made directly for his farmhouse. He had to take a few detours in order to avoid prowling zombies, and had no direct encounter with any of them.

Outside the farmhouse, the little zombie girl was still sitting there gazing at the sky, the rain dribbling across her upturned face and vacant, unblinking eyes. She was cross-legged in a pool; her dress soaking up the muddy water, the yellow and blue flowery fabric a shade of dull brown.

She was not alone. There were two other zombies on the porch, clawing at the boarded-up window nearest the door.

Davies did not recognize them at first, and it was only when they turned around in response to his approach that he identified the now soot-blackened and burnt faces.

Marie's parents.

When alive, they had visited the farmhouse only once before, and the occasion had turned into a shouting match. It had been Marie's idea, and she had prepared a special Sunday lunch for them all—a peace offering—but the meal went uneaten, and Davies had got progressively drunk. They were old-school Chapel folk from the valleys, rigidly respectable, with petty self-righteousness as their armor against "vice." They had worn their Sunday-best clothes, and had been to a Presbyterian Church of Wales service that morning, which they insisted on discussing at great length. Then there had been a row, with Davies telling them what he really thought of their moral code, and what they'd done to their daughter despite it. And they had replied in kind, with accusations flying back and forth.

Why had they come back to the farmhouse, a place they'd detested in life? Did they return in order to exact revenge upon him? And yet, they'd got exactly what they wanted. Marie had gone back to them, and not stayed with him.

Then why wasn't she here too? Had they come here looking for her?

They stepped off the porch and stumbled towards him, their faces twisted like a pair of gargoyles.

The dead girl turned towards them for a moment, drawn by the sound of their groaning cries.

Perhaps Marie had not gone back to them after all, he thought. Then why had she not returned to the farmhouse herself? Alive or dead?

Another flash of lightning, brighter than the sun, the stark horror revealed as shadows were obliterated. There were more zombies between the trees, with Bryn Owen and the others amongst them, and they seemed to be laughing insanely. Well, he thought, if zombies can scream, then why not laugh too?

Davies took the safety catch off of his shotgun.

The last resort.

He knelt down in the mud, propped the stock of the shotgun between his knees and thighs, and lowered his mouth over the muzzle. His right thumb found the trigger and he squeezed hard.

The sky turned black.

BOBBY CONROY COMES BACK FROM THE DEAD

Joe Hill

Joseph Hillström King was born in Bangor, Maine, in 1972. He is the second child of authors Stephen and Tabitha King.

Under the pseudonym "Joe Hill," he burst upon the literary scene with his acclaimed first collection of short stories, *20th Century Ghosts* (PS Publishing, 2005), and quickly followed it up with the *New York Times* best-selling novel *Heart-Shaped Box*. His latest novel is entitled *Horns*.

As a comic-book writer, he has contributed to Marvel Comics's *Spider-Man Unlimited*, and *Crown of Shadows* is the third in his Locke & Key miniseries from IDW Publishing, following *Welcome to Lovecraft* and *Head Games*.

Hill is a recipient of the World Fantasy Award, the Bram Stoker Award, two British Fantasy awards, the Ray Bradbury Fellowship, the William L. Crawford Award for Best New Fantasy Writer, and the Sydney J. Bounds Award for Best Newcomer.

At the age of ten, Hill appeared in the EC Comics–inspired anthology movie *Creepshow* (1982), scripted by his father and directed by a certain George A. Romero.

"I came close to making a novel out of 'Bobby Conroy,'" explains the author. "I had an idea it could be a very slim, bittersweet romantic comedy in the style of Laurie Colwin's ironic classic "Another Marvelous Thing." In the end, I didn't do it for what will probably seem an absurd reason—I'm not from Pennsylvania and mistrusted my ability to convincingly paint a portrait of Monroeville circa 1975. I knew just enough to skate through thirty pages, thought it best to leave it at that.

"Of course, the real love affair on display here is my twenty-two year fixation on *Dawn of the Dead*, a movie I've seen a truly absurd number of times. It's a long unrealized fantasy of mine to be cast as a zombie in one of George Romero's films and get paid a dollar a day to roll my eyes and drool blood.

"I guess it's time to admit I'm never going to have my shot at undead celebrity. Lacking that, this story will have to do . . ."

BOBBY DIDN'T KNOW HER AT FIRST. She was wounded, like him. The first thirty to arrive all got wounds. Tom Savini himself put them on.

Her face was a silvery blue, her eyes sunken into darkened hollows, and where her right ear had been was a ragged-edged hole, a gaping place that revealed a lump of wet red bone. They sat a yard apart on the stone wall around the fountain, which was switched off. She had her pages balanced on one knee—three pages in all, stapled together—and was looking them over, frowning with concentration. Bobby had read his while he was waiting in line to go into make-up.

Her jeans reminded him of Harriet Rutherford. There were patches all over them, patches that looked as if they had been made out of handkerchiefs; squares of red and dark blue, with paisley patterns printed on them. Harriet was always wearing jeans like that. Patches sewn into the butt of a girl's Levi's still turned Bobby on.

His gaze followed the bend of her legs down to where her blue jeans flared at the ankle, then on to her bare feet. She had kicked her sandals off, and was twisting the toes of one foot into the toes of the other. When he saw this he felt his heart lunge with a kind of painful-sweet shock.

"Harriet?" he said. "Is that little Harriet Rutherford who I used to write love poems to?"

She peered at him sideways, over her shoulder. She didn't need to answer, he knew it was her. She stared for a long, measuring moment, and then her eyes opened a little wider. They were a vivid, very undead green, and for a moment he saw a brightness in them, an unmistakable excitement. But it was the only sign she gave that she recognized him, and in another moment she turned her head away, went back to perusing her pages.

"No one ever wrote me love poems in high school," she said. "I'd remember. I would've died of happiness."

"In detention. Remember Billings stuck us with two weeks? The cooking show skit. You had a cucumber carved like a penis. You said marinate at slightly above room temperature for one hour and stick it in your pants. It was just the finest moment in the whole history of the Die Laughing Comedy Collective. Of which, you may recall, we were co-captains and due-paying members. In fact, I think we were the only due-paying members."

"We paid dues?"

"Yeah, we paid the other members. It was the only way to keep them from quitting."

"No," she said, and shook her head. "I have a good memory for the clubs I belonged to in high school and I wasn't ever in any comedy troupe."

"What clubs did you belong to?"

"The Bobby Conroy Hate Team. The Bobby Conroy Has a Little Dick Club. The Who Knows a Funny Story About Big Gay Bobby Conroy Society." She looked back down at the pages balanced on her knee. "Do you remember any details about these supposed poems?"

"How do you mean?"

"A line. Maybe if you could remember something about one of these poems—one line of heart-rending verse—it would all come flooding back to me."

He didn't know if he could at first; stared at her blankly, his tongue pressed to his lower lip, trying to call something back and his mind stubbornly blank.

Then he opened his mouth and began to speak, remembering as he went along: "*I love to watch you in the shower, I hope that's not obscene.*"

"*But when I see you soap your boobs, I get so sticky in my jeans!*" Harriet cried, turning her body towards him. "Bobby Conroy, *goddamn*, come here and hug me without screwing up my make-up."

He leaned towards her and put his arms around her narrow back. He shut his eyes and squeezed, feeling absurdly happy, maybe the happiest he had felt since moving back in with his parents. He had not spent a day in Monroeville when he didn't think about seeing her. He was depressed, he daydreamed about her, stories that began with exactly this moment—or not exactly *this* moment, he had not imagined them both made-up like partially decomposed corpses, but close enough.

When he woke in the morning, in his bedroom over his parents' garage, he felt flattened and listless. He'd lay on his lumpy mattress and stare at the skylights overhead. The skylights were milky with dust, and through them every sky appeared the same, a bland, formless white. Nothing in him wanted to get up, wanted to move past the first moments after opening his eyes. What made it worse was he still remembered what it felt like to wake up in that same bed with a teenager's sense of his own limitless possibilities, to wake up charged with enthusiasm for the day, no matter what had happened the day before. If he daydreamed about meeting Harriet again, and falling into their old friendship—and if these early morning daydreams sometimes turned explicitly sexual, if he remembered being with her in her father's shed, her back on the stained cement, her too-skinny legs pulled open, her socks still on—then at least it was something to stir his blood a little, get him going. All his other daydreams had thorns on them; handling them always threatened a sudden sharp prick of pain.

They were still holding each other when a boy spoke, close by. "Mom, who are you hugging?"

Bobby Conroy opened his eyes, shifted his stare to the right. A little blue-faced dead boy with limp black hair was staring morosely up at them. He wore a hooded sweatshirt, the hood pulled up.

Harriet's grip on Bobby relaxed. She was looking at the child too. Then, slowly, her arms slid away. Bobby's gaze held on the boy for an instant longer—the kid was no older than six—and then dropped to Harriet's hand, the wedding band on her ring finger.

Bobby looked back at the kid, forced a *hey-chumley* type smile. Bobby had been to over seven hundred auditions during his years in New York City, and he had a whole catalog of phony smiles.

"Hey chumley," Bobby said. "I'm Bobby Conroy. Your mom and me are old buddies from way back when Mastodons walked the earth."

"Bobby is my name too," the boy said. "Do you know a lot about dinosaurs? I'm a big dinosaur guy myself."

Bobby felt something, a shock to the heart, a sick pang that seemed to go right through the middle of him. He glanced at her face—didn't want to, couldn't help himself—and found Harriet watching him. Her smile was anxious and compressed.

"My husband picked it," she said. She was, for some reason, patting his leg. "After a Yankee. He's from Albany originally."

"I know about Mastodons," Bobby said to the boy, surprised to find his voice sounded just the same as it ever did. "Big hairy elephants the size of school buses. They once roamed the entire Pennsylvanian plateau, and left mountainous Mastodon poops everywhere, one of which later became Pittsburgh."

The kid grinned, and threw a quick glance at his mother, perhaps to appraise what she made of this off-hand reference to poop. She smiled indulgently.

Bobby saw the kid's hand and recoiled. "Ugh! Wow, that's the best wound I've seen all day. What is that, a fake hand?"

Three fingers were missing from the boy's left hand. Bobby grabbed it and yanked on it, expecting it to come off. But it was warm and fleshy under the blue make-up, and the kid pulled it out of Bobby's grip.

"No," he said. "It's just my hand. That's the way it is."

Bobby blushed so intensely his ears stung, and was grateful for his make-up. Harriet touched Bobby's wrist.

"He really doesn't have those fingers," she said.

Bobby looked at her, struggling to frame an apology. Her smile was a little fretful now, but she wasn't visibly angry with him, and the hand on his arm was a good sign.

"I stuck them into the table-saw but I don't remember because I was so little," the boy explained.

"Dean is in lumber," Harriet said.

"Is Dean staggering around here somewhere?" Bobby asked, craning his head and making a show of looking around, although of course he had no idea what Harriet's Dean might look like. The atrium at the center of the mall was crowded with other people like them, made-up to look like the recent dead. They sat together on benches, or stood together in groups, chatting, laughing at each other's wounds, or looking over the mimeographed pages they had been given of the screenplay. The mall was closed—doors of steel plate or Plexiglas pulled down in front of the entrances to the stores—no one in the place but the film crew and the undead.

"No, he dropped us off and went in to work."

"On a Sunday?"

"He owns his own yard."

It was as good a set-up for a punch line as he had ever heard, and he paused for a moment, searching for just the right one . . . and then it came to him that making wisecracks about Dean's choice of work to Dean's wife in front of Dean's five-year-old might be ill-advised, and never mind that he and Harriet had once been best friends and the royal couple of the Die Laughing Comedy Collective in their senior year in high school. Bobby said, "He does? Good for him."

"I like the big gross tear in your face," the little kid said, pointing at Bobby's brow. Bobby had a nasty scalp wound, the skin laid open to the lumpy bone. "Didn't you think the guy who made us into dead people was cool?"

Bobby had actually been a little creeped out by Tom Savini, who had told Bobby to keep his eye out for a guy walking around with a *great* looking pile of entrails in his arms. "They're kind of swinging from a wound in his stomach. You got to touch them. I squirted some K-Y on them to make them glisten like they're fresh, man, I grossed myself out. Now they feel just like something you'd yank out of a turkey. Hopefully he won't drag them around and get lint on them."

But Bobby could see what the kid meant about how he was cool. With his black leather jacket, motorcycle boots, black beard, and memorable eyebrows—thick black eyebrows that arched sharply upward, like Mr. Spock or Bela Lugosi—he looked like a death metal rock God.

Someone was clapping their hands. Bobby glanced around. The director, George Romero, stood close to the bottom of the curving staircase that wound down into the atrium from the second floor. He had stopped four steps up, so everyone could see him, but everyone would have been able to see him even if he came all the way to the bottom of the stairs. He was well over six feet tall and probably two hundred pounds, a bearish man with broad slumped shoulders and a dense beard, brown, peppered with silver. Bobby had noticed that many of the men working on the crew had beards. A lot of them had shoulder-length hair too, and wore army-navy castoffs and motorcycle boots like Savini, so that they resembled a band of counterculture revolutionaries.

Romero launched into a speech. He had a big booming confident voice and when he grinned, which was always, it made dimples in his cheeks, visible in spite of the beard. He asked if anyone present knew anything about making movies. A few people, Bobby included, raised their hands. Romero said thank God someone in this place does, and everyone laughed. He said he wanted to welcome them all to the world of big-budget Hollywood film-making, and everyone laughed at that too, because George Romero only made pictures in Pittsburgh, and everyone knew *Dawn of the Dead* was lower than low budget, it was a half-step above no-budget. He said he was grateful to them all for coming out today, and that for ten hours of grueling work, which would test them body and soul, they would be paid *in cash*, a sum so colossal he dare not say the number aloud, he couldn't say it, he could only show it. He held aloft a dollar bill, and there was more laughter. Then Tom Savini, up on the second floor, leaned over the railing, and shouted, "Don't laugh, that's more than most of us are getting paid to work on this bomb."

"Lots of people are in this film as a labor of love," George Romero said. "Tom is in it because he likes squirting pus on people." Some in the crowd moaned. "Fake pus! Fake pus!" Romero cried. "You *hope* it was fake pus," Savini intoned from somewhere above, but he was already moving away from the railing, out of sight.

More laughter. Bobby knew a thing or two about comic patter, and had a suspicion that this bit of the speech was rehearsed, and had been issued just this way, more than once.

Romero talked for a while about the plot. The recently dead were coming back to life; they liked to eat people; in the face of the crisis the government had collapsed, society was coming apart, people were panicking; four young heroes had picked this mall to hide out in. Bobby's attention wandered, he found himself looking down at the other Bobby, at Harriet's boy. Little Bob had a long, solemn face, dark chocolate eyes and lots of thick black hair, limp and disheveled. In fact, the kid bore a passing resemblance to Bobby himself, who also had brown eyes, a slim face, and a thick untidy mass of black hair on his head. Bobby found himself wondering if Dean looked like him; the thought made his blood race strangely. What if Dean dropped in to see how Harriet and little Bobby were doing, and the man turned out to be his exact twin? The thought was so alarming it made him feel briefly weak—but then he remembered he was made-up like a corpse, blue-face, scalp wound. Even if they looked exactly alike they wouldn't look anything alike.

Romero delivered some final instructions on how to walk like a zombie—he demonstrated by allowing his eyes to roll back in his head and his face to go slack—and then promised they'd be ready to roll on the first shot in a few minutes.

Harriet pivoted on her heel, turned to face him, her fist on her hip, eyelids fluttering theatrically. He turned at the same time, and they almost bumped into each other. She opened her mouth to speak but nothing came out. They were standing too close to each other, and the unexpected physical proximity seemed to throw her; all at once she didn't seem to know what it was she had been about to say. He didn't know what to say either, all thought suddenly wiped from his mind. She laughed, and shook her head, but the moment was somehow artificial, an expression of anxiety, not happiness.

"Let's set, pardner," she said. He remembered that when a skit wasn't going well, and she got rattled, she sometimes slipped into a big drawling John Wayne impersonation on stage as well, a nervous habit he had hated then and that he found, in that moment, indescribably endearing.

"Are we going to have something to do soon?" little Bob asked.

"Soon," she said. "Why don't you practice being a zombie? Go on, lurch around for a while."

Bobby and Harriet sat down at the edge of the fountain again. Her hands were small, bony fists on her thighs. She stared into her lap, her eyes blank, gaze directed inward. She was digging the toes of one bare foot into the toes of the other again.

He spoke. One of them had to say something.

"I can't believe you're married and you have a kid!" he said, in the same tone of happy astonishment he reserved for friends who had just told him they had been cast in a part he himself had auditioned for. "I love this kid you're dragging around with you. He's so cute. But then, who can resist a little kid who looks half-rotted?"

She seemed to come back from wherever she had been, smiled at him—almost shyly.

He went on, "And you better be ready to tell me everything about this Dean guy."

She nodded, looked down again, hair falling across her eyes, hiding them. "He's coming by later. He's going to take us out to lunch. You should come."

"That could be fun!" Bobby cried, and made a mental note to take his enthusiasm down a notch.

"He can be really shy the first time he meets someone, so don't expect too much."

Bobby waved a hand in the air: *pish-posh*. "It's going to be great. We'll have lots to talk about. I've always been fascinated with lumber yards and—plywood."

This was taking a chance, joshing her about the husband he didn't know. But she smirked and said:

"Everything you ever wanted to know about two-by-fours but were afraid to ask."

And for a moment they were both smiling, a little foolishly, knees almost touching. They had never really figured out how to talk to each other. They were always half-on-stage, trying to use whatever the other person said to set up the next punch-line. That much, anyway, hadn't changed.

"God I can't believe running into you here," she said. "I've wondered about you. I've thought about you a lot."

"You have?"

"I figured you'd be famous by now," she said.

"Hey, that makes two of us," Bobby said, and winked. Immediately he wished he could take the wink back. It was fake and he didn't want to be fake with her. He hurried on, answering a question she hadn't asked. "I'm settling in. Been back for three months. I'm staying with my parents for a while, kind of readapting to Monroeville."

She nodded, still regarding him steadily, with a seriousness that made him uncomfortable. "How's it going?"

"I'm making a life," Bobby lied.

.   .   .   .   .

In between set-ups, Bobby and Harriet and little Bob told stories about how they had died.

"I was a comedian in New York City," Bobby said, fingering his scalp wound. "Something tragic happened when I went on stage."

"Yeah," Harriet said. "Your act."

"Something that had never happened before."

"What, people laughed?"

"I was my usual brilliant self. People were rolling on the floor."

"Convulsions of agony."

"And then as I was taking my final bow—a terrible accident. A stagehand up in the rafters dropped a forty-pound sandbag right on my head. But at least I died to the sound of applause."

"They were applauding the stagehand," Harriet said.

The little boy looked seriously up into Bobby's face, and took his hand. "I'm sorry you got hit in the head." His lips grazed Bobby's knuckles with a dry kiss.

Bobby stared down at him. His hand tingled where little Bob's mouth had touched it.

"He's always been the kissiest, huggiest kid you ever met," Harriet said. "He's got all this pent-up affection. At the slightest sign of weakness he's ready to slobber on you." As she said this she ruffled little Bobby's hair. "What killed you, squirt?"

He held up his hand, waggled his stumps. "My fingers got cut off on Dad's table-saw and I bled to death."

Harriet went on smiling but her eyes seemed to film over just slightly. She fished around in her pocket and found a quarter. "Go get a gumball kid."

He snatched it and ran.

"People must think we're the most careless parents," she said, staring expressionlessly after her son. "But it was no one's fault about his fingers."

"Oh I'm sure," Bobby said. He thought his own voice sounded flat, lame. She didn't seem to notice. She didn't even seem to know he had spoken.

"The table saw was unplugged and he wasn't even two. He never plugged anything in before. We didn't know he knew how. Dean was right there with him. It just happened so fast. Do you know how many things had to go wrong, all at the same time for that to happen? Dean thinks the sound of the saw coming on scared him and he reached up to try and shut it off. He thought he'd be in trouble." She was briefly silent, watching her son work the gumball machine, then said, "I always thought about my kid—this is the one part of my life I'm going to get right. No indiscriminate fuck-ups about this. I was planning how when he was fifteen he'd make love to the most beautiful girl in school. How'd he be able to play five instruments and he'd blow everyone away with all his talent. How he'd be the funny kid who seems to know everyone." She paused again, and then added, "He'll be the funny kid now. The funny kid always has something wrong with him. That's why he's funny—to shift people's attention to something else."

In the silence that followed this statement, Bobby had several thoughts in rapid succession. The first was that *he* had been the funny kid when he was in school; did Harriet think there had been something wrong with *him* he had been covering for? Then he remembered they were *both* the funny kids, and thought: *what was wrong with us?*

It had to be something, otherwise they'd be together now and the boy at the gumball machine would be theirs. The thought which crossed his mind next was that, if little Bobby was *their* little Bobby, he'd still have ten fingers. He felt a seething dislike of Dean the lumber man, an ignorant squarehead whose idea of spending together-time with his kid probably meant taking him to the fair to watch a truck-pull.

An assistant director started clapping her hands and hollering down for the undead to get into their positions. Little Bob trotted back to them.

"Mom," he said, his gum in his cheek. "You didn't say how you died." Looking at her torn-off ear.

"I know," Bobby said. "She ran into this old friend at the mall and they got talking. You know, and I mean they *really* got talking. *Hours* of blab. Finally her old friend said, hey, I don't want to chew your ear off here. And your mom said, aw, don't worry about it . . ."

"A great man once said, lend me your ears," Harriet said. She smacked the palm of her hand hard against her forehead. "Why did I listen to him?"

.   .   .   .   .

Except for the dark hair, Dean didn't look anything like him. He was *short*. Bobby wasn't prepared for how short. He was shorter than Harriet, who was herself not much over five-and-a-half feet tall. When they kissed, Dean had to stretch his neck. He was compact, and solidly built, broad at the shoulders, deep through the chest, narrow at the hips. He wore thick glasses with grey plastic frames, the eyes behind them the color of unpolished pewter. They were shy eyes—his gaze met Bobby's when Harriet introduced them, darted away, returned and darted away again—not to mention old; at the corners of them the skin was creased in a web of finely-etched laugh lines. He was older than Harriet, maybe by as much as ten years.

They had only just been introduced when Dean cried suddenly, "Oh you're *that* Bobby! You're *funny* Bobby. You know we almost didn't name our *kid* Bobby because of you. I've had it drilled into me, if I ever run into you, I'm supposed to reassure you that naming him Bobby was my idea. 'Cause of Bobby Doerr. Ever since I was old enough to imagine having kids of my own I always thought—"

"I'm funny!" Harriet's son interrupted.

Dean caught him under the armpits and lofted him into the air. "You sure are!"

Bobby wasn't sure he wanted to have lunch with them, but Harriet looped her arm through his and marched him towards the doors out to the parking lot, and her shoulder—warm and bare—was leaning against his, so there was really no choice.

Bobby didn't notice the other people in the diner looking at him, and forgot they were in make-up until the waitress approached. She was barely out of her teens, with a terrific head of frizzy yellow hair that bounced as she walked.

"We're dead," little Bobby announced.

"Gotcha," the girl said, nodding and pointing her ball-point pen at them. "I'm guessing you either all work on the horror movie, or you already tried the special, which is it?"

Dean laughed, dry, bawling laughter. Dean was as easy a laugh as Bobby had ever met. Dean laughed at almost everything Harriet said, and most of what Bobby himself said. Sometimes he laughed so hard, the people at the next table stared in alarm. Once he had control of himself, he would apologize with unmistakable earnestness, his face flushed a delicate shade of rose, eyes gleaming and wet. That was when Bobby started to understand, when he started to see at least one possible answer to the question that had been on his mind ever since learning she was married to Dean who-owned-his-own-lumber-yard: *why him?* Well—he was a willing audience, there was that.

"So I thought you were acting in New York City," Dean said, at last. "What brings you back?"

"Failure," Bobby said.

"Oh—I'm sorry to hear that. What are you up to now? Are you doing some comedy locally?"

"You could say that. Only around here they call it substitute teaching for some wacky reason."

"Oh! You're teaching! How do you like it?"

"It's great. I always planned to work either in film or television or junior high. That I should finally make it so big subbing eighth grade gym—it's a dream come true."

Dean laughed, and chunks of pulverized chicken-fried steak flew out of his mouth. He blushed furiously, apologized, dabbed at the corners of his eyes.

"I'm sorry. This is awful," he said. "Food everywhere. You must think I'm a total pig."

"No, it's okay. Can I have the waitress bring you something? A glass of water? A trough?" He lifted his finger as a waitress—not theirs—went past. "Ma'am? Fresh bucket of slops here, when you get the chance."

Dean bent so his forehead was almost touching his plate, his laughter wheezy, asthmatic. "Stop. Really."

Bobby stopped, but not because Dean said. For the first time he had noticed Harriet's knee was knocking his under the table. He wondered if this was intentional, and the first chance he got he leaned back and looked. No, not intentional. She had kicked her sandals off and was digging the toes of one foot into the other, so fiercely that sometimes her right knee swung out and banged his.

"Wow, I would've loved to have a teacher like you. Someone who can make kids laugh," Dean said.

Bobby chewed and chewed, but couldn't tell what he was eating. It didn't have any taste.

Dean let out a shaky sigh, wiped the corners of his eyes again. "Of course, I'm not funny. I can't even remember knock-knock jokes. I'm not good for much else except working. And Harriet is *so* funny. Sometimes she puts on shows for Bobby and me, with these dirty socks on her hands, we get laughing so hard we can't breathe. She calls it the trailer park Muppet show. Sponsored by Pabst Blue Ribbon." He started laughing and thumping the table again. Harriet stared intently into her lap. Deån said, "I'd love to see her do that on Carson. This is—what do you call them, routines?—this could be a classic routine."

"Sure sounds it." Bobby said. "I'm surprised Ed McMahon hasn't already called to see if she's available."

. . . . .

When Dean dropped them back at the mall and left for the lumber yard, the mood was different. Harriet seemed distant, it was hard to draw her into any kind of conversation—not that Bobby felt like trying very hard. He was suddenly irritable. All the fun seemed to have gone out of playing a dead person for the day. It was mostly waiting—waiting for the gaffers to get the lights just so, for Tom Savini to touch up a wound that was starting to look a little too much like Latex, not enough like ragged flesh—and Bobby was sick of it. The sight of other people having a good time annoyed him. Several zombies stood in a group, playing hacky-sack with a quivering red spleen, and laughing. It made a juicy splat every time it hit the floor. Bobby wanted to snarl at them for being so merry. Hadn't any of them heard of method acting, Stanislavsky? They should all be sitting apart from one another, moaning unhappily and fondling giblets. He heard himself moan aloud, an angry frustrated sound, and little Bobby asked what was wrong. He said he was just practicing. Little Bob went to watch the hacky-sack game.

Harriet said, without looking at him, without any notable enthusiasm, "That was a good lunch, wasn't it?"

"*Sen*-sational," Bobby said, thinking *better be careful*. He was restless, charged with an energy he didn't know how to displace. "I feel like I really hit it off with Dean. He reminds me of my grandfather. I had this great grandfather who could wiggle his ears and who thought my name was Evan. He'd give me a quarter to stack wood for him, fifty cents if I'd do it with my shirt off. Say, how old *is* Dean?"

They had been walking together. Now Harriet stiffened, stopped. Her head swiveled towards him, but her hair was in front of her eyes, making it hard to read the expression in them. "He's nine years older than me. State your point."

"My point is nothing. I'm so glad you're happy."

"I *am* happy," Harriet said, her voice a half-octave too high.

"Did he get down on one knee when he proposed?"

Harriet nodded, her mouth crimped, suspicious.

"Did you have to help him up afterwards?" Bobby asked. His own voice was sounding a little off-key, too, and he thought *stop now*. It was like a cartoon, he saw Wile E. Coyote strapped to the front of a steam engine, jamming his feet down on the rails to try to brake the train, smoke boiling up from his heels, feet swelling, glowing red.

"Oh you prick," she said.

"I'm sorry!" he grinned, holding his hands palms-up in front of him. "Kidding, kidding. Funny Bobby, you know. I can't help myself." She hesitated—had been about to turn away—not sure whether she should believe him or not. Bobby wiped his mouth with the palm of his hand. "So we know what you do to make Dean laugh. What's he do to make you laugh? Oh that's right, he isn't *funny*. Well what's he do to make your heart race? Besides kiss you with his dentures out?"

"Leave me alone, Bobby," she said, but she wasn't trying to walk off. Instead she had gone rigid, her head ducked down, and turned away from him.

"No."

"Stop."

"Can't," he said, and suddenly he understood he was angry with her. "If he isn't funny he must be something. I need to know what."

"*Patient*," she said.

"Patient," Bobby repeated. It stunned him—that this could be her answer.

"With me."

"With you," he said.

"With Robert."

"Patient," Bobby said. Then he couldn't say anything more for a moment because he was out-of-breath. He felt suddenly that his make-up was itching on his face. He wished that when he started to press she had just walked away from him, or told him to fuck-off, or hit him even, wished she had responded with anything but *patient*. He swallowed. "Well that's not good enough." Knowing he couldn't stop now, the train was going into the canyon, Wile E. Coyote's eyes bugging three feet out of his head in terror. "I wanted to meet whoever you were with now and feel sick with jealousy, but instead I just feel sick. I wanted you to fall in love with someone good-looking and creative and brilliant, a novelist, a playwright, someone with a sense of humor and a fourteen-inch dong. Not a guy with a buzz cut and a lumber yard, who thinks erotic massage involves a tube of Ben Gay."

She smeared at the tears dribbling down her face with the backs of her hands. "I knew you'd hate him, but I didn't think you'd be mean."

"It's not that I hate him. What's to hate? He's not doing anything any other guy in his position wouldn't do. If I was eighty years old and about two feet tall, I'd *leap* at the chance to have a piece of ass like you. You bet he's patient. He better be. He ought to be down on his fucking knees every night, bathing your feet in sacramental oils, that you'd give him the time of day."

"You had your chance," she said. She was struggling not to let her crying slip out of control; the muscles in her face quivered with the effort, pulling her expression into a grimace.

"It's not about what chances I had," he said. "It's about what chances you had."

This time when she pivoted away from him, he let her go. She put her hands over her face. Her shoulders were jerking and she was making choked little sounds as she went. He watched her walk to the wall around the fountain where they had met earlier in the day. Then he remembered the boy and turned to look, his heart drumming hard, wondering what little Bobby might've seen or heard. But the kid was running down the broad concourse, kicking the spleen in front of him, which had now collected a mass of dust bunnies around it. Two other dead children were trying to kick it away from him.

Bobby watched them play for a while. A pass went wide, and the spleen skidded past him. He put a foot on it to stop it. It flexed unpleasantly beneath the sole of his shoe. The boys stopped three yards off, stood there breathing hard, awaiting him. He scooped it up.

"Go out," he said, and lobbed it to little Bobby, who made a basket catch and hauled for Wellby's SuperDrug with his head down and the others right behind him.

When he turned to peek at Harriet he saw her watching him, her palms pressed hard against her knees. He waited for her to look away, but she didn't, and finally he took her steady gaze as an invitation to approach.

He crossed to the fountain, sat down beside her. He was still working out how to begin his apology, when she spoke.

"I wrote you. You stopped writing back," she said. Her bare feet were wrestling with each other again.

"I hate how overbearing your right foot is," he said. "Why can't it give the left foot a little space?" But she wasn't listening to him.

"It didn't matter," she said. Her voice was congested and hoarse. The make-up was oil-based, and in spite of her tears, hadn't streaked. "I wasn't mad. I knew we couldn't have a relationship, just seeing each other when you came home for Christmas." She swallowed thickly. "I really thought someone would put you in their sitcom. Every time I thought about that—about seeing you on TV, and hearing people laugh when you said things—I'd get this big stupid smile on my face. I could float through a whole afternoon thinking about it. I don't understand what in the world could've made you come back to Monroeville."

But he had already said what in the world drew him back to his parents and his bedroom over the garage. Dean had asked in the diner, and Bobby had answered him truthfully.

One Thursday night, only last spring, he had gone on early in a club in the Village, called Nobody Move. He did his twenty minutes, earned a steady if-not-precisely-overwhelming murmur of laughter, and a spatter of applause when he came off. He found a place at the bar to hear some of the other acts. He was just about to slide off his stool and go home when Robin Williams leaped on stage. He was in town for SNL, cruising the clubs, testing material. Bobby quickly shifted his weight back onto his stool and sat listening, his pulse thudding heavily in his throat.

He couldn't explain to Harriet the import of what he had seen then. Bobby saw a man clutching the edge of a table with one hand, his date's thigh with the other, grabbing both so hard his knuckles were drained of all color. He was bent over with tears dripping off his face. He couldn't breathe. He wasn't laughing, he was making these desperate strangled sucking sounds—it was hilarity to the point of distress. The strangling man wagged his head from side to side, waved a hand frantically in the air, *stop, please, I can't, don't do this to me*. Robin Williams saw the suffocating man, broke away from a discourse on jerking off, pointed right at him, and shouted: "*You!* Yes, *you*, motherfucker! You get a free pass to every show I do for the rest of my fucking life!" And then there was a sound, not just laughter, not just applause. It was a low, thunderous rumble of pleasure, a sound so immense it was felt as much as heard, a thing that caused the bones of Bobby's chest to hum.

Bobby himself didn't laugh once, and when he left his stomach was churning. His feet fell strangely, heavily against the sidewalk, his feet seemed miles away from the rest of his body, and for some time he did not know his way home. When at last he was in his apartment, he sat on the edge of his bed, his suspenders pulled off, and his shirt unbuttoned, and for the first time felt things were hopeless. And none of this he knew how to say to Harriet; it was an understanding that could not be shared.

He saw something flash in her hand. She was jiggling some quarters.

"Going to call someone?" he asked.

"Dean," she said. "For a ride."

"Don't."

"I'm not staying. I can't stay."

He watched her tormented feet, toes struggling together, and finally nodded. They stood at the same time. They were, once again, standing uncomfortably close.

"See you then," she said.

"See you," he said. He wanted to reach for her hand, but didn't, wanted to say something, but couldn't think what.

"Is there a couple people around here who want to volunteer to get shot?" George Romero asked, from less than three feet away. "Its a guaranteed close-up in the finished film."

Bobby and Harriet put their hands up at the same time.

"Me," Bobby said.

"Me," said Harriet, stepping on Bobby's foot as she moved forward to get George Romero's attention. "Me!"

.   .   .   .   .

"It's going to be a great picture, Mr. Romero," Bobby said. They were standing shoulder to shoulder, making small talk, waiting for Savini to finish wiring Harriet with her squib. Bobby was already wired—in more than one sense of the word. "Someday everyone in Pittsburgh is going to claim they walked dead in this movie."

"You kiss ass like a pro," Romero said. "Do you have a show-biz background?"

"Six years off-Broadway," Bobby said. "Plus I played most of the comedy clubs."

Romero shot a finger at him and winked. "Ah, but now you're back in greater Pittsburgh. Good career move, kid. Stick around here, you'll be a star in no time."

Harriet skipped over to Bobby, her hair flouncing. "I'm going to get my tit blown off!"

"Magnificent," Bobby said. "People just have to keep on going, because you never know when something wonderful is going to happen."

George Romero led them to their marks, and walked them through what he wanted from them. They were down at the southern end of the mall, in front of Penny's. Lights pointed into silver spangly umbrellas, casting an even white glow, and a dry heat, over a ten-foot stretch of floor. The revolutionaries milled around the camera. A lumpy striped mattress rested on the floor, just to one side of a square pillar.

Harriet would get hit first, in the chest. She was supposed to jerk backwards, then keep coming, showing as little reaction to the shot as she could muster. Bobby would take the next bullet in the head and it would bring him down. The squib—a condom partially filled with cane syrup and food coloring—was hidden under one Latex fold of his scalp wound. The wires that would cause the Trojan to explode were threaded through his hair.

"You can slump first, and slide down and to the side," George Romero said. "Drop to one knee if you want, and then spill yourself out of the frame. If you're feeling a bit more acrobatic you can fall straight back, just be sure you hit the mattress. No one needs to get hurt."

It was just Bobby and Harriet in the shot, which would picture them from the waist up. The other extras lined the walls of the shopping mall corridor, watching them. Their stares, their steady murmuring, induced in Bobby a pleasurable burst of adrenaline. Tom Savini knelt on the floor, just outside the framed shot, with a hand-held metal box in hand, wires snaking across the floor towards Bobby and Harriet. Little Bob sat Indian-fashion next to him, his hands cupped under his chin, squeezing the spleen, his eyes shiny with anticipation. Savini had told little Bob all about what was going to happen, preparing the kid for the sight of blood bursting from his mother's chest, but little Bob wasn't worried. "I've been seeing gross stuff all day. It isn't scary. I like it." Savini was letting him keep the spleen as a souvenir.

"Roll," Romero said. Bobby twitched—what, they were rolling? Already? He only just gave them their marks! Christ, Romero was still standing in front of the camera!—and for an instant grabbed Harriet's hand. She squeezed his fingers, let go. Romero eased himself out of the shot. "Action."

Bobby rolled his eyes back in his head, rolled them back so far he couldn't see where he was going. He let his face hang slack. He took a plodding step forward.

"Shoot the girl," Romero said.

Bobby didn't see her squib go off, because he was a step ahead of her. But he heard it, a loud, ringing crack that echoed; and he smelled it, a sudden pungent whiff of gunpowder. Harriet grunted softly.

"Annnd," Romero said. "Now the other one."

It was like a gunshot going off next to his head. The bang of the blasting cap was so loud, it immediately deafened his eardrums. He snapped backwards, spinning on his heel. His shoulder slammed into something just behind him, he didn't see what. He caught a blurred glimpse of the square pillar next to the mattress, and in that instant was seized with a jolt of inspiration. He smashed his forehead into it on his way down, and as he reeled away, saw he had left a crimson flower on the white plaster.

He hit the mattress, the cushion springy enough to provide a little bounce. He blinked. His eyes were watering, creating a visual distortion, a subtle warping of things. The air above him was filled with blue smoke. The center of his head stung. His face was splattered with cool, sticky fluid. As the ringing in his ears faded, he simultaneously became aware of two things. The first was the sound, a low, subterranean bellow, a distant, steady roar of applause. The sound filled him like breath. George Romero was moving towards them, also clapping, smiling in that way that made dimples in his beard. At the periphery of his vision he saw little Bob leaping up and down, his fists raised over his head, Sylvester Stallone at the top of the steps leading to the public mezzanine in Philly, what a great movie that was. The second thing he noticed was Harriet curled against him, her hand on his chest. She was smiling, an easy contented smile like he hadn't seen at any other time, the whole day.

"What? Did I knock you down?" he asked.

"Fraid so," she said.

"I knew it was only a matter of time before I got you in bed with me," he said.

She stared into his face. Her blood-drenched bosom rose and fell against his side.

"You are so quick Bobby," she said.

Little Bob ran to the edge of the mattress and leaped onto it with them. Harriet got an arm underneath him, scooped him up, and rolled him into the narrow space between her and Bobby. Little Bob grinned and put his thumb in his mouth.

"Let's have a sleep over," Little Bob said. "Let's all sleep together."

"Why not?" Bobby said, and shut his eyes and dropped his head against the mattress. His face was close to the boy's head, and suddenly he was aware of the smell of little Bob's shampoo, a melon-flavored scent.

The next thing he knew, someone was twirling his hair. He opened his eyes again. Harriet's finger moved around and around, turning little circles in his hair. She continued smiling at him, watching him steadily across her son. His gaze drifted towards the ceiling, the banks of skylights, the crisp, blue sky beyond. Nothing in him wanted to get up, wanted to move past the next few moments. He wondered what Harriet did with herself when Dean was at work and little Bobby was at school. Tomorrow was a Monday; he didn't know if he would be teaching or free. He hoped free. The work week stretched ahead of him, empty of responsibilities or concerns, limitless in its possibilities. The three of them, Bobby, and the boy, and Harriet, lay on the mattress, their bodies pressed close together, and there was no movement but for their breathing.

George Romero turned back to them, shaking his head. "That was great, when you hit the pillar, and you left that big streak of gore. We should do it again, just the same way. This time you could leave some brains behind. What do you two kids say? Either one of you feel like a do-over?"

"Me," Bobby said.

"Me," said Harriet. "Me."

"Yes please," said little Bobby, around the thumb in his mouth.

"I guess it's unanimous," Bobby said. "Everyone wants a do-over."

THE CROSSING OF ALDO RAY

Weston Ochse

Weston Ochse (pronounced "Oaks") holds a Master of Fine Arts from National University in San Diego. He lives in southern Arizona and is the author of the zombie novel *Empire of Salt* from Abaddon Books.

He was awarded the 2005 Bram Stoker Award for his first novel, *Scarecrow Gods*, and has also been nominated for a Pushcart Prize for short fiction for his stories in *Appalachian Galapagos*. His other books include *Recalled to Life*, *The Golden Thread*, *Blaze of Glory*, and *The Track of the Storm*.

"'The Crossing of Aldo Ray' was inspired by late-night television," he reveals, "where the heroes always won, even in the most ridiculously dire straits."

Ochse wishes life could be that easy, but he knows the vicissitudes of living along the Mexican-American border don't always allow a hero to be a hero. So you will often find him walking quietly along the border fence, listening for the groans and tell-tale knocking that can only come from *los muertos*.

In the meantime, to keep in shape, he races tarantula wasps, wrestles rattlesnakes, and bakes in the noonday sun, so that when the time comes, he'll be ready to run.

"Deep in each man is the knowledge that something knows of his existence. Something knows, and cannot be fled nor hid from."
—Cormac McCarthy, *The Crossing*

IN THE LONG COLD EVENING with the darkness dripping from the sky, I stood among them all. I, Aldo Ray, was ready to cross. I was ready to die. I was ready to do anything so long as I could get home. I had to get to my son. He had been taken and here I was, caught on the wrong side of the border.

A breeze smelling of sage and tumbleweeds swept across us. I swayed with those around me, allowing the wind to push me as if I were a stalk of wheat or a wildflower along the side of the road. To do anything else would be human, and they were far removed from human.

So was I.

We moved forward into the fence. We pressed as one. I could feel it give. I could feel it groan. In answer, we all groaned, adding our miserable symphony to the wind that raced along the thin barrier of metal all the way to the Pacific Ocean on one side and the Gulf of Mexico on the other.

We had walked for two days, dragging, tripping, stumbling through torpid heat and bone-chilling cold. *El muertos* did not feel anything anymore, but for us *animados* it was all too real. We wanted to wipe the sweat from our faces and clutch our arms to our bodies, but we could not. *El caminar muertos* never would. The walking dead felt nothing. Nothing except the need to feed, to find that which they had lost, to move towards something they could no longer understand. And because they would not, neither could we—to survive meant mimicking as best we could this dance of the dead across the roiling sands of the Sonoran Desert.

Los Vaqueros began following us on the second day. They rode far out in the shadows of our crossing, careful not to let the *muertos* see their movement. Some said they were Mexican Army. Others that they were *enchantadors* and the reason for the *muertos*. Whatever they were, they could not really stop us. They just hovered on the edge of my vision, lean mirages twisting with an equine grace that left me longing to be alive once more.

But that was not to be. I was dead, or at least the *muertos* thought so. And that was the secret. They could not smell, nor did they seem to have any supernatural ability to realize that I was alive. But they could tell by movement the difference between *animado* and *muerto*. They could hear us and know from our speech that we were alive. The trick, as I had discovered on my two previous crossings, was to move like them, regardless of what might happen.

In front and behind me, I knew of four other *animados* like myself. Two of us were trying to get back to our families. Another worked for the *Zetas* out of Nuevo Laredo. He was a *sicario* and muled drugs across the border. The last was an *Americano* who had gotten drunk, been robbed, and sought to return to his home. It was an irony that he had to pretend to be a dead one of us in order to get back to where he belonged so he could live.

He had approached me a week before, after having sought me out in Puerto Peñasco, on the Sea of Cortez, where I was trying to earn enough money to pay the

Coyotes for safe passage across the fence. A shrimp-boat captain I knew pointed me out as one who knew how to cross.

"I need to get back," he had said.

"No way. *Usted está en América. Usted no puede pretender estar muerto muy bien.*"

"But I can pretend to be dead," he argued. "I'll do what it takes. All I want is to go home."

I still turned him down. How can someone from a land that is so alive be any good at pretending to be dead? And I would have never have shown him had I not gotten the call from *mi esposa* telling me that my son had disappeared from the playground. Some predator had stolen him and I needed to return. So I taught the *Americano*, also knowing that I might need him to help me if it came to that.

"Are you sure they can't tell I'm alive?"

I remember how remarkable it was that he never once disbelieved in the *muertos*. He took it for granted that they were real—so American to believe so easily.

Then we had lain on the ground pretending to be dead, our bodies covered in pig's blood and entrails until the herd had appeared. They came from the Black Sand, heading inexorably towards a lonely spot in the desert where it looked like the dunes met sky. When they came grunting and groaning over the top of us, the hardest thing was to keep still. We let them stagger above us, taking us for fellow *muertos*. The herd was halfway over me when in a state of electric terror I slowly lurched to my feet and joined them in their northbound shuffle.

That was two days ago. Two days of sweating and shitting and crying as I cramped and stumbled, so many times almost giving away my living condition. They never stopped so I never stopped, until we came to the fence the Americans had built. So many thought it was to keep people like me out. They had no idea about the Black Sand that was growing like a cancer through the old country, infecting all of those who walked across it, turning them into mad, hungry creatures.

We kept pushing against the fence. I felt the press of dead and rotting bodies against me. Teeth snapped near my ear. I watched beetles burrowing into the skin of the woman directly in front of me, someone's mother who was forever changed. Here and there pieces of them were missing, as older bodies had risen up while the Black Sand crept across the land. Some were nothing but dry bones and guitar-string tendons. Others had blown open, the heat expanding their bodies until the stitches along their torsos had snapped, peeling back the skin like their flesh were a strange, rare fruit that blossomed only on the march.

Suddenly a man screamed. It was the *sicario*. He had lost it. He shouted for the *muertos* to get away from him, for them to let him through. There was an uncomfortable rustling as they began to turn towards the flailing movements of one they had thought of as their own.

He screamed again, this time using my name. *If you want to see him again*, he shouted.

I turned with the *muertos*, just in time to watch one of them chew his ear off, as casually as a cow would munch a wild flower in a field.

The *sicario* pushed the thing that had once been a woman away and drew a pistol from beneath his poncho. He fired several shots towards the knees of those nearest him, sending them tumbling to the sand. He turned towards the barrier and did the same thing, until a pathway was cleared for him.

He hollered for me once again, but I could no more help him than I could help myself.

He leapt upon the dead, writhing bodies, using them as steppingstones for his last, desperate jump. He dropped the gun and grasped the top of the fence all in one gallant move. He began to heave himself up to the top, when one of the things grabbed his foot. It held him there, as a *muerto* child crawled up its back and sunk broken yellow teeth into the mule's leg.

The *sicario* screamed and kicked, but could not break free. The *muerto* child wrenched back its head and came away with meat, leaving red, shiny bone free to be tickled none so gently by the hot desert air. The *sicario* screeched incoherently. This time when he kicked out, he lost his grip and fell backwards. He hit the ground with a bone-jarring thud and was quickly lost from sight amongst the crush of the dead.

His screams were abruptly silenced, only to be replaced by the hungry groans of the *muertos* who were too far away to feed, but realized that a meal was being missed just beyond their grasp.

I groaned with them, at once both horrified by the death and relieved that it was not me.

Then I spied a camera atop the barrier. It sat several meters west of my herd and focused on the incident. The Americans saw everything. That they did not do anything was so much a part of who they were. I imagined them in some sort of immense building with a million monitors, watching everyone do everything, but doing nothing about it themselves. What good, I wondered, was all that technological superiority if it was never used?

As the weight of a dead old man pressed against me, I became aware of the packets taped to my ribs and chest. They contained I knew not what, but getting them to the other side was what the *sicario* told me would keep my son alive. They had found me soon after the *Americano* and co-opted both of us into their crime. For it was their car that my son had entered.

The barrier began to creak and bend. It was not designed for the weight of the herd. The excitement of the feast had brought more *muertos* forward until the press drove all the air from my lungs. I was desperate to breath, inhaling shallowly as I pushed with the rest. My head swam. For a moment I was no longer there, but transported to a time before.

"Aldo," came the plaintive cry down the telephone. "José is taken."

"What do you mean, taken?"

"He was at the playground with the other boys, then on the way home, he got into a car."

"What kind of car? Whose car?"

"A big one. A town car I think." The unspoken question was—did I know to whom it belonged?

"Did you call the police?"

"Of course not." She cursed through her sobs. "Aldo, you know we can't do that. Why such a question?"

"Have there been any calls?"

"Why would there be calls? Who would call?"

"I don't know."

My lie lay there, expanding into the silence. Finally she spoke once more.

"Get him back, Aldo. Do what you have to do to get him back. ¿Comprende?"

"Si," I had said. I had been about to tell her how much I loved her when the dial tone hit me like a blow in the gut. Do what you have to do to get him back, *she had said. So I had.*

The *Americano* began to sob. He was several feet to my left and I could feel the shudder of bodies as they turned towards him. The stress of being dead was too much for him, as I knew in my heart it would be.

He too had packets taped to him, as did the other like me who was returning to her family—a young woman who had been picked up in a raid on a processing plant in Illinois and deported. She had the longest way to travel, but her determination was that of a mother who had to return to her children. If I had to wager, it would be on her. If I had bet on the *Americano*, I would have lost.

I saw what would happen before he felt the teeth sink into his shoulder. A *muerto*, who reminded me of a shopkeeper I had known in Nogalas who sold overpriced rugs to *touristas*, began to chew on the *Americano* as if he were a rack of prime meat. First one bite and then another. The *Americano* screamed, the sound barely registering amidst the groans around us, as the herd once again pressed itself into the fence.

The obstruction before us began to shriek in protest. Reinforced metal, backed by rebars and steel-pilings, it was no match for the combined press of the dead. With a metallic scream, a section tore free and gave way. The first rows of *muertos* stumbled through the gap, as those behind trampled them to the ground. Limbs were crushed and broken as those who had fallen sought to stand while the others above them continued to shuffle forward.

I was far enough back to keep my balance. The groans increased as the *muertos* found the way ahead open. Like the cry of cattle about to stampede, they raised their heads and moaned towards the jet-black sky. I groaned with them, and in my lament felt compassion for those who were dead and about to die once more. The unfairness of it struck me, even though I could do nothing about it. That is what made me human, I supposed—the realization of what was being lost.

After the fence was breached, I lost sight of the *Americano*. We surged forward onto a flat plain. I had been here before. The terrain and location of the Black Sand almost ensured that the herd would end up at the same position along the border. To our left and right metal walls had been constructed like chutes in a cattle yard, guiding us onward to where I could see the *arroyo* begin. We shuffled and lurched forward. As always I wondered if the *muertos* knew where they were going. Did they have a goal, or were they as mindless as they seemed? What were they hungry for?

Then it happened.

I stumbled and fell to my knees. I was so caught up in my own thoughts that I had forgotten that I was supposed to be mindless and dead. A clumsy foot planted upon my back drove me into the ground. Another struck the back of my head and I must have blacked out for a moment.

Which is when I dreamed of Aldo Ray—not me, but my famous namesake. Tall where I was short, handsome where I was average bordering on ugly, blonde where I was black-haired, and white where I was brown. My mother had given me the name of her favorite American actor and hero in the hope that I would grow up to be like him—in the hope that his name would give me a head start on the American Dream. He had starred with James Coburn, John Wayne, Spencer Tracy, Katherine Hepburn and everyone who was anyone. With a name like that, how could I lose? He had been a hero during World War II, serving as a Frogman in the Pacific. With a past like that, how could I not succeed? Yet, as I told my mother, I could fail all too easily because a name does not make the man. She could have called me George Washington, but in the end I would always be reminded that Washington was not and had never had been Mexican. And therein lay the truth of it.

I came to my senses with a wetness down my back. It burned, as if someone had scraped the skin away. I wanted to touch there and see if I had been bitten, but I dared not. Any movement that was not that of a *muerto* would doom me to the same fate as the *sicario* and the *Americano*.

So I lurched to my feet again, using the press of bodies to propel me upwards and forward. My head ached, and my eyes felt dull. One of the packets had fallen loose and now hung free from my body, occasionally slapping my side as I stumbled onward.

Soon the steel walls were replaced by the sandy dirt embankments of the *arroyo* that rose up to twice the height of the tallest man. During the monsoon seasons the rain collected and rushed through the natural channel, seeking low ground and washing everything away in its path. Then it was dangerous, but not as dangerous as it was now. Now the water was replaced by the *muertos*, who were no less a natural force the storms that filled this conduit.

I noticed a change in my stride. My legs felt like they were no longer my own. The dull ache that had gripped them a day ago was now gone—to be replaced by a feeling of weightlessness, as if the limbs were no longer there.

Suddenly a gunshot rang out from far ahead. I knew it to be the beginning of the end, and the most dangerous part of the trek. The Border Patrol were taking aim at us, using their high-powered rifles to shoot us like chickens locked in a coop.

My hands lost their feeling as well. It was as if they belonged to someone else.

More gunshots followed the first. Although I could not see what was happening, I had witnessed it before on my first trip. Bullets were ripping through heads. Blood and bone was flying everywhere as marksmen found that sweet spot in the brain of the *muertos* that caused instant—and permanent—death. The fear I had was the fear only a living person could have. I had to hope and pray that I would not fall into the sights of a trigger-happy border guard.

I lost the feeling in my arms around the same time the minefield came into view. More than a hundred small rectangles were placed in the ground facing upwards. I knew that they were called Claymores and fired thousands of ball-bearings towards their targets, ripping them apart in an instant.

As the first ranks of *muertos* shuffled forward, night became day as a row of mines was triggered, shredding dead flesh. The surge halted for a moment as the flashes of light blinded the *muertos*. I think it scared them a little, too.

Yet still we pressed ahead.

I could no longer feel my body. It felt like I was walking in a dream where I moved but did not know how. A thought began to form in my brain, but it was hard to concentrate on such things.

I groaned and for the first time realized that I was hungry. The *muerto* in front of me had long ago rotted away, scraps of grey and green skin flapping as it moved. It did not appeal to me, but then I remembered the woman. I knew that she was somewhere forward and to the right of me. I willed my body to move in that direction, and began to jostle and push my way through the pressing mass of dead flesh.

The front ranks continued their forward momentum. This time they were allowed past the next two rows of mines until there were hundreds of *muertos* in the field. Then, as the mines were detonated, a supernova of sound and fury tore them apart, sending them skyward only to rain back down in a shower of body pieces and bone fragments.

I groaned again.

Somewhere in the back of my mind I knew I still had a son to save. I remembered the far-away words of *mi esposa* when she told me *to do what I had to do*. But I was becoming insatiably hungry. Instinctively, I sought out the woman I knew to be alive. Had the *muertos* known about her, they would be looking as well. But it was my secret, and she was mine.

When she came into view, the realization finally struck me. A burst of rational thought sparked through my dying brain cells as I now understood that I had somehow been bitten, perhaps when I was down, perhaps when I was not looking. A tiny part of me—that part that was still *animado*—screamed for the change to stop. It begged for a chance to save my child, who would most assuredly die without my delivery of the packets taped to my body. It cried out for a second chance to be human.

But the rest of me that had already died ignored my entreaty and cared only for its unholy appetite. No longer was my fuel the need to save my son. No longer was I to be Aldo Ray, the hero of the movies. Now I was a monster—hungry beyond hunger, and eager to sink my teeth into this woman with whom I had shared a conversation before all this had all started.

"Do you really think we can make it?" she had asked.

"Piece of cake," I had said. "Being dead is the easiest thing. It's being alive that's hard."

We had laughed at the joke, then covered ourselves in pig's blood and waited for the herd to cross over us. At the time it all seemed like no big deal.

I pushed through the last few of my fellow *muertos* and staggered up beside her. She turned her head minutely, recognizing me out of the corner of her eye. But I was not what she expected. Her gaze widened as she realized what I had become. I could see the terror in her understanding that she would never make it back to her family.

She tried to back away as I leaned towards her. The hunger was overpowering. I was close enough to take away her face, but instead I lightly kissed her cheek.

That surprised us both, and soon she was swept away in the press of bodies. For a brief moment humanity sparked again inside me. The last thing I remembered about myself was who I was—my name, and who my mother had wanted me to be.

Aldo Ray.

And then the hunger took me over until I exploded in a shower of light and heat. And as I rained down over the desert, I finally knew where the Black Sand came from. I knew from what it was born. It was from a hunger far older and far deeper than any of us. And it was growing. And it would soon take over us all. And I became one with the land, and was greeted by fellow *muertos* as they too rained down and joined me in the *arroyo*—a monsoon of the dead, and us flowing nowhere, forever.

OBSEQUY
David J. Schow

David J. Schow is a short story writer, novelist, screenwriter (television and film), columnist, essayist, editor, photographer, and winner of the World Fantasy and International Horror Guild awards (for short fiction and nonfiction, respectively).

His association with New Line Cinema includes such horror icons as Freddy Kreuger (*A Nightmare on Elm Street: Freddy's Nightmares* and an episode of the TV series *Freddy's Nightmares*), Leatherface (*Leatherface: Texas Chainsaw Massacre III* and the story for *The Texas Chainsaw Massacre: The Beginning*), and the eponymous Critters (*Critters 3* and *Critters 4*). His most recent film credit is *The Hills Run Red* starring William Sadler.

In 1994 he co-wrote the screenplay for the modern classic *The Crow* and has since worked with such directors as Alex Proyas, James Cameron, E. Elias Merhige, Rupert Wainwright, Mick Garris, and William Malone. He wrote more than forty installments of his popular "Raving & Drooling" column for *Fangoria* magazine, later collected in the book *Wild Hairs*.

For the premiere season of Showtime Networks's *Masters of Horror*, Schow adapted his own short story "Pick Me Up" for director Larry Cohen, and for Season 2 he wrote "We All Scream for Ice Cream" (based on a story by John Farris) for director Tom Holland.

Among his more recent books are the novels *Gun Work* and *Internecine*, and the short story collections *Zombie Jam* and *Havoc Swims Jaded*. He has appeared on many documentaries and DVD supplements, contributing material to *Creature from the Black Lagoon*, *Incubus*, *Reservoir Dogs*, *From Hell*, *The Shawshank Redemption*, *The Dirty Dozen,* and the two-disc reissue of *Dark City*.

He is currently on the verge of his next book script or chaotic house renovation.

As Schow explains, "'Obsequy' was originally written to demonstrate the difference between a "half-hour's worth of story" versus an hour for the benefit of several TV executives. Now, I know what you're thinking: That would be like trying to train a dog to eat with a fork. And you would be right. The good part is the story came to life on its own and didn't need TV for anything.

"One indirect result was that I was asked to rewrite the French film *Les revenants* (released in the U.S. as *They Came Back*) for an American production company. As

American re-takes of foreign horror movies are mandated to provide *lots of explanations* for everything going on, I had to invent these. The reaction I got on my somewhat anti-linear take was . . . horrifying.

"Horror fiction seems to spawn more dumbass 'rules' than any other kind of writing, and one of the dumbest is the assumed 'requirement' of a twist ending, going all the way back to H. H. Munro. This story is also the result of a long rumination on how stories are sometimes scuttled or diminished by succumbing to such 'rules.'

"Another land mine is use of the zombie archetype, which has become polluted with extra-stupid assumptions derived from an endless mudslide of movies featuring resurrected corpses who want to eat your brain. That's fine, but it's not what I wanted to explore here."

DOUG WALCOTT'S NEED FOR A CHANGE of perspective seemed simple: *Haul ass out of Triple Pines, pronto. Start the next chapter of my life. Before somebody else makes the decision for you, in spades.*

He grimly considered the shovel in his grasp, clotted with mulchy grave dirt. Spades, right. It was the moment Doug knew he could not go on digging up dead people, and it was only his first day on the job. Once he had been a teacher, with a teacher's penchant for seeing structure and symbols in everything. *Fuck all that,* he thought. *Time to get out. Time to bail, now.*

"I've got to go," he said, almost mumbling, his conviction still tentative.

Jacky Tynan had stepped down from his scoop-loader and ambled over, doffing his helmet and giving his brow a mop. Jacky was a simple, basically honest guy; a spear carrier in the lives of others with more personal color. Content with burgers and beer, satellite TV and dreams of a someday-girlfriend, Jacky was happy in Triple Pines.

"Yo, it's Douglas, right?" Jacky said. Everybody had been introduced shortly after sunrise. "What up?" He peeled his work gloves and rubbed his hands compulsively until tiny black sweatballs of grime dropped away like scattered grains of pepper.

"I've got to go," Doug repeated. "I think I just quit. I've got to tell Coggins I'm done. I've got to get out of here."

"Graves and stuff getting to ya, huh?" said Jacky. "You should give it another day, at least. It ain't so bad."

Doug did not meet Jacky's gaze. His evaluation of the younger man harshened, more in reaction against the locals, the natives, the people who fit into a white trash haven such as Triple Pines. They would hear the word "cemetery" and conclude "huge downer." They would wax prosaic about this job being perverse, therefore unhealthy. To them, digging up long-deceased residents would be that sick stuff. They all acted and reacted strictly according to the playbook of cliché. Their retinue of perception was so predictable that it was almost comically dull. Jacky's tone suggested that he was one of those people with an almost canine empathy to discord; he could smell when something had gone south.

Doug fought to frame some sort of answer. It was not the funereal atmosphere. The stone monuments, the graves, the loam were all exceptionally peaceful. Doug felt no connection to the dearly departed here . . . with one exception, and one was sufficient.

"It's not the work," Doug said. "It's me. I'm overdue to leave this place. The town, not the cemetery. And the money doesn't matter to me any more."

Jacky made a face as though he had whiffed a fart. "You don't want the money, man? Hell, this shit is easier than workin' the paper mill or doin' stamper time at the plant, dude." The Triple Pines aluminum plant had vanished into Chapter Eleven a decade ago, yet locals still talked about it as if it were still a functioning concern.

The people in Triple Pines never saw what was right in front of them. Or they refused to acknowledge anything strange. That was the reason Doug had to eject. He had to jump before he became one of them.

One of them . . .

A week ago, Doug had not been nearly so philosophical. Less than a week from now, and he would question his own sanity.

Craignotti, the job foreman, had seen Jacky and Doug not working—that is to say, not excavating—and already he was humping his trucker bulk over the hilltop to yell at them. Doug felt the urge to just pitch his tools and helmet and run, but his rational side admitted that there were protocols to be followed and channels to be taken. He would finish out his single day, then do some drinking with his workmates, then try to decide whether he could handle one more day. He was supposed to be a responsible adult, and responsible adults adhered to protocol and channels as a way of reinforcing the gentle myth of civilization.

Whoa, dude, piss on all that, Jacky might say. *Just run.* But Jacky rarely wrestled with such complexities. Doug turned to meet Craignotti with the fatalism of a man who has to process a large pile of tax paperwork.

A week ago, things had been different. Less than a week from now, these exhumations would collide with every one of them, in ways they could not possibly predict.

. . . . .

Frank Craignotti was one of those guys who loved their beer, Doug had observed. The man had a *relationship* with his Pilsner glass, and rituals to limn his interaction with it. Since Doug had started haunting Callahan's, he had seen Craignotti in there every night—same stool at the end of the bar, same three pitchers of tap beer, which he emptied down his neck in about an hour-and-a-half. Word was that Craignotti had been a long-haul big-rig driver for a major nationwide chain of discount stores, until the company pushed him to the sidelines on account of his disability. He had stepped down from the cab of his sixteen-wheeler on a winding mountain road outside of Triple Pines (for reasons never explained; probably to relieve himself among Nature's bounty) and had been sideswiped by a car that never saw him standing there in the rain. Presently he walked with a metal cane because after his surgery one leg had come up shorter than the other. There were vague noises of lawsuits and settlements. That had all happened before Doug wound up inside Callahan's as a regular, and so it maintained the tenuous validity of small-town gossip. It was as good a story as any.

Callahan's presented a nondescript face to the main street of Triple Pines, its stature noted solely by a blue neon sign that said BAR filling up most of a window whose sill probably had not been dusted since 1972. There was a roadhouse fifteen miles to the north, technically "out of town," but its weak diversions were not worth the effort. Callahan's flavor was mostly clover-colored Irish horse apples designed to appeal to all the usual expectations. Sutter, the current owner and the barman on most weeknights, had bought the place when the original founders had wised up and gotten the hell out of Triple Pines. Sutter was easy to make up a story about. To Doug he looked like a career criminal on the run who had found his perfect hide in Triple Pines. The scar bisecting his lower lip had probably come from a knife fight. His skin was like mushrooms in the fridge the day before you decide to throw them out. His eyes were set back in his skull, socketed deep in bruise-colored shadow.

Nobody in Triple Pines really knew anything bona fide about anybody else, Doug reflected.

Doug's first time into the bar as a drinker was his first willful act after quitting his teaching job at the junior high school that Triple Pines shared with three other communities. All pupils were bussed in from rural route pickups. A year previously, he had effortlessly scored an emergency credential and touched down as a replacement instructor for History and Geography, though he took no interest in politics unless they were safely in the past. It was a rote gig that mostly required him to ramrod disinterested kids through memorizing data that they forgot as soon as they puked it up on the next test. He had witnessed firsthand how the area, the towns, and the school system worked to crush initiative, abort insight, and nip talent. The model for the Triple Pines secondary educational system seemed to come from some early 1940s playbook, with no imperative to change anything. The kids here were all white and mostly poor to poverty level, disinterested and leavened to dullness. Helmets for the football team always superceded funds for updated texts. It was the usual, spirit-deflating story. Doug spent the term trying to kick against this corpse, hoping to provoke life signs. Past the semester break, he was just hanging on for the wage. Then, right as summer vacation loomed, Shiela Morgan had deposited herself in the teacher's lounge for a conference.

Doug had looked up from his newspaper. The local rag was called the *Pine Grove Messenger* (after the adjacent community). It came out three times weekly and was exactly four pages long. Today was Victoria Day in Canada. This week's Vocabulary Building Block was "ameliorate."

"Sheila," he said, acknowledging her, not really wanting to. She was one of the many hold-backs in his classes. Hell, many of Triple Pines' junior high schoolers already drove their own cars to battle against the citadel of learning.

"Don't call me that," Shiela said. "My name's *Brittany.*"

Doug regarded her over the top of the paper. They were alone in the room. "Really."

"Totally," she said. "I can have my name legally changed. I looked it up. I'm gonna do it, too. I don't care what anybody says."

Pause, for bitter fulfillment: One of his charges had actually *looked something up*.

Further pause, for dismay: Shiela had presented herself to him wearing a shiny vinyl mini as tight as a surgeon's glove, big-heeled boots that laced to the knee, and a leopard top with some kind of boa-like fringe framing her breasts. There was a scatter of pimples between her collarbones. She had ratty black hair and too much eye kohl. Big lipstick that had tinted her teeth pink. She resembled a hillbilly's concept of a New York streetwalker, and she was all of fourteen-years-old.

Mara Corday, Doug thought. *She looks like a Goth-slut version of Mara Corday. I am a dead man.*

Chorus girl and pin-up turned B-movie *femme fatale*, Mara Corday had decorated some drive-in low-budgeters of the late 1950s. *Tarantula. The Giant Claw. The Black Scorpion.* She had been a *Playboy* Playmate and familiar of Clint Eastwood. Sultry and sex-kittenish, she had signed her first studio contract while still a teenager. She, too, had changed her name.

Sheila wanted to be looked at, and Doug avoided looking. At least her presentation was a relief from the third-hand, Sears & Roebuck interpretation of banger and skatepunk styles that prevailed among most of Triple Pines other adolescents. In that tilted moment, Doug realized what he disliked about the dunnage of rap and hip-hop: all those super-badasses looked like they were dressed in gigantic baby clothes. Sheila's ass was broader than the last time he had not-looked. Her thighs were chubbing. The trade-off was bigger tits. Doug's heartbeat began to accelerate. *Why am I looking?*

"Sheila—"

"*Brittany.*" She threw him a pout, then softened it, to butter him up. "Lissen, I wanted to talk to you about that test, the one I missed? I wanna take it over. Like, not to cheat it or anything, but just to kinda . . . take it over, y'know? Pretend like that's the *first* time I took it?"

"None of the other students get that luxury, and you know that."

She fretted, shifting around in her seat, her skirt making squeaky noises against the school-issue plastic chair. "I know, I know, like, right? That's like, totally not usual, I know, so that's why I thought I'd ask you about it first?"

Sheila spent most of her schooling fighting to maintain a low C-average. She had won a few skirmishes, but the war was already a loss.

"I mean, like, you could totally do a new test, and I could like study for it, right?"

"You should have studied for the original test in the first place."

She wrung her hands. "I know, I know that, but . . . well let's just say it's a lot of bullshit, parents and home and alla that crap, right? I couldn't like do it then but I could now. My mom finds out I blew off the test, she'll beat the shit outta me."

"Shouldn't you be talking to a counselor?"

"Yeah, right? No thanks. I thought I'd like go right to the source, right? I mean, you like me and stuff, right?" She glanced toward the door, revving up for some kind of Big Moment that Doug already dreaded. "I mean, I'm flexible; I thought that, y'know, just this one time. I'd do anything. Really. To fix it. Anything."

She uncrossed her legs, from left on right to right on left, taking enough time to make sure Doug could see she had neglected to factor undergarments into her abbreviated ensemble. The move was so studied that Doug knew exactly which movie she had gotten it from.

There are isolated moments in time that expand to gift you with a glimpse of the future, and in that moment Doug saw his tenure at Triple Pines take a big centrifugal swirl down the cosmic toilet. The end of life as he knew it was embodied in the bit of anatomy that Sheila referred to as her "cunny."

"You can touch it if you want. I won't mind." She sounded as though she was talking about a bizarre pet on a leash.

Doug had hastily excused himself and raced to the bathroom, his four-page newspaper folded up to conceal the fact that he was strolling the hallowed halls of the school, semi-erect. He rinsed his face in a basin and regarded himself in a scabrous mirror. *Time to get out. Time to bail. Now.*

He flunked Sheila, and jettisoned himself during summer break, never quite making it to the part where he actually *left* Triple Pines. Later he heard Sheila's mom had gone ballistic and put her daughter in the emergency ward at the company clinic for the paper mill, where her father had worked since he was her age. Local residual scuttlebutt had it that Sheila had gotten out of the hospital and mated with the first guy she could find who owned a car. They blew town like fugitives and were arrested several days later. Ultimately, she used her pregnancy to force the guy to sell his car to pay for her train fare to some relative's house in the Dakotas, end of story.

Which, naturally, was mostly hearsay anyway. Bar talk. Doug had become a regular at Callahan's sometime in early July of that year, and by mid-August he looked at himself in another mirror and thought, *you bagged your job and now you have a drinking problem, buddy. You need to get out of this place.*

That was when Craignotti had eyeballed him. Slow consideration at reptile brain-speed. He bombed his glass at a gulp and rose; he was a man who always squared his shoulders when he stood up, to advise the talent of the room just how broad his chest was. He stumped over to Doug without his walking stick, to prove he didn't really need it. He signaled Sutter, the cadaverous bartender, to deliver his next pitcher of brew to the stool next to Doug's.

After some preliminary byplay and chitchat, Craignotti beered himself to within spitting distance of having a point. "So, you was a teacher at the junior high?"

"Ex-teacher. Nothing bad. I just decided I had to relocate."

"Ain't what I heard." Every time Craignotti drank, his swallows were half-glass capacity. One glassful, two swallows, rinse and repeat. "I heard you porked one of your students. That little slut Sheila Morgan."

"Not true."

Craignotti poured Doug a glass of beer to balance out the Black Jack he was consuming, one slow finger at a time. "Naah, it ain't what you think. I ain't like that. Those little fucking whores are outta control anyway. They're fucking in goddamned grade school, if they're not all crackheads by then."

"The benefits of our educational system." Doug toasted the air. If you drank enough, you could see lost dreams and hopes, swirling there before your nose, demanding sacrifice and tribute.

"Anyhow, point is that you're not working, am I right?"

"That is a true fact." Doug tasted the beer. It chased smooth.

"You know Coggins, the undertaker here?"

"Yeah." Doug had to summon the image. Bald guy, ran the Triple Pines funeral home and maintained the Hollymount Cemetery on the outskirts of town. Walked around with his hands in front of him like a preying mantis.

"Well, I know something a lotta people around here don't know yet. Have you heard of the Marlboro Reservoir?" It was the local project that would not die. It had last been mentioned in the *Pine Grove Messenger* over a year previously.

"I didn't think that plan ever cleared channels."

"Yeah, well, it ain't for you or me to know. But they're gonna build it. And there's gonna be a lotta work. Maybe bring this shithole town back to life."

"But I'm leaving this shithole town," said Doug. "Soon. So you're telling me this because—?"

"Because you look like a guy can keep his trap shut. Here's the deal: this guy Coggins comes over and asks me to be a foreman. For what, I say. And he says—now get this—in order to build the reservoir, for some reason I don't know about, they're gonna have to move the cemetery to the other side of Pine Grove—six fucking *miles*. So he needs guys to dig up all the folks buried in the cemetery, and catalogue 'em, and bury 'em again on the other side of the valley. Starts next Monday. The pay is pretty damned good for the work, and almost nobody needs to know about it. I ain't about to hire these fucking deadbeats around here, these dicks with the muscle cars, 'cept for Jacky Tynan, 'cos he's a good worker and don't ask questions. So I thought, I gotta find me a few more guys that are, like, responsible, and since you're leaving anyhow . . ."

Long story short, that's how Doug wound up manning a shovel. The money was decent and frankly, he needed the bank. "Answer me one question, though," he said to Craignotti. "Where did you get all that shit about Sheila Morgan, I mean, why did you use that to approach me?"

"Oh, that," said Craignotti. "She told me. Was trying to trade some tight little puddy for a ride outta town." Craignotti had actually said *puddy*, like Sylvester the Cat. *I tot I taw* . . . "I laughed in her face; I said, what, d'you think I'm some kinda baby-raper? I woulda split her in half. She threw a fit and went off and fucked a bunch of guys who were less discriminating. Typical small-time town-pump *scheiss*. She musta lost her cherry when she was twelve. So I figured you and me had something in common—we're probably the only two men in town who haven't plumbed *that* hole. Shit, we're so fucking honest, folks around here will think we're queer."

Honor and ethics, thought Doug. Wonderful concepts, those were.

· · · · ·

There were more than a thousand graves in Hollymount Cemetery, dating back to the turn of the 19th century. Stones so old that names had weathered to vague indentations in granite. Plots with no markers. Minor vandalism. The erosion of time and climate. Coggins, the undertaker, had collated a master name sheet and stapled it to a gridded map of the cemetery, presenting the crew picked by Craignotti with a problem rather akin to solving a huge crossword puzzle made out of dead people. Doug paged through the list until he found Michelle Farrier's name. He had attended her funeral, and sure enough—she was still here.

After his divorce from Marianne (the inevitable ex-wife), he had taken to the road, but had read enough Kerouac to know that the road held nothing for him. A stint as a blackjack dealer in Vegas. A teaching credential from L.A.; he was able to put that in his pocket and take it anywhere. Four months after his arrival in Triple Pines, he attended the funeral of the only friend he had sought to develop locally—Michelle Farrier, a runner just like him.

In the afterblast of an abusive and ill-advised marriage, Michelle had come equipped with a six-year-old daughter named Rochelle. Doug could easily see the face of the mother in the child, the younger face that had taken risks and sought adventure and brightened at the prospect of sleeping with rogues. Michelle had touched down in Triple Pines two months away from learning she was terminally ill. Doug had met them during a seriocomic bout of bathroom-sharing at Mrs. Ives' rooming house, shortly before he had rented a two-bedroom that had come cheap because there were few people in town actively seeking better lodgings, and fewer who could afford to move up. Michelle remained game, as leery as Doug of getting involved, and their gradually kindling passion filled their evenings with a delicious promise. In her kiss lurked a hungry romantic on a short tether, and Doug was working up the nerve to invite her and Rochelle to share his new home when the first talk of doctor visits flattened all other concerns to secondary status. He watched her die. He tried his best to explain it to Rochelle. And Rochelle was removed, to grandparents somewhere in the Bay Area. She wept when she said goodbye to Doug. So had Michelle.

Any grave but that one, thought Doug. *Don't make me dig that one up. Make that someone else's task.*

He knew enough about mortuary tradition to know it was unusual for an undertaker like Coggins to also be in charge of the cemetery. However, small, remote towns tend not to view such a monopoly on the death industry as a negative thing. Coggins was a single stranger for the populace to trust, instead of several. Closer to civilization, the particulars of chemical supply, casket sales, and the mortician's craft congregated beneath the same few conglomerate umbrellas, bringing what had been correctly termed a "Tru-Value hardware" approach to what was being called the "death industry" by the early 1990s. Deceased Americans had become a cash crop at several billion dollars per annum . . . not counting the flower arrangements. Triple Pines still believed in the mom-and-pop market, the corner tavern, the one-trade-fits-all handyman.

Doug had been so appalled at Michelle's perfunctory service that he did a bit of investigative reading-up. He discovered that most of the traditional accoutrements of the modern funeral were aimed at one objective above all—keeping morticians and undertakers in business. Not, as most people supposed, because of obscure health imperatives, or a misplaced need for ceremony, or even that old favorite, religious ritual. It turned out to be one of the three or four most expensive costs a normal citizen could incur during the span of an average, conventional life— another reason weddings and funerals seemed bizarrely similar. It was amusing to think how simply the two could be confused. Michelle would have been amused, at least. She had rated one of each, neither very satisfying.

Doug would never forget Rochelle's face, either. He had gotten to play the role of father to her for about a week and change, and it had scarred him indelibly. Given time, her loss, too, was a strangely welcome kind of pain.

Legally, disinterment was a touchy process, since the casket containing the remains was supposed to be technically "undamaged" when removed from the earth. This meant Jacky and the other backhoe operators could only skim to a certain depth—the big scoops—before Doug or one of his co-workers had to jump in with a shovel. Some of the big concrete grave liners were stacked three deep to a plot; at least, Craignotti had said something about three being the limit. They looked like big, featureless refrigerators laid on end, and tended to crumble like plaster. Inside were the burial caskets. Funeral publicists had stopped calling them coffins about forty years ago. "Coffins" were boxes shaped to the human form, wide at the top, slim at the bottom, with the crown shaped like the top half of a hexagon. "Coffins" evoked morbid assumptions, and so were replaced in the vernacular with "caskets"—nice, straight angles, with no Dracula or Boot Hill associations. In much the same fashion, "cemeteries" had become "memorial parks." People did everything they could, it seemed, to deny the reality of death.

Which explained the grave liners. Interment in coffins, caskets, or anything else from a wax-coated cardboard box to a shroud generally left a concavity in the lawn, once the body began to decompose, and its container, to collapse. In the manner of a big, mass-produced, cheap sarcophagus, the concrete grave liners prevented the depressing sight of . . . er, depressions. Doug imagined them to be manufactured by the same place that turned out highway divider berms; the damned things weighed about the same.

Manning his shovel, Doug learned a few more firsthand things about graves. Like how it could take eight hours for a single digger, working alone, to excavate a plot to the proper dimensions. Which was why Craignotti had been forced to locate operators for no fewer than three backhoes on this job. Plus seven "scoopers" in Doug's range of ability. The first shift, they only cleared fifty final resting-places. From then on, they would aim for a hundred stiffs per working day.

Working. Stiffs. Rampant, were the opportunities for gallows humor.

Headstones were stacked as names were checked off the master list. BEECHER, LEE, 1974-2002—HE PROTECTED AND SERVED. GUDGELL, CONROY, 1938-2003—DO NOT GO GENTLY. These were newer plots, more recent deaths. These were people who cared about things like national holidays or presidential elections, archetypal Americans from fly-over country. But in their midst, Doug was also a cliché—the drifter, the stranger. If the good folk of Triple Pines (the living ones, that is) sensed discord in their numbers, they would actively seek out mutants to scotch. Not One of Us.

He had to get out. Just this job, just a few days, and he could escape. It was better than being a mutant, and perhaps getting lynched. He moved on to STOWE, DORMAND R., 1940-1998—LOVING HUSBAND, CARING FATHER. Not so recent. Doug felt a little bit better.

They broke after sunset. That was when Doug back-checked the dig list and found a large, red X next to Michelle Farrier's name.

. . . . .

"This job ain't so damned secret," said Joe Hopkins, later, at Callahan's. Their after-work table was five: Joe, Jacky, Doug, and two more guys from the shift, Miguel Ayala and Boyd Cooper. Craignotti sat away from them, at his accustomed roost near the end of the bar. The men were working on their third pitcher. Doug found that no amount of beer could get the taste of grave dirt out of the back of his throat. Tomorrow, he'd wear a bandana. *Maybe.*

"You working tomorrow, or not, or what?" said Craignotti. Doug gave him an if-come answer, and mentioned the bandana. Craignotti had shrugged. In that moment, it all seemed pretty optional, so Doug concentrated on becoming mildly drunk with a few of the crew working the—heh—graveyard shift.

Joe was a musclebound ex-biker type who always wore a leather vest and was rarely seen without a toothpick jutting from one corner of his mouth. He had cultivated elaborate moustaches which he waxed. He was going grey at the temples. His eyes were dark, putting Doug in mind of a gypsy. He continued: "What I mean is, nobody's supposed to know about this little relocation. But they guys in here know, even if they don't talk about it. The guys who run the Triple Pines bank sure as shit know. It's a public secret. Nobody talks about it, is all."

"I bet the mayor's in on it, too," said Miguel. "All in, who cares? I mean, I had to pick mushrooms once for a buck a day. This sure beats the shit out of that."

"Doesn't bother you?" said Boyd Cooper, another of the backhoe jockeys. Older, pattern baldness, big but not heavy. Bull neck and cleft chin. His hands had seen a lifetime of manual labor. It had been Boyd who showed them how to cable the lids off the heavy stone grave liners, instead of bringing in the crane rig used to emplace them originally. This group's unity as mutual outcasts gave them a basic common language, and Boyd always cut to the gristle. "Digging up dead people?"

"Nahh," said Jacky, tipping his beer. "We're doing them a favor. Just a kind of courtesy thing. Moving 'em so they won't be forgotten."

"I guess," said Joe, working his toothpick. He burnished his teeth a lot with it. Doug noticed one end was stained with a speck of blood, from his gums.

"You're the teacher," Boyd said to Doug. "You tell us. Good thing or bad thing?"

Doug did not want to play arbiter. "Just a job of work. Like re-sorting old files. You notice how virtually no one in Triple Pines got cremated? They were all buried. That's old-fashioned, but you have to respect the dead. Laws and traditions."

"And the point is . . .?" Boyd was looking for validation.

"Well, not everybody is entitled to a piece of property when they die, six by three by seven. That's too much space. Eventually we're going to run out of room for all our dead people. Most plots in most cemeteries are rented, and there's a cap on the time limit, and if somebody doesn't pay up, they get mulched. End of story."

"Wow, is that true?" said Jacky. "I thought you got buried, it was like, forever."

"Stopped being that way about a hundred years ago," said Doug. "Land is worth too much. You don't process the dead and let them use up your real estate without turning a profit."

Miguel said, "That would be un-American." He tried for a chuckle but it died.

"Check it out if you don't believe me," said Doug. "Look it up. Behind all that patriotic rah-rah-rah about community brotherhood and peaceful gardens, it's all about capital gains. Most people don't like to think about funerals or cemeteries because, to them, it's morbid. That leaves funeral directors free to profiteer."

"You mean Coggins?" said Joe, giving himself a refill.

"Look, Coggins is a great example," said Doug. "In the outside world, big companies have incorporated most aspects of the funeral. Here, Coggins runs the mortuary, the cemetery, everything. He can charge whatever he wants, and people will pay for the privilege of shunting their grief and confusion onto him. You wouldn't believe the mark-up on some of this stuff. Caskets are three times wholesale. Even if they put you in a cardboard box—which is called an 'alternative container,' by the way—the charge is a couple of hundred bucks."

"Okay, that settles it," said Miguel. When he smiled big, you could see his gold tooth. "We all get to live forever, because we can't afford to die."

"There used to be a riddle," said Doug. "What is it: the man who made it didn't want it, the man who bought it had no use for it, and the man who used it didn't know it. What is it?"

Jacky just looked confused.

. . . . .

His head honeycombed with domestic beer, Doug tried not to lurch or slosh as he navigated his way out of Callahan's. The voice coming at him out of the fogbound darkness might well have been an aural hallucination. Or a wish fulfillment.

"Hey stranger," it said. "Walk a lady home?"

The night yielded her to him. She came not as he had fantasized, nor as he had seen her in dreams. She wore a long-sleeved, black, lacy thing with a neck-wrap collar, and her hair was up. She looked different but her definitive jawline and frank, grey gaze were unmistakable.

"That's not you," he said. "I'm a tiny bit intoxicated, but not enough to believe it's you." *Yet.* There was no one else on the street to confirm or deny; no validation from fellow inebriates or corroboration from independent bystanders. Just Doug, the swirling night, and a woman who could not be the late Michelle Farrier, whom he had loved. He had only accepted that he loved her after she died. It was more tragic that way, more delusionally romanticist. Potent enough to wallow in. A weeper, produced by his brain while it was buzzing with hops and alcohol.

She bore down on him, moving into focus, and that made his grief worse. "Sure it's me," she said. "Look at me. Take a little bit of time to get used to the idea."

He drank her in as though craving a narcotic. Her hair had always been long, burnished sienna, deftly razor-thinned to layers that framed her face. Now it was pinned back to exhibit her gracile neck and bold features. He remembered the contour of her ears. She smiled, and he remembered exactly how her teeth set. She brought with her the scent of night-blooming jasmine. If she was a revenant, she had come freighted with none of the corruption of the tomb. If she was a mirage, the light touch of her hand on his wrist should not have felt so corporeal.

Her touch was not cold.

"No," said Doug. "You died. You're gone."

"Sure, darling—I don't deny that. But now I'm back, and you should be glad."

He was still shaking his head. "I *saw* you die. I helped *bury* you."

"And today, you helped *un*-bury me. Well, your buddies did."

She had both hands on him, now. This was the monster movie moment when her human visage melted away to reveal the slavering ghoul who wanted to eat his brain and wash it down with a glass of his blood. Her sheer *presence* almost buckled his knees.

"How?"

"Beats me," she said. "We're coming back all over town. I don't know exactly how it all works, yet. But that stuff I was buried in—those *cerements*—were sort of depressing. I checked myself out while I was cleaning up. Everything seems to be in place. Everything works. Except for the tumor; that kind of withered away to an inert little knot, in the grave. I know this is tough for you to swallow, but I'm here, and goddammit, I missed you, and I thought you'd want to see me."

"I think about you every day," he said. It was still difficult to meet her gaze, or to speed-shift from using the accustomed past tense.

"Come on," she said, linking arms with him.

"Where?" Without delay his guts leaped at the thought that she wanted to take him back to the cemetery.

"Wherever. Listen, do you recall kissing me? See if you can remember how we did that."

She kissed him with all the passion of the long-lost, regained unexpectedly. It was Michelle, all right—alive, breathing, returned to him whole.

No one had seen them. No one had come out of the bar. No pedestrians. Triple Pines tended to roll up the sidewalks at 7:00 p.m.

"This is . . . nuts," he said.

She chuckled. "As long as you don't say it's distasteful." She kissed him again. "And of course you remember that other thing we never got around to doing?"

"Antiquing that roll-top desk you liked, at the garage sale?" His humor was helping him balance. His mind still wanted to swoon, or explode.

"Ho, ho, very funny. I am so glad to see you right now that I'll spell it out for you, Doug." She drew a tiny breath of consideration, working up nerve, then puffed it out. "Okay: I want to hold your cock in my hand and feel you get hard, *for me*. That was the dream, right? That first attraction, where you always visualize the other person naked, fucking you, while your outer self pretends like none of that matters?"

"I didn't think that," Doug fibbed. Suddenly his breath would not draw.

"Yes you did," Michelle said. "I did, too. But I was too chicken to act. That's all in the past." She stopped and smacked him lightly on the arm. "Don't give me that lopsided look, like *I'm* the one that's crazy. Not now. Not after I died, thinking you were the best damned thing I'd found in a long time."

"Well, there was Rochelle," said Doug, remembering how cautiously they had behaved around her six-year-old daughter.

"My little darling is not here right now," she said. "I'd say it's time to fulfill the fantasy, Doug. Mine, if not yours. We've wasted enough life, and not everybody gets a bonus round."

"But—" Doug's words, his protests had bottlenecked between his lungs. (And for-crap-sake *why* did he feel the urge to *protest* this?)

"I know what you're trying to say. I *died*." Another impatient huff of breath— living breath. "I can't explain it. I don't know if it's temporary. But I'll tell you one thing I do know: All that shit about the 'peace' of the grave? It doesn't exist. It's not a release, and it's not oblivion. It's like a nightmare that doesn't conveniently end when you wake up, because you're not *supposed* to wake up, ever! And you know what else? When you're in the grave, you can hear every goddamned footfall of the living, above you. Trust me on that one."

"Jesus . . ." he said.

"Not Jesus. Neither Heaven nor Hell. Not God. Not Buddha, not Allah, not Yahweh. Nothing. That's what waits on the other side of that headstone. No pie in the sky by and by when you die. No Nirvana. No Valhalla. No Tetragrammaton. No Zeus or Jove or any of their buddies. Nothing. Maybe that's why we're coming back—there's nothing out there, beyond. Zero. Not even an echo. So kiss me again. I've been cold and I've been still, and I need to make love to you. Making love; that sounds like we're manufacturing something, doesn't it? Feel my hand. There's living blood in there. Feel my heart; it's pumping again. I've felt bad things moving around inside of me. That happens when you're well and truly dead. Now I'm back. And I want to feel *other* things moving around inside of me. You."

Tomorrow, Doug would get fired as a no-show after only one day on the job. Craignotti would replace him with some guy named Dormand R. Stowe, rumored to be a loving husband and a caring father.

．　．　．　．　．

One of the most famous foreign pistols used during the Civil War was the Le Mat Revolver, a cap and ball weapon developed by a French-born New Orleans doctor, unique in that it had two barrels—a cylinder which held nine .40 caliber rounds fired through the upper barrel, and revolved around the lower, .63 caliber barrel, which held a charge of 18 or 20-gauge buckshot. With a flick of the thumb, the shooter could re-align the hammer to fall on the lower barrel, which was essentially a small shotgun, extremely deadly at close range, with a kick like an enraged mule. General J. E. B. Stuart had carried one. So had General P. G. T. Beauregard. As an antique firearm, such guns in good condition were highly prized. Conroy Gudgell cherished his; it was one of the stars of his modest home arsenal, which he always referred to as his "collection." His big mistake was showing his wife how to care for it. How to clean it. How to load it. How to fire it, you know, "just in case." No one was more surprised than Conroy when his loving wife, a respected first-grade teacher in Triple Pines, blew him straight down to Hell with his own collectible antique.

Ellen Gudgell became a widow at sixty-one years of age. She also became a Wiccan. She was naked, or "sky-clad," when she burned the braided horsehair whip in her fireplace after murdering Conroy. Firing the Le Mat had broken her right wrist; she'd had to make up a story about that. With her left hand she had poured herself a nice brandy, before working herself up into enough lather to phone the police, in tears, while most of Conroy's head and brains were cooling in various corners of his basement workshop. A terrible accident, oh my lord, it's horrible, please come. She kept all the stuff about Earth Mother religious revelations to herself.

She treated Constable Dickey (Triple Pines' head honcho of law enforcement) as she would one of her elementary school charges. Firm but fair. Matronly, but with just the right salting of manufactured hysteria. Conroy had been working with his gun collection in the basement when she heard a loud boom, she told the officer. She panicked and broke her wrist trying to move what was left of him, and now she did not know what to do, and she needed help.

And the local cops had quite neatly taken care of all the rest. Ellen never had to mention the beatings she had suffered under the now-incinerated whip, or that the last fifteen years of their sex life had consisted mostly of rape. When not teaching school, she used her free time—that is, her time free of Conroy's oppression—to study up on alternate philosophies, and when she found one that made sense to her, it wasn't long before she decided to assert her new self.

After that, the possibilities seemed endless. She felt as though she had shed a chrysalis and evolved to a form that made her happier with herself.

Therefore, no one was more surprised than Ellen when her husband Conroy thumped up the stairs, sundered head and all, to come a-calling more than a year after she thought she had definitively killed the rotten sonofabitch. His face looked exactly as it had when Coggins, the undertaker, had puttied and waxed it back into a semblance of human, dark sub-dermal lines inscribing puzzle pieces in rough assembly. The parts did not move in correct concert when Conroy spoke to her, however. His face was disjointed and broken, his eyes, oddly fixed.

"Time for some loving," is what Conroy said to her first.

Ellen ran for the gun cabinet, downstairs.

"Already thought of that," said Conroy, holding up the Le Mat.

He did not shoot her in the head.

· · · · ·

Despite the fact that Lee Beecher's death had been inadvertent, one of those Act of God things, Constable Lon Dickey had always felt responsible. Lee had been a hometown boy, Dickey had liked him, and made him his deputy; ergo, Lee had been acting as a representative of the law on Dickey's behalf, moving a dead deer out of the middle of the road during a storm. Some local asshole had piled into the animal and left it for dead, which constituted Triple Pines' only known form of hit-and-run. If you'd had to guess the rest of the story, Dickey thought, you'd say *and another speeding nitwit had hit Lee.* Nope. Struck by *lightning,* for christ's sake. Hit by a thunderbolt out of the ozone and killed deader than snakeshit on the spot, fried from the inside out, cooked and discarded out near the lumber yard which employed about a quarter of Triple Pines' blue-collar workforce.

Lee had been buried in his uniform. A go-getter, that kid. Good footballer. Instead of leaving Triple Pines in his rearward dust, as so many youngsters ached to do, Lee had stuck close to home, and enthusiastically sought his badge. It was worth it to him to be called an "officer," like Dickey. Death in Triple Pines was nearly always accidental, or predictable—no mystery. This was not the place where murderers or psychos lived. In this neck of the woods, the worst an officer might have to face would be the usual rowdiness—teenagers, or drunks, or drunk teenagers—and the edict to act all authoritative if there was a fire or flood or something naturally disastrous.

Beecher's replacement was a guy named James Trainor, shit-hot out of the academy in Seattle and fulminating to enforce. Too stormtrooper for Triple Pines; too ready to pull his sidearm for a traffic stop. Dickey still had not warmed up to him, smelling the moral pollution of citified paranoia.

Feeling like a lazy lion surveying his domain, Dickey had sauntered the two blocks back to the station from the Ready-Set Dinette, following his usual cheeseburger late-lunch. (The food at Callahan's, a block further, was awful—the burgers as palatable as pucks sliced off a Duraflame log.) Time to trade some banter with RaeAnn, who ran the police station's desk, phones and radios. RaeAnn was a stocky chunk of bottle-blonde business with multiple chins and an underbite, whose choice of corrective eyewear did not de-emphasize her Jimmy Durante nose. In no way was RaeAnn a temptation, and Dickey preferred that. Strictly business. RaeAnn was fast, efficient, and did not bring her problems to work. Right now she was leaning back at her station with her mouth wide open, which seemed strange. She resembled a gross caricature of one of those mail-order blowjob dolls.

Before he could ask what the hell, Dickey saw the bullet hole in the center of her forehead. Oh.

"Sorry I'm a little bit late, Chief," said Lee Beecher. He had grave dirt all over his moldy uniform, and his face was the same flash-fried nightmare that had caused Coggins to recommend a closed-casket service. Beecher had always called Dickey "Chief."

Deputy Trainor was sprawled behind Dickey's desk, his cap over his eyes, his tongue sticking out, and a circlet of five .357 caliber holes in his chest. Bloodsmear on the bulletin board illustrated how gracelessly he had fallen, hit so hard one of his boots had flown off. The late Lee Beecher had been reloading his revolver when Dickey walked in.

"I had to shoot RaeAnn, she was making too much bother," said Beecher. His voice was off, dry and croaky, buzzing like a reed.

Dickey tried to contain his slow awe by muttering the names of assorted deities.

His hand wanted to feel the comfort of his own gun.

"How come you replaced me, Chief?" said the late Lee Beecher. "Man, I didn't quit or nothing. You replaced me with some city boy. That wasn't our deal. I thought you liked me."

"I—" Dickey stammered. "Lee, I . . ." He just could not force out words. This was too wrong.

"You just put me in the dirt." The late Lee Beecher shook his charred skull with something akin to sadness. He snapped home the cylinder on his pistol, bringing the hammer back to full cock in the same smooth move. "Now I'm gonna have to return the favor. Sorry, Chief."

Constable Dickey was still trying to form a whole sentence when the late Lee Beecher gave him all six rounds. Up at RaeAnn's desk, the radio crackled and the switchboard lit up with an influx of weird emergency calls, but there was no one to pay any attention, or care.

. . . . .

Doug's current home barely fit the definition. It had no more character than a British row flat or a post-war saltbox. It was one of the basic, ticky-tacky clapboard units thrown up by the Triple Pines aluminum plant back when they sponsored company housing, and abandoned to fall apart on its own across slow years once the plant folded. It had a roof and indoor plumbing, which was all Doug had ever required of a residence, because addresses were disposable. It had storm shutters and a rudimentary version of heat, against rain and winter, but remained drafty. Its interior walls were bare and still the same vague green Doug had always associated with academia. The bedroom was sort of blue, in the same mood.

He regretted his cheap sheets, his second-hand bed, his milk-crate nightstand. He had strewn some candles around to soften the light, and fired up a portable, radiant oil heater. The heat and the light diffused the stark seediness of the room, just enough. They softened the harsh edges of reality.

There had been no seduction, no ritual libations, no teasing or flirting. Michelle had taken him the way the Allies took Normandy, and it was all he could muster to keep from gasping. His pelvis felt hammered and his legs seemed numb and far away. She was alive, with the warm, randy needs of the living, and she had plundered him with a greed that cleansed them both of any lingering recriminations.

No grave rot, no mummy dust. Was it still necrophilia when the dead person moved and talked back to you?

"I have another blanket," he said. His left leg was draped over her as their sweat cooled. He watched candle-shadows dance on the ceiling, making monster shapes.

"I'm fine," she said. "Really."

They bathed. Small bathtub, lime-encrusted shower-head. It permitted Doug to refamiliarize himself with the geometry of her body, from a perspective different than that of the bedroom. He felt he could never see or touch *enough* of her; it was a fascination for him.

There was nothing to eat in the kitchen, and simply clicking on the TV seemed faintly ridiculous. They slept, wrapped up in each other. The circumstance was still too fragile to detour into lengthy, dissipate conversations about need, so they slept, and in sleeping, found a fundamental innocence that was already beyond logic—a *feeling* thing. It seemed right and correct.

Doug awoke, his feet and fingertips frigid, in the predawn. He added his second blanket and snuggled back into Michelle. She slept with a nearly beatific expression, her breath—real, living—coming in slow tidal measures.

The next afternoon Doug sortied to the market to stock up on some basics and find some decent food that could be prepared in his minimal kitchen. In the market, he encountered Joe Hopkins, from the digging crew. Doug tried unsuccessfully to duck him. He wanted to do nothing to break the spell he was under.

But Joe wanted to talk, and cornered him. He was holding a fifth of bourbon like he intended to make serious use of it, in due course.

"There was apparently a lot of activity in the cemetery last night," he said, working his toothpick from one corner of his mouth to the other. Both ends were wet and frayed. "I mean, after we left. We went back this morning, things were moved around. Some graves were disrupted. Some were partially re-filled. It was a mess, like a storm had tossed everything. We had to spend two hours just to get back around to where we left off."

"You mean, like vandalism?" said Doug.

"Not exactly." Joe had another habit, that of continually smoothing his upper lip with his thumb and forefinger, as though to keep his moustache in line when he wasn't looking. To Doug, it signaled nervousness, agitation, and Joe was too brawny to be agitated about much for very long. "I tried to figure it, you know—what alla sudden makes the place not creepy, but threatening in a way it wasn't, yesterday. It's the feeling you'd have if you put on your clothes and alla sudden thought that, hey, somebody *else* has been wearing my clothes, right?"

Doug thought of what Michelle had said, about the dead hearing every footfall of the living above them.

"What I'm saying is, I don't blame you for quitting. After today, I'm thinking the same thing. Every instinct I have tells me to just jump on my bike and ride the fuck out of here as fast as I can go. And, something else? Jacky says he ran into a guy last night, a guy he went to high school with. They were on the football team together. Jacky says the guy died four years ago in a Jeep accident. But the he *saw* him, last night, right outside the bar after you left. Not a ghost. He wasn't that drunk. Then, this morning, Craignotti says something equally weird: That he saw a guy at the diner, you know the Ready-Set? Guy was a dead ringer for Aldus Champion, you know the mayor who died in 2003 and got replaced by that asshole selectman, whatsisname—?"

"Brad Ballinger," said Doug.

"Yeah. I been here long enough to remember that. But here's the thing: Craignotti checked, and today Ballinger was nowhere to be found, and he ain't on vacation or nothing. And Ballinger is in bed with Coggins, the undertaker, somehow. Notice how that whole Marlboro Reservoir thing went into a coma when Champion was mayor? For a minute I thought Ballinger had, you know, had him whacked or something. But now Champion's back in town—a guy Craignotti swears isn't a lookalike, but *the* guy. So now I think there was some heavy-duty money changing hands under a lot of tables, and the reservoir is a go, except nobody is supposed to talk about it, and now we're out there, digging up the whole history of Triple Pines as a result."

"What does this all come to?" Doug really wanted to get back to Michelle. She might evaporate or something if left alone too long.

"I don't know, that's the fucked up thing." Joe tried to shove his busy hands into his vest pockets, then gave up. "I'm not smart enough to figure it out, whatever it is . . . so I give it to you, see if any lightbulbs come on. I'll tell you one thing. This afternoon I felt scared, and I ain't felt that way since I was paddy humping."

"We're both outsiders, here," said Doug.

"Everybody on the dig posse in an outsider, man. Check *that* out."

"Not Jacky."

"Jacky don't pose any threat because he don't know any better. And even him, he's having fucking hallucinations about his old school buddies. Listen: I ain't got a phone at my place, but I got a mobile. Do me a favor—I mean, I know we don't know each other that well—but if you figure something out, give me a holler?"

"No problem." They traded phone numbers and Joe hurried to pay for his evening's sedation. As he went, he said, "Watch your ass, cowboy."

"You, too."

Doug and Michelle cooked collaboratively. They made love. They watched a movie together both had seen separately. They made more love. They watched the evening sky for several hours until chilly rain began to sheet down from above, then they repaired inside and continued to make love. The Peyton Place antics of the rest of the Triple Pines community, light years away from their safe, centered union, could not have mattered less.

·   ·   ·   ·

The trick, as near as Billy Morrison could wrassle it, was to find somebody and pitch them into your hole as soon as you woke up. Came back. Revived. Whatever.

So he finished fucking Vanessa Billings. "Bill-ing" her, as his cohort Vance Thompson would crack, heh. Billy had stopped "billing" high school chicks three years ago, when he died. Now he was billing a Billings, wotta riot.

Billy, Vance, and Donna Christiansen had perished inside of Billy's Boss 302 rebuild, to the tune of Black Sabbath's "The Mob Rules" on CD. The car was about half grey primer and fender-fill, on its way back to glory. The CD was a compilation of metal moldies. No-one ever figured out how the car had crashed, up near a trailer suburbia known as Rimrock, and no one in authority gave much of a turd, since Billy and his fellow losers hailed from "that side" of town, rubbing shoulders with an open-fire garbage dump, an auto wrecking yard, and (although Constable Dickey did not know it) a clandestine crack lab. The last sensation Billy experienced as a living human was the car sitting down hard on its left front as the wheel flew completely off. The speed was ticketable and the road, wet as usual, slick as mayonnaise. The car flipped and tumbled down an embankment. Billy dimly recalled seeing Donna snap in half and fly through the windshield before the steering column punched into his chest. The full tank ruptured and spewed a meandering piss-line of gasoline all the way down the hill. Vance's cigarette had probably touched it off, and the whole trash-compacted mess had burned for an hour before new rain finally doused it and a lumberyard worker spotted the smoke.

Their plan for the evening had been to destroy a bottle of vodka in the woods, then Billy and Vance would do Donna from both ends. Donna dug that sort of thing when she was sufficiently wasted. When they awoke several years later in their unearthed boxes, they renewed their pleasure as soon as they could scare up some more liquor. They wandered into a roadside outlet known as the 1-Stop Brew Shoppe and Vance broke bottles over the head of the proprietor until the guy stopping breathing. Then Donna lit out for the Yard, a quadrangle of trees and picnic benches near most of the churches in town. The Yard was Triple Pines' preferred salon for dropouts fond of cannabis, and Donna felt certain she could locate an old beau or two lingering among the waistoids there. Besides, she could bend in interesting new ways, now.

Billy had sought and duly targeted Vanessa Billings, one of those booster/cheerleader bitches who would never have anything to do with his like. She had graduated in '02 and was still—*still!*—living in her parents' house. It was a kick to see her jaw gape in astonishment at the sight of him. *Omigod, you like DIED!* It was even more of a kick to hold her by the throat and fuck her until she croaked, the stuck-up little cuntling. Getting Vanessa out of her parents' house caused a bit of ruckus, so Billy killed them, too.

Ultimately, the trio racked up so many new corpses to fill their vacant graves they needed to steal a pickup truck to ferry them all back to Hollymount. Their victims would all be back soon enough, and the fun could begin again.

None of them had a precise cognition of what they needed to do. It was more along the lines of an ingrained need—like a craving—to take the heat of the living to avoid reverting to the coldness of death. That, and the idea of refreshing their grave plots with new bodies. Billy had always had more cunning than intelligence, but the imperatives were not that daunting. Stupid dogs learned tricks in less time.

Best of all, after he finished billing Billings, Billy found he *still* had a boner. Death was apparently better than Viagara; he had an all-night hard-on. And since the night was still a toddler, he began to hunt for other chicks he could bill.

The sun came up. The sun went down. Billy thought of that rhyme about how the worms *play pinochle on your snout*. Fucking worms. How about the worms *eat your asshole inside-out*. For starters. Billy had been one super-sized organ smorgasbord, and had suffered every delicious bite. Now a whole fuckload of Triple Pines' good, upstanding citizens were going to pay, pay, pay.

. . . . .

As day and night blended and passed, Triple Pines continued to mutate.

Over at the Ready-Set Dinette, a pink neon sign continued to blink the word EAT, just as it had before things changed in Triple Pines.

Deputy Lee Beecher (the late) and RaeAnn (also the late) came in for lunch as usual. The next day, Constable Dickey (recently deceased) and the new deputy, James Trainor (ditto), joined them.

Vanessa Billings became Billy Morrison's main squeeze, and what with Vance and Donna's hangers-on, they had enough to form a new kind of gang. In the next few days, they would start breaking windows and setting fires.

Over at Callahan's, Craignotti continued to find fresh meat for the digging crew as the original members dropped out. Miguel Ayala had lasted three days before he claimed to have snagged a better job. Big Boyd Cooper stuck—he was a rationalist at heart, not predisposed to superstitious fears or anything else in the path of Getting the Job Done. Jacky Tynan had apparently taken sick.

Joe had packed his saddlebags and gunned his panhead straight out of town, without calling Doug, or anyone.

In the Gudgell household, every day, a pattern commenced. In the morning, Conroy Gudgell would horsewhip his treacherous wife's naked ass, and in the evening, Ellen Gudgell would murder her husband, again and again, over and over.

The blood drenching the inside of their house was not ectoplasm. It continued to accrete, layer upon layer, as one day passed into another.

. . . . .

In the middle of the night, Doug felt askew on the inside, and made the mistake of taking his own temperature with a thermometer.

Eighty-seven-point-five degrees.

"Yeah, you'll run a little cold," said Michelle, from behind him. "I'm sorry about that. It's sort of a downside. Or maybe you caught something. Do you feel sick?"

"No, I—" Doug faltered. "I just feel shagged. Weak."

"You're not a weak man."

"Stop it." He turned, confrontational. He did not want to do anything to alienate her. But. "This is serious. What if I start losing core heat? Four or five degrees is all it takes, then I'm as dead as a Healthy Choice entrée. What the hell is happening, Michelle? What haven't you told me?"

"I don't *know,*" she said. Her eyes brightened with tears. "I'm not *sure.* I didn't come back with a goddamned manual. I'm afraid that if I go ahead and do the *next* thing, the thing I feel I'm supposed to do . . . that I'll lose you."

Panic cinched his heart. "What's the next thing?!"

"I was avoiding it. I was afraid to bring it up. Maybe I was enjoying this too much, what we have right now, in this isolated bubble of time."

He held her. She wanted to reject simple comfort, but succumbed. "Just . . . tell me. Say it, whatever it is. Then it's out in the world and we can deal with it."

"It's about Rochelle."

Doug nodded, having prepared for this one. "You miss her. I know. But we can't do anything about it. There'd be no way to explain it."

"I want her back." Michelle's head was down, the tears coursing freely now.

"I know, baby, I know . . . I miss her, too. I wanted you guys to move in with me. Both of you. From here we could move anywhere, so long as it's out of this deathtrap of a town. Neither of us likes it here very much. I figured, in the course of time—"

She slumped on the bed, hands worrying each other atop her bare legs. "It was my dream, through all those hours, days, that things had happened differently, and we had hooked up, and we all got to escape. It would be great if you were just a means to an end; you know—just another male guy-person, to manipulate. Great if I didn't care about you; great if I didn't actually love you."

"I had to explain your death to Rochelle. There's no going back from that one. Look at it this way: she's with your mother, and she seemed like a nice lady."

When her gaze came up to meet his, her eyes were livid. "You don't know anything," she said, the words constricted and bitter. "Sweet, kindly old Grandma Farrier? She's a fucking sadist who has probably shot pornos with Rochelle by now."

"What?!" Doug's jaw unhinged.

"She is one sick piece of shit, and her mission was always to get Rochelle away from me, into her clutches. I ran away from home as soon as I could. And when I had Rochelle, I swore that bitch would never get her claws on my daughter. And you just . . . handed her over."

"Now, wait a minute, Michelle . . ."

She overrode him. "No—it's not your fault. She always presented one face to the world. Her fake face. Her human masque. Inside the family with the doors closed, it was different. You saw the masque. You dealt with the masque. So did Rochelle. Until Grandma could actually strap the collar on, she had to play it sneaky. Her real face is from a monster who needed to be inside a grave decades ago. I should know—she broke me in with a heated glass dildo when I was nine."

"Holy shit. Michelle, why didn't you tell me this before?"

"Which 'before'? Before now? Or before I died? Doug, I died not knowing you were as good as you are. I thought I could never make love to anybody, ever again. I concentrated on moving from place to place to keep Rochelle off the radar."

Doug toweled his hands, which were awash in nervous perspiration, yet irritatingly cold. Almost insensate. He needed to assuage her terror, to fix the problem, however improbable; like Boyd Cooper, to Get the Job Done. "Okay. Fine. I'll just go get her back. We'll figure something out."

"I can't ask you to do that."

"Better yet, how about we *both* go get her? Seeing you ought to make Grandma's brain hit the floor."

"That's the problem, Doug. It's been the problem all along. *I can't leave here.*

None of us can. If we do . . . if any of us goes outside of Triple Pines . . ."

"You don't mean 'us' as in you-and-me. You're talking about us as in the former occupants of Hollymount Cemetery, right?"

She nodded, more tears spilling. "I need you to fuck me. And I need you to love me. And I was hoping that you could love me enough so that I didn't have to force you to take my place in that hole in the ground, like all the rest of the goddamned losers and dim bulbs and fly-over people in Triple Pines. I want you to go to San Francisco, and get my daughter back. But if you stay here—if you go away and come back here—eventually I'll use you up anyway. I've been taking your heat, Doug, a degree at a time. And eventually you would die, and then resurrect, and then you would be stuck here too. An outsider, stuck here. And no matter what anyone's good intentions are, it would also happen to Rochelle. I can't kill my little girl. And I can't hurt you any more. It's killing me, but—what a joke—I can't die."

She looked up, her face a raw, aching map of despair. "You see?"

Michelle had not been a local, either. But she had died here, and become a permanent resident in the Triple Pines boneyard. The population of the town was slowly shifting balance. The dead of Triple Pines were pushing out the living, seeking that stasis of small town stability where once again, everyone would be the same. What happened in Triple Pines had to stay in Triple Pines, and the Marlboro Reservoir was no boon to the community. It was going to service coastal cities; Doug knew this in his gut, now. In all ways, for all concerned, Triple Pines was the *perfect* place for this kind of thing to transpire, because the outside world would never notice, or never care.

With one grating exception. Which suggested one frightening solution.

Time to get out. Time to bail, now.

"Don't you see?" she said. "If you don't get out now, you'll never get out. Get out, Doug. Kiss me one last time and get out. Try to think of me fondly."

His heart smashed to pieces and burned to ashes, he kissed her. Her tears lingered on his lips, the utterly real *taste* of her. Without a word further, he made sure he had his wallet, got in his car, and drove. He could be in San Francisco in six hours, flat-out.

He could retrieve Rochelle, kidnap her if that was what was required. He could bring her back here to die, and be reunited with her mother. Then he could die, too. But at least he would be with them, in the end. Or he could put it behind him, and just keep on driving.

The further he got from Triple Pines, the warmer he felt.

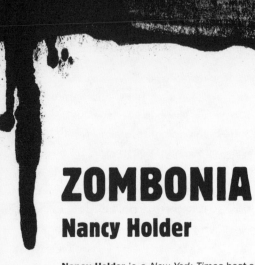

ZOMBONIA
Nancy Holder

Nancy Holder is a *New York Times* best-selling author (*Wicked: Witch and Curse* and *Wicked: Resurrection*, co-authored with Debbie Viguie). She has received four Bram Stoker Awards for her fiction and has written material for *Saving Grace*, *Buffy the Vampire Slayer*, *Smallville*, *Hulk*, *Hellboy*, and other tie-in franchises.

In addition to the popular Wicked series, she is also co-writing a new young-adult vampire series, Crusade, for Simon & Schuster. She also writes Possessions, another young-adult horror series, for Penguin Razorbill.

The author lives in San Diego with her daughter, Belle, their cats, David and Kitten Snow Vampire, and Panda Monium Holder, a Cardigan Welsh Corgi.

"I wrote this story out of sheer glee and sent it to my English editor, Mr. Jones, because it seems to me that Brits have more fun than Americans—and zombies must have more fun than the living.

"Oh, to be a zombie, now that spring is here."

I WANT YOU TO KNOW that the best thing that ever happened to me was this breakout of zombie fever or whatever the hell you call it.

I read this article that said that people get depressed when they can't bounce back—either cuz they don't have the right life skills (like if one of their parents was an alcoholic) or else they're just too overwhelmed and/or tired. Like if you're jumping up and down on the Great Trampoline of Life, and all of a sudden you say, "Oh, fuck it" and you fall down and you can't get back up again.

And speaking of fucked . . . there we were, fleeing—just going nuts in a blind panic. Not enough food or water, not even batteries, and the radio busted. And I got separated from everyone else (and I have never heard from any of them again), but I staggered on and on. I was sure I would dry up in the desert, and I pictured myself sprawled in the sand like this big hunk of people jerky for some zombie with the constitution of a friggin' camel to chew on.

But I'm struggling on in the blackest of the black nights of blackdom, thinking *this is it*, when I hit a rise, crawled up it, and gazed down with blistered eyeballs on the full-bore beauty of civilization.

Holy moly, I thought I was hallucinating! I woulda wet my pants if there'd been enough liquid in my body. It was a fabulosity of food, clothing, and shelter. A bunch of mobile homes and Winnebagos surrounded by lights, generators, and half-naked men with big stud-muscles and great tans.

People. The smell of real food, like maybe grilled cheese sandwiches. I thought I'd stumbled onto some *Road Warrior* movie. I lay there panting, squinting for a look at James Bond or Vin Diesel. Then my vision started to blur and I started to die. Everything began imploding, sagging, draining. And I thought, *Rats*. Ironic, since a rat, at that moment, might have saved my life. Rat, or rat jerky.

Someone saw me, and they yelled, and everyone trained their honkin' big guns on me. I couldn't even move my hand to wave, couldn't talk.

I don't remember being carried to Surfer Bob's double-wide, but I was, and after I got better they showed me around and asked me if I wanted to stay.

They already had too many cooks and gardeners and like that and, frankly, I know shit about fixing stuff. So I made myself a sign and put it outside the double-wide that said WILL FUCK FOR FOOD, and now they called me the Head of the Entertainment Committee.

Ha! Last joke's on me!

You see, I am not exactly a good-looking woman. I'm marginal at best. I had some bad times back in the world—a few wrong turns, nothing you need to know much about—and here was a chance to start over, big-time.

And, dude, I did.

We all did.

We did all our Type "A" bullshit during the light, and then every day at dusk, we made a huge pot of rabbit stew or chili or tacos and whipped on those generators— *weeeaaauauuaau*, sounded like a Texas chain saw rally—and all the lights in town blazed on. From trailer to trailer we had strings of chili pepper lights, cow lights, Christmas lights. People burned lights in all the rooms of their mobiles, gleaming in the clear desert sky. It was the most beautiful thing you had ever seen.

And we lit bonfires—zombies hate fire—and we danced and screwed and ate and drank ourselves crazy, speaking of camels. Every night was one commodious, ever-lasting keggery-Gregory-Peccary.

We used to swap stories about how we got to town—stuff we'd seen. One lady told us how her kids told her they were outside playing tag with "the new kid."

Turns out it was a zombie that chomped down on her little Jennifer and Jason. She had to shoot them both in the brains.

Or the story this guy told about his buds playing chicken with this one zombie. And the zombie fooled them into getting too close, and chomp-chomp-*chomporama!* He was the sole survivor, just like that old song by Michael Bolton or the Bee Gees, whoever, I dunno.

Me, I had never even *seen* a zombie, so maybe that was why it used to shake me up when someone would pass through—a lone guy, a couple, maybe a family— and they would go nuts and yell at us and say things like, "You should prepare yourselves! You should build fences! You don't know what's coming!"

Our all-night fiestas gave them the jim-jams. Here the world was coming to an end and Big Barbara and the mayor, J. P. Alderman Alderson, were trading salsa recipes and Steamin' Screamin' Kevin the Magical Dancing Bear was playing David Byrne records as loud as he could. What were we, *nuts?*

So I used to listen to these people, many of whom had actually seen zombies. And the way they described them—white-faced and staring and rotting and hungry, hungry, hungry, teeth chattering away like those wind-up toys and all that groaning—that would make me lose my rhythm whether I was learning the Lambada or having sex with someone (speaking of groaning) in Surfer Bob's double-wide for an extra helping of Big Barbara's Six Gun Six Fart Chili. And that brought me down in a major way, believe it, dude.

So after a while we imposed censorship, which was okay, and we got more particular about letting people immigrate. That is to say, hang with us. A couple of people left—were urged to leave—the ones who didn't like the status quo. Screw 'em and the trailers they rode in on. And the rest of us regulars kept on keeping on, bouncing on Life's well-sprung trampoline.

And speaking of well-sprung, which by the way rhymes with "well-hung," I have not yet mentioned Surfer Bob. He was the love of my life, my true White Knight, my Prince Charming. He was from Malibu and he never lost his tan, his surfer's knees, or his accent. He was the most laid-back of all us laid-back townsfolk, and just about no matter what you said, his answer was always, "Cool!"

YOU: "Bob, it's your turn to stand guard."

FB: "Cool!"

YOU: "Bob, you gotta drive two hundred miles to get more juice for the generators."

FB: "Cool!"

YOU (well, actually, ME, that is to say, JUANITA): "Bob, you gotta vacate cuz the mayor wants to 'visit' me in private."

FB: "Cool!"

See what I mean? You gotta love a guy like that.

So like I said, I kept thinking: If this is what happens when lots of zombies start devouring lots of folks, talk about your serendipity! I had friends, an important position (well, actually dozens of 'em, ha-ha) and I had never eaten better in my life.

Then these really downer people came through with a captured zombie, and I saw the problem—meltdown, freak city, and talk about your blind panic!—and I still think it was the right thing the Mayor did, cuz otherwise more people would have gotten killed. And besides, it was quick.

Soon enough we got the bodies buried, said our little prayers, and then we all bounced back—*boing!*—on our trampolines. Before you knew it, we were back to partying, partying on, and it seemed our little festivals lasted from one dawn to the next. We did not stopping partying; and Big Barbara was running around screaming and saying something about us all giving in to hysteria, how we were sick! We were sick!

WE WERE SICK!

And that scene was fast, too.

And the next thing I know, the mayor was saying, "It has come to my attention that we have all been infected with the zombie virus, and the proof is that we look like hell and we ate Big Barbara last night. I just finished devouring my wife in my Airstream, and I can see Juanita over there drooling over Surfer Bob like he was a T-bone."

And you know what? He was so righteously right-on right!

These days our little community is known by many names: Zombietown, Casa de Zombies or Zombia. But mostly people just call it Zombonia.

We still have our parties, and we still light our lights, even though we skip the fires. And I still fuck, but not for food. And it's going to last forever.

Most definitely the best thing that ever happened to me!

As my hunky and darling and finger-lickin' good Surfer Bob (his heart was still beating and everybody teased me about that, also because he had a jones during the entire banqueteria) used to say, "Cool!"

So, hey, baby, disco down to stone soul city!

If you're bummed about the solid state of the world, haul your sweet, throbbin' brainpan out here to Zombonia. We're here for you, dudes and dudettes. We'll help you out.

Especially if you want to start over.

Big Time!

COOL AIR

H. P. Lovecraft

Howard Phillips Lovecraft was born in Providence, Rhode Island, in 1890. A life-long antiquarian who had an interest in astronomy, his early work was initially published in the amateur press.

His tales of horror and the macabre did not see print professionally until the early 1920s, and even then the bulk of his work appeared in such pulp magazines as *Weird Tales*, along with a handful of hardcover anthologies.

Following his untimely death in 1937, Lovecraft's work was initially kept in print by Arkham House publishers, and today his fiction—notably the influential "Cthulhu Mythos"—is known all over the world and forms the basis for countless books, movies, comics, collectibles, and role-playing games.

The author wrote "Cool Air" in March 1928 during a miserable stay in New York City. Although obviously influenced by Edgar Allan Poe's story "The Facts in the Case of M. Valdemar," Lovecraft himself later claimed that his inspiration for the story came from Arthur Machen's "The Novel of the White Powder." There is also no doubt that the tale reflected the author's own abnormal sensitivity to the cold.

Weird Tales editor Farnsworth Wright inexplicably rejected the story, even though Lovecraft considered it "not nearly so bad as many he has taken," and it eventually appeared in the penultimate March 1928 issue of *Tales of Magic and Mystery*, a classy-looking but short-lived pulp that ran for just five issues. Following Lovecraft's death, Wright did eventually purchase the story, and he used it in the September 1939 edition of *Weird Tales*.

Lovecraft's story was the unofficial basis for EC Comics's "Baby . . . It's Cold Inside!" in *Vault of Horror* No.17 (February/March, 1951), and artist Bernie Wrightson adapted it for the second issue of Pacific Comics's *Berni Wrightson: Master of the Macabre* (August, 1983).

Rod Serling scripted an adaptation directed by Jeannot Szwarc for the 1971 NBC-TV series *Night Gallery*, and the story also formed the basis for Shusuke Kaneko's episode "The Cold" in the Lovecraftian omnibus movie *Necronomicon* (1993). Bryan Moore directed a fifty-minute version in 1999, while Serdge Rodnunsky's *Chill* (2007) was also loosely based on Lovecraft's classic tale.

YOU ASK ME TO EXPLAIN why I am afraid of a draught of cool air; why I shiver more than others upon entering a cold room, and seem nauseated and repelled when the chill of evening creeps through the heat of a mild autumn day. There are those who say I respond to cold as others do to a bad odour, and I am the last to deny the impression. What I will do is to relate the most horrible circumstance I ever encountered, and leave it to you to judge whether or not this forms a suitable explanation of my peculiarity.

It is a mistake to fancy that horror is associated inextricably with darkness, silence, and solitude. I found it in the glare of mid-afternoon, in the clangour of a metropolis, and in the teeming midst of a shabby and commonplace rooming-house with a prosaic landlady and two stalwart men by my side. In the spring of 1923 I had secured some dreary and unprofitable magazine work in the city of New York; and being unable to pay any substantial rent, began drifting from one cheap boarding establishment to another in search of a room which might combine the qualities of decent cleanliness, endurable furnishings, and very reasonable price. It soon developed that I had only a choice between different evils, but after a time I came upon a house in West Fourteenth Street which disgusted me much less than the others I had sampled.

The place was a four-story mansion of brownstone, dating apparently from the late forties, and fitted with woodwork and marble whose stained and sullied splendour argued a descent from high levels of tasteful opulence. In the rooms, large and lofty, and decorated with impossible paper and ridiculously ornate stucco cornices, there lingered a depressing mustiness and hint of obscure cookery; but the floors were clean, the linen tolerably regular, and the hot water not too often cold or turned off, so that I came to regard it as at least a bearable place to hibernate 'til one might really live again. The landlady, a slatternly, almost bearded Spanish woman named Herrero, did not annoy me with gossip or with criticisms of the late-burning electric light in my third floor front hall room; and my fellow-lodgers were as quiet and uncommunicative as one might desire, being mostly Spaniards a little above the coarsest and crudest grade. Only the din of street cars in the thoroughfare below proved a serious annoyance.

I had been there about three weeks when the first odd incident occurred. One evening at about eight I heard a spattering on the floor and became suddenly aware that I had been smelling the pungent odour of ammonia for some time. Looking about, I saw that the ceiling was wet and dripping; the soaking apparently proceeding from a corner on the side toward the street. Anxious to stop the matter at its source, I hastened to the basement to tell the landlady; and was assured by her that the trouble would quickly be set right.

"Doctair Muñoz," she cried as she rushed upstairs ahead of me, "he have speel hees chemicals. He ees too seeck for doctair heemself—seecker and seecker all the time—but he weel not have no othair for help. He ees vairy queer in hees seeckness— all day he take funnee-smelling baths, and he cannot get excite or warm. All hees own housework he do—hees leetle room are full of bottles and machines, and he do not work as doctair. But he was great once—my fathair in Barcelona have hear of heem—and only joost now he feex a arm of the plumber that get hurt of sudden. He nevair go out, only on roof, and my boy Esteban he breeng heem hees food and laundry and mediceens and chemicals. My God, the sal-ammoniac that man use for to keep heem cool!"

Mrs. Herrero disappeared up the staircase to the fourth floor, and I returned to my room. The ammonia ceased to drip, and as I cleaned up what had spilled and opened the window for air, I heard the landlady's heavy footsteps above me. Dr. Muñoz I had never heard, save for certain sounds as of some gasoline-driven mechanism; since his step was soft and gentle. I wondered for a moment what the strange affliction of this man might be, and whether his obstinate refusal of outside aid were not the result of a rather baseless eccentricity. There is, I reflected tritely, an infinite deal of pathos in the state of an eminent person who has come down in the world.

I might never have known Dr. Muñoz had it not been for the heart attack that suddenly seized me one forenoon as I sat writing in my room. Physicians had told me of the danger of those spells, and I knew there was no time to be lost; so remembering what the landlady had said about the invalid's help of the injured workman, I dragged myself upstairs and knocked feebly at the door above mine. My knock was answered in good English by a curious voice some distance to the right, asking my name and business; and these things being stated, there came an opening of the door next to the one I had sought.

A rush of cool air greeted me; and though the day was one of the hottest of late June, I shivered as I crossed the threshold into a large apartment whose rich and tasteful decoration surprised me in this nest of squalor and seediness. A folding couch now filled its diurnal role of sofa, and the mahogany furniture, sumptuous hangings, old paintings, and mellow bookshelves all bespoke a gentleman's study rather than a boarding-house bedroom. I now saw that the hall room above mine— the "leetle room" of bottles and machines which Mrs. Herrero had mentioned—was merely the laboratory of the doctor; and that his main living quarters lay in the spacious adjoining room whose convenient alcoves and large contiguous bathroom permitted him to hide all dressers and obtrusively utilitarian devices. Dr. Muñoz, most certainly, was a man of birth, cultivation, and discrimination.

The figure before me was short but exquisitely proportioned, and clad in somewhat formal dress of perfect cut and fit. A high-bred face of masterful though not arrogant expression was adorned by a short iron-grey full beard, and an old-fashioned pince-nez shielded the full, dark eyes and surmounted an aquiline nose which gave a Moorish touch to a physiognomy otherwise dominantly Celtiberian. Thick, well-trimmed hair that argued the punctual calls of a barber was parted gracefully above a high forehead; and the whole picture was one of striking intelligence and superior blood and breeding.

Nevertheless, as I saw Dr. Muñoz in that blast of cool air, I felt a repugnance which nothing in his aspect could justify. Only his lividly inclined complexion and coldness of touch could have afforded a physical basis for this feeling, and even these things should have been excusable considering the man's known invalidism. It might, too, have been the singular cold that alienated me; for such chilliness was abnormal on so hot a day, and the abnormal always excites aversion, distrust, and fear.

But repugnance was soon forgotten in admiration, for the strange physician's extreme skill at once became manifest despite the ice-coldness and shakiness of his bloodless-looking hands. He clearly understood my needs at a glance, and ministered to them with a master's deftness; the while reassuring me in a finely modulated though oddly hollow and timbreless voice that he was the bitterest of sworn enemies to death, and had sunk his fortune and lost all his friends in a lifetime of bizarre experiment devoted to its bafflement and extirpation. Something of the benevolent fanatic seemed to reside in him, and he rambled on almost garrulously as he sounded my chest and mixed a suitable draught of drugs fetched from the smaller laboratory room. Evidently he found the society of a well-born man a rare novelty in this dingy environment, and was moved to unaccustomed speech as memories of better days surged over him.

His voice, if queer, was at least soothing; and I could not even perceive that he breathed as the fluent sentences rolled urbanely out. He sought to distract my mind from my own seizure by speaking of his theories and experiments; and I remember his tactfully consoling me about my weak heart by insisting that will and consciousness are stronger than organic life itself, so that if a bodily frame be but originally healthy and carefully preserved, it may through a scientific enhancement of these qualities retain a kind of nervous animation despite the most serious impairments, defects, or even absences in the battery of specific organs. He might, he half jestingly said, some day teach me to live—or at least to possess some kind of conscious existence—without any heart at all! For his part, he was afflicted with a complication of maladies requiring a very exact regimen which included constant cold. Any marked rise in temperature might, if prolonged, affect him fatally; and the frigidity of his habitation—some fifty-five or fifty-six degrees Fahrenheit—was maintained by an absorption system of ammonia cooling, the gasoline engine of whose pumps I had often heard in my own room below.

Relieved of my seizure in a marvellously short while, I left the shivery place a disciple and devotee of the gifted recluse. After that I paid him frequent over-coated calls; listening while he told of secret researches and almost ghastly results, and trembling a bit when I examined the unconventional and astonishingly ancient volumes on his shelves. I was eventually, I may add, almost cured of my disease for all time by his skilful ministrations. It seems that he did not scorn the incantations of the mediaevalists, since he believed these cryptic formulae to contain rare psychological stimuli which might conceivably have singular effects on the substance of a nervous system from which organic pulsations had fled. I was touched by his account of the aged Dr. Torres of Valencia, who had shared his earlier experiments and nursed him through the great illness of eighteen years before, whence his present disorders proceeded. No sooner had the venerable practitioner saved his colleague than he himself succumbed to the grim enemy he had fought. Perhaps the strain had been too great; for Dr. Muñoz made it whisperingly clear—though not in detail—that the methods of healing had been most extraordinary, involving scenes and processes not welcomed by elderly and conservative Galens.

As the weeks passed, I observed with regret that my new friend was indeed slowly but unmistakably losing ground physically, as Mrs. Herrero had suggested. The livid aspect of his countenance was intensified, his voice became more hollow and indistinct, his muscular motions were less perfectly coördinated, and his mind and will displayed less resilience and initiative. Of this sad change he seemed by no means unaware, and little by little his expression and conversation both took on a gruesome irony which restored in me something of the subtle repulsion I had originally felt.

He developed strange caprices, acquiring a fondness for exotic spices and Egyptian incense 'til his room smelled like a vault of a sepulchred Pharaoh in the Valley of Kings. At the same time, his demands for cold air increased, and with my aid he amplified the ammonia piping of his room and modified the pumps and feed of his refrigerating machine 'til he could keep the temperature as low as thirty-four or forty degrees, and finally even twenty-eight degrees; the bathroom and laboratory, of course, being less chilled, in order that water might not freeze, and that chemical processes might not be impeded. The tenant adjoining him complained of the icy air from around the connecting door, so I helped him fit heavy hangings to obviate the difficulty. A kind of growing horror, of outré and morbid cast, seemed to possess him. He talked of death incessantly, but laughed hollowly when such things as burial or funeral arrangements were gently suggested.

All in all, he became a disconcerting and even gruesome companion; yet in my gratitude for his healing I could not well abandon him to the strangers around him, and was careful to dust his room and attend to his needs each day, muffled in a heavy ulster which I bought especially for the purpose. I likewise did much of his shopping, and gasped in bafflement at some of the chemicals he ordered from druggists and laboratory supply houses.

An increasing and unexplained atmosphere of panic seemed to rise around his apartment. The whole house, as I have said, had a musty odour; but the smell in his room was worse, and in spite of all the spices and incense, and the pungent chemicals of the now incessant baths which he insisted on taking unaided, I perceived that it must be connected with his ailment, and shuddered when I reflected on what that ailment might be. Mrs. Herrero crossed herself when she looked at him, and gave him up unreservedly to me; not even letting her son Esteban continue to run errands for him. When I suggested other physicians, the sufferer would fly into as much of a rage as he seemed to dare to entertain. He evidently feared the physical effect of violent emotion, yet his will and driving force waxed rather than waned, and he refused to be confined to his bed. The lassitude of his earlier ill days gave place to a return of his fiery purpose, so that he seemed about to hurl defiance at the death-daemon even as that ancient enemy seized him. The pretence of eating, always curiously like a formality with him, he virtually abandoned; and mental power alone appeared to keep him from total collapse.

He acquired a habit of writing long documents of some sort, which he carefully sealed and filled with injunctions that I transmit them after his death to certain persons whom he named—for the most part lettered East Indians, but including a once celebrated French physician now generally thought dead, and about whom the most inconceivable things had been whispered. As it happened, I burned all these papers undelivered and unopened. His aspect and voice became utterly frightful, and his presence almost unbearable. One September day an unexpected glimpse of him induced an epileptic fit in a man who had come to repair his electric desk lamp; a fit for which he prescribed effectively whilst keeping himself well out of sight. That man, oddly enough, had been through the terrors of the Great War without having incurred any fright so thorough.

Then, in the middle of October, the horror of horrors came with stupefying suddenness. One night about eleven the pump of the refrigerating machine broke down, so that within three hours the process of ammonia cooling became impossible.

Dr. Muñoz summoned me by thumping on the floor, and I worked desperately to repair the injury while my host cursed in a tone whose lifeless, rattling hollowness surpassed description. My amateur efforts, however, proved of no use; and when I had brought in a mechanic from a neighbouring all-night garage, we learned that nothing could be done until morning, when a new piston would have to be obtained. The moribund hermit's rage and fear, swelling to grotesque proportions, seemed likely to shatter what remained of his failing physique; and once a spasm caused him to clap his hands to his eyes and rush into the bathroom. He groped his way out with face tightly bandaged, and I never saw his eyes again.

The frigidity of the apartment was now sensibly diminishing, and at about five in the morning, the doctor retired to the bathroom, commanding me to keep him supplied with all the ice I could obtain at all-night drug stores and cafeterias. As I would return from my sometimes discouraging trips and lay my spoils before the closed bathroom door, I could hear a restless splashing within, and a thick voice croaking out the order for "More—more!" At length a warm day broke, and the shops opened one by one. I asked Esteban either to help with the ice-fetching while I obtained the pump piston, or to order the piston while I continued with the ice; but instructed by his mother, he absolutely refused.

Finally I hired a seedy-looking loafer whom I encountered on the corner of Eighth Avenue to keep the patient supplied with ice from a little shop where I introduced him, and applied myself diligently to the task of finding a pump piston and engaging workmen competent to install it. The task seemed interminable, and I raged almost as violently as the hermit when I saw the hours slipping by in a breathless, foodless round of vain telephoning, and a hectic quest from place to place, hither and thither by subway and surface car. About noon I encountered a suitable supply house far downtown, and at approximately one-thirty that afternoon arrived at my boarding-place with the necessary paraphernalia and two sturdy and intelligent mechanics. I had done all I could, and hoped I was in time.

Black terror, however, had preceded me. The house was in utter turmoil, and above the chatter of awed voices I heard a man praying in a deep basso. Fiendish things were in the air, and lodgers told over the beads of their rosaries as they caught the odour from beneath the doctor's closed door. The lounger I had hired, it seems, had fled screaming and mad-eyed not long after his second delivery of ice: perhaps as a result of excessive curiosity. He could not, of course, have locked the door behind him; yet it was now fastened, presumably from the inside. There was no sound within save a nameless sort of slow, thick dripping.

Briefly consulting with Mrs. Herrero and the workmen despite a fear that gnawed my inmost soul, I advised the breaking down of the door; but the landlady found a way to turn the key from the outside with some wire device. We had previously opened the doors of all the other rooms on that hall, and flung all the windows to the very top. Now, noses protected by handkerchiefs, we tremblingly invaded the accursed south room which blazed with the warm sun of early afternoon.

A kind of dark, slimy trail led from the open bathroom door to the hall door, and thence to the desk, where a terrible little pool had accumulated. Something was scrawled there in pencil in an awful, blind hand on a piece of paper hideously smeared as though by the very claws that traced the hurried last words. Then the trail led to the couch and ended unutterably.

What was, or had been, on the couch I cannot and dare not say here. But this is what I shiveringly puzzled out on the stickily smeared paper before I drew a match and burned it to a crisp; what I puzzled out in terror as the landlady and two mechanics rushed frantically from that hellish place to babble their incoherent stories at the nearest police station. The nauseous words seemed well-nigh incredible in that yellow sunlight, with the clatter of cars and motor trucks ascending clamorously from crowded Fourteenth Street, yet I confess that I believed them then. Whether I believe them now I honestly do not know. There are things about which it is better not to speculate, and all that I can say is that I hate the smell of ammonia, and grow faint at a draught of unusually cool air.

"The end," ran that noisome scrawl, "is here. No more ice—the man looked and ran away. Warmer every minute, and the tissues can't last. I fancy you know—what I said about the will and the nerves and the preserved body after the organs ceased to work. It was good theory, but couldn't keep up indefinitely. There was a gradual deterioration I had not foreseen. Dr. Torres knew, but the shock killed him. He couldn't stand what he had to do; he had to get me in a strange, dark place when he minded my letter and nursed me back. And the organs never would work again. It had to be done my way—artificial preservation—*for you see I died that time eighteen years ago.*"

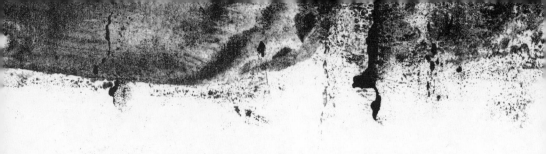

CALL FIRST

Ramsey Campbell

Ramsey Campbell was born in Liverpool, England, where he still lives with his wife Jenny. After working as a tax officer from 1962 to 1966, and as a library assistant from 1966 to 1973, he became a full-time writer.

His first book, a collection of stories entitled *The Inhabitant of the Lake and Less Welcome Tenants*, was published by August Derleth's legendary Arkham House imprint in 1964. Since then his novels have included *The Doll Who Ate His Mother*, *The Face That Must Die*, *The Parasite*, *The Nameless*, *Incarnate*, *The Claw* (a.k.a. *Night of the Claw*), *Obsession*, *The Hungry Moon*, *The Influence*, *Ancient Images*, *Midnight Sun*, *The Count of Eleven*, *The Long Lost*, *The One Safe Place*, *The House on Nazareth Hill*, *The Last Voice They Hear*, *Pact of the Fathers*, *The Darkest Part of the Woods*, *The Overnight*, *Secret Story*, *The Grin of the Dark*, *Thieving Fear*, *Creatures of the Pool*, and *The Seven Days of Cain*.

His short fiction has been collected in such volumes as *Demons by Daylight*, *The Height of the Scream*, *Dark Companions*, *Scared Stiff*, *Waking Nightmares*, *Dark Companions*, *Cold Print*, *Alone with the Horrors*, *Strange Things and Stranger Places*, *Ghosts and Grisly Things*, *Told by the Dead*, and *Just Behind You*. He has edited a number of anthologies, including *Superhorror* (a.k.a. *The Far Reaches of Fear*), *New Terrors*, *New Tales of the Cthulhu Mythos*, *Fine Frights: Stories That Scared Me*, *Uncanny Banquet*, *Meddling with Ghosts*, and *Gathering the Bones: Original Stories from the World's Masters of Horror* (with Dennis Etchison and Jack Dann).

Ramsey Campbell has won multiple World Fantasy Awards, British Fantasy Awards, and Bram Stoker Awards, and is a recipient of the World Horror Convention Grand Master Award, the Horror Writers Association Lifetime Achievement Award, the Howie Award of the H. P. Lovecraft Film Festival for Lifetime Achievement, and the International Horror Guild's Living Legend Award. A film reviewer for BBC Radio Merseyside since 1969, he is also president of both the British Fantasy Society and the Society of Fantastic Films.

"In late 1973, my agent, Kirby McCauley, gave me the news that Marvel Comics was looking to publish horror comics and to use short stories in-between the graphic tales," Campbell recalls. "They apparently wanted stories no more than 1,800 words long using the classic figures—vampires, zombies, and the like—of horror fiction.

"It sounded like a challenge and energized me to write, if I recall correctly, six such tales in January 1974. Some I wrote in just a day, others—such as "Call First"—in two days each.

"Off they went to Kirby, but Marvel had decided not to use prose tales after all. Charlie Grant bought one, but Kirby snaffled "Call First" for his own anthology.

"It's a story of mine that always goes down well when I read it aloud, and when she was at high school, the Canadian artist Adriana Capozzi learned it by heart and recited the entire tale. With fans like (and as delightful as) that, I must be doing something right, yes?"

IT WAS THE OTHER porters who made Ned determined to know who answered the phone in the old man's house.

Not that he hadn't wanted to know before. He'd felt it was his right almost as soon as the whole thing had begun, months ago. He'd been sitting behind his desk in the library entrance, waiting for someone to try to take a bag into the library so he could shout after them that they couldn't, when the reference librarian ushered the old man up to Ned's desk and said "Let this gentleman use your phone." Maybe he hadn't meant every time the old man came to the library, but then he should have said so. The old man used to talk to the librarian and tell him things about books even he didn't know, which was why he let him phone. All Ned could do was feel resentful. People weren't supposed to use his phone, and even he wasn't allowed to phone outside the building. And it wasn't as if the old man's calls were interesting. Ned wouldn't have minded if they'd been worth hearing.

"I'm coming home now." That was all he ever said; then he'd put down the receiver and hurry away. It was the way he said it that made Ned wonder. There was no feeling behind the words, they sounded as if he were saying them only because he had to, perhaps wishing he needn't. Ned knew people talked like that: his parents did in church and most of the time at home. He wondered if the old man was calling his wife, because he wore a ring on his wedding-finger, although in the claw where a stone should be was what looked like a piece of yellow fingernail. But Ned didn't think it could be his wife; each day the old man came he left the library at the same time, so why would he bother to phone?

Then there was the way the old man looked at Ned when he phoned: as if he didn't matter and couldn't understand, the way most of the porters looked at him. That was the look that swelled up inside Ned one day and made him persuade one of the other porters to take charge of his desk while Ned waited to listen in on the old man's call. The girl who always smiled at Ned was on the switchboard, and they listened together. They heard the phone in the house ringing then lifted, and the old man's call and his receiver going down: nothing else, not even breathing apart from the old man's. "Who do you think it is?" the girl said, but Ned thought she'd laugh if he said he didn't know. He shrugged extravagantly and left.

Now he was determined. The next time the old man came to the library Ned phoned his house, having read what the old man dialed. When the ringing began its pulse sounded deliberately slow, and Ned felt the pumping of his blood rushing ahead. Seven trills and the phone in the house opened with a violent click. Ned held his breath, but all he could hear was his blood thumping in his ears. "Hello," he said and after a silence, clearing his throat, "Hello!" Perhaps it was one of those answering machines people in films used in the office. He felt foolish and uneasy greeting the wide silent metal ear, and put down the receiver. He was in bed and falling asleep before he wondered why the old man should tell an answering machine that he was coming home.

The following day, in the bar where all the porters went at lunchtime, Ned told them about the silently listening phone. "He's weird, that old man," he said, but now the others had finished joking with him they no longer seemed interested, and he had to make a grab for the conversation. "He reads weird books," he said. "All about witches and magic. Real ones, not stories."

"Now tell us something we didn't know," someone said, and the conversation turned its back on Ned. His attention began to wander, he lost his hold on what was being said, he had to smile and nod as usual when they looked at him, and he was thinking: they're looking at me like the old man does. I'll show them. I'll go in his house and see who's there. Maybe I'll take something that'll show I've been there. Then they'll have to listen.

But next day at lunchtime, when he arrived at the address he'd seen on the old man's library card, Ned felt more like knocking at the front door and running away. The house was menacingly big, the end house of a street whose other windows were brightly bricked up. Exposed foundations like broken teeth protruded from the mud that surrounded the street, while the mud was walled in by a five-storey crescent of flats that looked as if it had been designed in sections to be fitted together by a two-year-old. Ned tried to keep the house between him and the flats, even though they were hundreds of yards away, as he peered in the windows.

All he could see through the grimy front window was bare floorboards; when he coaxed himself to look through the side window, the same. He dreaded being caught by the old man, even though he'd seen him sitting behind a pile of books ten minutes ago. It had taken Ned that long to walk here; the old man couldn't walk so fast, and there wasn't a bus he could catch. At last he dodged round the back and peered into the kitchen: a few plates in the sink, some tins of food, an old cooker. Nobody to be seen. He returned to the front, wondering what to do. Maybe he'd knock after all. He took hold of the bar of the knocker, trying to think what he'd say, and the door opened.

The hall leading back to the kitchen was long and dim. Ned stood shuffling indecisively on the step. He would have to decide soon, for his lunch-hour was dwindling. It was like one of the empty houses he'd used to play in with the other children, daring each other to go up the tottering stairs. Even the things in the kitchen didn't make it seem lived in. He'd show them all. He went in. Acknowledging a vague idea that the old man's companion was out, he closed the door to hear if they returned.

On his right was the front room; on his left, past the stairs and the phone, another of the bare rooms he'd seen. He tiptoed upstairs. The stairs creaked and swayed a little, perhaps unused to anyone of Ned's weight. He reached the landing, breathing heavily, feeling dust chafe his throat. Stairs led up to a closed attic door, but he looked in the rooms off the landing.

Two of the doors which he opened stealthily showed him nothing but boards and flurries of floating dust. The landing in front of the third looked cleaner, as if the door were often opened. He pulled it towards him, holding it up all the way so it didn't scrape the floor, and went in.

Most of it didn't seem to make sense. There was a single bed with faded sheets. Against the walls were tables and piles of old books. Even some of the books looked disused. There were black candles and racks of small cardboard boxes. On one of the tables lay a single book. Ned padded across the fragments of carpet and opened the book in a thin path of sunlight through the shutters.

Inside the sagging covers was a page which Ned slowly realized had been ripped from the Bible. It was the story of Lazarus. Scribbles that might be letters filled the margins, and at the bottom of the page: "p. 491." Suddenly inspired, Ned turned to that page in the book. It showed a drawing of a corpse sitting up in his coffin, but the book was all in the language they sometimes used in church: Latin. He thought of asking one of the librarians what it meant. Then he remembered that he needed proof he'd been in the house. He stuffed the page from the Bible into his pocket.

As he crept swiftly downstairs, something was troubling him. He reached the hall and thought he knew what it was. He still didn't know who lived in the house with the old man. If they lived in the back perhaps there would be signs in the kitchen. Though if it was his wife, Ned thought as he hurried down the hall, she couldn't be like Ned's mother, who would never have left torn strips of wallpaper hanging at shoulder height from both walls. He'd reached the kitchen door when he realized what had been bothering him. When he'd emerged from the bedroom, the attic door had been open.

He looked back involuntarily, and saw a woman walking away from him down the hall.

He was behind the closed kitchen door before he had time to feel fear. That came only when he saw that the back door was nailed rustily shut. Then he controlled himself. She was only a woman, she couldn't do much if she found him. He opened the door minutely. The hall was empty.

Halfway down the hall he had to slip into the side room, heart punching his chest, for she'd appeared again from between the stairs and the front door. He felt the beginnings of anger and recklessness, and they grew faster when he opened the door and had to flinch back as he saw her hand passing. The fingers looked famished, the color of old lard, with long yellow cracked nails. There was no nail on her wedding-finger, which wore a plain ring. She was returning from the direction of the kitchen, which was why Ned hadn't expected her.

Through the opening of the door he heard her padding upstairs. She sounded barefoot. He waited until he couldn't hear her, then edged out into the hall. The door began to swing open behind him with a faint creak, and he drew it stealthily closed. He paced towards the front door. If he hadn't seen her shadow creeping down the stairs he would have come face to face with her.

He'd retreated to the kitchen, and was near to panic, when he realized she knew he was in the house. She was playing a game with him. At once he was furious. She was only an old woman, her body beneath the long white dress was sure to be as thin as her hands, she could only shout when she saw him, she couldn't stop him leaving. In a minute he'd be late for work. He threw open the kitchen door and swaggered down the hall.

The sight of her lifting the phone receiver broke his stride for a moment. Perhaps she was phoning the police. He hadn't done anything, she could have her Bible page back. But she laid the receiver beside the phone. Why? Was she making sure the old man couldn't ring?

As she unbent from stooping to the phone she grasped two uprights of the banisters to support herself. They gave a loud splintering creak and bent together. Ned halted, confused. He was still struggling to react when she turned towards him, and he saw her face. Part of it was still on the bone.

He didn't back away until she began to advance on him, her nails tearing new strips from both walls. All he could see was her eyes, unsupported by flesh. His mind was backing away faster than he was, but it had come up against a terrible insight. He even knew why she'd made sure the old man couldn't interrupt until she'd finished. His calls weren't like speaking to answering machine at all. They were exactly like switching off a burglar alarm.

JOE AND ABEL IN THE FIELD OF REST

Lisa Morton

Lisa Morton lives in North Hollywood, California. She is a screenwriter (*Meet the Hollow-heads*, *Blood Angels*, and *Glass Trap*, among others), the author of four nonfiction books, and a prolific scribe of short fiction, with recent appearances in *Cemetery Dance* magazine and the anthologies *Unspeakable Horror* and *The Bleeding Edge*. In 2009 she edited *Midnight Walk*, an original anthology of terror and suspense from Darkhouse Publishing.

Morton won the 2006 Bram Stoker Award for Short Fiction, and two years later she also received the Stoker Award for Nonfiction (for *A Hallowe'en Anthology: Literary and Historical Writings over the Centuries*). Her first novel, *The Castle of Los Angeles*, was published in 2009 by Gray Friar Press, and a novella, *The Lucid Dreaming*, is available from Bad Moon Books.

"I've always been interested in writing about non-romantic love," reveals the author, "a love for a friend or a parent, a pet, even a precious object.

"The idea of writing a story about the love a man feels for a walking corpse presented a bit more of a challenge than usual: How do you make the man (Joe) into a real character whom audiences can relate to? And how do you tell a story about this love while still keeping it firmly in a zombie milieu, complete with action and suspense?

"The key was Joe—I thought about him for a long time, until I felt as if I knew him, and when I sat down to finally write the story everything else fell into place with surprising ease."

IT WAS STILL DARK when Joe suddenly sat up in bed, chest hitching, calling out, "Da?"

Then, as he sat in the pre-dawn gloom, breath slowing, he focused on the house, on the bed, on himself, and remembered:

Da was gone. He'd died a year ago; his ashes now rested in the urn above the fireplace.

Before Joe could stop to really wonder what had awakened him, he heard it: A thud on the front door of the house, followed by another, and another. Something was outside, knocking against the steel-reinforced door with rhythmic determination.

For a moment, absurdly, Joe had an urge to cry. Of course Da was long gone, replaced by the constant threat of *them*. Of course Joe was completely alone, in a house without electricity and only an inch of metal between him and something that thought of him as nothing but meat.

Joe briefly considered waiting until dawn; he thought the door would hold. But without a clock, he had no way of knowing how far off sunrise was, and there was still a small, nagging doubt tugging him away from sleep.

So he slid from his cooling sheets, lit a propane lantern, and made his way down the hallway and past the living room to the front door. Once there, he picked up the loaded rifle he always kept waiting.

He paused, listening, but heard no indication that there was more than a single one of them out there. This should be an easy in-and-out, then—he'd let the thing in, then take it out.

Joe placed the lantern on the side entry table, checked the gun (even though he'd checked it just before bed, as he did every night), and stepped back slightly from the door. He set his feet apart and reached forward, cautiously, carefully, knowing this would depend on timing. He finally took a deep breath, darted a hand forward and turned the lock and the doorknob, then leapt back, whipping up the rifle.

Almost immediately the door crashed in and a dead thing was grappling with Joe, too close to shoot, its flaking fingers reaching for him, jaw slack and venting a hungry howl. Joe tried to back away, but hit a wall. He swung the rifle until the barrel was facing down and used it to hold his aggressor back. He gave a push and the gaping nightmare staggered. Joe raised the rifle as a club, and it went off as the stock hit the dead man's head. He felt powder burn his leg, but he had no time to see if he'd been shot. Instead he swung again, then changed his hold on the gun and drove the rifle's stock butt-first into the other's forehead. Bone cracked beneath the blow, and all sound ceased. One more ramming and Joe stepped back as his attacker dropped, truly dead at last.

Joe smacked the gun into its head three more times to be sure.

Then he remembered the open door, swung the rifle around and grabbed the lantern. He saw one other figure outside and waited until it came closer. A single efficient shot and it went down. He looked at the corpse beneath him, kicked the stiff body out the door, then closed and barred it again.

Safe once more, Joe walked into the kitchen, intending to grab rags and water to clean, but instead he dropped into one of the old peeling chairs and let the gun fall from nerveless fingers.

"Da . . ." he whispered before slumping into the chair, too tired to do anymore.

．　．　．　．　．

In the morning, Joe ate his usual sparse breakfast of canned fruit, goat's milk and nuts, then opened the door carefully. He'd gotten started later than usual today, having decided to wait until the sun was completely up so he could spot any more of them.

Walkers.

When they'd first appeared six months ago, he hadn't known what to call them. He was a simple man and had no vocabulary to apply to reanimated corpses that sought to consume the living. He'd watched the first few days of the plague on the television, then broadcasting had stopped and power had followed. Joe and his father had been largely self-sufficient for years, selling crops from their little farm for the few necessities they didn't already have. Then Da had died, and Joe had continued on the same way, growing corn and potatoes and walnuts, until the world had died.

Newly acquired by its own kind.

It had taken an accident to tell Joe how to stop them. One of the things had been bludgeoned by a heavy, swinging pulley in the barn, and it was the first one Joe had seen really die. After that he'd learned how to deal with them easily, with a single shot from his old rifle.

He'd barricaded his house first. Then, after losing all of his pigs and most of his goats, he'd fortified the barn to protect the remaining livestock. Joe had never been a reader, but a few cautious trips to the nearest library—empty now, forgotten, silent—had taught him how to put up stronger fencing, set up a hothouse, and cast his own bullets. Soon he'd fortified the entire farm, with a chain link boundary lifted from the nearest large hardware store and an extra supply of guns and ammo.

And he basically lived the way he'd always lived—tending crops and livestock until the sun set, then eating a simple final meal before collapsing into bed, sleeping eight hours, and rising to start again.

Except now he was alone.

When Da had been alive, they had never spoken much, two taciturn men who spent their energies on work. But there had been *two* of them. It had been enough. Two was all Joe could remember—his mother had died when he was only four, and he no longer had any memory of her. Somehow, though, he thought she'd been worn out by this life, wrung out early and left to die a husk.

At least she hadn't come back.

Joe had never put much thought into the mechanics of why some came back and some didn't. He occasionally arose in the morning and saw a walker raking its dry fingers over his fence, and had some moment of dull shock when he realized he'd once known the fingers' owner.

Jenny from the convenience store . . . the pastor I used to see in the market . . .

After Joe got past the moment of surprise, he shot them in the head. And then he took their bodies to the Field of Rest.

That was what he called it, at least. In reality it was a pit he'd dug with the backhoe in the half-acre at the far northwest corner of the farm where nothing would grow—the land was stony and barren, not even good for grazing. One day Joe had used precious gallons of fuel (although he'd never regretted it) to dig the twenty-foot deep pit, three-dozen yards in diameter. From then on, he'd thrown the dead walkers into the pit, waiting until the bottom was lined with enough to shovel in a layer of dirt.

The Field of Rest was only ten feet deep now.

A quick scan of his fence today showed Joe where they'd broken through last night. They'd pushed in a section near the Field of Rest. He shot another walker at the perimeter (*I used to see her at the feed store, didn't I?*), then set to work repairing and strengthening the fence.

It was afternoon by the time he was done. Joe went back to the house to eat his small lunch (*almost out of the jerky*), then released the three remaining goats from the barn and retrieved a wheelbarrow. He loaded up last night's two dead walkers, then made his way out to the Field. It was a warm day, late in May, and he was sweating by the time he reached the edge of the pit.

He set down the wheelbarrow, preparing to dump its contents, when he heard something—scrabbling. Moaning.

A walker. In the pit.

Joe carefully leaned over the edge and saw it. Moving, at the bottom, clawing at the dirt wall just below him.

It was trapped, and he paused to examine it. He thought he knew it—a young man, no more than twenty-seven or twenty-eight, friendly, stout, bearded face (the beard now hung in tattered clumps from a decaying jaw), used to drive a truck, stopped at the pub every once in a while . . .

Strange name like something from the Bible—Abraham? No . . . Abel. That was it. Abel.

Joe realized this one must have entered with the rest last night and staggered into the pit. He saw that one leg indeed bent strangely, forcing the thing to support most of its dead weight on the remaining limb. It stared up at Joe and moaned softly, desperately scratching at the dirt walls in a futile, desperate attempt to climb.

Joe looked down at it thoughtfully. He'd left his rifle back in the house. He'd have to go back and get it. He'd have to aim carefully, since the shot would be a high angle from overhead and he didn't want to waste a bullet he couldn't retrieve.

"Abel . . ." Joe muttered.

The thing in the pit stopped mewling for a moment. It looked up at Joe, curiously . . . and in that moment, regardless of what would come after, Joe knew he wouldn't be putting a bullet into Abel's brain.

He dumped the dead walkers into the pit, watched idly as Abel turned away long enough to investigate. When Abel realized the bodies were dead and decayed, he turned his attention back to Joe, renewing his efforts to reach something warm and vital.

The sun was limning the western horizon when Joe finally remembered the rest of his chores and left the Field—and Abel—behind.

·   ·   ·   ·   ·

Joe visited Abel every day for the next three weeks.

He didn't put much thought into what compelled him to look at the thing in the pit—whether it was curiosity or boredom or something else he wouldn't name. He just knew he found some value in sitting by the edge, looking down, eventually talking to the walker.

It began as idle thoughts, about the weather, or the food, or the crops. But before long Joe was unleashing entire monologues on his captive companion. He talked about his life, about how well he and Da had worked together, how they hadn't needed anyone else, how they'd taught themselves to do important and necessary things. Once or twice Joe started to talk about watching the cancer take Da, how it'd eaten him away until he'd been little more than taut skin over bones when he'd died. How he'd obeyed Da's wishes and had him cremated.

How he was glad now that he had.

Meanwhile, Abel grew weaker and weaker, down there on the dirt floor, until his bad leg would support him no longer and he slid to a sitting position on the floor, tattered fingertips still drawing runnels around him. He stared up at Joe, mirroring Joe's own hunger, and Joe felt a compassion he'd experienced only once in his life—when as a child he'd rescued a lamb from an irrigation ditch.

And when Joe shot more walkers outside the fence, he carted them to a far corner of the Field of Rest, unwilling to hurl them down atop Abel.

One morning he awoke to find one of the three remaining goats had died during the night. Whether from old age or sickness Joe didn't know, and he didn't think about it as he methodically butchered the goat, placing some of the meat in his homemade smoker to preserve, and carving a portion for his dinner that night. He'd eat well for a change.

After he'd cooked the goat steak, he walked to the Field of Rest, steaming plate in one hand and a bucket in the other. When he reached the edge, he set both down and peered through dusk's gloom.

"Good evening, Abel. We're eating together tonight."

With that he emptied the bucket—which contained the parts of the goat he couldn't eat—into the pit, then sat down with his own plate.

Abel uttered a dry moan, then crept across the floor to clutch at the remains. Joe watched, enjoying his own repast, as Abel shoveled the pieces into his mouth. When Joe had gnawed his meat down to the bone, so had Abel, and they both finished—Joe sated and Abel renewed.

Apparently the meal had given the walker fresh strength, because he stood again, limping on his shattered limb to the wall below Joe. But this time he simply stood and looked up, a small sound escaping from his decayed mouth.

"You're welcome, Abel," Joe said, looking down into the pit and smiling.

. . . . .

A week after that, the weather turned hot and Joe sweated as he worked among his crops. Even though he had a hat and plenty of water, he could feel a few exposed parts burning beneath the cruel sun.

Then he heard a motor.

He froze, thinking perhaps it was merely an insect drone, but no—there it was, nearing. He spun and looked past the fence where the road ran, and sure enough— he spotted the glint of metal on something approaching.

Numb, Joe stood where he was and watched a huge, black, boxy vehicle approach. Someone had welded chicken wire over the windows, including the front, and Joe could see that some of the glass in the rear had been shattered.

The car's brakes suddenly squealed and it skidded to a stop just on the other side of the fence, perhaps a hundred feet from Joe. After a beat the driver's door was thrown back, and a tall, skinny young man leapt out. He took two, three steps toward Joe and stopped, peering.

They stared at each other for what seemed like hours, uncomprehending, each the first living human being the other had seen in weeks. Finally the driver broke the silence by calling out to Joe:

"Are you human?"

Joe blinked in surprise, tried to clear his throat, but it was suddenly too dry for words. He simply nodded.

"Do you have any spare food?"

Again, a silent nod. The driver's body suddenly relaxed and he gripped the car door to steady himself. Joe waved to his left and finally found his voice: "Gate's that way."

The young man nodded, grinned at Joe, and then happily climbed back into his car. Joe began to trudge toward the gate, simply astonished.

Behind him, in the Field of Rest, Abel groaned.

· · · · ·

His name was Harrison, Harrison Melcher, but everyone called him "Sonny." He was twenty-three years old and had worked as a print model until everything had fallen apart. He'd been driving ever since, looking for survivors, food, anything, but fuel was getting harder to find and he knew he'd have to stop soon. He hadn't eaten in two days.

He said all this around mouthfuls of Joe's pickled vegetables and two baked potatoes and a small portion of goat jerky. Joe listened and just nodded or shook his head when asked questions, like whether he lived alone (a nod) and if he knew of other survivors (a shake) and if it was safe here (another nod).

By the time Sonny had finished eating, the sun was setting and he asked Joe if he could stay the night. He could sleep in his car, which he'd been doing every night for the last month. He wouldn't impose.

In the end Joe offered him Da's room, despite the dust that had built up since Da had passed on. Sonny was nonetheless grateful, and fell asleep almost instantly.

Joe stayed up most of the night, his routine interrupted, his mind struggling to process the surprising flood of thoughts and emotions that swept through him. He sat at the kitchen table, sipping a cup of mulberry leaf tea and listening to the sound of Sonny's snoring. Da had snored, too, although it'd been louder than Sonny's. Probably because Sonny was younger.

Joe didn't really know. In fact, he suddenly became aware of just how little he knew about anyone else. So he listened carefully as Sonny talked more about himself the next day.

· · · · ·

About how he'd left home at eighteen, lived on the streets for two years before someone asked him to model, had just been starting to make some real money when all the shit hit. He talked about his lover Willum, who'd been attacked in front of Sonny's eyes one day. He talked about how he'd seen one camp of survivors behind barbed wire, but had moved on when he'd heard screaming from within. He talked about how he'd run out of food and ammunition at almost the same time, and how every store he'd stopped at in the last week had been stripped bare.

Joe listened to it all, and tried to process a life so different from his. He'd never had a job other than farming, enough money for a vacation, or a lover. Sonny was almost like some mythical creature to him, something he could barely relate to as his own species.

Then Sonny asked if he could stay.

"I really don't know where else to go," he said, and Joe was uncomfortable as he saw tears stream down Sonny's cheeks. "The cities are dead, the countryside's dead, there's no more gas or food . . . I could stay here with you. I can make myself useful. Teach me anything. I can learn to farm, we can grow twice as much together, right?"

He'd reached out then and touched Joe's hand.

Joe had stared in mute disbelief. No one but Da had ever touched him before. It was a light touch, and quickly withdrawn, but it left Joe stunned, unable to reply or even move.

Sonny must have sensed Joe's discomfort, because he abruptly wiped his eyes and stood, turning away. "Sorry, man . . . I know it's a lot to ask . . . hey, if it's okay, I'm just going for a walk."

Sonny walked out of the kitchen, and Joe continued to sit, still looking down at his hand.

Could Sonny stay here? Could he become a part of Joe's life? Joe knew he couldn't replace Da, but perhaps he could help. They could work the farm together, and with Abel they could—

What? Joe stopped and realized that he hadn't factored in Abel yet.

Joe's pondering was interrupted by the sound of running feet and panting. He looked up as Sonny burst into the kitchen, sweating, eyes wide. "Hey, man, you got one of *them* outside—one of the dead things—in some kind of pit out there—" Sonny waved an indiscriminate hand wildly in the air, indicating every direction at once.

Joe didn't say anything.

Sonny took an anxious step forward. "I don't have any ammo left . . . we've gotta shoot that thing—" His eyes darted around Joe's house, then fixed on something:

The rifle. By the front door, where Joe always left it, loaded.

Sonny grabbed the rifle and ran from the house.

Joe was instantly on his feet, running after Sonny and the gun. Sonny was younger and in good shape, and he easily outdistanced Joe as they both raced for the Field of Rest. Sonny reached the edge of the hole easily 200 feet in front of Joe, and Joe could only watch, running in slow-motion dread, as Sonny pulled back the rifle's bolt, lifted the gun to his eye, and aimed down.

An incoherent shout from Joe startled Sonny into lowering the gun, and he watched in perplexity as Joe reached him, gasping for air. "What—?!"

Joe put a hand on the barrel. "You can't shoot Abel."

Sonny gazed at him in disbelief for a moment, then burst into laughter. "He's fucking dead, don't you get that?! If you don't put a bullet in his head, he'll eventually dig his way out of there and turn you into a meal—"

Joe didn't answer, except to give a solid tug on the rifle, but Sonny didn't relinquish his grip.

"You're crazy."

Joe yanked harder on the gun, but this time Sonny stepped back and pulled the gun firmly away. "No way, man. No way am I giving you this gun."

In the pit, Abel looked up and cried out.

That was all Joe needed. He lunged for Sonny, barreling into him like a runaway bull. The action surprised Sonny, and although he was bigger than Joe he went down. They both fell to the rocky earth, grappling for the gun, hands pushing, feet kicking, the uneven surface jabbing them both as they rolled one way, then another. At one point the gun went off, and Joe couldn't tell if one of them had been hit. He drove his fingers into Sonny's eye sockets, and the other man screamed, involuntarily releasing his hold on both gun and Joe. Joe took advantage of the moment to scrabble back, finding the gun, raising it and cocking it as Sonny sat up, screaming, blood gushing down his face.

Then Joe pulled the trigger.

．　．　．　．　．

It was twilight before Joe finished, but he felt a surprising warmth flood through him, a serenity he thought he'd never known.

His full stomach protested slightly against the strange contents, but Joe had been surprised to find the taste reasonably pleasant. Below him, Abel still gnawed on an arm bone, dark blood smearing his ravaged face.

"You were right, Abel. It's good."

Abel finished eating and suddenly stopped to stare at the grisly bones he now held. Joe watched, peering through the gathering darkness, thinking that something had happened to Abel—something had awakened in him that Joe hadn't seen before. Abel jabbed the pointed end of the bones into the earth, and created a sizable furrow as he pulled the bone towards him.

He looked up at Joe, and Joe thought he saw Abel smile.

Abel hauled himself to his unsteady feet and ambled to the side of the pit just beneath Joe. Joe bent over to watch as Abel, reinvigorated by his meal, determinedly jammed arm bones into the dirt, causing a sizable clod to fall. He did it again and again, and within a few moments several feet of the wall above him had crumbled. At this rate, Joe knew it wouldn't be long until Abel would create enough of a pathway to crawl up—that soon he'd be out of the Field of Rest and back to the world's surface.

Joe saw the rifle by his side, and for a second an image flashed in his mind's eye—an image of fighting Sonny for the gun, of the gun going off and Sonny falling back, dead. Murdered.

Joe's reverie was interrupted by the sound of more of the soil falling away below him. He looked up into the clear evening sky, and thought about how pleasant it would be to pass the warm night here, in the open, under the forgiving stars.

He lay back to wait.

MIDNIGHT AT THE BODY FARM

Brian Keene

Brian Keene's most recent books include *Urban Gothic*, *Castaways*, *Unhappy Endings*, *Dark Hollow*, and *Ghost Walk*.

He also writes comic books for Marvel Comics and DC Comics, as well as short stories, video game scripts, and more. His books have been translated into German, Polish, French, and Taiwanese. Several of his novels and stories have been optioned for film, one of which, *The Ties That Bind*, premiered on DVD in 2009.

The winner of two Bram Stoker Awards, Keene's work has been featured in such diverse venues as the *New York Times*, CNN.com, *Publisher's Weekly*, The History Channel, *The Howard Stern Show*, *Fangoria*, and *Rue Morgue Magazine*. He lives in Pennsylvania with his wife and two sons.

"The idea for this story came from a conversation with an old childhood friend named Susan Repasky," recalls the author. "Susan is a high school chemistry teacher, and often uses scenarios from my stories and novels as the basis for her student's classroom experiments.

"She told me about a real-life body farm, and commented, 'I bet you could do something with that.' She was right.

"The story takes place in the same 'world' as my novel *Dead Sea* and first appeared in a special collectible Lettered Edition of that book."

THE DEAD OUTSIDE the body farm's security fence were much more lively than the ones inside the compound. They smelled just as bad, though.

"My God . . ."

Hector Bolivar took a last sip of cold instant coffee, and watched their efforts.

Both types of dead were dangerous. The corpses on the body farm didn't move, but they posed a danger through microbes and disease. Following established procedures and wearing the proper protective gear negated these threats, but such protocols offered little protection against the dead outside. The new dead were different. They moved. Bit. Clawed. And while they spread disease like the farm's inhabitants, the more prevalent danger was that they'd eat you long before infection set in.

When the zombies finally tore through the razor wire and made it onto the property, Bolivar ran for the building's exit. He jumped into a battery-powered golf cart, started the engine, and pulled away, heading towards the forest.

The body farm's massive acreage held many different kinds of landscape—forests, thickets, grassland, ponds and streams. They'd even built a man-made desert near the rear of the property. But sand dunes would offer little cover. He'd be safer among the trees.

The zombies plodded along in slow pursuit. Bolivar grinned, despite his terror. As long as he could outrun them, he'd be okay.

Before Hamelin's Revenge—a name the media gave the disease in reference to the rats that had spawned it—eradicated all of mankind's achievements and reduced them to meat, Bolivar had been a leading Forensic Anthropologist and head of the National Institute for Justice's "body farm"—a secure, twenty-acre parcel of land in rural Virginia. The compound's purpose had been to advance the study of decomposition on the human body in relation to climate, weather and exposure to the elements. The body farm had provided every possibility for research—snow, rain, heat, and other conditions. Professionals from the Federal, State, and local levels—criminologists, medical examiners, coroners, pathologists, biological anthropologists, homicide investigators, the armed forces, and even Hollywood filmmakers and special effects creators—had regularly visited the site in the pursuit of science and better law enforcement (or more realistic effects, in the case of the movie people). They'd studied how climate, insects, plants, and other factors advanced or slowed decay. The bodies were donated by families, universities, and medical research institutes.

The facility had once operated with a staff of twenty and usually contained at least two-hundred corpses. Now it was just Bolivar. And the corpse count had just doubled.

The cart's top speed was five miles per hour, but it was still faster than his pursuers. The zombies fell far behind as Bolivar drove into the darkness. The moon and stars were hidden behind a thick cover of clouds. The air was hot. Sticky. It felt heavy and charged. Bolivar had no doubt there would be a thunderstorm before morning. The cloying atmosphere made the stench that much worse. In his rush to leave, he'd forgotten his protective gear. He was used to the smell of decomposition, of course, but that didn't make the reeking miasma any more pleasant. Coughing, he breathed through his mouth.

The headlights flashed off a corpse in an advanced stage of decay. The body was propped up against a tree. A small red tag fluttered from a stake next to it, denoting how long it had been there, the cause of death, and other factors. The legs had turned to soup and spread out all over the grass like melted candle wax.

Upon reaching the woods, he turned off the cart and walked towards the edge of the forest. The space between the trees was shadowed and silent. Bolivar shivered in the heat. As he crept into the woods, his pulse beat faster. Sweat ran into his eyes and dripped from his nose.

A branch snapped to his left. Bolivar spun around, but couldn't see anything in the darkness. He suppressed the urge to cry out. Instead, he crouched down and waited.

More branches snapped. Something rustled nearby. There was a wet, phlegm-filled snort, and then a shape emerged from the shadows.

A deer.

The body farm had wildlife, of course. That was part of the studies. He'd seen deer on the grounds before—had watched them with his colleagues from their office windows. But as it drew closer, Bolivar saw that this deer was different. It was dead. Even though he couldn't see it very well, he could smell the rot and hear the flies buzzing around it. Hamelin's Revenge had jumped species. First the rats, then humans, and now deer.

My God, he thought, *if it manages to infect avian life forms . . .*

The deer made an awkward lunge for him. Bolivar dodged it easily enough and scampered backward—straight into another congealing corpse. Wetness soaked into his pants and shirt. His hands clawed through something warm with the consistency of tapioca pudding. The stench was horrible. Bolivar raised his arms to shield himself. Gore dripped from them.

The zombie attacked.

And then the only thing left on the body farm were two types of dead.

DEAD TO THE WORLD
Gary McMahon

Gary McMahon's fiction has appeared in award-winning magazines and anthologies on both sides of the Atlantic and has been reprinted in both *The Mammoth Book of Best New Horror* and *The Year's Best Fantasy and Horror*.

He is the British Fantasy Award–nominated author of *Rough Cut*, *All Your Gods Are Dead*, *Dirty Prayers*, *How to Make Monsters*, and *Rain Dogs*, and he edited the 2008 anthology of original novelettes entitled *We Fade to Grey*.

Forthcoming are the collections *Pieces of Midnight*, *Different Skins*, and *To Usher, the Dead*, and McMahon's first mass-market novel, *Hungry Hearts*, was published by Abaddon Books in late 2009.

"When the editor contacted me about submitting a story to this zombie anthology, his timing could not have been better," recalls McMahon. "I'd just handed in my zombie novel *Hungry Hearts* to the editor at Abaddon Books, and I still had all things undead very much on my mind.

"I got to work that very day, and as the story began to take shape it struck me as being something like George Romero's *Land of the Dead* meets Cormac McCarthy's *The Road*—with its themes of loneliness, despair, duty, and, of course, what we might do if a zombie apocalypse were to actually occur, and then what might happen once the living became a minority . . ."

I STAND AT THE TOPMOST WINDOW of our fortified house, looking out at the dead. They are clearly defined in the moonlight; clumsy figures draped in rags and peeling tatters of skin. They are the first ones I have seen in quite some time, but their appearance was always inevitable.

They will never leave us alone.

We have been in the old farmhouse for two weeks, now—enough time for Coral to have recovered from the badly twisted ankle she sustained when we were running from an infested warehouse district, and to finish what little food we found in the place when we arrived.

Coral is downstairs now, packing. We travel light; everything we once owned has now been abandoned, other than crucial items like water bottles, a tin opener, knives and the gun.

I watch the dead as they stumble around amongst the trees, sniffing us out. It was quiet here when we first arrived, with no traces of anyone in the immediate vicinity, but now they have discovered us. I wonder if they can smell our living flesh, or perhaps the blood in our veins? They must have developed some kind of hunting instinct over the past ten years since the term "dead" began to mean something different from simply an end to walking about. They always find us, no matter how far and how fast we run.

We were both active political campaigners back then, before things changed. We attended rallies and marches for world peace and hunger; worked with charities to help Third World countries with massive debts, unstable regimes, and little hope of helping themselves. In short, and to borrow a phrase from an old song, we cared a lot.

That term, the Third World, has been outdated since the Cold War ended in the early 1990s. During that unique state of drama and conflict after World War II, when it seemed that the opposing blocs of the Soviets and the Western World were destined to blow us all to hell, the Third World countries watched and starved and wondered just who might help them.

Now, I know what that really means—to watch helplessly as forces beyond your control reshape and destroy everything you have ever known and believed in.

I think of all this now, as I watch the scattered dead walk through the darkened tree line and approach the fence that borders the farmhouse property. It occurs to me that what we have now is a kind of Fourth World—a group of (dead) people aligned with no political viewpoint or ideology, and whose needs have been honed down to the basic drive to feed. To feed on the rest of us . . . to feed on the living.

I turn away from the window—from the moonlight and the dark ground and the stumbling, staggering corpses—and walk out of the room, shutting the door quietly behind me as I head for the stairs. I am afraid to make a sound. The next sound I hear might be that of my own mind snapping.

"Have you checked all the rooms up there?" Coral looks up from fastening the rucksacks as I enter the downstairs living room. Her face is too pale, too thin. We haven't eaten in three days and her hunger has now become a visible thing, a terrifying luminescence that shines from beneath her sallow skin.

I nod. "There's nothing left up there. We have everything. Where's the gun? I saw a few of them out there, coming out of the woods."

She points towards the corner of the room, where the rifle is propped up against cushions on a dusty armchair. We do not have much ammunition left, and I doubt that we will be lucky enough to stumble on any before what we do have runs out completely. This is rural England not downtown Los Angeles. The best we can hope for is to find some old farmer's shotgun in another of the abandoned properties we continually hop between like frogs on lily pads.

I cross the room and pick up the rifle. Ten years ago I had never held a gun, would not have known how to fire one. These days I am an efficient marksman. I have to be, to save on bullets. "Won't be long," I say, leaving the room and going back up the stairs.

Back at the window I see that the dead have already come closer to the fence. One of them is even attempting to climb, but having only one arm seems a hindrance to his progress. There are four of them in total—the one trying to climb over the fence and three others who stand watching him, their bodies limp and ragged.

I raise the rifle and take aim, enjoying its heft at my shoulder. The sight line is perfect; an unrestricted view from the high window. I caress the trigger, waiting until the right moment, when my heart seems to stop beating for a second to allow me to take the shot. I pull the trigger. The tallest one—who is wearing some kind of dark overalls—twitches backwards as the side of his head explodes in a shock of dark matter. He takes three tiny backward steps before hitting the ground.

The other two do not even glance in his direction. I take them down with a shot each, heads going up like watermelons stuffed with cherry bombs.

Then I shoot the one on the fence. He hangs there, trapped in the razor wire, what is left of his brains leaking out of the large wound in what remains of his forehead.

I pull the gun back inside and secure the window, pulling the shutters tight and testing that they are solid. Then I go back downstairs to my wife.

Coral is sitting in the same dusty armchair where previously she'd put the gun. She is weeping quietly, her narrow shoulders hitching. "We can't keep doing this," she says, between almost silent sobs. "We can't go on."

I go to her but am unable to offer the comfort she needs. We are beyond all that—the world has gone past such small intimacies, tiny shows of affection. Instead I kneel down in front of her, placing my hands on her thighs. "We *have* to go on. There's nothing else to do. We've run out of food here, now. The choice is simple—we either stay here and die, or we move and put off dying for a few more weeks or months."

The silence in the room feels like an invasion of some kind: it robs us of our ability to communicate at any effective level. We have become strangers, travelling companions, little more than a couple of empty shells shuffling along in search of something that no longer exists.

"I miss the baby," she says, finally looking me in the eye. Her cheeks are wet. Her lips quiver. She has not mentioned the baby since she miscarried, and I was forced to lay the squawking undead thing to rest. I had hoped that she might have pushed all thoughts of the baby—no name, just "the baby"—from her mind to focus on the immediate business of survival. But no, if I am honest I have known all along that she could never forget what happened. I have watched her mind slowly crumple, like a deflating balloon, for months now, since it happened.

"We . . . we can't talk about that. Things are different now. There was no baby." I stand up and back away, appalled by my own lack of humanity, my utter inability to even discuss that terrible evening. "I'll get the other water bottles."

I leave her there in the darkness, clasping at her face with hands that have become talons. In the kitchen I pick up the two plastic bottles of well water and stuff them into the third small rucksack. Then I walk back through the house to the living room, where Coral is now standing in the shadows by the big boarded-up window, staring at the drapes.

"We need to go now," I say, not without compassion.

She turns to face me. Her tears have all dried up. She walks to my side, her face taut and filled with hate. We walk together to the front door, where I tug loose the timbers and open the door. I go first, scanning the area outside, and Coral follows me in silence, her eyes burning holes into my back.

·　·　·　·　·

We walk to the edge of the property, open the gate, and take the small road through the trees, passing within a few yards of the dead folk I shot earlier. A large crow is perched on the chest of one of the fallen corpses. It looks up as we pass by, and then lowers its beak into the mass of decayed flesh and bone to continue its scant meal.

Coral walks at my side, a constant companion through the darkness. She says nothing and I am glad of the breakdown in communication. There is no longer room for sentiment in this world. We must all be hard as stone, cold as a rifle barrel.

I hear no sounds of life as we continue along the road, the trees on either side of us stirring in a slight breeze. Dark clusters of leaves wave in the night, branches heave and creak, and somewhere deep inside the wood a bough breaks, falling to the ground with a soft thud.

The only light out here is that of the moon and the stars. The electricity supply failed years ago, and the only sources of power that remain now are from privately-operated generators. Soon there will be no-one left to run them; the dead already outnumber the living, and it cannot be long until they dominate the planet.

I think again of those developing countries all those years ago, and the committees

I sat on, the fund-raisers I organized to help them—starving people living in tumble-down shacks, entire families surviving for days on a handful of rice.

What of this Fourth World nation? What will happen when *their* food runs out, when there is nobody left alive for them to kill and eat? Will they simply rot down to nothing, the process accelerated because they have nothing to consume? What will the world be like when there are no living people left on its surface, when the only feet who tread this land are those of the long dead?

I glance again at Coral, but she is staring straight ahead, her eyes narrowed and her mouth a grim line in her face. Her hair is long and greasy, her teeth rotten and her breath stale. If I did not know her and simply caught sight of her out here, I would assume that she was one of them—one of the dead. Is this how I look as well?

When I think of what we have now become, I am filled with a sense of depression that seems almost pleasurable. At least it is some kind of emotional response. Previously I had thought myself incapable of even this small thing.

Coral takes a folded map from her back pocket and lifts it up to her face, where she can study its lines and symbols. Her pace slows while she examines the map, and I watch the trees for movement. I am uneasy that we have not yet encountered any of the dead. The fact that four of them were hanging around at the fence must mean that there are more nearby.

"There's a small community of some sort about three miles down the road. There might be some canned stuff in a cupboard someone forgot, or a stash in one of the houses." Her voice is hard, like stones rubbing up against each another in a shallow ditch.

"It's worth a try. If we don't find food soon, we're going to die."

"Is that all you care about? Survival at any cost?" The tone of her voice does not change—the question is asked in the same way she spoke about the town or village. "Existing no matter how much of you has already died?"

"To be honest, I don't even care about that anymore. It's just something to do, a target to aim for. We have two options . . . die now or die later. As soon as I stop seeing the point of dying later, I'll sit down on the ground and swallow a bullet from this rifle." I say all this without feeling. It is simply how it is, the way we have to be now. It is what we are.

She says no more on the subject. I can tell that she is angry but does not have the energy to rage against me and my stupid, ill-thought-out philosophy.

The trees are like dark shapes cut out of night by a child. They make a jagged black outline across the slightly lighter sky. The stars are tiny splatters against this backdrop, spilled paint from the same child's art box. At one time I would have thought the sight beautiful, but now it is just another thing that I can see. None of these sights makes any kind of genuine impression upon me. I watch them without truly seeing them.

The road is long and straight. We might reach the end or we might not, it matters little in the scheme of things. But we must continue. Forward motion is all we have, all we live for. There is nothing else. I do not even care about the community Coral saw on the map. We will either get there or we won't, and there will be a forgotten few cans of food or there won't.

It matters not.

I see them as we approach a rusted, abandoned flatbed truck lying in a ditch. There are four or five of them, milling about in the middle of the road, walking in small circles like bored shoppers waiting at the back of a lengthy queue. We keep walking. There is no point in running. The only way is forward. I feel Coral tense at my side and hear the sharp intake of breath as she counts them. I unsling the rifle from my shoulder with practiced ease—an almost graceful movement that probably makes me look like I have handled firearms my entire life.

"This could get messy," she says, slipping the baseball bat from her pack. She picked it up in a sports shop in an out-of-town shopping center almost two months ago. It is already stained dark with blood.

I think what hurts Coral most is going against her natural instincts. She is a giver, a helper, and this new selfish mode of existence is something she finds it impossible to reconcile with her old identity as someone who could never stop giving. Back before the world began to die, it was she who convinced me to give my time to charitable causes, to find ways to help my fellow man—serving in late-night soup kitchens, advising in cramped offices for poorly funded causes. She won me over with her caring manner, and all the love she had to give scared the hell out of me and made me feel small in a world grown so large with troubles.

If she could, I think Coral would set up a charity for the dead. Bring-and-buy sales, sit-ins at the local council offices—equal rights for the undead. Instead, she is forced to bring the ones she meets to extinction with her baseball bat, or with the gun that I now bring around and point at the group in the road. Coral loathes herself for having become such a proficient assassin.

"Try not to let them suffer," she whispers, as she always does. Part of her problem is that she still sees them as human. She cannot divorce the living from the dead, and this, I fear, will be her undoing. It might also be mine.

As soon as they see us the dead people begin to move in our direction. None of them are too fresh, so their progress is slow and bewildered, like the movements of a group of ailing senior citizens in line for a free dinner. One of them, I notice, is sitting on the ground, and when he fails to stand I realize why. He has no legs, just a torso, and he pulls himself along on his hands, mouth open in a hungry leer.

I shoot him first, for purely aesthetic reasons. Then, striding forward like a gunslinger from some old Western movie, I begin to take the rest of them down, shot after shot after shot . . . They make strange sounds in their throats, as if they are attempting to speak—half-words, near-sentences that might in fact be nothing of the kind. I aim for the heads—nobody knows why the brains are the only sure targets—and watch as shattered bone dances white in the air, mixed with a red so dark it is almost black.

A female is the last of the bunch, looming towards us with skeletal arms outstretched and claw-like hands clutching. Slow-moving, yet lethal if she is allowed within touching distance, the female opens her mouth and hisses like a snake. Her face is mostly mottled skull, with barely any flesh left to cling to its sharp angles. Coral steps in and swings the bat, almost taking off the female's head with a single blow. The skull leans so far sideways on the decayed strings of neck muscle that one cheek touches an exposed shoulder blade. Coral swings again, this time completing the job. The skull parts with the ropy gristle, tumbling to the ground where the female's left foot, in mid-step, kicks it like a football. The body takes one more stride before going down like a sack of dried offal.

Coral is crying. She always cries when she kills. It is her charitable nature, the part of her old self that she is unwilling to lose. Unlike me, she prefers to remain human, and sees these tears as purification, a cleansing of her soul after committing such indecent acts to prolong our tedious survival.

"Come on," I say, worried that there are more of them lurking in the trees. They are mostly slow and very dumb—dim-witted and not even possessing enough intelligence to carry out a coordinated attack. But in enough numbers they can be dangerous. If enough of them attack at once, it is easy to be overpowered, and they will take you down and eat you. If they leave enough of you to get back up and walk, you will become one of them.

We reach the village at sunset. A small group of cottages lining one side of the road, with a post office and a corner shop flanked by concrete posts. It is barely large enough to be called a village at all, and there are no signs of life. The shop has already been looted, while the post office is a blackened heap of bricks and charred timbers. Whoever did this is long gone, and probably dead by now. I cannot recall the last time we saw a living person. There must be so few of us left.

Again I wonder what will happen when there are none, and if in fact Coral and I might be the last living people in the country, or perhaps in the world. The thought, rather than terrifying, is strangely comforting. When at last we are gone, I imagine the whole planet becoming that mythical Fourth World I considered earlier—filled with rotting corpses with nothing to eat. Unable to help themselves, their bodies falling apart and filling the earth with dust. Valleys of dust. Rivers of dust. Dust that will remain undisturbed for all eternity.

"It's the same as everywhere else. Nothing. No food. No people. Just . . . fucking . . . nothing . . ." Coral falls to her knees, dropping her bag, and pummels the ground with her fists, drawing blood. I watch in silence, unable to help her and unwilling to even try. She sprawls on her belly and wails, a verbalization of her inadequacy, her inability to help herself and anyone else. But can't she see that there is no-one left to help?

I walk over to the little grocery shop and step through the shattered doorway. The shelves are empty, the counter smashed beyond repair. Refrigerators are overturned. A microwave lies disemboweled on the floor next to a pile of empty snack wrappers. The shop has been thoroughly cleaned-out of all supplies but for a single dented can of garden peas, which sits on a shelf like a bad joke. I imagine someone laughing as they placed it there, impressed by their own vicious humor.

I reach out and pick up the can. It is better than nothing, but only just. I stuff the can into my pack and leave the shop, wishing that I could remember how to cry. I am thinking of the baby—the stillborn whose eyes turned upon me and whose mouth opened to snap with toothless gums at my shaking fingers—and even then I am unable to connect with my emotions. Coral, however, is still on the ground, still weeping, her hands still bloodied and ragged. "I'll get some plasters," I say, reaching into my pack.

"Bastard!" she snarls, and I can only agree with her assessment.

. . . . .

Later that night, after a meal of cold peas and bitter memories, I awake in the darkness and the mattress beside me is cold and empty. I close my eyes and try to get back to sleep, but something whispers for my attention—a gentle breeze, perhaps through an open window, or a door that has not been shut when someone went outside.

I lift myself from the bed and put on my clothes—no rush, no hurry. Whatever has happened has happened. Whatever will be will be. There is no room now for sentimental thoughts and actions, for love and tenderness. These are the times of the closed hand, the hard fist, and each decision is tougher than the last. This is the Fourth World.

I pick up the gun and drift through the room like a ghost, slipping through the doorway to the upstairs landing of the small house at the end of the row—beyond the burned-out post office and the shop with its empty shelves and scattered furnishings. Standing at the top of the stairs, I can see that the front door is open. Pale moonlight spills across the welcome mat. That slight breezes trickles in through the gap.

I step gently down the stairs, through the doorway, and out into the night. The air is fresh and smells so very clean, like a promise of salvation. But I know not to trust such positive thoughts, and cast them gladly from my mind.

I walk along the narrow street—the houses and cottages to my left—my bare feet soundless on the cold, dense tarmac, the rifle held at port arms. There is sweat on my back, stones in my heart, and death is perched like a big black bird upon my shoulder.

She is there, in the darkness and moonlight, kneeling down in the middle of the road. Coral, my wife—a woman I can no longer allow myself to know and to love. Beyond the road, where she is kneeling, is a dark grove of trees. She is staring at the trees, at the blackness between their broad trunks, her arms held out as if in supplication, or welcome.

I move slowly, afraid to confront the moment, but realizing deep down that I cannot turn away. All I have is forward motion, momentum. When this ceases to be enough, I will slip the rifle barrel into my mouth and taste the darkness for one final time.

A dark bird plummets from the sky and perches on a nearby rock—it is a crow, possibly even the same one we saw yesterday, at the farm. Yesterday now seems so far away. For ten years we have kept up the charade, this pretence of life, and now it is all coming apart. The center is unable to hold. Ten years of shambling forward, never looking back, becoming even more dead than the dead things we are trying to outrun.

I continue walking towards the spot where my wife is on her knees, committing some self-created act of atonement. Darkness blooms around her, like a black mist, and I walk into it—a willing witness to whatever scene she has chosen to perform.

I can now see that Coral's body is shaking, as if she is having some kind of fit. But still her hands are raised, lifted to the heavens. As I get closer I see the figures—two of them, with more standing behind. Thin and wiry, shrouded in the darkness of the grove of trees. The one at the front is leaning down in front of my wife, his withered white hands buried in her stomach up to the wasted wrists to access the charity she is willingly giving. He pulls the moist red offerings from the cavity of her gut, lifting them to his lips and rubbing them across his chin as he begins to feast.

I raise the rifle and move in a tight curve, coming towards the scene from the side. It is this positioning that enables me to see that Coral is still alive and that she is weeping . . . and beneath the tears is a calm, beatific smile.

The worst thing, in Coral's case, was the fact that she had to turn against her true nature and become utterly selfish. But she could not do that—she was unable to put herself first. Always one for compassion, at the very last she is still giving of herself. My charitable wife . . . my little bleeding heart—the very organ which, even now, is being removed from her chest by dead hands and brought up to a grinning dead mouth.

Perhaps the baby was the final straw? Maybe my own failure to be there for her, putting my own survival first instead, was the final blow to her already weakened defenses?

And even now, right at the end, I continue to fail her. I fail her yet again.

Quickly I lift the rifle and take aim, then fire a single bullet into the back of her head. There will be no solidarity here, no politic with the dead. The back of her skull comes apart and her blood anoints those she wished to help, bathing them in her desire to share. For even at the moment of her death, Coral just can't stop giving.

. . . . .

I remain in the house for days afterwards, becoming gradually weaker with hunger. A sense of sorrow trickles slowly into me like water spilled on porous stone. At last there is a semblance of emotion. I miss Coral—her constant presence at my side— even though at the end she hated me.

I stay beneath the bedclothes after the second day, not even going downstairs to use the toilet. The bed begins to smell and the sheets are soaking wet, but I am long past caring. The sun rises and sets, the window lightens and darkens, my mind wanders. I remember green fields and children playing, couples walking hand-in-hand and the promise of a future that was not dead . . .

I lose count of the days, slipping between sleeping and wakefulness as easily as closing my eyes. The room is a mirage and the walls seem to shimmer. When I hear the noise downstairs—a crashing splintering sound—I suspect that it is the dead breaking in to finish me off. At last they have found me. I hope they choke on my gristle and that my bones shatter and stab them in the brain.

Footsteps on the stairs—slow, uneven, stumbling. The door opens . . . the room goes dark.

When I open my eyes again I am no longer alone. There is a man standing by the bed. He is not dead. His hair is brown and clean, and the overalls he wears are freshly washed. I can tell by the overpowering smell of soap that he has been well looked after. I stare at him, waiting for something to happen.

"How do you feel?"

I can barely answer. "Bad."

"I'm sorry that we couldn't come sooner. We've been watching you for days, weighing up the situation and waiting for the area to clear. To be safe." His face barely moves as he speaks. There is a name-tag on his chest pocket, but I am too tired to read what it says.

"Who are you?" I whisper.

"I'm part of a collective. We have been hiding out for years, stockpiling supplies. Everything we have is shared equally between the members of the group." His eyes blink.

"What do you want?"

"We can offer you food and shelter . . . a life, of sorts. All you need to do is work with us, become *one of us*." His hands clench at his sides. "Help us to re-build something good."

"How long have you been watching us?"

"A few days. We had to be sure . . . be safe."

"Did you see what happened to my wife?"

He pauses before answering. "I'm sorry. I wish we could've come earlier, but it wasn't safe. I'm sorry."

Sorry. I have never met anyone so sorry in my whole life.

"Not. Safe." I stare at him, knowing that this has all come much too late to mean anything. "And you have food and shelter?"

"Yes. We have those things, and much more." He lifts his left hand, which clasps a small sack that I had not noticed before. Cans and bottles rattle and sing as he shakes it at arm's length, almost teasing me.

My response surprises me almost as much as him.

"I don't want your . . . fucking . . . *charity*." I pull down the bedclothes and use the rifle hidden beneath the stained sheets to shoot him in the head. I smile as the blood sprays and his knees buckle, toppling him to the floor. The sack rolls from his lifeless fingers, spilling its precious contents across the floorboards.

After a long time I finally get out of bed and cross the room. There is food and water and, even better, medicine. It is no longer charity—now that he is unable to offer these things freely, it is simply so much found goods. Now they are mine.

Days later, after the food and the water and the drugs, I am feeling much better. My mind is clear and my body has regained some strength. I still cannot think of a good enough reason to swallow a bullet, so instead I will go looking for the man's comrades. And when I find them, I will show them what it means to be sorry.

Only then can I rest—when the world truly belongs to the dead.

THE LONG DEAD DAY
Joe R. Lansdale

Joe R. Lansdale is the multiple-award-winning author of thirty novels and more than 200 short stories, articles, and essays. He has written screenplays, teleplays, and comic-book scripts and teaches creative writing and screenplay writing occasionally at Stephen F. Austin State University.

His novels include *Act of Love, Dead in the West, Magic Wagon, The Nightrunners, The Drive-In: A "B" Movie with Blood and Popcorn Made in Texas* and *The Drive-In 2: Not Just One of Them Sequels, Cold in July, Tarzan: The Lost Adventure* (with Edgar Rice Burroughs), *Freezer Burn*, the Edgar Award–winning *The Bottoms, A Fine Dark Line, Sunset and Sawdust, Lost Echoes*, and *Leather Maiden*. He is also the author of such short story collections as *By Bizarre Hands, Stories by Mama Lansdale's Youngest Boy, Bestsellers Guaranteed, Writer of the Purple Rage, A Fistful of Stories (and Articles), High Cotton, Bumper Crop*, and *The Shadows Kith and Kin*. His best-selling series of quirky crime novels featuring mismatched investigators Hap Collins and Leonard Pine comprises such titles as *Savage Season, Mucho Mojo, The Two-Bear Mambo, Bad Chili, Rumble Tumble, Captains Outrageous*, and *Vanilla Ride*.

Lansdale has been an editor or co-editor of several anthologies, including *Best of the West, New Frontiers, Razored Saddles* (with Pat LoBrutto), *Dark at Heart* (with Karen Lansdale), *Weird Business: A Horror Comics Anthology* (with Rick Klaw), *The Horror Hall of Fame: The Stoker Winners, Retro-Pulp Tales*, and *Lords of the Razor*.

His novella *Bubba Ho-tep* was filmed in 2002, produced and directed by Don Coscarelli and starring Bruce Campbell and Ossie Davis. A sequel is currently in development, and Lansdale's story "Incident on and Off a Mountain Road" became the first episode of Showtime Networks' *Masters of Horror* series, from the same director.

Lansdale has won the British Fantasy Award and seven Bram Stoker Awards. In 2007 he received the Grand Master Award from the World Horror Convention. He is the founder of the martial arts system Shen Chuan and has been in the International Martial Arts Hall of Fame four times. He lives in East Texas with his wife, Karen.

"'The Long Dead Day' is a short-short," observes the author, "but I think it has impact, like an ice pick to the brain. It was written in a sudden flush of excitement."

SHE SAID A DOG BIT HER, but we didn't find the dog anywhere. It was a bad bite, though, and we dressed it with some good stuff and wrapped it with some bandages, and then poured alcohol over that, letting it seep in, and, she, being ten, screamed and cried. She hugged up with her mama, though, and in a while she was all right, or as all right as she could be.

Later that evening, while I sat on the wall and looked down at the great crowd outside the compound, my wife, Carol, called me down from the wall and the big gun. She said Ellen had developed a fever, that she could hardly keep her eyes open, and the bite hurt.

Carol took her temperature, said it was high, and that to touch her forehead was to almost burn your hand. I went in then, and did just that, touched her forehead. Her mother was right. I opened up the dressing on the wound, and was amazed to see that it had turned black, and it didn't really look like a dog bite at all. It never had, but I wanted it to, and let myself be convinced that was just what it was, even if there had been no dog we could find in the compound. By this time, they had all been eaten. Fact was, I probably shot the last one around; a beautiful Shepard, that when it saw me wagged its tail. I think when I lifted the gun he knew, and didn't care. He just sat there with his mouth open in what looked like a dog's version of a smile, his tail beating. I killed him first shot, to the head. I dressed him out without thinking about him much. I couldn't let myself do that. I loved dogs. But my family needed to eat. We did have the rabbits we raised, some pigeons, a vegetable garden, but it was all very precarious.

Anyway, I didn't believe about the dog bite, and now the wound looked really bad. I knew the real cause of it, or at least the general cause, and it made me sick to think of it. I doctored the wound again, gave her some antibiotics that we had, wrapped it and went out. I didn't tell Carol what she was already thinking.

I got my shotgun and went about the compound, looking. It was a big compound, thirty-five acres with a high wall around it, but somehow, someone must have breached the wall. I went to the back garden, the one with trees and flowers where our little girl liked to play. I went there and looked around, and found him sitting on one of the benches. He was just sitting. I guess he hadn't been the way he was for very long. Just long enough to bite my daughter. He was about her age, and I knew then, being so lonely, she had let him in. Let him in through the bolted back door. I glanced over there and saw she had bolted it back. I realized then that she had most likely been up on the walk around the wall and had seen him down there, not long of turning, looking up wistfully. He could probably still talk then, just like anyone else, maybe even knew what he was doing, or maybe not. Perhaps he thought he was still who he once was, and thought he should get away from the others, that he would be safe inside.

It was amazing none of the others had forced their way in. Then again, the longer they were what they were, the slower they became, until finally they quit moving altogether. Problem with that was, it took years.

I looked back at him, sitting there, the one my daughter had let in to be her playmate. He had come inside, and then he had done what he had done, and now my daughter was sick with the disease, and the boy was just sitting there on the bench, looking at me in the dying sunlight, his eyes black as if he had been beat, his face grey, his lips purple.

He reminded me of my son. He wasn't my son, but he reminded me of him. I had seen my son go down among them, some, what was it, five years before. Go down in a flash of kicking legs and thrashing arms and squirting liquids. That was when we lived in town, before we found the compound and made it better. There were others then, but they were gone now. Expeditions to find others they said. Whatever, they left, we never saw them again.

Sometimes at night I couldn't sleep for the memory of my son, Gerald, and sometimes in my wife's arms, I thought of him, for had it not been such a moment that had created him?

The boy rose from the bench, stumble-stepped toward me, and I shot him. I shot him in the chest, knocking him down. Then I rushed to him and shot him in the head, taking half of it away.

I knew my wife would have heard the shot, so I didn't bother to bury him. I went back across the compound and to the upper apartments where we lived. She saw me with the gun, opened her mouth as if to speak, but nothing came out.

"A dog," I said. "The one who bit her. I'll get some things, dress him out and we'll eat him later."

"There was a dog," my wife said.

"Yes, a dog. He wasn't rabid. And he's pretty healthy. We can eat him."

I could see her go weak with relief, and I felt both satisfied and guilty at the same time. I said, "How is she?"

"Not much better. There was a dog, you say."

"That's what I said, dear."

"Oh, good. Good. A dog."

I looked at my watch. My daughter had been bitten earlier that day, and it was almost night. I said, "Why don't you go get a knife, some things for me to do the skinning, and I'll dress out the dog. Maybe she'll feel better, she gets some meat in her."

"Sure," Carol said. "Just the thing. She needs the protein. The iron."

"You bet," I said.

She went away then, down the stairs, across the yard to the cooking shed. I went upstairs, still carrying the gun.

Inside my daughter's room, I saw from the doorway that she was grey as cigarette ash. She turned her head toward me.

"Daddy," she said.

"Yes, dear," I said, and put the shotgun against the wall by the door and went over to her.

"I feel bad."

"I know."

"I feel different."

"I know."

"Can anything be done? Do you have some medicine?"

"I do."

I sat down in the chair by the bed. "Do you want me to read to you?"

"No," she said, and then she went silent. She lay there not moving, her eyes closed.

"Baby," I said. She didn't answer.

I got up then and went to the open door and looked out. Carol, my beautiful wife, was coming across the yard, carrying the things I'd asked for. I picked up the shotgun and made sure it was loaded with my daughter's medicine. I thought for a moment about how to do it. I put the shotgun back against the wall. I listened as my wife come up the stairs.

When she was in the room, I said, "Give me the knife and things."

"She okay?"

"Yes, she's gone to sleep. Or she's almost asleep. Take a look at her."

She gave me the knife and things and I laid them in a chair as she went across the room and to the bed.

I picked up the shotgun, and as quietly as I could, stepped forward and pointed it to the back of my wife's head and pulled the trigger. It was over instantly. She fell across the bed on our dead child, her blood coating the sheets and the wall.

She wouldn't have survived the death of a second child, and she sure wouldn't have survived what was about to happen to our daughter.

I went over and looked at Ellen. I could wait, until she opened her eyes, till she came out of the bed, trying for me, but I couldn't stomach that. I didn't want to see that. I took the shotgun and put it to her forehead and pulled the trigger. The room boomed with the sound of shotgun fire again, and the bed and the room turned an even brighter red.

I went outside with the shotgun and walked along the landing, walked all the way around, came to where the big gun was mounted. I sat behind it, on the swivel stool, leaned the shotgun against the protecting wall. I sat there and looked out at the hundreds of them, just standing there, looking up, waiting for something.

I began to rotate and fire the gun. Many of them went down. I fired until there was no more ammunition. Reloaded, I fired again, my eyes wet with tears. I did this for some time, until the next rounds of ammunition were played out. It was like swatting at a hive of bees. There always seemed to be more.

I sat there and tried not to think about anything. I watched them. Their shapes stretched for miles around, went off into the distance in shadowy bulks, like a horde of rats waiting to board a cargo ship.

They were eating the ones I had dropped with the big gun.

After awhile the darkness was total and there were just the shapes out there. I watched them for a long time. I looked at the shotgun propped against the retaining wall. I looked at it and picked it up and put it under my chin, and then I put it back again.

I knew, in time, I would have the courage.

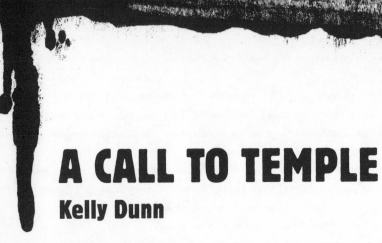

A CALL TO TEMPLE

Kelly Dunn

Kelly Dunn has worked as a university instructor, hearse dealer, and stage actress, but is glad to have found her calling as a writer.

A professional print journalist and editor covering a variety of subjects from workplace issues to entertainment news, her short fiction has appeared in *Necrotic Tissue*, *Aberrant Dreams*, and the Lisa Morton–edited anthology *Midnight Walk*.

"A dear friend of mine invited me to attend one of her young daughter's dance classes," recalls Dunn. "While the child danced, carefree and safe, my friend and I discussed a murder case unfolding in a nearby town.

"Another little girl, about the same age as my friend's daughter, had been abducted, brutally tortured and slain by a sexual predator. 'I don't know how that girl's mother is coping,' my friend said. 'I can't imagine life without my child.'

"The conversation got me to thinking about the kind of love that is completely entwined in another human being's existence. What happens when your baby is given up for lost? I wrote this story to explore just how far a parent can—or should—go for a beloved child."

"WHY ARE YOU SITTING HERE in the dark?" Dr. Rubin's words startled Hannah Levinson, and she shifted in the wingback chair where she had been instructed to wait, vaguely wondering how the natural light in the tiny office could have faded without her realizing it. She thought she had been studying the various diplomas displayed on the walls, but the tiny lettering inside the frames had long since blurred into the evening's deepening indigo.

The doctor seated himself, not behind the desk as she expected, but in the matching chair next to her.

"How is he, doctor?"

Dr. Rubin took a deep breath. "Mrs. Levinson, you need to prepare yourself." In the fluorescents' inadequate illumination the doctor's face looked waxen and washed out. "I'm very sorry, but the therapy is not successful."

Hannah's stomach upset became a flood of full-fledged nausea. "What? What did you say?"

"The therapy has not had any effect on your son's condition. I'm terribly sorry."

Hannah clenched and unclenched her nail-bitten hands, willing the circulation back into them. "Well, what are the options? Can you do another stem-cell transplant?"

"I'm afraid not."

"But why? I told you I want Sam to have every chance. I don't care what it costs. I—"

"It simply isn't possible. We've done everything we can, but we haven't been able to stop the—the decomposition. Do you understand?"

Comprehension clutched Hannah's insides with icy fingers, but she feigned ignorance. "So? What's the next step? The next phase of treatment?"

Dr. Rubin slumped a little in his chair. "At this point, your son's condition is simply too advanced."

"But I brought him to you immediately after the attack! They say you're the best there is! That's why I brought Sam here instead of to the military hospital!"

"I think I explained to you that the adults who contract this particular, um . . . disorder, have not responded to any treatment whatsoever. They suffer. They become a danger to themselves and others. That is why the hospitals are under government order to perform immediate euthanasia. Now because of your son's age and our philosophy here, I was willing to try an experimental treatment. Stem cells have sometimes worked wonders in young children. But he's at the point where his body, his tissues, have begun to die. You see?" He leaned forward, and Hannah noticed for the first time the strands of silver in his hair and beard.

"I'm very sorry, but Sam's heart is no longer beating. It will be hard for you to accept, but your son is dead."

"How *dare* you. My son is not dead!"

"But—"

"After all you've put him through, you're trying to tell me you want to throw a seven-year-old child into the garbage? Isn't he still moving and looking around? What about that? And what about his *soul?*"

The doctor leaned back in his chair, considering for a moment. "As far as Sam's consciousness goes, things like his personality, his awareness, we believe that these may exist in some way. But his brain has been damaged, and it is only going to get worse. From here on, his body will continue to deteriorate. If Sam understands what's happening at all, it is only in the most primitive sense." The doctor sighed. "I know how difficult this must be for you, but it's better for you to know the truth."

"Why can't you just give him more time?"

"Mrs. Levinson, you've got to be realistic . . ."

The cold inside Hannah had turned into white-hot rage. "You think I don't know what this is all about? This sick contest to see who can have the most dead bodies to their credit? Well, you are not going to get Sam away from me. You haven't even given him a chance!"

Dr. Rubin spoke soothingly, gently. "You know that this clinic does not follow the same policy as the hospitals do, nor are we under government control, technically speaking. We understand how traumatic this is for you. All of us here at the clinic have lost loved ones because of this crisis. And that's why we were willing to take the great risk we did in treating your son."

His eyes appeared moist and he turned his head away, seemingly lost in a moment of mourning. Hannah followed his gaze to the window. In it, a wan reflection of the room and themselves wavered against a backdrop of night. Her conscience nagged at her. Dr. Rubin had told her at the very beginning that he stood to lose everything—his funding, his clinic, his medical license, even his freedom—if the authorities discovered that he'd treated Sam instead of destroying him. The doctor was looking at her again, studying her face, her eyes.

"What about the other option we discussed?" he asked. "Have you thought about that as a possibility?"

Hannah could no longer hold back tears of indignation, of grief. She hated to be weak at this moment when she so needed to be strong for herself and for Sam, but her loathing for her own frailty made the tears fall faster. "That's your solution? Your payment for all the chances you took? For me to leave him here all by himself so he can be your own personal lab rat?"

Dr. Rubin began to look upset. "It's not like that. Please, it's all right. Please." He handed her tissues, not speaking, until Hannah got her emotions under control. When she sat quietly once more he tried again.

"Please just hear me out. Your son's youth, the fact that he is in the relatively early stages of decline, it all means that he is eligible for the program I told you about. It may be the best way to—"

"This is totally unacceptable."

"There is nothing we can do to make him well. But there is something he might be able to do for others. Who knows?"

Hannah stood up. She let all her fury come into her voice: "I'm going to see my son. *Right now.*"

She fumbled with the handle, finally flung the door open, marched down the hall to the elevator, got in, and punched the CLOSE button so that Dr. Rubin had to squeeze in between the doors. They nearly slammed on him before the sensor kicked in and the doors slid apart. He stepped into the elevator, breathless, but Hannah didn't care. He had pushed her too far.

She ignored the doctor as the elevator climbed, kept ignoring him as the elevator doors opened onto another hallway. Nurses drifted by, ghostly in head-to-toe coverings of face shields, surgical masks, surgical aprons and lab coats. For Hannah they did not exist. Only the room numbers deserved her attention. Not this one, not this one. This one. And then she stood next to the bed, where her little boy lay.

Sam's eyes were open, but they had lost that fixed intensity they'd had right after the attack, when she'd brought him to Temple Medical Clinic in the first place. Hannah's heart melted. Sam looked so frail, so defenseless.

"He's still under complete sedation." Dr. Rubin stood beside her, gazing down at the boy. Casually he moved behind her to shut and lock the door. "Won't you at least consider it?" he asked. "You know the vicious cycle of this disease will only continue unless . . ."

"Look at him, Doctor. He's the only child I'll ever have."

"And he's the only child we have ever had, as well. Of course, we wish we could get more adult subjects, too. They're all important. But your child is just the right age, at just the right stage. Don't you know what this could mean? If we could only find out how this disease takes hold in the brain, we might find a cure. For *all* children. For the world."

"A cure? As far as I'm concerned, you haven't even tried to cure Sam."

The doctor tapped his lips with a forefinger. "Tell me something. If you could be sure, absolutely sure, that Sam was beyond all hope, what would you say then?"

"I really can't picture myself ever thinking my son is beyond hope. I've had enough of this. I'm taking Sam home. Tonight."

"That will not be possible, Mrs. Levinson. This disease is highly communicable, and—"

"And? And?" She felt her breathing speed into hyperventilation. "And what if I went to the police right now and told them you did a horrible unauthorized experiment on my son? What would *you* say then?"

For an awful moment Hannah could only hear her own heart beating as Dr. Rubin frowned, transforming his pleasant face into a mask of irritation, frustration, and, Hannah thought, ruthlessness. But when he spoke again it was only to ask another question.

"Do you really want to take Sam home?"

"I don't want to. I *intend* to."

"Let us understand each other. My purpose is not to deprive you of your son. I am only trying to spare you some pain. Caring for Sam will only be burden for you, and it won't help him."

"I think I should decide what's helping him."

The doctor cocked his head to one side as if listening to an internal suggestion. "All right. I'll help you get him out of here, if that's what you want. But there will have to be some conditions . . ."

. . . . .

The alarm went off. A newscaster announced the time and date as Hannah got out of bed. Two weeks since Sam had come home.

Pulling on whatever clothing came to hand, she went to the kitchen, drank some water, and prepared a syringe and an IV bag for Sam. She had learned to medicate him first thing in the morning, injecting the meds into the nutrient fluid. The drugs would drip with the first feeding into the tube that burrowed like a worm under the skin of his chest. By the time the drip had finished, he would be calm, and she could get him out of bed.

"There's so much we don't know," Dr. Rubin had said as he gave Hannah a crash course on how to change the IV bags and keep the feeding tube clean. "Nothing in their bodies works the way it should, and yet they still have—appetites. The tube will keep him hydrated and fed, but he will still be aggressive. You'll have to be careful."

Hannah forced herself to look cheerful as she entered Sam's room and took care of the feeding, though she couldn't be sure if he saw her smile. She knew she should have put on the protective clothing Dr. Rubin had given her, but she hated the sense of distance created by the gloves, the mask, the long surgical apron.

"Good morning, precious boy."

The figure on the bed did not respond. His thick black hair, which had fallen out during the chemotherapy he'd been given to prepare his body for the stem cells, showed no sign of growing back. His shriveled scalp lent an alien aspect to his baby face. Hannah checked to make sure the safety harness holding Sam down on the bed was still secure. Then she took a bottle from the nightstand and put drops in Sam's filmy eyes. A dark murky grey had replaced their once-beatific blue, spreading to the whites around the irises. When her hand moved above his face, he opened his mouth, straining to get closer to her arm. As a toddler he used to reach up from his bed like this to kiss her. If his mouth reached her now, though, it would not be a kiss he delivered, but his own sickness. She tried not to look inside his parted lips. The gums and tongue had turned black.

She sat by Sam's bedside, waiting for the drugs to take effect. When the boy stopped trying to turn his head to bite her, she removed his stockinette compression garments and sprayed an insect repellent all over Sam's body—the expensive one the doctor had recommended. So far, her efforts seemed to be helping. True, Sam's complexion had faded from its perfect roses-and-lilies hue to a greenish lividity, but for the most part the skin remained unbroken. When she had to look at Sam she concentrated on that, instead of agonizing over the deep wound near his right shoulder. It had been stitched up, but the sight of it still made her sick.

"Almost done, Sam," she told him as she put fresh compression garments on him. The abdomen was the tricky part, for it had puffed out, making his childish physique resemble a pudgy old man's. She involuntarily groaned with disgust at the rancid smell of the gases that escaped as she adjusted and arranged his body. But it was all right. It wasn't Sam's fault.

Finally, for safety's sake, she pulled the flannel cover, like a little sleeping bag, over his feet, all the way up to his neck, and fastened the Velcro straps all the way around. Then she carried him to the living room. As she put him down in a cushy armchair, his ever-open eyes turned to her. Hannah thought, *not alive, but watching*, as if the boy were merely a statue of a child who could observe her actions. "Come back to life, little boy," she whispered.

Sam stayed where Hannah put him, staring blankly at the kids' show she put on the television for him. She got a little respite now that she allowed the TV to do some of the work. For the first few days after Sam came home she had tried to engage him with his favorite books and toys. But he didn't even respond to *Green Eggs and Ham*, his favorite storybook since he was four years old, when he started reading. Hannah remembered his baby voice sounding out, "S-A-M, Sssss-aaaa-mmmmm, S-a-m, Sam!" and his shriek of delight when he realized that the name he had just read was his own. She wondered if he would be physically capable of speaking now, even if he still had the mental capacity. He had not said a single word since the attack.

But at least he remained, for the moment, quiet and apparently calm. Her schedule and system would suffice for the time being. Good, because she simply could not go another day without taking a shower. Her skin itched, and she could not help reaching up to touch her limp, greasy hair. As she raised her arm she became aware of how badly she stank, her own body odor rising under the stench of Sam's rot. Until now she had felt she had to watch him every second. But he would be all right, all snugly wrapped-up in his little cover. There was no way he could move, especially with the tranquilizers working in his system. Another feeding wouldn't be due for two hours yet. Plenty of time. Her tired body craved the hot, soothing water.

With her bedroom door open, she could see Sam clearly in the room beyond. Sitting. Still.

Stepping inside the doorway, Hannah put a clean pair of jeans, underwear, and a tank top on her bed, then undressed. She flinched as she met her own eyes in the dresser mirror. When she had become pregnant, finally, at forty, she had still considered herself young. She thought of her husband, his gentle smile and comforting arms eternally out of reach. The diseased creatures hadn't killed Sam's father. The shock and stress of a world turned upside-down had. Perhaps the same was happening to her. When had she gotten those lines between her eyes and around her mouth? When had her face and body started to droop, as if testifying to her unhappiness?

I'm just tired, she decided. *I'll feel better after my shower.*

But the warm water didn't wash away Hannah's anxiety. Turning around in the stall, she thought about the attack on Sam. It was really her fault. Why hadn't she foreseen that the park would be too dangerous?

Sam loved the park. It stood in the exact center of the planned community, surrounded by houses, gates, and trained personnel who had always kept the problems at bay. Though the park was within walking distance of the house, Hannah drove Sam there. Just to be safe. The boy enjoyed the swings, but he liked the sandbox best. It was a beautiful day, the streets quiet. They had the park to themselves.

Hannah let Sam run to the other side of the playground and jump into the sandbox. He immediately started digging, pushing sand up here, punching holes in the shifting surface there. Hannah sat down on a bench and turned her face up toward the sun. It felt so good, and when she closed her eyes she remembered a better time. She could hear the little sound effects Sam made as he played. Then he started chattering.

Hannah opened her eyes and saw that another child had joined Sam in the sand. Hannah wondered whose little boy it could be. He looked a bit too big to be playing with a seven-year-old like Sam. In fact, he didn't look like a very nice boy at all. Even from here you could see the grime on his face and arms, his ripped clothing, his . . .

Hannah got up and started walking toward the sandbox. Then she started to run. As she got closer she saw Sam reach over to grab a spade stuck in the sand, saw the strange child lunge, sinking what remained of its teeth deep into Sam's upper chest, near the shoulder.

Hannah swooped down and grabbed Sam, kicking the creature as hard as she could. Sand flew. Her kick made virtually no impact. The thing stood up. It had been a boy of perhaps twelve or thirteen years old, but it was almost as tall as Hannah. It lurched forward.

As Hannah screamed, a shot rang out. A bullet hit the creature right between the eyes. The force knocked its head sideways on its shoulders. Its body fell out of the sandbox.

Hannah turned around and saw a woman in a green uniform—one of the military police—running toward the playground from the street. Hannah cradled Sam close, grateful that he had a slim, slight build for his age. Pushing his chest to hers, she tried desperately to conceal Sam's mangled chest while he screamed in pain and terror. She could feel his blood soaking into her T-shirt.

Oh God, it won't work, it won't work, she thought as the MP reached the park's border. *She'll see, and then . . .* Hannah knew what the MP would do if she figured out what had happened to Sam.

The MP got closer and closer. Hannah trembled, trying to come up with an excuse, an evasion, an escape. Then the MP reached them, ran right past them without even looking. Hannah turned to stare at the MP's retreating back. On the opposite street, a female figure, a decaying wreck of a woman, staggered around the corner, the MP in hot pursuit.

Hannah did not wait to see the result. She carried Sam to her car, ripped his pants off, wrapped them around his chest to stanch the bleeding, and drove him to Temple Medical Clinic.

The clinic terrified her, but anything resembling a hospital always did. As Sam lay on a gurney the medical team rushed about, machines beeped and instruments clattered. She had never felt so helpless.

A tremendous crash jolted Hannah out of her memories. She stopped the shower and stood there, listening. Silence. What had happened? Into the bathroom drifted the sinister music of scattering glass.

Hannah jumped out of the shower, wrapping a towel around her body as she scampered to the bedroom doorway, looking into the living room. The chair where Sam had sat so calmly stood empty. On the floor lay the little flannel cover, intact, its Velcro straps still fastened. The plate-glass window looking into the backyard, however, had been shattered, its remains glittering on the brick patio, along with those of the TV. Beyond the wreckage, she caught a glimpse of the perpetrator himself as he pushed through the gate.

Hannah dropped the towel, raced to the bedroom, and threw on her jeans, tank top, and track shoes. Before she left the house she fetched another syringe and the tranquilizer, and picked the flannel cover off the floor as she ran, ripping open the Velcro straps as she went. By the time she got through the gate herself, her son had disappeared.

What if some trigger-happy neighbor—or worse, an officer, saw him? In her mind's eye she relived how the MP had fired on the thing attacking her son without warning or regard. She needed help, experts, but she knew she would have to take care of this herself. One of Dr. Rubin's conditions raced through her mind. "If anything should happen, if he should hurt someone or if someone should hurt him, we will deny any and all involvement. You and your son were never here."

She had to think logically. Where would Sam go, if he could? Wasn't he still a child? Maybe the playground?

Hannah headed there. As she crossed a street two blocks from the playground she caught sight of Sam trundling down the sidewalk. She put all her strength into a sprint. Then she saw the baby.

Not a baby, really, but a little girl—perhaps four years old—on the same length of sidewalk as Sam. The world went into slow motion. In the time it took Hannah to get to Sam she saw the little girl's overturned tricycle and skinned knee, saw a bored-looking teenage girl sunning herself on a patch of grass, just now raising her head at the sound of running footsteps, and then Hannah got close enough to see the back of Sam's head—close enough to see the eight tiny holes that had been drilled into the boy's skull in order introduce the stem cells.

She jumped into a flying tackle, using the flannel to shield herself as she brought Sam down. As soon as he hit the pavement, Hannah panicked. *What if I've hurt him?*

Sam rolled over, and Hannah found herself lying under him, the boy on his hands and knees on her chest.

"Sam! Sam!" She called to him again and again. His response was not the pitiful cry of a hurt or hungry child, but the screech of a thwarted beast. As she reached for him he flopped and wriggled, snapping at her arms and trying to get past the flannel she jammed into his face whenever he moved.

"*Sam!*" But it was not a name any more, it was a plea for some kind of sanity. Nothing mattered now but getting this creature under control before it succeeded in infecting her. It snarled and snapped, its body impossibly heavy, its smell bringing countless retches to her throat.

With all her might Hannah shoved her son off her and threw the cover over his head, then down past his arms, as far down his legs as she could, before wrapping one of the straps around his legs, immobilizing him. She filled the syringe and quickly injected Sam—she didn't care where, it didn't matter, so long as it made him quiet. She looked up and down the empty sidewalk. The four-year-old and her keeper had evidently fled.

Hannah tried to catch her breath. When had she lost control? When had her son turned from someone who needed compassion and care to some kind of monster? She remembered the feel of his body on top of hers, the malevolence radiating from every inch of him. Her own life didn't matter, but what if he had caused that little girl to become what he was? The vicious cycle, Dr. Rubin had called it. Without knowing it, Hannah had been a part of that cycle, had made Sam a part of it. It had started with her. Somehow, she had to help end it too.

Would she have the courage to shoot a bullet through Sam's head, or allow a stranger to do the deed? That would end Sam's suffering. But she could not believe that her son had gone through so much to so little purpose. She thought of all the knowledge he would never gain, all the fun he would never have; the family he would never know, the man he would never be. And she made her choice.

As Hannah drove back to the Temple Medical Clinic, she tried to feel the anguish she had felt before, but all her emotions now seemed submerged. Her sadness had broken into fragmented reflections, her anger into transient gleams.

At the clinic, Dr. Rubin summoned two orderlies, who put Sam on a gurney. "They're taking him to his new room," the doctor said. Once again, he asked her to wait in his office. The twilight deepened around Hannah, but this time she felt no agony of suspense. When Dr. Rubin opened the door, she stood up, ready to walk with him to see Sam.

Gooseflesh prickled Hannah's arms as the doctor ushered her into the room. Her little boy lay quiet, a pillow under his head. The restraints holding him to the bed had been discreetly covered with a blue blanket. They stood together, the medical man and the mother, looking down at the child.

Dr. Rubin spoke. "It is little ones like this who will save this world, if it can be saved."

In spite of everything that had happened Hannah felt a stir of separation anxiety. "I—I've never left him alone before."

"He won't be alone. I'll give you a moment."

Hannah heard the doctor leave the room, the door clicking shut behind him. Sam looked brave and hurt, his flesh ghastly from the beating it had taken during their tussle on the sidewalk. He had that watching-statue stare again, the visionary gaze of the starving child who sees nothing but the next sumptuous, imagined meal.

"I'm sorry, Sam. I so wanted the best for you. I just . . . I love you so much, I couldn't let you go. But now I have to believe that you can help the doctors and the other kids. Can you do that? Can you help the kids for Mama?"

Though Sam said nothing, it seemed their recent struggle had brought them closer. Hannah could feel his growing need for human flesh. Though she had not prayed in years a fragment of Psalm circulated in her mind: *I will lift up mine eyes unto the hills. From whence cometh my help?* She remembered her little Sam, the affectionate boy who kissed her constantly, who played and read his own name with delight, the child who loved to build new worlds in the sandbox. Someday soon he would wake into a world without plague and pestilence, where innocence would be restored. Yes, Sam had gone beyond hope, past her love, to a place where only faith in a cure validated his existence.

And *her* existence—what would become of it now? The years dropped away before her into emptiness. No son to love. No child who would grow into a man, perhaps with a family of his own, a family she could share. Like Sam, she would be doomed to suffer a hunger that could never be satisfied. How selfish it would be to simply go on living as an empty shell, without purpose or plan.

Sam turned his head a little, the clouded eyes staring at her. *He's so hungry, so lost,* Hannah thought. How could she even think of abandoning him? No matter what, children always needed their mothers. Sam needed her, even now. She just hadn't been prepared for all it meant.

Instinctively she lowered her hand towards the bed. Sam's mouth opened, his blackened tongue protruding between his lips in anticipation. As her fingertips caressed his cheek, Sam turned his head and closed his teeth around her forearm. Blood flowed. She remembered Sam's birth and how the doctors had cut her open in order to bring her son forth. On that day, a new life had begun for the two of them. And now, as Sam gave her the only kiss that remained to him, their journey would start anew.

"I'll be with you forever, little boy," she told him. The room seemed to fill with light as Sam ripped and ravaged.

Dr. Rubin should be pleased. He'd have another test subject soon.

HAECKEL'S TALE

Clive Barker

Clive Barker was born in Liverpool, England, where he went to all the same schools as John Lennon before attending Liverpool University. He now lives in California with his partner, photographer David Armstrong, and their daughter, Nicole.

The author of around thirty books, including the six *Books of Blood* collections, *The Damnation Game*, *Weaveworld*, *Cabal*, *The Great and Secret Show*, *Imajica*, *The Thief of Always*, *Everville*, *Sacrament*, *Galilee*, *Coldheart Canyon: A Hollywood Ghost Story*, *Mister B. Gone*, *The Adventures of Mr. Maximillian Bacchus and His Travelling Circus*, and the *New York Times* best-selling Arabat series, he is one of the leading writers of contemporary horror and fantasy, as well as being an acclaimed artist, playwright, film producer and director.

As a filmmaker, he created the hugely influential *Hellraiser* franchise in 1987 and went on to direct *Nightbreed* and *Lord of Illusions*. Barker also executive produced the Oscar-winning *Gods and Monsters*, while the Candyman series, along with *Underworld*, *Rawhead Rex*, *Quicksilver Highway*, *Saint Sinner*, *The Midnight Meat Train*, *Book of Blood*, *Dread*, and the video games *Undying*, *Demonik*, and *Jericho* are all based on his concepts.

The following story was one of two by Barker adapted for the Showtime Network's series *Masters of Horror* by creator Mick Garris. It was directed by John McNaughton (*Henry: Portrait of a Serial Killer*) after original director Roger Corman had to pull out because of a back injury.

"I was between novels and I was thinking of doing a collection of short stories," explains the author. "'Haeckel's Tale' is one of four or five that I finished. Part of it was a desire for me to just revisit the old Clive and see whether he was still living at the same address."

PURRUCKER DIED LAST week, after a long illness. I never much liked the man, but the news of his passing still saddened me. With him gone I am now the last of our little group; there's no-one left with whom to talk over the old times. Not that I ever did; at least not with him. We followed such different paths, after Hamburg. He became a physicist, and lived mostly, I think, in Paris. I stayed here in Germany, and worked with Herman Helmholtz, mainly working in the area of mathematics, but occasionally offering my contribution to other disciplines. I do not think I will be remembered when I go. Herman was touched by greatness; I never was. But I found comfort in the cool shadow of his theories. He had a clear mind, a precise mind. He refused to let sentiment or superstition into his view of the world. I learned a good deal from that.

And yet now, as I think back over my life to my early twenties (I'm two years younger than the century, which turns in a month), it is not the times of intellectual triumph that I find myself remembering; it is not Helmholtz's analytical skills, or his gentle detachment.

In truth, it is little more than the slip of a story that's on my mind right now. But it refuses to go away, so I am setting it down here, as a way of clearing it from my mind.

. . . . .

In 1822, I was—along with Purrucker and another eight or so bright young men— the member of an informal club of aspirant intellectuals in Hamburg. We were all of us in that circle learning to be scientists, and being young had great ambition, both for ourselves and for the future of scientific endeavor. Every Sunday we gathered at a coffee-house on the Reeperbahn, and in a back room which we hired for the purpose, fell to debate on any subject that suited us, as long as we felt the exchanges in some manner advanced our comprehension of the world. We were pompous, no doubt, and very full of ourselves; but our ardor was quite genuine. It was an exciting time. Every week, it seemed, one of us would come to a meeting with some new idea.

It was an evening during the summer—which was, that year, oppressively hot, even at night—when Ernst Haeckel told us all the story I am about to relate. I remember the circumstances well. At least I think I do. Memory is less exact than it believes itself to be, yes? Well, it scarcely matters. What I remember may as well *be* the truth. After all, there's nobody left to disprove it. What happened was this: towards the end of the evening, when everyone had drunk enough beer to float the German fleet, and the keen edge of intellectual debate had been dulled somewhat (to be honest we were descending into gossip, as we inevitably did after midnight), Eisentrout, who later became a great surgeon, made casual mention of a man called Montesquino. The fellow's name was familiar to us all, though none of us had met him. He had come into the city a month before, and attracted a good deal of attention in society, because he claimed to be a necromancer. He could speak with and even raise the dead, he claimed, and was holding seances in the houses of the rich. He was charging the ladies of the city a small fortune for his services.

The mention of Montesquino's name brought a chorus of slurred opinions from around the room, every one of them unflattering. He was a contemptuous cheat and a sham. He should be sent back to France—from whence he'd come—but not before the skin had been flogged off his back for his impertinence.

The only voice in the room that was not raised against him was that of Ernst Haeckel, who in my opinion was the finest mind amongst us. He sat by the open window—hoping perhaps for some stir of a breeze off the Elbe on this smothering night—with his chin laid against his hand.

"What do you think of all this, Ernst?" I asked him.

"You don't want to know," he said softly.

"Yes we do. Of course we do."

Haeckel looked back at us. "Very well then," he said. "I'll tell you."

His face looked sickly in the candlelight, and I remember thinking—distinctly thinking—that I'd never seen such a look in his eyes as he had at that moment. Whatever thoughts had ventured into his head, they had muddied the clarity of his gaze. He looked fretful.

"Here's what I think," he said. "That we should be careful when we talk about necromancers."

"Careful?" said Purrucker, who was an argumentative man at the best of times, and even more volatile when drunk. "Why should we be *careful* of a little French prick who preys on our women? Good Lord, he's practically stealing from their purses!"

"How so?"

"Because he's telling them he can raise the dead!" Purrucker yelled, banging the table for emphasis.

"And how do we know he cannot?"

"Oh now Haeckel," I said, "you don't believe—"

"I believe the evidence of my eyes, Theodor," Haeckel said to me. "And I saw— once in my life—what I take to be proof that such crafts as this Montesquino professes are real."

The room erupted with laughter and protests. Haeckel sat them out, unmoving. At last, when all our din had subsided, he said: "Do you want to hear what I have to say or don't you?"

"Of *course* we want to hear," said Julius Linneman, who doted on Haeckel; almost girlishly, we used to think.

"Then listen," Haeckel said. "What I'm about to tell you is absolutely true, though by the time I get to the end of it you may not welcome me back into this room, because you may think I am a little crazy. More than a little perhaps."

The softness of his voice, and the haunted look in his eyes, had quieted everyone, even the volatile Purrucker. We all took seats, or lounged against the mantelpiece, and listened. After a moment of introspection, Haeckel began to tell his tale. And as best I remember it, this is what he told us.

"Ten years ago I was at Wittenberg, studying philosophy under Wilhem Hauser. He was a metaphysician, of course; monkish in his ways. He didn't care for the physical world; it didn't touch him, really. And he urged his students to live with the same asceticism as he himself practices. This was of course hard for us. We were very young, and full of appetite. But while I was in Wittenberg, and under his watchful eye, I really tried to live as close to his precepts as I could.

"In the spring of my second year under Hauser, I got word that my father—who lived in Luneburg—was seriously ill, and I had to leave my studies and return home. I was a student. I'd spent all my money on books and bread. I couldn't afford the carriage fare. So I had to walk. It was several days' journey, of course, across the empty heath, but I had my meditations to accompany, and I was happy enough. At least for the first half of the journey. Then, out of nowhere there came a terrible rainstorm. I was soaked to the skin, and despite my valiant attempts to put my concern for physical comfort out of my mind, I could not. I was cold and unhappy, and the rarifications of the metaphysical life were very far from my mind.

"On the fourth or fifth evening, sniffling and cursing, I gathered some twigs and made a fire against a little stone wall, hoping to dry myself out before I slept. While I was gathering moss to make a pillow for my head an old man, his face the very portrait of melancholy, appeared out of the gloom, and spoke to me like a prophet.

"'It would not be wise for you to sleep here tonight,' he said to me.

"I was in no mood to debate the issue with him. I was too fed up. 'I'm not going to move an inch,' I told him. 'This is an open road. I have very right to sleep here if I wish to.'

"'Of course you do,' the old man said to me. 'I didn't say the right was not yours. I simply said it wasn't wise.'

"I was a little ashamed of my sharpness, to be honest. 'I'm sorry,' I said to him. 'I'm cold and I'm tired and I'm hungry. I meant no insult.'

"The old man said that none was taken. His name, he said, was Walter Wolfram.

"I told him my name, and my situation. He listened, then offered to bring me back to his house, which he said was close by. There I might enjoy a proper fire and some hot potato soup. I did not refuse him, of course. But I did ask him, when I'd risen, why he thought it was unwise for me to sleep in that place.

"He gave me such a sorrowful look. A heart-breaking look, the meaning of which I did not comprehend. Then he said: 'You are a young man, and no doubt you do not fear the workings of the world. But please believe me when I tell you there are nights when it's not good to sleep next to a place where the dead are laid.'

"'The dead?' I replied, and looked back. In my exhausted state I had not seen what lay on the other side of the stone wall. Now, with the rain-clouds cleared and the moon climbing, I could see a large number of graves there, old and new intermingled. Usually such a sight would not have much disturbed me. Hauser had taught us to look coldly on death. It should not, he said, move a man more than the prospect of sunrise, for it is just as certain, and just as unremarkable. It was good advice when heard on a warm afternoon in a classroom in Wittenberg. But here—out in the middle of nowhere, with an old man murmuring his superstitions at my side—I was not so certain it made sense.

"Anyway, Wolfram took me home to his little house, which lay no more than half a mile from the necropolis. There was the fire, as he'd promised. And the soup, as he'd promised. But there also, much to my surprise and delight, wife, Elise.

"She could not have been more than twenty-two, and easily the most beautiful woman I had ever seen. Wittenberg had its share of beauties, of course. But I don't believe its streets ever boasted a woman as perfect as this. Chestnut hair, all the way down to her tiny waist. Full lips, full hips, full breasts. And such eyes! When they met mine they seemed to consume me.

"I did my best, for decency's sake, to conceal my admiration, but it was hard to do. I wanted to fall down on my knees and declare my undying devotion to her, there and then.

"If Walter noticed any of this, he made no sign. He was anxious about something, I began to realize. He constantly glanced up at the clock on the mantel, and looked towards the door.

"I was glad of his distraction, in truth. It allowed me to talk to Elise, who—though she was reticent at first—grew more animated as the evening's proceeded. She kept plying me with wine, and I kept drinking it, until sometime before midnight I fell asleep, right there amongst the dishes I'd eaten from."

At this juncture, somebody in our little assembly—I think it may have been Purrucker—remarked that he hoped this wasn't going to be a story about disappointed love, because he really wasn't in the mood. To which Haeckel replied that the story had absolutely nothing to do with love in any shape or form. It was a simple enough reply, but it did the job: it silenced the man who'd interrupted, and it deepened our sense of foreboding.

The noise from the café had by now died almost completely; as had the sounds from the street outside. Hamburg had retired to bed. But we were held there, by the story, and by the look in Ernst Haeckel's eyes.

"I awoke a little while later," he went on, "but I was so weary and so heavy with wine, I barely opened my eyes. The door was ajar, and on the threshold stood a man in a dark cloak. He was having a whispered conversation with Walter. There was, I thought, an exchange of money; though I couldn't see clearly. Then the man departed. I got only the merest glimpse of his face, by the light thrown from the fire. It was not the face of a man I would like to quarrel with, I thought. Nor indeed even meet. Narrow eyes, sunk deep in fretful flesh. I was glad he was gone. As Walter closed the door I lay my head back down and almost closed my eyes, preferring that he not know I was awake. I can't tell you exactly why. I just knew that something was going on I was better not becoming involved with.

"Then, as I lay there, listening, I hear a baby crying. Walter called for Elise, instructing her to calm the infant down. I didn't hear her response. Rather, I heard it, I just couldn't make any sense of it. Her voice, which had been soft and sweet when I'd talked with her, now sounded strange. Through the slits of my eyes I could see that she'd gone to the window, and was staring out, her palms pressed flat against the glass.

"Again, Walter told her to attend to the child. Again, she gave him some guttural reply. This time she turned to him, and I saw that she was by no means the same woman as I'd conversed with. She seemed to be in the early stages of some kind of fit. Her color was high, her eyes wild, her lips drawn back from her teeth.

"So much that had seemed, earlier, evidence of her beauty and vitality now looked more like a glimpse of the sickness that was consuming her. She'd glowed too brightly; like someone consumed by a fever, who in that hour when all is at risk seems to burn with a terrible vividness.

"One of her hands went down between her legs and she began to rub herself there, in a most disturbing manner. If you've ever been to a madhouse you've maybe seen some of the kind of behavior she was exhibiting.

"'Patience,' Walter said to her, 'everything's being taken care of. Now go and look after the child.'

"Finally she conceded to his request, and off she went into the next room. Until I'd heard the infant crying I hadn't even realized they had a child, and it seemed odd to me that Elise had not made mention of it. Lying there, feigning sleep, I tried to work out what I should do next. Should I perhaps pretend to wake, and announce to my host that I would not after all be accepting his hospitality? I decided against this course. I would stay where I was. As long as they thought I was asleep they'd ignore me. Or so I hoped.

"The baby's crying had now subsided. Elise's presence had soothed it.

"'Make sure he's had enough before you put him down,' I heard Walter say to her. 'I don't want him waking and crying for you when you're gone.'

"From this I gathered that she was breast-feeding the child; which fact explained the lovely generosity of her breasts. They were plump with milk. And I must admit, even after the way Elise had looked when she was at the window, I felt a little spasm of envy for the child, suckling at those lovely breasts.

"Then I returned my thoughts to the business of trying to understand what was happening here. Who was the man who'd come to the front door? Elise's lover, perhaps? If so, why was Walter *paying* him? Was it possible that the old man had hired this fellow to satisfy his wife, because he was incapable of doing the job himself? Was Elise's twitching at the window simply erotic anticipation?

"At last, she came out of the infant's room, and very carefully closed the door. There was a whispered exchange between the husband and wife, which I caught no part of, but which set off a new round of questions in my head. Suppose they were conspiring to kill me? I will tell you, my neck felt very naked at that moment . . .

"But I needn't have worried. After a minute they finished their whispering and Elise left the house. Walter, for his part, went to sit by the fire. I heard him pour himself a drink, and down it noisily; then pour himself another. Plainly he was drowning his sorrows; or doing his best. He kept drinking, and muttering to himself while he drank. Presently, the muttering became tearful. Soon he was sobbing.

"I couldn't bear this any longer. I raised my head off the table, and I turned to him.

"'Herr Wolfram,' I said, '. . .what's going on here?'

"He had tears pouring down his face, running into his beard.

"'Oh my friend,' he said, shaking his head, 'I could not begin to explain. This is a night of unutterable sadness.'

"'Would you prefer that I left you to your tears?' I asked him.

"'*No*,' he said. 'No, I don't want you to go out there right now.'

"I wanted to know why, of course. Was there something he was afraid I'd see?

"I had risen from the table, and now went to him. 'The man who came to the door—'

"Walter's lip curled at my mention of him. 'Who is he?' I asked.

"'His name is Doctor Skal. He's an Englishman of my acquaintance.'

"I waited for further explanation. But when none was forthcoming, I said: 'And a friend of your wife's.'

"'No,' Walter said. 'It's not what you think it is.' He poured himself some more brandy, and drank again. 'You're supposing they're lovers. But they're not. Elise has not the slightest interest in the company of Doctor Skal, believe me. Nor indeed in any visitor to this house.'

"I assumed this remark was a little barb directed at me, and I began to defend myself, but Walter waved my protestations away.

"'Don't concern yourself,' he said, 'I took no offence at the looks you gave my wife. How could you not? She's a very beautiful woman, and I'd be surprised if a young man such as yourself *didn't* try to seduce her. At least in his heart. But let me tell you, my friend: you could never satisfy her.' He let this remark lie for a moment. Then he added: 'Neither, of course, could I. When I married her I was already too old to be a husband to her in the truest sense.'

"'But you have a baby,' I said to him.

"'The boy isn't mine,' Walter replied.

"'So you're raising this infant, even though he isn't yours?'

"'Yes.'

"'Where's the father?'

"'I'm afraid he's dead.'

"'Ah.' This all began to seem very tragic. Elise pregnant, the father dead, and Walter coming to the rescue, saving her from dishonor. That was the story constructed in my head. The only part I could not yet fit into this neat scheme was Doctor Skal, whose cloaked presence at the door had so unsettled me.

"'I know none of this is my business—' I said to Walter.

"'And better keep it that way,' he replied.

"'But I have one more question.'

"'Ask it.'

"'What kind of Doctor is this man Skal?'

"'Ah.' Walter set his glass down, and stared into the fire. It had not been fed in a while, and now was little more than a heap of glowing embers. 'The esteemed Doctor Skal is a necromancer. He deals in a science which I do not profess to understand.' He leaned a little closer to the fire, as though talking of the mysterious man had chilled him to the marrow. I felt something similar. I knew very little about the work of a necromancer, but I knew that they dealt with the dead.

"I thought of the graveyard, and of Walter's first words to me:

"'*It would not be wise for you to sleep here tonight.*'

"Suddenly, I understood. I got to my feet, my barely sobered head throbbing. 'I know what's going on here,' I announced. 'You paid Skal so that Elise could speak to the dead! To the man who fathered her baby.' Walter continued to stare into the fire. I came close to him. 'That's it, isn't it? And now Skal's going to play some miserable trick on poor Elise to make her believe she's talking to a spirit.'

"'It's *not* a trick,' Walter said. For the first time during this grim exchange he looked up at me. 'What Skal does is real, I'm afraid to say. Which is why you should stay in here until it's over and done with. It's nothing you need ever—'

"He broke off at that moment, his thought unfinished, because we heard Elise's voice. It wasn't a word she uttered, it was a sob; and then another, and another, I knew whence they came, of course. Elise was at the graveyard with Skal. In the stillness of the night her voice carried easily.

"'Listen to her,' I said.

"'Better not,' Walter said.

"I ignored him, and went to the door, driven by a kind of morbid fascination. I didn't for a moment believe what Walter had said about the necromancer. Though much else that Hauser had taught me had become hard to believe tonight, I still believed in his teachings on the matter of life and death. The soul, he'd taught us, was certainly immortal. But once it was released from the constraints of flesh and blood, the body had no more significance than a piece of rotted meat. The man or woman who had animated it was gone, to be with those who had already left this life. There was, he insisted, no way to call that spirit back. And nor therefore— though Hauser had never extrapolated this far—was there any validity in the claims of those who said that they could commune with the dead.

"In short, Doctor Skal was a fake: this was my certain belief. And poor distracted Elise was his dupe. God knows what demands he was making of her, to have her sobbing that way! My imagination—having first dwelt on the woman's charms shamelessly, and then decided she was mad—now re-invented her a third time, as Skal's hapless victim. I knew from stories I'd heard in Hamburg what power charlatans like this wielded over vulnerable women. I'd heard of some necromancers who demanded that their seances be held with everyone as naked as Adam, for purity's sake! Others who had so battered the tender hearts of their victims with their ghoulishness that the women had swooned, and been violated in their swoon. I pictured all this happening to Elise. And the louder her sobs and cries became the more certain I was that my worst imaginings were true.

"At last I couldn't bear it any longer, and I stepped out into the darkness to get her.

"Herr Wolfram came after me, and caught hold of my arm. 'Come back into the house!' he demanded. 'For pity's sake, leave this alone *and come back into the house!*'

"Elise was shrieking now. I couldn't have gone back in if my life had depended upon it. I shook myself free of Wolfram's grip and started out for the graveyard. At first I thought he was going to leave me alone, but when I glanced back I saw that though he'd returned into the house he was now emerging again, cradling a musket in his arms. I thought at first he intended to threaten me with it, but instead he said:

"'Take it!' offering the weapon to me.

"'I don't intend to kill anybody!' I said, feeling very heroic and self-righteous now that I was on my way. 'I just want to get Elise out of this damn Englishman's hands.'

"'She won't come, believe me,' Walter said. 'Please take the musket! You're a good fellow. I don't want to see any harm come to you.'

"I ignored him and strode on. Though Walter's age made him wheeze, he did his best to keep up with me. He even managed to talk, though what he said—between my agitated state and his panting—wasn't always easy to grasp.

"'She has a sickness . . . she's had it all her life . . . what did I know? . . . I loved her . . . wanted her to be happy . . .'

"'She doesn't sound very happy right now,' I remarked.

"'It's not what you think . . . it is and it isn't . . . oh God, please come back to the house!'

"'I said no! I don't want her being molested by that man!'

"'You don't understand. We couldn't begin to please her. Neither of us.'

"'So you hire Skal to service her Jesus!'

"I turned and pushed him hard in the chest, then I picked up my pace. Any last doubts I might have entertained about what was going on in the graveyard were forgotten. All this talk of necromancy was just a morbid veil drawn over the filthy truth of the matter. Poor Elise! Stuck with a broken down husband, who knew no better way to please than to give her over to an Englishman for an occasional pleasuring. Of all things, an Englishman! As if the English knew anything about making love.

"As I ran, I envisaged what I'd do when I reached the graveyard. I imagined myself hopping over the wall and with a shout racing at Skal, and plucking him off my poor Elise. Then I'd beat him senseless. And when he was laid low, and I'd proved just how heroic a fellow I was, I'd go to the girl, take her in my arms, and show her what a good German does when he wants to make a woman happy.

"Oh, my head was spinning with ideas, right up until the moment that I emerged from the corner of the trees and came in sight of the necropolis . . ."

Here, after several minutes of headlong narration, Haeckel ceased speaking. It was not for dramatic effect, I think. He was simply preparing himself, mentally, for the final stretch of his story. I'm sure that none of us in that room doubted that what lay ahead would not be pleasant. From the beginning this had been a tale overshadowed by the prospect of some horror. None of us spoke; that I do remember. We sat there, in thrall to the persuasions of Haeckel's tale, waiting for him to begin again. We were like children.

After a minute or so, during which time he stared out of the window at the night sky (though seeing, I think, nothing of its beauty) he turned back to us and rewarded our patience.

"The moon was full and white," he said. "It showed me every detail.

"There were no great, noble tombs in this place, such as you'd see at the Ohlsdorf Cemetery; just coarsely carved headstones and wooden crosses. And in their midst, a kind of ceremony was going on. There were candles set in the grass, their flames steady in the still air. I suppose they made some kind of circle—perhaps ten feet across—in which the necromancer had performed his rituals. Now, however, with his work done, he had retired some distance from this place. He was sitting on a tombstone, smoking a long, Turkish pipe, and watching.

"The subject of his study, of course, was Elise. When I had first laid eyes on her I had guiltily imagined what she would look like stripped of her clothes. Now I had my answer. There she was, lit by the gold of the candle flames and the silver of the moon. Available to my eyes in all her glory.

"But oh God! What she was doing turned every single drop of pleasure I might have taken in her beauty to the bitterest gall.

"Those cries I'd heard—those sobs that had made my heart go out to her—they weren't provoked by the pawings of Doctor Skal, but by the touch of the dead. The dead, raised out of their dirt to pleasure her! She was squatting, and there between her legs was a face, pushed up out of the earth. A man recently buried, to judge by his condition, the flesh still moist on the bone, and the tongue—Jesus, the tongue!—still flicking between his bared teeth.

"If this had been all it would have been enough. But it was not all. The same grotesque genius that had inspired the cadaver between her legs into this resemblance of life, had also brought forth a crop of smaller parts—pieces of the whole, which had wormed their way out of the grave by some means or other. Bony pieces, held together with leathery sinew. A rib-cage, crawling around on its elbows; a head, propelled by a whiplash length of stripped spine; several hands, with some fleshless lengths of bone attached. There was a morbid bestiary of these things And they were all upon her, or waiting their turn to be upon her.

"Nor did she for a moment protest their attentions. Quite the contrary. Having climbed off the corpse that was pleasuring her from below, she rolled over onto her back and invited a dozen of these pieces upon her, like a whore in a fever, and they came, oh God they came, as though they might have out of her the juices that would return them to wholesomeness.

"Walter, by now, had caught up with me.

"'I warned you,' he said.

"'You knew this was happening?'

"'Of course I knew. I'm afraid it's the only way she's satisfied.'

"'What is she?' I said to him.

"'A woman,' Walter replied.

"'No natural woman would endure *that*,' I said. 'Jesus! Jesus!'

"The sight before me was getting worse by the moment. Elise was up on her knees in the grave dirt now, and a second corpse—stripped of whatever garments he had been buried in—was coupling with her, his motion vigorous, his pleasure intense, to judge by the way he threw back his putrefying head. As for Elise, she was kneading her full tits, directing arcs of milk into the air so that it rained down on the vile menagerie cavorting before her. Her lovers were in ecstasy. They clattered and scampered around in the torrents, as though they were being blessed.

"I took the musket from Walter.

"'Don't hurt her!' he begged. 'She's not to blame.'

"I ignored him, and made my way towards the yard, calling to the necromancer as I did so.

"'Skal! *Skal!*

"He looked up from his meditations, whatever they were, and seeing the musket I was brandishing, immediately began to protest his innocence. His German wasn't good, but I didn't have any difficulty catching his general drift. He was just doing what he'd been paid to do, he said. He wasn't to blame.

"I clambered over the wall and approached him through the graves, instructing him to get to his feet. He got up, his hands raised in surrender. Plainly he was terrified that I was going to shoot him. But that wasn't my intention. I just wanted to stop this obscenity.

"'Whatever you did to start this, *undo it!*' I told him.

"He shook his head, his eyes wild. I thought perhaps he didn't understand so I repeated the instruction.

"Again, he shook his head. All his composure was gone. He looked like a shabby little cut-purse who'd just been caught in the act. I was right in front of him, and I jabbed the musket in his belly. If he didn't stop this, I told him, I'd shoot him.

"I might have done it too, but for Herr Wolfram, who had clambered over the wall and was approaching his wife, calling her name.

"'Elise . . . please, Elise . . . you should come home.'

"I've never in my life heard anything as absurd or as sad as that man calling to his wife. '*You should come home . . .*'

"Of course she didn't listen to him. Didn't *hear* him, probably, in the heat of what she was doing, and what was being done to her.

"But her *lovers* heard. One of the men who'd been raised up whole, and was waiting his turn at the woman, started shambling towards Walter, waving him away. It was a curious thing to see. The corpse trying to shoo the old man off. But Walter wouldn't go. He kept calling to Elise, the tears pouring down his face. Calling to her, calling to her—

"I yelled to him to stay away. He didn't listen to me. I suppose he thought if he got close enough he could maybe catch hold of her arm. But the corpse came at him, still waving its hands, still shooing, and when Walter wouldn't be shooed the thing simply knocked him down. I saw him flail for a moment, and then try to get back up. But the dead—or pieces of the dead—were everywhere in the grass around his feet. And once he was down, they were upon him.

"I told the Englishman to come with me, and I started off across the yard to help Walter. There was only one ball in the musket, so I didn't want to waste it firing from a distance, and maybe missing my target. Besides I wasn't sure what I was going to fire at. The closer I got to the circle in which Elise was crawling around—still being clawed and petted—the more of Skal's unholy handiwork I saw. Whatever spells he'd cast here, they seemed to have raised every last dead thing in the place. The ground was crawling with bits of this and that; fingers, pieces of dried up flesh with locks of hair attached; wormy fragments that were beyond recognition.

"By the time we reached Walter, he'd already lost the fight. The horrors he'd paid to have resurrected—ungrateful things—had torn him open in a hundred places. One of his eyes had been thumbed out, there was a gaping hole in his chest.

"His murderers were still working on him. I batted a few limbs off him with the musket, but there were so many it was only a matter of time, I knew, before they came after me. I turned around to Skal, intending to order him again to bring this abomination to a halt, but he was springing off between the graves. In a sudden surge of rage, I raised the musket and I fired. The felon went down, howling in the grass. I went to him. He was badly wounded, and in great pain, but I was in no mood to help him. He was responsible for all this. Wolfram dead, and Elise still crouching amongst her rotted admirers; all of this was Skal's fault. I had no sympathy for the man.

"'What does it take to make this stop?' I asked him. '*What are the words?*'

"His teeth were chattering. It was hard to make out what he was saying. Finally I understood.

"'When . . . the . . . sun . . . comes up . . .' he said to me.

"'You can't stop it any other way?'

"'No,' he said. 'No . . . other . . . way . . .'

"Then he died. You can imagine my despair. I could do nothing. There was no way to get to Elise without suffering the same fate as Walter. And anyway, she wouldn't have come. It was an hour from dawn, at least. All I could do was what I did: climb over the wall, and wait. The sounds were horrible. In some ways, worse than the sight. She must have been exhausted by now, but she kept going. Sighing sometimes, sobbing sometimes, moaning sometimes. Not—let me make it perfectly clear—the despairing moan of a woman who understands that she is in the grip of the dead. This was the moan of a deeply pleasured woman; a woman in bliss.

"Just a few minutes before dawn, the sounds subsided. Only when they had died away completely did I look back over the wall. Elise had gone. Her lovers lay around in the ground, exhausted as perhaps only the dead can be. The clouds were lightening in the East. I suppose resurrected flesh has a fear of the light, because as the last stars crept away so did the dead. They crawled back into the earth, and covered themselves with the dirt that had been shoveled down upon their coffins . . ."

Haeckel's voice had become a whisper in these last minutes, and now it trailed away completely. We sat around not looking at one another, each of us deep in thought. If any of us had entertained the notion that Haeckel's tale was some invention, the force of his telling—the whiteness of his skin, the tears that had now and then appeared in his eyes—had thrust such doubts from us, at least for now.

It was Purrucker who spoke first, inevitably. "So you killed a man," he said. "I'm impressed."

Haeckel looked up at him. "I haven't finished my story," he said.

"Jesus . . ." I murmured, ". . . what else is there to tell?"

"If you remember, I'd left all my books, and some gifts I'd brought from Wittenberg for my father, at Herr Wolfram's house. So I made my way back there. I was in a kind of terrified trance, my mind still barely able to grasp what I'd seen.

"When I got to the house I heard somebody singing. A sweet lilting voice it was. I went to the door. My belongings were sitting there on the table where I'd left them. The room was emptying. Praying that I'd go unheard, I entered. As I picked up my philosophy books and my father's gift the singing stopped.

"I retreated to the door but before I could reach the threshold Elise appeared, with her infant in her arms. The woman looked the worse for her philanderings, no question about that. There were scratches all over her face, and her arms, and on the plump breast at which the baby now sucked. But marked as she was, there was nothing but happiness in her eyes. She was sweetly content with her life at that moment.

"I thought perhaps she had no memory of what had happened to her. Maybe the necromancer had put her into some kind of trance, I reasoned; and now she'd woken from it the past was all forgotten.

"I started to explain to her. 'Walter . . .' I said.

"'Yes, I know—' she replied. 'He's dead.' She smiled at me; a May morning smile. 'He was old,' she said, matter-of-factly. 'But he was always kind to me. Old men are the best husbands. As long as you don't want children.'

"My gaze must have gone from her radiant face to the baby at her nipple, because she said:

"'Oh, this isn't Walter's boy.'

"As she spoke she tenderly teased the infant from her breast, and it looked my way. There it was: life-in-death, perfected. Its face was shiny pink, and its limbs fat from its mother's milk, but its sockets were deep as the grave, and its mouth wide, so that its teeth, which were not an infant's teeth, were bared in a perpetual grimace.

"The dead, it seemed, had given her more than pleasure.

"I dropped the books, and the gift for my father there on the doorstep. I stumbled back out into the daylight, and I ran—oh God in Heaven, I ran!—afraid to the very depths of my soul. I kept on running until I reached the road. Though I had no desire to venture past the graveyard again, I had no choice: it was the only route I knew, and I did not want to get lost, I wanted to be home. I wanted a church, an altar, piety, prayers.

"It was not a busy thoroughfare by any means, and if anyone had passed along it since day-break they'd decided to leave the necromancer's body where it lay beside the wall. But the crows were at his face, and foxes at his hands and feet. I crept by without disturbing their feast."

Again, Haeckel halted. This time, he expelled a long, long sigh. "And that, gentlemen, is why I advise you to be careful in your judgments of this man Montesquino."

He rose as he spoke, and went to the door. Of course we all had questions, but none of us spoke then, not then. We let him go. And for my part, gladly. I'd enough of these horrors for one night.

· · · · ·

Make of all this what you will. I don't know to this day whether I believe the story or not (though I can't see any reason why Haeckel would have *invented* it. Just as he'd predicted, he was treated very differently after that night; kept at arm's length). The point is that the thing still haunts me; in part, I suppose, *because* I never made up my mind whether I thought it was a falsehood or not. I've sometimes wondered what part it played in the shaping of my life: if perhaps my cleaving to empiricism—my devotion to Helmholtz's methodologies—was not in some way the consequence of this hour spent in the company of Haeckel's account.

Nor do I think I was alone in my preoccupation with what I heard.

Though I saw less and less of the other members of the group as the years went by, on those occasions when we did meet up the conversation would often drift round to that story, and our voices would drop to near-whispers, as though we were embarrassed to be confessing that we even remembered what Haeckel had said.

A couple of members of the group went to some lengths to pluck holes in what they'd heard, I remember; to expose it as nonsense. I think Eisentrout actually claimed he'd retraced Haeckel's journey from Wittenberg to Luneburg, and claimed there was no necropolis along the route. As for Haeckel himself, he treated these attacks upon his veracity with indifference. We had asked him to tell us what he thought of necromancers, and he'd told us. There was nothing more to say on the matter.

And in a way he was right. It was just a story told on a hot night, long ago, when I was still dreaming of what I would become.

And yet now, sitting here at the window, knowing I will never again be strong enough to step outside, and that soon I must join Purrucker and the others in the earth, I find the terror coming back to me; the terror of some convulsive place where death has a beautiful woman in its teeth, and she gives voice to bliss. I have, if you will, fled Haeckel's story over the years; hidden my head under the covers of reason. But here, at the end, I see that there is no asylum to be had from it; or rather, from the terrible suspicion that it contains a clue to the ruling principle of the world.

THE RULEBOOK
Christopher Fowler

Christopher Fowler's first thriller was the 1988 bestseller *Roofworld*. Subsequent novels include *Rune*, *Spanky*, *Psychoville*, *Disturbia*, and the Bryant & May series of classic mysteries featuring two elderly, argumentative detectives.

His short fiction has been collected in *Bureau of Lost Souls*, two volumes of *City Jitters*, *Sharper Knives*, *Flesh Wounds*, *Personal Demons*, *Uncut*, *The Devil in Me*, and *Demonized*.

Fowler has worked in the movie industry for more than thirty years. He has written comedy and drama for BBC Radio, has a weekly column in the *Independent on Sunday* newspaper, and has written articles and columns for *The Times*, *Time Out*, *Black Static*, *Smoke*, *Pure*, *Dazed and Confused*, *The Big Issue*, and many others, including penning BBC Radio 1's first-ever broadcast drama in 2005.

His 1997 graphic novel for DC Comics was the critically acclaimed *Menz Insana*, while his short story "The Master Builder" became a CBS-TV movie entitled *Through the Eyes of a Killer* starring Tippi Hedren and Marg Helgenberger.

In fact, the author has achieved several ridiculous schoolboy fantasies, including releasing a Christmas pop single, writing a stage show, being used as the model for a Batman villain, appearing in *The Pan Book of Horror Stories*, and standing in for James Bond. He lives in glass penthouse overlooking London's King's Cross area.

The author's fiction has been regularly nominated for awards, including the Bram Stoker Award and the Dilys Award. His collection *Old Devil Moon* received both the 2008 Edge Hill Award and the British Fantasy Award, while *The Victoria Vanishes* won the 2009 Last Laugh Award for a humorous crime novel at Bristol CrimeFest.

"My agent was pleased with the way my schoolboy memoir, *Paperboy*, turned out," explains Fowler, "although I think the chapter eulogizing *Famous Monsters of Filmland* probably bored her.

"She suggested I write a teen book of horror, but I lacked the confidence. Kids are allergic to me—they come out in bruises. I live on a roof with a low balcony just in case one decides to visit. But I thought I'd try to create a decent horror frisson with a short tale.

"I decided to dodge the embarrassment of an oldie getting down with the kids by avoiding slang, Twitter, or anything else that would be over in about two hours' time, and instead wrote pretty much the way I think, which seems to have worked. Plus, kids love rules—it's why they're so good with computers. So, I thought, let's have a rulebook, then see what happens when the rules are broken—simple.

"So simple, in fact, that I've started writing a series of horror novels for teens—the first, *Hellion*, is out soon."

EVERY HOUSE HAS A RULEBOOK. It's not an actual book, but it has rules you're not supposed to break. In our house the rulebook appeared after my Dad went away. Here are some of the rules:

Never leave the back gate unbolted.

Put the lid down on the toilet seat when you've finished.

If you want to get something down from the top shelf don't stack the furniture to reach it. Your cousin Freddie died like that.

Don't touch the boiler in the kitchen, you'll burn yourself.

Reading under the bedsheets with a torch will hurt your eyes.

The Internet does not replace real friends.

Don't say "Bollocks" even though your Grandad says it all the time.

Just because everyone else has got one doesn't mean that you should have one too.

When you ask for seconds and can't finish them, remember there are people starving in Africa.

Television doesn't go on until you've finished your homework.

Pressing 6 on the speed-dial will call Auntie Pauline in Australia, she has verbal diarrhea and it will come out of your pocket money.

Every time you blaspheme, an angel gets a nosebleed.

Don't touch the cat's tray without washing your hands afterwards.

Don't ever put a lightbulb in the microwave again.

On holiday, there was another set of rules:

Don't go in the sea until an hour after you've eaten.

Always keep an eye on the tide.

Only go into an amusement arcade if you're prepared to lose money.

A stick of rock can pull your fillings out.

If you feel carsick tell Mum at once, don't leave it too late and do it down the window.

There's no need to drop a brick on a jellyfish. It can still feel pain even though it hasn't got a face.

. . . . .

Soon I made up my own rulebook. These were rules I just seemed to know by instinct, or felt were probably true. Here are some of them:

If you don't reach the bottom of the stairs before the toilet finishes flushing, the Thing That Lives in the Landing Cupboard will come after you.

You can ruin next door's TV reception by throwing balls of silver foil at their satellite dish.

Every time you squash an insect, God makes a mark in his book against you.

If you die at home while your Mum is away there will be nobody to feed the cat, and it will eat your eyes.

There is a horror film that can make you go mad if you watch it.

And:

Dad is still checking up on you, even though he isn't here.

Then, in the summer of my twelfth birthday, I learned a new rule.

Don't tell the neighbors that Mr. Hill murdered his wife.

It was a game, really. I don't think I believed that Mr. Hill had really murdered his wife, but I hated him because he had a dead grey eye like the guy in *Pirates of the Caribbean* and had painted all his flowerpots in Arsenal stripes and he kept my football whenever it went over his fence. He probably had footballs enough to open a branch of JD Sports.

On Bonfire Night Mr. Hill had a huge row with his wife. I heard her in the hall, yelling, "Do you know how painful this is, or what it's doing to me? I'm not going to stay in this house another minute." Then she left. She dragged a huge suitcase out to the front step and climbed into a waiting taxi, and he slammed the door behind her. Two months before this I had heard a lot of banging and crashing in their house one night, so I figured they had been fighting for a long time.

I was the only one who saw her leave. When I told my best friend Andy about the row, I exaggerated the story a little bit. I told him that I had seen Mr. Hill hit his wife with a shovel before burying her in the back garden while everyone else was watching the fireworks.

I told Andy not to tell anyone else, so by nightfall everyone in the street had heard the story, and as the days went on it became even more exaggerated to include all kinds of gross stuff. He'd cut off his wife's hands and buried them in his Arsenal pots, he'd used her spleen to decorate his Christmas tree, he kept her head on a stick in his shed and cast a spell on it to make it predict the football results.

I saw Mr. Hill staring through his kitchen window with laser-vision that could have melted a hole in the glass, and I knew the story had reached him, so I stayed out of his way after that. I thought he might kill me as well, because by now I believed my own story.

"You mustn't go around telling people lies about Mr. Hill," said my Mum one day. "His wife left him and he's very upset about that, without you making things worse by telling everyone he's a murderer."

There had always been a damp patch on my bedroom wall near the ceiling. It was dark grey and furry, and shaped like the Isle of Wight. One day there was an amazing storm. The rain fell sideways. Water came in through the back door and all our gutters overflowed, soaking my ceiling. The grey furry patch grew to the size of France and then part of the ceiling fell down, so my Mum called a company called AA-1 Roofs. They were called AA-1 so they would be the first people listed in the alphabetical telephone directory under ROOF REPAIRS, but now that everyone used Google they weren't at the top of the list anymore, so they were really cheap.

They came in to do the work, but told me and Mum to move out for the weekend because the air was unhealthy and the house needed to dry out for a bit.

"The good news," said my Mum, "is that Mr. Hill has to go into hospital, and says we can stay there."

"Why is he going to hospital?" I asked.

"He's having something done to his bladder."

"Gross. Can't we stay in a hotel?" I asked.

"No, too expensive."

"Bugger."

"Mind your language." My Mum collected the keys, and on Friday evening we went next door.

.   .   .   .   .

How can I describe Mr. Hill's house?

The hall was as dark as a tunnel to the center of the earth. There was a framed photo on the wall of a really old man that turned out to be a picture of Mr. Hill's grandmother. The living room smelled of wet dogs. It was full of little china ornaments of poodles, Dalmatians, bulldogs, every kind of dog. There were piles of magazines about dogs and dog shows, and there were long brown dog hairs everywhere, but get this, *he didn't own a dog*. I could see why Mrs. Hill had run away from him.

Every room was painted in a different shade of brown paint. Either he was color-blind or couldn't be bothered to match up the tins. There was a clock in the hall that ticked very slowly, like someone hobbling painfully towards the grave. In the hall cupboard I found my footballs. He had let the air out of them and folded them on a shelf like pairs of pants. Weird.

Mr. Hill had a son who had grown up and left home, and now that he lived alone he didn't bother cleaning up anymore. My Mum saw this as a challenge, and decided to give the place a spring-clean. I think she actually looked forward to our weekend of living next door, charging around with a mop and bucket.

"Think of it as a holiday," she told me, but a holiday is amusements and sunburn and the beach, not getting covered in dog hair in someone else's smelly, creepy house.

"You can play wherever you like," she said, "except in the room at the end of the upstairs hall. Mr. Hill says you're not allowed to go in there under any circumstances. It's one of his rules." So Mr. Hill had a rulebook too.

I went out into the garden and stayed there, but there was nothing to do. Weirdly the garden was the opposite of the house, so perfectly kept that there weren't even any insects in it. Eventually it was time to go to bed. There were three rooms upstairs. The smallest was Mr. Hill's son's room, which was now mine. Then came Mr Hill's room, which was where my Mum would sleep. Finally there was the big double room at the front of the house which nobody ever used and I wasn't allowed to go into Under Any Circumstances.

I stood outside this door and sniffed the keyhole. The dog-smell was coming from inside. I put my ear against the door and listened. I could hear faint breathing—in, gurgle, out, in, gurgle, out—like someone with a very bad cold and no tissues. I called Mum up and made her listen but she couldn't hear anything.

"Nothing at all?" I said, shocked. "You really can't hear anything?"

"No," she said.

"You wait till you want me to hear something." Disgusted, I went to my room.

Mr. Hill's son must have been about five when he left home to get a job, because his bedroom was full of stupid fluffy rabbits and realistic-looking puppies. I washed and got into my PJs and listened to the house. It creaked and clicked and rattled in the wind, so I couldn't get to sleep. My duffel coat on the door looked like a hunchbacked monster in the dark, and even though I knew it was just my coat, it bothered me. I must have drifted off for a few minutes, because I remember running through a jungle. Some kind of animal was after me. I heard claws scratching at the door.

At 11:45 p.m. my Mum looked in and said "Why are you still awake?" I don't know how she knew; she's sort of psychic like that.

"I can't sleep," I told her. "Listen to all the noise."

She cocked an ear. "That's just the rain falling on the dustbins."

"It doesn't sound like that on our dustbins."

She gave me a funny look. "You okay?"

"I think I had a bad dream," I told her. "I was being chased."

She came and on the edge of the bed. "It's because you're in a strange house. Was my little soldier afraid?"

"No, I was fine."

"Okay, I'll let you get some rest."

"I hate it here."

"Give me a break, Paul. It's just for two nights. Go to sleep."

The rest of the night I lay wide awake, watching the bedroom door. Finally I buried myself deep in bed with the pillows pulled up around my ears.

At seven o'clock it was supposed to get light, but it didn't. The rain had turned to thick wet fog. You could usually hear traffic outside but today there was complete silence. The fog had blinded and deafened our street, like someone had thrown a blanket over it.

I checked the door for scratch-marks. Nothing. I got dressed when I smelled Mum burning the toast. Mr. Hill's kitchen was bright yellow because it was the room where he smoked, and all the nicotine had stained the ceiling. I wondered what it made his food taste like.

Mum had tried to poach eggs in Mr. Hill's microwave and they had exploded. She said "You know I've never been good at breakfast. It's a horrible day. You'll be better off staying indoors."

There was no way I was going to do that. I spent almost the whole day outside on my bike, but by the evening it was bucketing down with rain again, and thunder rolled in the distance. We ate beans on toast and watched some rubbish dancing show my Mum liked. The storm was getting closer because I counted the gaps between the flash and the bang, and they were shorter each time.

My Mum's mobile rang. It was Mr. Hill. He needed some bathroom stuff to be brought to the hospital, so my Mum agreed to take it to him on her scooter. "I don't want you coming with me," she said, "it's raining too hard. Do you want to stay up until I'm back? You've got your computer games."

This was very good news, as it was already late. "Drive slowly. Don't rush back," I told her. "I'll be fine."

"Don't open the door to anyone, okay? And stay out of the end room. I know what you're like."

"I don't know what you mean." I tried to look innocent.

"Yeah, right. Butter wouldn't melt in your mouth."

After an hour by myself, I got tired of blasting monsters on my game—actually I was stuck at the first boss and was fed up with repeating the same level over and over. So I went upstairs and had a good nose in a few drawers. Mr. Hill had a dressing table full of really good stuff, including a red penknife with about a million attachments, a huge ring of keys, some really weird comics in plastic bags called *Out of This World*, several watches and a tobacco tin full of old metal puzzles.

I wanted to look in the room at the end of the hall, because I knew it would take an act of bravery to do so. My Dad used to say "Are you a man or a mouse? Squeak up." We'd laugh a lot about that one. When he told me not to do something, I didn't do it. With Mum it was different. Sometimes I deliberately did the opposite of what she asked.

Tonight was one of those occasions.

I wasn't scared, even though I was sure I could hear something breathing behind the door. Even though it smelled like something had died in the room. I stood outside the brown-painted door for along time, listening to the falling rain, listening for the in-gurgle-out breathing. I made a list in my head of all the terrible things that could be inside, so that I'd be prepared for the worst when I opened the door. I decided it could be any one of the following:

Mrs. Hill had come back to the house to beg his forgiveness for leaving, and her husband had pretended to forgive her before locking her up in a cage and feeding her dog food.

Mr. Hill kept a pack of starving dogs in the room, and if I opened the door they would spring out and tear me to pieces.

Mr. Hill had created a human being out of bits of dog, sewing all the parts together and bringing his creature to life with electricity. He had to keep it locked up because it was really angry all the time.

None of these situations were very likely, but they were all I could come up with. What else breathed and smelled like dead animals?

Finally I decided there was only one way to find out. Wrapping my fingers around the handle, I pushed down on it.

The door didn't budge. It was locked.

Then I remembered the keys in Mr. Hill's desk. I went to the drawer and took out the great ring. Returning to the door, I tried each one in turn.

I tried the coolest-looking keys first, but none fit. Six. Seven. Eight. Nine. The tenth key was the smallest, and worked. The lock wasn't very big. Maybe there wasn't something trying to get out of the room after all. As I pushed open the door and tried to find the light switch, the animal smell overpowered me and I heard the breathing more loudly.

Then I saw it, a huge hair-covered outline against the rainy window. It had a bristly snout and pointed ears like an Alsatian. In the light from the street lamp outside I could see the raised arms, the long curved claws, the great tongue that hung out from between yellow teeth. I knew the truth then:

Mr. Hill was a werewolf.

He hadn't gone to hospital, he had tricked my Mum and lured her away, leaving me alone with him. He knew I would come to the room. He was going to catch me and suck the meat from my bones.

Then I found the light switch. The lampshade in the middle of the ceiling glowed orange, removing the dark from the room.

Mr. Hill wasn't a werewolf after all.

The room was full of dead animals, and there was a huge book on his desk called *Taxidermy for Beginners*.

Mr. Hill had a secret hobby. He stuffed dead animals. Lots of people used to do it. The noise I had mistaken for breathing was the hiss of a cooling unit which was breathing cold air over his creations.

I opened the book and began to read:

.   .   .   .   .

Taxidermy Specimens—Preservation and Mounting. The taxidermist must remove the skin of the dead animal, then tan it and treat it. The animal's bones and muscles are posed in place with wires. The body is molded in plaster to make a cast, then re-covered with skin. Artificial eyes are then added as real ones would rot.

.   .   .   .   .

I put down the book and looked around the room. A dozen dogs, a badger, four cats, some bats and foxes stared back at me with shining marble eyes. There was also an owl with no eyes and a duck without a beak. The big creature I saw by the window was a molting brown bear, mounted on its back legs and frozen in mid-roar. There was another flash of lightning.

In jars by the window were some of the creatures' pink innards. No wonder Mr. Hill didn't tell anyone about what he was doing.

Just then, there was a huge bang of thunder and all the lights in the street went out.

I watched in horror as the great head of the bear slowly turned its head toward me, its black eyes glittering with life. Its jaw slowly widened and it drooled saliva. I dropped the ring of keys.

A new sound took over from the hissing of the cooling unit. This time it really was breathing. A lot of breathing. I looked down and saw a bat creeping toward me on the tips of its wings. I jumped backwards in fright. A half-finished dog was coming up behind me, although it had difficulty walking because its legs were only wire and bone, and screwed-up newspapers stuck out from the gap in its stomach.

A huge centipede curled and stretched by my hand. Several rats dropped onto the desktop and scampered around me into the hall. Little patches of dried fur were falling off the bear as it lumbered toward me, shoving all the other creatures out of the way. A cat yowled in pain as he stood on its foot. The dogs whimpered. The foxes cried like babies. All these animals were hurting.

There was a crash as the stand that had been propping up the great bear fell over. All the animals were on the move. I could smell their stale breath, the sawdust and balls of newspaper than had taken the place of their entrails. I could feel their pain. They were creeping, hopping, staggering in terrible angry pain.

I stumbled backwards as the bear lunged for the door.

The house was in total darkness. I ran along the hall but caught the banister against my hip and fell onto my knees. I could hear the creatures coming out of the front bedroom. I heard scratching, scampering, thumping, whimpering, growling. They were coming closer every second. A perfectly preserved tarantula threw itself onto my back. I could feel its hairy legs pattering against the nape of my neck.

Knowing that I could not reach the stairs in time, I climbed to my feet and ran back to my room, but the animals were very close now. I dived inside and shoved the door shut, just as the bear wrapped its great clawed paw around the jamb and tried to push its way inside. He was forcing it open to let all the smaller creatures in. I kicked the door hard on his paw until he withdrew it with a great roar. And there I stayed, pushed against the door, until eventually the scratching and clawing stopped, and it sounded like they went away.

I didn't know what to do. Should I risk opening the door? I knew I'd be anxious until I had checked, so I slowly opened it and looked out.

The hall was empty. The door to the front bedroom was still unlocked, and the big ring of keys was on the floor, exactly where I had dropped it. But I hadn't imagined the stuffed animals. They filled the room, crouching or standing on every surface, and they still smelled bad. The bear was facing back to the window now, where it had been to start with. But there was something floating in the air—sawdust settling, like they had only just got back into position before I opened the door.

I went to the landing window and stared down into the street, or rather the nearest part of it, as the rest had completely disappeared in the fog.

As I stood watching, a figure slowly came into view and opened the front garden gate, but it wasn't my Mum. Whoever it was seemed to be having trouble walking, like they had sprained their ankle. A few moments later I heard the front door open and shut. Someone was climbing the stairs. I heard feet thumping and dragged on the stairs, coming nearer, and a strange *crick-crack* noise.

Mrs. Hill was standing at the end of the hall in a green rain hat and Wellington boots. Her head was down. I couldn't see her eyes.

"I saw your mother go out, Paul," she said. "I want to talk to you for a minute." Her voice was dry and whispery, as though her vocal chords had rusted.

As she walked toward me she dripped rain everywhere. She took off her hat and scratched her fingers through her hair. Mrs. Hill was blonde and bonier than I remembered, like she'd been on a diet and hiding indoors for months. She stopped about three feet in front of me.

She smelled like mildew, like something that had been left past its sell-by date at the back of the fridge, and there was another smell too, the same dog smell about her like the bear, but I figured it was because her hair was wet. I couldn't move any further back, because the room of stuffed animals was behind me.

I asked her if she wanted a cup of tea.

Slowly she raised her head. Her skin was as yellow and dry as an old newspaper. I looked in her eyes and saw glittering blue marbles, like a doll's. The left one was cracked. It had turned up and rolled in a little, so that I could see the damp blackness inside her socket.

"What have you been telling people about me?"

"Nothing," I lied. "It was a mistake."

"You told the street that my husband killed me with a shovel on Bonfire Night and buried me in the garden. Don't lie to me."

"No, I only told Andy, no-one else. As for the thing about your head being cut off and stuck on a pole in the shed, the story just got sort of stretched as it went around."

She fumbled blindly with her handbag, snapping it open to dig out a handkerchief. Mopping the rain from her face, she smeared paint from her lips. "You saw me leave on Bonfire Night. I didn't come back."

"Okay." I wasn't interested in what they got up to. Anything to make her go. Reaching down, she placed a hand on my shoulder and gripped it tightly. Her fingers were so bony that it felt like being pinched by crab claws. There was nothing in her that was alive, no beating heart, no pulsing blood, just cold leathery flesh.

"Mr. Hill saved me. Two months before Bonfire Night I had an accident. I fell down the stairs and broke my neck, and he saved me. I don't want to see him hurt. Do you understand?"

"I understand."

Suddenly she bent down close to me. "No more lies, Paul. That's one of my rules. No more lies or I will come back and find you. I will take out your guts and fill the space with straw and sawdust." She stretched open her mouth and I saw right inside. There was newspaper at the back of it, sticking up out of her throat.

She released her bruising grip and turned to leave, her knees crick-cracking. When she went to put on her rain hat I saw the stitches, a neat dark row of them behind each ear.

She walked as if she was in great pain. As she slowly went down the stairs I noticed the seams of uneven stitches that ran down the backs of her legs. I could see the wires poking out of her fingertips as she gripped the stair-rail. Her skin seemed to have been sewn back too tightly, like a cover on a sofa that didn't quite fit.

The front door opened and closed. I watched her hobble sadly down the empty street and disappear piece by piece into the fog.

The sawdust settled. The house was silent once more, as if wild things had returned to sleeping death. As I sat in the kitchen waiting for Mum to come back, I looked out into the foggy front garden, fearful of what I might now be able to see.

The world has a rulebook. One of the rules is:

The dead can't be brought back to life.

Sometimes the rulebook is wrong.

BLACK CANAAN
Robert E. Howard

Robert E. Howard was born and raised in rural Texas, where he lived all his life.

The son of a pioneer physician, he began writing professionally at the age of fifteen. Three years later he sold his first story to the legendary pulp magazine *Weird Tales*.

A prolific and proficient author, he published Westerns, sports stories, horror tales, true confessions, historical adventures, and detective thrillers while developing a series of heroic characters with whom he would forever be identified—Solomon Kane, King Kull, Bran Mak Morn, and, of course, Conan the Cimmerian. Between 1932 and 1935, Howard wrote twenty-one sword and sorcery adventures of Conan, ranging in length from 3,500 words to 75,000 words.

When he learned that his beloved mother had slipped into a terminal coma, he committed suicide in June 1936 at the age of thirty.

That same month, "Black Canaan" was published in *Weird Tales*. It was billed as "A tale of the Southern swamps, and voodoo brought from blackest Africa—a spine-freezing, blood-chilling story of a beautiful quadroon girl who wielded bitter magic," and was one of a number of "regional" horror stories (including "The Horror from the Mound" and "Pigeons from Hell") that the author had sold to the magazine before his untimely death.

Although Howard was probably not an overt racist, the story is very much of its time and contemporary readers may find themselves uncomfortable with some of the language used. However, it should be remembered that these terms were in common usage back when the story was first published more than seventy years ago.

That one caveat notwithstanding, the novella that follows is as exciting and horrific as any of the author's best work and, in keeping with Howard's ability to reinvent some of the classic horror concepts, it features a very unusual and original interpretation of the reanimated dead.

I. Call from Canaan

"TROUBLE ON TULAROOSA CREEK!" A warning to send cold fear along the spine of any man who was raised in that isolated back-country, called Canaan, that lies between Tularoosa and Black River—to send him racing back to that swamp-bordered region, wherever the word might reach him.

It was only a whisper from the withered lips of a shuffling black crone, who vanished among the throng before I could seize her; but it was enough. No need to seek confirmation; no need to inquire by what mysterious, black-folk way the word had come to her. No need to inquire what obscure forces worked to unseal those wrinkled lips to a Black River man. It was enough that the warning had been given and understood.

Understood? How could any Black River man fail to understand that warning? It could have but one meaning—old hates seething again in the jungle-deeps of the swamplands, dark shadows slipping through the cypress, and massacre stalking out of the black, mysterious village that broods on the moss-festooned shore of sullen Tularoosa.

Within an hour New Orleans was falling further behind me with every turn of the churning wheel. To every man born in Canaan, there is always an invisible tie that draws him back whenever his homeland is imperiled by the murky shadow that has lurked in its jungled recesses for more than half a century.

The fastest boats I could get seemed maddeningly slow for that race up the big river, and up the smaller, more turbulent stream. I was burning with impatience when I stepped off on the Sharpsville landing, with the last fifteen miles of my journey yet to make. It was past midnight, but I hurried to the livery stable where, by tradition half a century old, there is always a Buckner horse, day or night.

As a sleepy black boy fastened the cinches, I turned to the owner of the stable, Joe Lafely, yawning and gaping in the light of the lantern he upheld. "There are rumors of trouble on Tularoosa?"

He paled in the lantern-light.

"I don't know. I've heard talk. But you people in Canaan are a shut-mouthed clan. No one *outside* knows what goes on in there—"

The night swallowed his lantern and his stammering voice as I headed west along the pike.

The moon set red through the black pines. Owls hooted away off in the woods, and somewhere a hound howled his ancient wistfulness to the night. In the darkness that foreruns dawn I crossed Nigger Head Creek, a streak of shining black fringed by walls of solid shadows. My horse's hooves splashed through the shallow water and clinked on the wet stones, startlingly loud in the stillness. Behind Nigger Head

Creek began the country men called Canaan.

Heading in the same swamp, miles to the north, that gives birth to Tularoosa, Nigger Head flows due south to join Black River a few miles west of Sharpsville, while the Tularoosa runs westward to meet the same river at a higher point. The trend of Black River is from northwest to southeast; so these three streams form the great irregular triangle known as Canaan.

In Canaan lived the sons and daughters of the white frontiersmen who first settled the country, and the sons and daughters of their slaves. Joe Lafely was right; we were an isolated, shut-mouthed breed. Self-sufficient, jealous of our seclusion and independence.

Beyond Nigger Head the woods thickened, the road narrowed, winding through unfenced pinelands, broken by live-oaks and cypresses. There was no sound except the soft clop-clop of hoofs in the thin dust, the creak of the saddle. Then someone laughed throatily in the shadows.

I drew up and peered into the trees. The moon had set and dawn was not yet come, but a faint glow quivered among the trees, and by it I made out a dim figure under the moss-hung branches. My hand instinctively sought the butt of one of the dueling-pistols I wore, and the action brought another low, musical laugh, mocking yet seductive. I glimpsed a brown face, a pair of scintillant eyes, white teeth displayed in an insolent smile.

"Who the devil are you?" I demanded.

"Why do you ride so late, Kirby Buckner?" Taunting laughter bubbled in the voice. The accent was foreign and unfamiliar; a faintly negroid twang was there, but it was rich and sensuous as the rounded body of its owner. In the lustrous pile of dusky hair a great white blossom glimmered palely in the darkness.

"What are you doing here?" I demanded. "You're a long way from any darky cabin. And you're a stranger to me.

"I came to Canaan since you went away," she answered. "My cabin is on the Tularoosa. But now I've lost my way. And my poor brother has hurt his leg and cannot walk."

"Where is your brother?" I asked, uneasily. Her perfect English was disquieting to me, accustomed as I was to the dialect of the black folk.

"Back in the woods, there—far back!" She indicated the black depths with a swaying motion of her supple body rather than a gesture of her hand, smiling audaciously as she did so.

I knew there was no injured brother, and she knew I knew it, and laughed at me. But a strange turmoil of conflicting emotions stirred in me. I had never before paid any attention to a black or brown woman. But this quadroon girl was different from any I had ever seen. Her features were regular as a white woman's, and her speech was not that of a common wench. Yet she was barbaric, in the open lure of her smile, in the gleam of her eyes, in the shameless posturing of her voluptuous body. Every gesture, every motion she made set her apart from the ordinary run of women; her beauty was untamed and lawless, meant to madden rather than to soothe, to make a man blind and dizzy, to rouse in him all the unreined passions that are his heritage from his ape ancestors.

I hardly remember dismounting and tying my horse. My blood pounded suffocatingly through the veins in my temples as I scowled down at her, suspicious yet fascinated.

"How do you know my name? Who *are* you?"

With a provocative laugh, she seized my hand and drew me deeper into the shadows. Fascinated by the lights gleaming in her dark eyes, I was hardly aware of her action.

"Who does not know Kirby Buckner?" she laughed. "All the people of Canaan speak of you, white or black. Come! My poor brother longs to look upon you!" And she laughed with malicious triumph.

It was this brazen effrontery that brought me to my senses. Its cynical mockery broke the almost hypnotic spell in which I had fallen.

I stopped short, throwing her hand aside, snarling: "What devil's game are you up to, wench?"

Instantly the smiling siren was changed to a blood-mad jungle cat. Her eyes flamed murderously, her red lips writhed in a snarl as she leaped back, crying out shrilly. A rush of bare feet answered her call. The first faint light of dawn struck through the branches, revealing my assailants, three gaunt black giants. I saw the gleaming whites of their eyes, their bare glistening teeth, the sheen of naked steel in their hands.

My first bullet crashed through the head of the tallest man, knocking him dead in full stride. My second pistol snapped—the cap had somehow slipped from the nipple. I dashed it into a black face, and as the man fell, half stunned, I whipped out my bowie knife and closed with the other. I parried his stab and my counter-stroke ripped across the belly-muscles. He screamed like a swamp-panther and made a wild grab for my knife wrist, but I stuck him in the mouth with my clenched left fist, and felt his lips split and his teeth crumble under the impact as he reeled backward, his knife waving wildly. Before he could regain his balance I was after him, thrusting, and got home under his ribs. He groaned and slipped to the ground in a puddle of his own blood.

I wheeled about, looking for the other. He was just rising, blood streaming down his face and neck. As I started for him he sounded a panicky yell and plunged into the underbrush. The crashing of his blind flight came back to me, muffled with distance. The girl was gone.

II. The Stranger on Tularoosa

The curious glow that had first showed me the quadroon girl had vanished. In my confusion I had forgotten it. But I did not waste time on vain conjecture as to its source, as I groped my way back to the road. Mystery had come to the pinelands and a ghostly light that hovered among the trees was only part of it.

My horse snorted and pulled against his tether, frightened by the smell of blood that hung in the heavy damp air. Hoofs clattered down the road, forms bulked in the growing light. Voices challenged.

"Who's that? Step out and name yourself, before we shoot!"

"Hold on, Esau!" I called. "It's me—Kirby Buckner"

"Kirby Buckner, by thunder!" ejaculated Esau McBride, lowering his pistol. The tall rangy forms of the other riders loomed behind him.

"We heard a shot," said McBride. "We was ridin' patrol on the roads around Grimesville like we've been ridin' every night for a week now—ever since they killed Ridge Jackson."

"Who killed Ridge Jackson?"

"The swamp niggers. That's all we know. Ridge come out of the woods early one mornin' and knocked at Cap'n Sorley's door. Cap'n says he was the color of ashes. He hollered for the Cap'n for God's sake to let him in, he had somethin' awful to tell him. Well, the Cap'n started down to open the door, but before he'd got down the stairs he heard an awful row among the dogs outside, and a man screamed he reckoned was Ridge. And when he got to the door, there wasn't nothin' but a dead dog layin' in the yard with his head knocked in, and the others all goin' crazy. They found Ridge later, out in the pines a few hundred yards from the house. From the way the ground and the bushes was tore up, he'd been dragged that far by four or five men. Maybe they got tired of haulin' him along. Anyway, they beat his head into a pulp and left him layin' there."

"I'll be damned!" I muttered. "Well, there's a couple of niggers lying back there in the brush. I want to see if you know them. I don't."

A moment later we were standing in the tiny glade, now white in the growing dawn. A black shape sprawled on the matted pine needles, his head in a pool of blood and brains. There were wide smears of blood on the ground and bushes on the other side of the little clearing, but the wounded black was gone.

McBride turned the carcass with his foot.

"One of them niggers that came in with Saul Stark," he muttered.

"Who the devil's that?" I demanded.

"Strange nigger that moved in since you went down the river last time. Come from South Carolina, he says. Lives in that old cabin in the Neck—you know, the shack where Colonel Reynolds' niggers used to live."

"Suppose you ride on to Grimesville with me, Esau," I said, "and tell me about this business as we ride. The rest of you might scout around and see if you can find a wounded nigger in the brush."

They agreed without question; the Buckners have always been tacitly considered leaders in Canaan, and it came natural for me to offer suggestions. Nobody gives *orders* to white men in Canaan.

"I reckoned you'd be showin' up soon," opined McBride, as we rode along the whitening road. "You usually manage to keep up with what's happenin' in Canaan."

"What *is* happening?" I inquired. "I don't know anything. An old black woman dropped me the word in New Orleans that there was trouble. Naturally I came home as fast as I could. Three strange niggers waylaid me—" I was curiously disinclined to mention the woman. "And now you tell me somebody killed Ridge Jackson. What's it all about?"

"The swamp niggers killed Ridge to shut his mouth," announced McBride. "That's the only way to figure it. They must have been close behind him when he knocked on Cap'n Sorley's door. Ridge worked for Cap'n Sorley most of his life; he thought a lot of the old man. Some kind of deviltry's bein' brewed up in the swamps, and Ridge wanted to warn the Cap'n. That's the way I figure it."

"Warn him about what?"

"We don't know," confessed McBride. "That's why we're all on edge. It must be an uprisin'."

That word was enough to strike chill fear into the heart of any Canaan-dweller. The blacks had risen in 1845, and the red terror of that revolt was not forgotten, nor the three lesser rebellions before it, when the slaves rose and spread fire and slaughter from Tularoosa to the shores of Black River. The fear of a black uprising lurked for ever in the depths of that forgotten back-country; the very children absorbed it in their cradles.

"What makes you think it might be an uprising?" I asked.

"The niggers have all quit the fields, for one thing. They've all got business in Goshen. I ain't seen a nigger nigh Grimesville for a week. *The town niggers have pulled out.*"

In Canaan we still draw a distinction born in antebellum days. Town niggers are descendants of the house-servants of the old days, and most of them live in or near Grimesville. There are not many, compared to the mass of "swamp niggers" who dwell on tiny farms along the creeks and the edge of the swamps, or in the black village of Goshen, on the Tularoosa. They are descendants of the field-hands of other days, and, untouched by the mellow civilization which refined the natures of the house-servants, they remain as primitive as their African ancestors.

"Where have the town niggers gone?" I asked.

"Nobody knows. They lit out a week ago. Probably hidin' down on Black River. If we win, they'll come back. If we don't, they'll take refuge in Sharpsville."

I found his matter-of-factness a bit ghastly, as if the actuality of the uprising were an assured fact.

"Well, what have you done?" I demanded.

"Ain't much we could do," he confessed. "The niggers ain't made no open move, outside of killin' Ridge Jackson; and we couldn't prove who done that, or why they done it.

"They ain't done nothin' but clear out. But that's mighty suspicious. We can't keep from thinkin' Saul Stark's behind it."

"Who is this fellow?" I asked.

"I told you all I know, already. He got permission to settle in that old deserted cabin on the Neck; a great big black devil that talks better English than I like to hear a nigger talk. But he was respectful enough. He had three or four big South Carolina bucks with him, and a brown wench which we don't know whether she's his daughter, sister, wife or what. He ain't been in to Grimesville but that one time, and a few weeks after he came to Canaan, the niggers begun actin' curious. Some of the boys wanted to ride over to Goshen and have a show-down, but that's takin' a desperate chance."

I knew he was thinking of a ghastly tale told us by our grandfathers of how a punitive expedition from Grimesville was once ambushed and butchered among the dense thickets that masked Goshen, then a rendezvous for runaway slaves, while another red-handed band devastated Grimesville, left defenseless by that reckless invasion.

"Might take all the men to get Saul Stark," said McBride. "And we don't dare leave the town unprotected. But we'll soon have to—hello, what's this?"

We had emerged from the trees and were just entering the village of Grimesville, the community center of the white population of Canaan. It was not pretentious. Log cabins, neat and white-washed, were plentiful enough. Small cottages clustered about big, old-fashioned houses which sheltered the rude aristocracy of that backwoods democracy. All the "planter" families lived "in town." "The country" was occupied by their tenants, and by the small independent farmers, white and black.

A small log cabin stood near the point where the road wound out of the deep forest. Voices emanated from it, in accents of menace, and a tall lanky figure, rifle in hand, stood at the door.

"Howdy, Esau!" this man hailed us. "By golly, if it ain't Kirby Buckner! Glad to see you, Kirby."

"What's up, Dick?" asked McBride.

"Got a nigger in the shack, tryin' to make him talk. Bill Reynolds seen him sneakin' past the edge of town about daylight, and nabbed him."

"Who is it?" I asked.

"Tope Sorley. John Willoughby's gone after a blacksnake."

With a smothered oath I swung off my horse and strode in, followed by McBride. Half a dozen men in boots and gun-belts clustered about a pathetic figure cowering on an old broken bunk. Tope Sorley (his forebears had adopted the name of the family that owned them, in slave days) was a pitiable sight just then. His skin was ashy, his teeth chattered spasmodically, and his eyes seemed to be trying to roll back into his head.

"Here's Kirby!" ejaculated one of the men as I pushed my way through the group. "I'll bet he'll make this coon talk!"

"Here comes John with the blacksnake!" shouted someone, and a tremor ran through Tope Sorley's shivering body.

I pushed aside the butt of the ugly whip thrust eagerly into my hand.

"Tope," I said, "you've worked one of my father's farms for years. Has any Buckner ever treated you any way but square?"

"Nossuh," came faintly.

"Then what are you afraid of? Why don't you speak up? Something's going on in the swamps. You know, and I want you to tell us why the town niggers have all run away, why Ridge Jackson was killed, why the swamp niggers are acting so mysteriously."

"And what kind of devilment that cussed Saul Stark's cookin' up over on Tularoosa!" shouted one of the men.

Tope seemed to shrink into himself at the mention of Stark.

"I don't dast," he shuddered. "He'd put me in de swamp!"

"Who?" I demanded. "Stark? Is Stark a conjer man?"

Tope sank his head in his hands and did not answer. I laid my hand on his shoulder.

"Tope," I said, "you know if you'll talk, we'll protect you. If you don't talk, I don't think Stark can treat you much rougher than these men are likely to. Now spill it—what's it all about?"

He lifted desperate eyes.

"You-all got to lemme stay here," he shuddered. "And guard me, and gimme money to git away on when de trouble's over."

"We'll do all that," I agreed instantly. "You can stay right here in this cabin, until you're ready to leave for New Orleans or wherever you want to go."

He capitulated, collapsed, and words tumbled from his livid lips.

"Saul Stark's a conjer man. He come here because it's way off in back-country. He aim to kill all de white folks in Canaan—"

A growl rose from the group, such a growl as rises unbidden from the throat of the wolf-pack that scents peril.

"He aim to make hisself king of Canaan. He sent me to spy dis mornin' to see if Mistah Kirby got through. He sent men to waylay him on de road, cause he knowed Mistah Kirby was comin' back to Canaan. Niggers makin' voodoo on Tularoosa, for weeks now. Ridge Jackson was goin' to tell Cap'n Sorley; so Stark's niggers foller him and kill him. That make Stark mad. He ain't want to kill Ridge; he want to put him in de swamp with Tunk Bixby and de others."

"What are you talking about?" I demanded.

Far out in the woods rose a strange, shrill cry, like the cry of a bird. But no such bird ever called before in Canaan. Tope cried out as if in answer, and shriveled into himself. He sank down on the bunk in a veritable palsy of fear.

"That was a signal!" I snapped. "Some of you go out there."

Half a dozen men hastened to follow my suggestion, and I returned to the task of making Tope renew his revelations. It was useless. Some hideous fear had sealed his lips. He lay shuddering like a stricken animal, and did not even seem to hear our questions. No one suggested the use of the blacksnake. Anyone could see the negro was paralyzed with terror.

Presently the searchers returned empty-handed. They had seen no one, and the thick carpet of pine needles showed no foot-prints. The men looked at me expectantly. As Colonel Buckner's son, leadership was expected of me.

"What about it, Kirby?" asked McBride. "Breckinridge and the others have just rode in. They couldn't find that nigger you cut up."

"There was another' nigger I hit with a pistol," I said. "Maybe he came back and helped him. "Still I could not bring myself to mention the brown girl. "Leave Tope alone. Maybe he'll get over his scare after a while. Better keep a guard in the cabin all the time. The swamp niggers may try to get him as they got Ridge Jackson. Better scour the roads around the town, Esau; there may be some of them hiding in the woods."

"I will. I reckon you'll want to be gettin' up to the house, now, and seein' your folks."

"Yes. And I want to swap these toys for a couple of .44s. Then I'm going to ride out and tell the country people to come into Grimesville. If it's to be an uprising, we don't know when it will commence."

"You're not goin' alone!" protested McBride.

"I'll be all right," I answered impatiently. "All this may not amount to anything, but it's best to be on the safe side. That's why I'm going after the country folks. No, I don't want anybody to go with me. Just in case the niggers do get crazy enough to attack the town, you'll need every man you've got. But if I can get hold of some of the swamp niggers and talk to them, I don't think there'll be any attack."

"You won't get a glimpse of them," McBride predicted.

III. Shadows Over Canaan

It was not yet noon when I rode out of the village westward along the old road. Thick woods swallowed me quickly. Dense walls of pines marched with me on either hand, giving way occasionally to fields enclosed with straggling rail fences, with the log cabins of the tenants or owners close by, with the usual litters of tow-headed children and lank hound dogs.

Some of the cabins were empty. The occupants, if white, had already gone into Grimesville; if black they had gone into the swamps, or fled to the hidden refuge of the town niggers, according to their affiliations. In any event, the vacancy of their hovels was sinister in its suggestion.

A tense silence brooded over the pinelands, broken only by the occasional wailing call of a plowman. My progress was not swift, for from time to time I turned off the main road to give warning to some lonely cabin huddled on the bank of one of the many thicket-fringed creeks. Most of these farms were south of the road; the white settlements did not extend far to the north; for in that direction lay Tularoosa Creek with its jungle-grown marshes that stretched inlets southward like groping fingers.

The actual warning was brief; there was no need to argue or explain. I called from the saddle: "Get into town; trouble's brewing on Tularoosa." Faces paled, and people dropped whatever they were doing: the men to grab guns and jerk mules from the plow to hitch to the wagons, the women to bundle necessary belongings together and shrill the children in from their play. As I rode I heard the cow-horns blowing up and down the creeks, summoning men from distant fields—blowing as they had not blown for a generation, a warning and a defiance which I knew carried to such ears as might be listening in the edges of the swamplands. The country emptied itself behind me, flowing in thin but steady streams toward Grimesville.

The sun was swinging low among the topmost branches of the pines when I reached the Richardson cabin, the westernmost "white" cabin in Canaan. Beyond it lay the Neck, the angle formed by the junction of Tularoosa with Black River, a jungle-like expanse occupied only by scattered negro huts.

Mrs. Richardson called to me anxiously from the cabin stoop.

"Well, Mr. Kirby, I'm glad to see you back in Canaan! We been hearin' the horns all evenin', Mr. Kirby. What's it mean? It—it ain't—"

"You and Joe better get the children and light out for Grimesville," I answered. "Nothing's happened yet, and may not, but it's best to be on the safe side. All the people are going."

"We'll go right now!" she gasped, paling, as she snatched off her apron. "Lord, Mr. Kirby, you reckon they'll cut us off before we can git to town?"

I shook my head. "They'll strike at night, if at all. We're just playing safe. Probably nothing will come of it."

"I bet you're wrong there," she predicted, scurrying about in desperate activity. "I been hearin' a drum beatin' off toward Saul Stark's cabin, off and on, for a week now. They beat drums back in the Big Uprisin'. My pappy's told me about it many's the time. The nigger skinned his brother alive. The horns was blowin' all up and down the creeks, and the drums was beatin' louder'n the horns could blow. You'll be ridin' back with us, won't you, Mr. Kirby?"

"No; I'm going to scout down along the trail a piece."

"Don't go too far. You're liable to run into old Saul Stark and his devils. Lord! *Where* is that man? Joe! *Joe!*"

As I rode down the trail her shrill voice followed me, thin-edged with fear.

Beyond the Richardson farm pines gave way to live-oaks. The underbrush grew ranker. A scent of rotting vegetation impregnated the fitful breeze. Occasionally I sighted a nigger hut, half hidden under the trees, but always it stood silent and deserted. Empty nigger cabins meant but one thing: the blacks were collecting at Goshen, some miles to the east on the Tularoosa; and that gathering, too, could have but one meaning.

My goal was Saul Stark's hut. My intention had been formed when I heard Tope Sorley's incoherent tale. There could be no doubt that Saul Stark was the dominant figure in this web of mystery. With Saul Stark I meant to deal. That I might be risking my life was a chance any man must take who assumes the responsibility of leadership.

The sun slanted through the lower branches of the cypresses when I reached it—a log cabin set against a background of gloomy tropical jungle. A few steps beyond it began the uninhabitable swamp in which Tularoosa emptied its murky current into Black River. A reek of decay hung in the air; grey moss bearded the trees, and poisonous vines twisted in rank tangles.

I called: "Stark! Saul Stark! Come out here!"

There was no answer. A primitive silence hovered over the tiny clearing. I dismounted, tied my horse and approached the crude, heavy door. Perhaps this cabin held a clue to the mystery of Saul Stark; at least it doubtless contained the implements and paraphernalia of his noisome craft. The faint breeze dropped suddenly. The stillness became so intense it was like a physical impact. I paused, startled; it was as if some inner instinct had shouted urgent warning.

As I stood there every fiber of me quivered in response to that subconscious warning; some obscure, deep-hidden instinct sensed peril, as a man senses the presence of the rattlesnake in the darkness, or the swamp panther crouching in the bushes. I drew a pistol, sweeping the trees and bushes, but saw no shadow or movement to betray the ambush I feared. But my instinct was unerring; what I sensed was not lurking in the woods about me; it was inside the cabin—*waiting*. Trying to shake off the feeling, and irked by a vague half-memory that kept twitching at the back of my brain, I again advanced. And again I stopped short, with one foot on the tiny stoop, and a hand half advanced to pull open the door. A chill shivering swept over me, a sensation like that which shakes a man to whom a flicker of lightning has revealed the black abyss into which another blind step would have hurled him. For the first time in my life I knew the meaning of fear; I knew that black horror lurked in that sullen cabin under the moss-bearded cypresses—a horror against which every primitive instinct that was my heritage cried out in panic.

And that insistent half-memory woke suddenly. It was the memory of a story of how voodoo men leave their huts guarded in their absence by a powerful ju-ju spirit to deal madness and death to the intruder. White men ascribed such deaths to superstitious fright and hypnotic suggestion. But in that instant I understood my sense of lurking peril; I comprehended the horror that breathed like an invisible mist from that accursed hut. I sensed the reality of the ju-ju, of which the grotesque wooden images which voodoo men place in their huts are only a symbol.

Saul Stark was gone; but he had left a Presence to guard his hut.

I backed away, sweat beading the backs of my hands. Not for a bag of gold would I have peered into the shuttered windows or touched that unbolted door. My pistol hung in my hand, useless I knew against the *Thing* in that cabin. What it was I could not know, but I knew it was some brutish, soulless entity drawn from the black swamps by the spells of voodoo. Man and the natural animals are not the only sentient beings that haunt this planet. There are invisible *Things*—black spirits of the deep swamps and the slimes of the river beds—the negroes know of them . . .

My horse was trembling like a leaf and he shouldered close to me as if seeking security in bodily contact. I mounted and reined away, fighting a panicky urge to strike in the spurs and bolt madly down the trail.

I breathed an involuntary sigh of relief as the somber clearing fell away behind me and was lost from sight. I did not, as soon as I was out of sight of the cabin, revile myself for a silly fool. My experience was too vivid in my mind. It was not cowardice that prompted my retreat from that empty hut; it was the natural instinct of self-preservation, such as keeps a squirrel from entering the lair of a rattlesnake.

My horse snorted and shied violently. A gun was in my hand before I saw what had startled me. Again a rich musical laugh taunted me.

She was leaning against a bent tree-trunk, her hands clasped behind her sleek head, insolently posing her sensuous figure. The barbaric fascination of her was not dispelled by daylight; if anything, the glow of the low-hanging sun enhanced it.

"Why did you not go into the ju-ju cabin, Kirby Buckner?" she mocked, lowering her arms and moving insolently out from the tree.

She was clad as I had never seen a swamp woman, or any other woman, dressed. Snakeskin sandals were on her feet, sewn with tiny sea-shells that were never gathered on this continent. A short silken skirt of flaming crimson molded her full hips, and was upheld by a broad bead-worked girdle. Barbaric anklets and armlets clashed as she moved, heavy ornaments of crudely hammered gold that were as African as her loftily piled coiffure. Nothing else she wore, and on her bosom, between her arching breasts, I glimpsed the faint lines of tattooing on her brown skin.

She posed derisively before me, not in allure, but in mockery. Triumphant malice blazed in her dark eyes; her red lips curled with cruel mirth. Looking at her then I found it easy to believe all the tales I had heard of torture and mutilations inflicted by the women of savage races on wounded enemies. She was alien, even in this primitive setting; she needed a grimmer, more bestial background, a background of steaming jungle, reeking black swamps, flaring fires and cannibal feasts, and the bloody altars of abysmal tribal gods.

"Kirby Buckner!" She seemed to caress the syllables with her red tongue, yet the very intonation was an obscene insult. "Why did you not enter Saul Stark's cabin? It was not locked! Did you fear what you might see there? Did you fear you might come out with your hair white like an old man's, and the drooling lips of an imbecile?"

"What's in that hut?" I demanded.

She laughed in my face, and snapped her fingers with a peculiar gesture.

"One of the ones which come oozing like black mist out of the night when Saul Stark beats the ju-ju drum and shrieks the black incantation to the gods that crawl on their bellies in the swamp."

"What is he doing here? The black folk were quiet until he came."

Her red lips curled disdainfully. "Those black dogs? They are his slaves. If they disobey he kills them, *or puts them in the swamp*. For long we have looked for a place to begin our rule. We have chosen Canaan. You whites must go. And since we know that white people can never be driven away from their land, we must kill you all."

It was my turn to laugh, grimly.

"They tried that, back in '45."

"They did not have Saul Stark to lead them, then," she answered calmly.

"Well, suppose they won? Do you think that would be the end of it? Other white men would come into Canaan and kill them all."

"They would have to cross water," she answered. "We can defend the rivers and creeks. Saul Stark will have many *servants in the swamps* to do his bidding. He will be king of black Canaan. No one can cross the waters to come against him. He will rule his tribe, as his fathers ruled their tribes in the Ancient Land."

"Mad as a loon!" I muttered. Then curiosity impelled me to ask: "Who is this fool? What are you to him?"

"He is the son of a Kongo witch-finder, and he is the greatest voodoo priest out of the Ancient Land," she answered, laughing at me again. "I? You shall leant who *I* am, tonight in the swamp, in the House of Damballah."

"Yes?" I grunted. "What's to prevent me from taking you into Grimesville with me? You know the answers to questions I'd like to ask."

Her laughter was like the slash of a velvet whip.

"*You* drag me to the village of the whites? Not all death and hell could keep me from the Dance of the Skull, tonight in the House of Damballah. You are my captive, already." She laughed derisively as I started and glared into the shadows about me. "No one is hiding there. I am alone, and you are the strongest man in Canaan. Even Saul Stark fears you, for he sent me with three men to kill you before you could reach the village. Yet you are my captive. I have but to beckon, so"—she crooked a contemptuous finger—"and you will follow to the fires of Damballah and the knives of the torturers."

I laughed at her, but my mirth rang hollow. I could not deny the incredible magnetism of this brown enchantress; it fascinated and impelled, drawing me toward her, beating at my will-power. I could not fail to recognize it any more than I could fail to recognize the peril in the ju-ju hut.

My agitation was apparent to her, for her eyes flashed with unholy triumph.

"Black men are fools, all but Saul Stark," she laughed. "White men are fools, too. I am the daughter of a white man, who lived in the hut of a black king and mated with his daughters. I know the strength of white men, and their weakness. I failed last night when I met you in the woods, but now I cannot fail!" Savage exultation thrummed in her voice. "By the blood in your veins I have snared you. The knife of the man you killed scratched your hand—seven drops of blood that fell on the pine needles have given me your soul! I took that blood, and Saul Stark gave me the man who ran away. Saul Stark hates cowards. With his hot, quivering heart, and seven drops of your blood, Kirby Buckner, deep in the swamps I have made such magic as none but the Bride of Damballah can make. Already you feel its urge! Oh, you are strong! The man you fought with the knife died less than an hour later. But you cannot fight me. Your blood makes you my slave. I have put a conjurment upon you."

By heaven, it was not mere madness she was mouthing! Hypnotism, magic, call it what you will, I felt its onslaught on my brain and will—a blind, senseless impulse that seemed to be rushing me against my will to the brink of some nameless abyss.

"I have made a charm you cannot resist!" she cried. "When I call you, you will come! Into the deep swamps you will follow me. You will see the Dance of the Skull and you will see the doom of a poor fool who sought to betray Saul Stark—who dreamed he could resist the Call of Damballah when it came. Into the swamp he goes tonight, with Tunk Bixby and the other four fools who opposed Saul Stark. You shall see that. You shall know and understand your own doom. And then you too shall go into the swamp, into darkness and silence deep as the darkness of nighted Africa! But before the darkness engulfs you there will be sharp knives, and little fires—oh, you will scream for death, even for the death that is beyond death!"

With a choking cry I whipped out a pistol and leveled it full at her breast. It was cocked and my finger was on the trigger. At that range I could not miss. But she looked full into the black muzzle and laughed—laughed—laughed, in wild peals that froze the blood in my veins.

And I sat there like an image pointing a pistol I could not fire! A frightful paralysis gripped me. I knew, with numbing certainty, that my life depended on the pull of that trigger, but I could not crook my finger—not though every muscle in my body quivered with the effort and sweat broke out on my face in clammy beads.

She ceased laughing, then, and stood looking at me in a manner indescribably sinister.

"You cannot shoot me, Kirby Buckner," she said quietly. "I have enslaved your soul. You cannot understand my power, but it has ensnared you. It is the Lure of the Bride of Damballah—the blood I have mixed with the mystic waters of Africa drawing the blood in your veins. Tonight you will come to me, in the House of Damballah."

"You lie!" My voice was an unnatural croak bursting from dry lips. "You've hypnotized me, you she-devil, so I can't pull this trigger. But you can't drag me across the swamps to you."

"It is you who lie," she returned calmly. "You know you lie. Ride back toward Grimesville or wherever you will, Kirby Buckner. But when the sun sets and the black shadows crawl out of the swamps, you will see me beckoning you, and you will follow me. Long I have planned your doom, Kirby Buckner, since first I heard the white men of Canaan talking to you. It was I who sent the word down the river that brought you back to Canaan. Not even Saul Stark knows of my plans for you.

"At dawn Grimesville shall go up in flames, and the heads of the white men will be tossed in the blood-running streets. But tonight is the Night of Damballah, and a white sacrifice shall be given to the black gods. Hidden among the trees you shall watch the Dance of the Skull—and then I shall call you forth—to die! And now, go fool! Run as far and as fast as you will. At sunset, wherever you are, you will turn your footsteps toward the House of Damballah!"

And with the spring of a panther she was gone into the thick brush, and as she vanished the strange paralysis dropped from me. With a gasped oath I fired blindly after her, but only a mocking laugh floated back to me.

Then in a panic I wrenched my horse about and spurred him down the trail. Reason and logic had momentarily vanished from my brain, leaving me in the grasp of blind primitive fear. I had confronted sorcery beyond my power to resist. I had felt my will mastered by the mesmerism in a brown woman's eyes. And now one driving urge overwhelmed me—a wild desire to cover as much distance as I could before that low-hanging sun dipped below the horizon and the black shadows came crawling from the swamps.

And yet I knew I could not outrun the grisly specter that menaced me. I was like a man fleeing in a nightmare, trying to escape from a monstrous phantom which kept pace with me despite my desperate speed.

I had not reached the Richardson cabin when above the drumming of my flight I heard the clop of hoofs ahead of me, and an instant later, sweeping around a kink in the trail, I almost rode down a tall, lanky man on an equally gaunt horse.

He yelped and dodged back as I jerked my horse to its haunches, my pistol presented at his breast.

"Look out, Kirby! It's me—Jim Braxton! My God, you look like you'd seen a ghost! What's chasin' you?"

"Where are you going?" I demanded, lowering my gun.

"Lookin' for you. Folks got worried as it got late and you didn't come in with the refugees: I 'lowed I'd light out and look for you. Miz Richardson said you rode into the Neck. Where in tarnation you been?"

"To Saul Stark's cabin."

"You takin' a big chance. What'd you find there?"

The sight of another white man had somewhat steadied my nerves. I opened my mouth to narrate my adventure, and was shocked to hear myself saying, instead: "Nothing. He wasn't there."

"Thought I heard a gun crack, a while ago," he remarked, glancing sharply at me sidewise.

"I shot at a copperhead," I answered, and shuddered. This reticence regarding the brown woman was compulsory; I could no more speak of her than I could pull the trigger of the pistol aimed at her. And I cannot describe the horror that beset me when I realized this. The conjer spells the black men feared were not lies, I realized sickly; demons in human form *did* exist who were able to enslave men's will and thoughts.

Braxton was eyeing me strangely.

"We're lucky the woods ain't full of black copperheads," he said. "Tope Sorley's pulled out."

"What do you mean?" By an effort I pulled myself together.

"Just that. Tom Breckinridge was in the cabin with him. Tope hadn't said a word since you talked to him. Just laid on that bunk and shivered. Then a kind of holler begun way out in the woods, and Tom went to the door with his rifle-gun, but couldn't see nothin'. Well, while he was standin' there he got a lick on the head from *behind*, and as he fell he seen that crazy nigger Tope jump over him and light out for the woods. Tom he taken a shot at him, but missed. Now what do you make of that?"

"The Call of Damballah!" I muttered, a chill perspiration beading my body. "God! The poor devil!"

"Huh? What's that?"

"For God's sake let's not stand here mouthing! The sun will soon be down!" In a frenzy of impatience I kicked my mount down the trail. Braxton followed me, obviously puzzled. With a terrific effort I got a grip on myself. How madly fantastic it was that Kirby Buckner should be shaking in the grip of unreasoning terror! It was so alien to my whole nature that it was no wonder Jim Braxton was unable to comprehend what ailed me.

"Tope didn't go of his own free will," I said. "That call was a summons he couldn't resist. Hypnotism, black magic, voodoo, whatever you want to call it, Saul Stark has some damnable power that enslaves men's will-power. The blacks are gathered somewhere in the swamp, for some kind of a devilish voodoo ceremony, which I have reason to believe will culminate in the murder of Tope Sorley. We've got to get to Grimesville if we can. I expect an attack at dawn."

Braxton was pale in the dimming light. He did not ask me where I got my knowledge.

"We'll lick 'em when they come; but it'll be slaughter."

I did not reply. My eyes were fixed with savage intensity on the sinking sun, and as it slid out of sight behind the trees I was shaken with an icy tremor. In vain I told myself that no occult power could draw me against my will. If she had been able to compel me, why had she not forced me to accompany her from the glade of the ju-ju hut? A grisly whisper seemed to tell me that she was but playing with me, as a cat allows a mouse almost to escape, only to be pounced upon again.

"Kirby, what's the matter with you?" I scarcely heard Braxton's anxious voice. "You're sweatin' and shakin' like you had the aggers. What—hey, what you stoppin' for?"

I had not consciously pulled on the rein, but my horse halted, and stood trembling and snorting, before the mouth of a narrow trail which meandered away at right angles from the road we were following—a trail that led north.

"Listen!" I hissed tensely.

"What is it?" Braxton drew a pistol. The brief twilight of the pinelands was deepening into dusk.

"Don't you hear it?" I muttered. "Drums! Drums beating in Goshen!"

"I don't hear nothin'," he mumbled uneasily. "If they was beatin' drums in Goshen you couldn't hear 'em this far away."

"Look there!" my sharp sudden cry made him start. I was pointing down the dim trail, at the figure which stood there in the dusk less than a hundred yards away. There in the dusk I saw her, even made out the gleam of her strange eyes, the mocking smile on her red lips. "Saul Stark's brown wench!" I raved, tearing at my scabbard. "My God, man, are you stone-blind? Don't you see her?"

"I don't see nobody!" he whispered, livid. "What are you talkin' about, Kirby?"

With eyes glaring I fired down the trail, and fired again, and yet again. This time no paralysis gripped my arm. But the smiling face still mocked me from the shadows. A slender, rounded arm lifted, a finger beckoned imperiously; and then she was gone and I was spurring my horse down the narrow trail, blind, deaf and dumb, with a sensation as of being caught in a black tide that was carrying me with it as it rushed on to a destination beyond my comprehension.

Dimly I heard Braxton's urgent yells, and then he drew up beside me with a clatter of hoofs, and grabbed my reins, setting my horse back on its haunches. I remember striking at him with my gun-barrel, without realizing what I was doing. All the black rivers of Africa were surging and foaming within my consciousness, roaring into a torrent that was sweeping me down to engulf me in an ocean of doom.

"Kirby, are you crazy? This trail leads to Goshen!"

I shook my head dazedly. The foam of the rushing waters swirled in my brain, and my voice sounded far away. "Go back! Ride for Grimesville! I'm going to Goshen."

"Kirby, you're mad!"

"Mad or sane, I'm going to Goshen this night," I answered dully. I was fully conscious. I knew what I was saying, and what I was doing. I realized the incredible folly of my action, and I realized my inability to help myself. Some shred to sanity impelled me to try to conceal the grisly truth from my companion, to offer a rational reason for my madness. "Saul Stark is in Goshen. He's the one who's responsible for all this trouble. I'm going to kill him. That will stop the uprising before it starts."

He was trembling like a man with the ague.

"Then I'm goin' with you."

"You must go on to Grimesville and warn the people," I insisted, holding to sanity, but feeling a strong urge begin to seize me, an irresistible urge to be in motion—to be riding in the direction toward which I was so horribly drawn.

"They'll be on their guard," he said stubbornly. "They won't need my warnin'. I'm goin' with you. I don't know what's got in you, but I ain't goin' to let you die alone among these black woods."

I did not argue. I could not. The blind rivers were sweeping me on—on—on! And down the trail, dim in the dusk, I glimpsed a supple figure, caught the gleam of uncanny eyes, the crook of a lifted finger . . . Then I was in motion, galloping down the trail, and I heard the drum of Braxton's horse's hoofs behind me.

IV. The Dwellers in the Swamp

Night fell and the moon shone through the trees, blood-red behind the black branches. The horses were growing hard to manage.

"They got more sense'n us, Kirby," muttered Braxton.

"Panther, maybe," I replied absently, my eyes searching the gloom of the trail ahead.

"Naw, t'ain't. Closer we get to Goshen, the worse they git. And every time we swing nigh to a creek they shy and snort."

The trail had not yet crossed any of the narrow, muddy creeks that criss-crossed that end of Canaan, but several times it had swung so close to one of them that we glimpsed the black streak that was water glinting dully in the shadows of the thick growth. And each time, I remembered, the horses showed signs of fear.

But I had hardly noticed, wrestling as I was with the grisly compulsion that was driving me. Remember, I was not like a man in a hypnotic trance. I was fully aware, fully conscious. Even the daze in which I had seemed to hear the roar of black rivers had passed, leaving my mind clear, my thoughts lucid. And that was the sweating hell of it: to realize my folly clearly and poignantly, but to be unable to conquer it. Vividly I realized that I was riding to torture and death, and leading a faithful friend to the same end. But on I went. My efforts to break the spell that gripped me almost unseated my reason, but on I went. I cannot explain my compulsion, any more than I can explain why a sliver of steel is drawn to a magnet. It was a black power beyond the ring of white man's knowledge; a basic, elemental thing of which formal hypnotism is but scanty crumbs, spilled at random. A power beyond my control was drawing me to Goshen, and beyond; more I cannot explain, any more than the rabbit could explain why the eyes of the swaying serpent draw him into its gaping jaws.

We were not far from Goshen when Braxton's horse unseated its rider, and my own began snorting and plunging.

"They won't go no closer!" gasped Braxton, fighting at the reins.

I swung off, threw the reins over the saddle-horn.

"Go back, for God's sake, Jim! I'm going on afoot."

I heard him whimper an oath, then his horse was galloping after mine, and he was following me on foot. The thought that he must share my doom sickened me, but I could not dissuade him; and ahead of me a supple form was dancing in the shadows, luring me on—on—on . . .

I wasted no more bullets on that mocking shape. Braxton could not see it, and I knew it was part of my enchantment, no real woman of flesh and blood, but a hell-born will-o'-the-wisp, mocking me and leading me through the night to a hideous death. A "sending," the people of the Orient, who are wiser than we, call such a thing.

Braxton peered nervously at the black forest walls about us, and I knew his flesh was crawling with the fear of sawed-off shotguns blasting us suddenly from the shadows. But it was no ambush of lead or steel I feared as we emerged into the moonlit clearing that housed the cabins of Goshen.

The double line of log cabins faced each other across the dusty street. One line backed against the bank of Tularoosa Creek. The black stoops almost overhung the black waters. Nothing moved in the moonlight. No lights showed, no smoke oozed up from the stick-and-mud chimneys. It might have been a dead town, deserted and forgotten.

"It's a trap!" hissed Braxton, his eyes blazing slits. He bent forward like a skulking panther, a gun in each hand. "They're layin' for us in them huts!"

Then he cursed, but followed me as I strode down the street. I did not hail the silent huts. I *knew* Goshen was deserted. I felt its emptiness. Yet there was a contradictory sensation as of spying eyes fixed upon us. I did not try to reconcile these opposite convictions.

"They're gone," muttered Braxton, nervously. "I can't smell 'em. I can always smell niggers, if they're a lot of 'em, or if they're right close. You reckon they've gone to raid Grimesville?"

"No," I muttered. "They're in the House of Damballah."

He shot a quick glance at me.

"That's a neck of land in the Tularoosa about three miles west of here. My grandpap used to talk about it. The niggers held their heathen palavers there back in slave times. You ain't—Kirby—you—"

"Listen!" I wiped the icy sweat from my face. "*Listen!*"

Through the black woodlands the faint throb of a drum whispered on the wind that glided up the shadowy reaches of the Tularoosa.

Braxton shivered. "It's them, all right. But for, God's sake, Kirby—*look out!*"

With an oath he sprang toward the houses on the bank of the creek. I was after him just in time to glimpse a dark clumsy object scrambling or tumbling down the sloping bank into the water. Braxton threw up his long pistol, then lowered it, with a baffled curse. A faint splash marked the disappearance of the creature. The shiny black surface crinkled with spreading ripples.

"What was it?" I demanded.

"A nigger on his all-fours!" swore Braxton. His face was strangely pallid in the moonlight. "He was crouched between them cabins there, watchin' us!"

"It must have been an alligator." What a mystery is the human mind! I was arguing for sanity and logic, I, the blind victim of a compulsion beyond sanity and logic. "A nigger would have to come up for air."

"He swum under the water and come up in the shadder of the bresh where we couldn't see him," maintained Braxton. "Now he'll go warn Saul Stark."

"Never mind!" The pulse was thrumming in my temples again, the roar of foaming water rising irresistibly in my brain. "I'm going—straight through the swamp. For the last time, go back!"

"No! Sane or mad, I'm goin' with you!"

The pulse of the drum was fitful, growing more distinct as we advanced. We struggled through jungle-thick growth; tangled vines tripped us; our boots sank in scummy mire. We were entering the fringe of the swamp which grew deeper and denser until it culminated in the uninhabitable morass where the Tularoosa flowed into Black River, miles farther to the west.

The moon had not yet set, but the shadows were black under the interlacing branches with their mossy beards. We plunged into the first creek we must cross, one of the many muddy streams flowing into the Tularoosa. The water was only thigh-deep, the moss-clogged bottom fairly firm. My foot felt the edge of a sheer drop, and I warned Braxton: "Look out for a deep hole; keep right behind me."

His answer was unintelligible. He was breathing heavily, crowding close behind me. Just as I reached the sloping bank and pulled myself up by the slimy, projecting roots, the water was violently agitated behind me. Braxton cried out incoherently, and hurled himself up the bank, almost upsetting me. I wheeled, gun in hand, but saw only the black water seething and whirling, after his thrashing rush through it.

"What the devil, Jim?"

"Somethin' grabbed me!" he panted. "Somethin' out of the deep hole. I tore loose and busted up the bank. I tell you, Kirby, something's follerin' us! Somethin' that swims under the water."

"Maybe it was that nigger you saw. These swamp people swim like fish. Maybe he swam up under the water to try to drown you."

He shook his head, staring at the black water, gun in hand.

"It *smelt* like a nigger, and the little I saw of it *looked* like a nigger. But it didn't *feel* like any kind of a human."

"Well, it was an alligator then," I muttered absently as I turned away. As always when I halted, even for a moment, the roar of peremptory and imperious rivers shook the foundations of my reason.

He splashed after me without comment. Scummy puddles rose about our ankles, and we stumbled over moss-grown cypress knees. Ahead of us there loomed another, wider creek, and Braxton caught my arm.

"Don't do it, Kirby!" he gasped. "If we go into that water, it'll git us sure!"

"What?"

"I don't know. Whatever it was that flopped down that bank back there in Goshen. The same thing that grabbed me in that creek back yonder. Kirby, let's go back."

"Go back?" I laughed in bitter agony. "I wish to God I could! I've got to go on. Either Saul Stark or I must die before dawn."

He licked dry lips and whispered, "Go on, then; I'm with you, come heaven or hell." He thrust his pistol back into its scabbard, and drew a long keen knife from his boot. "Go ahead!"

I climbed down the sloping bank and splashed into the water that rose to my hips. The cypress branches bent a gloomy, moss-trailing arch over the creek. The water was black as midnight. Braxton was a blur, toiling behind me. I gained the first shelf of the opposite bank and paused, in water knee-deep, to turn and look back at him.

Everything happened at once, then. I saw Braxton halt short, staring at something on the bank behind me. He cried out, whipped out a gun and fired, just as I turned. In the flash of the gun I glimpsed a supple form reeling backward, a brown face fiendishly contorted. Then in the momentary blindness that followed the flash, I heard Jim Braxton scream.

Sight and brain cleared in time to show me a sudden swirl of the murky water, a round, black object breaking the surface behind Jim—and then Braxton gave a strangled cry and went under with a frantic thrashing and splashing. With an incoherent yell I sprang into the creek, stumbled and went to my knees, almost submerging myself. As I struggled up I saw Braxton's head, now streaming blood, break the surface for an instant, and I lunged toward it. It went under and another head appeared in its place, a shadowy black head. I stabbed at it ferociously, and my knife cut only the blank water as the thing dipped out of sight.

I staggered from the wasted force of the blow, and when I righted myself, the water lay unbroken about me. I called Jim's name, but there was no answer. Then panic laid a cold hand on me, and I splashed to the bank, sweating and trembling. With the water no higher than my knees I halted and waited, for I knew not what. But presently, down the creek a short distance, I made out a vague object lying in the shallow water near the shore.

I waded to it, through the clinging mud and crawling vines. It was Jim Braxton, and he was dead. It was not the wound in his head which had killed him. Probably he had struck a submerged rock when he was dragged under. But the marks of strangling fingers showed black on his throat. At the sight a nameless horror oozed out of that black swamp and coiled itself clammily about my soul; for no human fingers ever left such marks as those.

I had seen a head rise in the water, a head that looked like that of a negro, though the features had been indistinct in the darkness. But no man, white or black, ever possessed the fingers that had crushed the life out of Jim Braxton. The distant drum grunted as if in mockery.

I dragged the body up on the bank and left it. I could not linger longer, for the madness was foaming in my brain again, driving me with white-hot spurs. But as I climbed the bank, I found blood on the bushes, and was shaken by the implication.

I remembered the figure I had seen staggering in the flash of Braxton's gun. *She* had been there, waiting for me on the bank, then—not a spectral illusion, but the woman herself, in flesh and blood! Braxton had fired at her, and wounded her. But the wound could not have been mortal; for no corpse lay among the bushes, and the grim hypnosis that dragged me onward was unweakened. Dizzily I wondered if she could be killed by mortal weapons.

The moon had set. The starlight scarcely penetrated the interwoven branches. No more creeks barred my way, only shallow streams, through which I splashed with sweating haste. Yet I did not expect to be attacked. Twice the dweller in the depths had passed me by to attack my companion. In icy despair I knew I was being saved for the grimmer fate. Each stream I crossed might be hiding the monster that killed Jim Braxton. Those creeks were all connected in a network of winding waterways. It could follow me easily. But my horror of it was less than the horror of the jungle-born magnetism that lurked in a witch-woman's eyes.

And as I stumbled through the tangled vegetation, I heard the drum rumbling ahead of me, louder and louder, a demoniacal mockery. Then a human voice mingled with its mutter, in a long-drawn cry of horror and agony that set every fiber of me quivering with sympathy. Sweat coursed down my clammy flesh; soon my own voice might be lifted like that, under unnamable torture. But on I went, my feet moving like automatons, apart from my body, motivated by a will not my own.

The drum grew loud, and a fire glowed among the black trees. Presently, crouching among the bushes, I stared across the stretch of black water that separated me from a nightmare scene. My halting there was as compulsory as the rest of my actions had been. Vaguely I knew the stage for horror had been set, but the time for my entry upon it was not yet. When the time had come, I would receive my summons.

A low, wooded island split the black creek, connected with the shore opposite me by a narrow neck of land. At its lower end the creek split into a network of channels threading their way among hummocks and rotting logs and moss-grown, vine-tangled clumps of trees. Directly across from my refuge the shore of the island was deeply indented by an arm of open, deep black water. Bearded trees walled a small clearing, and partly hid a hut. Between the hut and the shore burned a fire that sent up weird twisting snake-tongues of green flames. Scores of black people squatted under the shadows of the overhanging branches. When the green fire lit their faces it lent them the appearance of drowned corpses.

In the midst of the glade stood a giant negro, an awesome statue in black marble. He was clad in ragged trousers, but on his head was a band of beaten gold set with a huge red jewel, and on his feet were barbaric sandals. His features reflected titanic vitality no less than his huge body. But he was all negro—flaring nostrils, thick lips, ebony skin. I knew I looked upon Saul Stark, the conjure man.

He was regarding something that lay in the sand before him, something dark and bulky that moaned feebly. Presently, lifting his head, he rolled out a sonorous invocation across the black waters. From the blacks huddled under the trees there came a shuddering response, like a wind wailing through midnight branches. Both invocation and response were framed in an unknown tongue—a guttural, primitive language.

Again he called out, this time a curious high-pitched wail. A shuddering sigh swept the black people. All eyes were fixed on the dusky water. And presently an object rose slowly from the depths. A sudden trembling shook me. It looked like the head of a negro. One after another it was followed by similar objects until five heads reared above the black, cypress-shadowed water. They might have been five negroes submerged except for their heads—but I knew this was not so. There was something diabolical here. Their silence, motionlessness, their whole aspect was unnatural. From the trees came the hysterical sobbing of women, and someone whispered a man's name.

Then Saul Stark lifted his hands, and the five heads silently sank out of sight.

Like a ghostly whisper I seemed to hear the voice of the African witch: "*He puts them in the swamp!*"

Stark's deep voice rolled out across the narrow water: "And now the Dance of the Skull, to make the conjer sure!"

What had the witch said? "*Hidden among the trees you shall watch the Dance of the Skull!*"

The drum struck up again, growling and rumbling. The blacks swayed on their haunches, lifting a wordless chant. Saul Stark paced measuredly about the figure on the sand, his arms weaving cryptic patterns. Then he wheeled and faced toward the other end of the glade. By some sleight of hand he now grasped a grinning human skull, and this he cast upon the wet sand beyond the body. "Bride of Damballah!" he thundered. "The sacrifice awaits!"

There was an expectant pause; the chanting sank. All eyes were glued on the farther end of the glade. Stark stood waiting, and I saw him scowl as if puzzled. Then as he opened his mouth to repeat the call, a barbaric figure moved out of the shadows.

At the sight of her a chill shuddering shook me. For a moment she stood motionless, the firelight glinting on her gold ornaments, her head hanging on her breast. A tense silence reigned and I saw Saul Stark staring at her sharply. She seemed to be detached, somehow, standing aloof and withdrawn, head bent strangely.

Then, as if rousing herself, she began to sway with a jerky rhythm, and presently whirled into the mazes of a dance that was ancient when the ocean drowned the black kings of Atlantis. I cannot describe it. It was bestiality and diabolism set to motion, framed in a writhing, spinning whirl of posturing and gesturing that would have appalled a dancer of the Pharaohs. And that cursed skull danced with her; rattling and clashing on the sand, it bounded and spun like a live thing in time with her leaps and prancings.

But there was something amiss. I sensed it. Her arms hung limp, her drooping head swayed. Her legs bent and faltered, making her lurch drunkenly and out of time. A murmur rose from the people, and bewilderment etched Saul Stark's black countenance. For the domination of a conjure man is a thing hinged on a hair-trigger. Any trifling dislocation of formula or ritual may disrupt the whole web of his enchantment.

As for me, I felt the perspiration freeze on my flesh as I watched the grisly dance. The unseen shackles that bound me to that gyrating she-devil were strangling, crushing me. I knew she was approaching a climax, when she would summon me from my hiding-place, to wade through the black waters to the House of Damballah, to my doom.

Now she whirled to a floating stop, and when she halted, poised on her toes, she faced toward the spot where I lay hidden, and I knew that she could see me as plainly as if I stood in the open; knew, too, somehow, that only she knew of my presence. I felt myself toppling on the edge of the abyss. She raised her head and I saw the flame of her eyes, even at that distance. Her face was lit with awful triumph. Slowly she raised her hand, and I felt my limbs begin to jerk in response to that terrible magnetism. She opened her mouth—

But from that open mouth sounded only a choking gurgle, and suddenly her lips were dyed crimson. And suddenly, without warning, her knees gave way and she pitched headlong into the sands.

And as she fell, so I too fell, sinking into the mire. Something burst in my brain with a shower of flame. And then I was crouching among the trees, weak and trembling, but with such a sense of freedom and lightness of limb as I never dreamed a man could experience. The black spell that gripped me was broken; the foul incubus lifted from my soul. It was as if light had burst upon a night blacker than African midnight.

At the fall of the girl a wild cry rose from the blacks, and they sprang up, trembling on the verge of panic. I saw their rolling white eyeballs, their bared teeth glistening in the firelight. Saul Stark had worked their primitive natures up to a pitch of madness, meaning to turn this frenzy, at the proper time, into a fury of battle. It could as easily turn into a hysteria of terror. Stark shouted sharply at them.

But just then the girl in a last convulsion, rolled over on the wet sand, and the firelight shone on a round hole between her breasts, which still oozed crimson. Jim Braxton's bullet had found its mark.

From the first I had felt that she was not wholly human; some black jungle spirit sired her, lending her the abysmal subhuman vitality that made her what she was. She had said that neither death nor hell could keep her from the Dance of the Skull. And, shot through the heart and dying, she had come through the swamp from the creek where she had received her death-wound to the House of Damballah. And the Dance of the Skull had been her death dance.

Dazed as a condemned man just granted a reprieve, at first I hardly grasped the meaning of the scene that now unfolded before me.

The blacks were in a frenzy. In the sudden, and to them inexplicable, death of the sorceress they saw a fearsome portent. They had no way of knowing that she was dying when she entered the glade. To them, their prophetess and priestess had been struck down under their very eyes, by an invisible death. This was magic blacker than Saul Stark's wizardry—and obviously hostile to them.

Like fear-maddened cattle they stampeded. Howling, screaming, tearing at one another they blundered through the trees, heading for the neck of land and the shore beyond. Saul Stark stood transfixed, heedless of them as he stared down at the brown girl, dead at last. And suddenly I came to myself, and with my awakened manhood came cold fury and the lust to kill. I drew a gun, and aiming in the uncertain firelight, pulled the trigger. Only a click answered me. The powder in the cap-and-ball pistols was wet.

Saul Stark lifted his head and licked his lips. The sounds of flight faded in the distance, and he stood alone in the glade. His eyes rolled whitely toward the black woods around him. He bent, grasped the man-like object that lay on the sand, and dragged it into the hut. The instant he vanished I started toward the island, wading through the narrow channels at the lower end. I had almost reached the shore when a mass of driftwood gave way with me and I slid into a deep hole.

Instantly the water swirled about me, and a head rose beside me; a dim face was close to mine—the face of a negro—*the face of Tunk Bixby*. But now it was inhuman; as expressionless and soulless as that of a catfish; the face of a being no longer human, and no longer mindful of its human origin.

Slimy, misshapen fingers gripped my throat, and I drove my knife into the sagging mouth. The features vanished in a wave of blood; mutely the thing sank out of sight, and I hauled myself up the bank, under the thick bushes.

Stark had run from his hut, a pistol in his hand. He was staring wildly about, alarmed by the noise he had heard, but I knew he could not see me. His ashy skin glistened with perspiration. He who had ruled by fear was now ruled by fear. He feared the unknown hand that had slain his mistress; feared the negroes who had fled him; feared the abysmal swamp which had sheltered him, and the monstrosities he had created. He lifted a weird call that quavered with panic. He called again as only four heads broke the water, but he called in vain.

But the four heads began to move toward the shore and the man who stood there. He shot them one after another. They made no effort to avoid the bullets. They came straight on, sinking one by one. He had fired six shots before the last head vanished. The shots drowned the sounds of my approach. I was close behind him when he turned at last.

I know he knew me; recognition flooded his face and fear went with it, at the knowledge that he had a human being to deal with. With a scream he hurled his empty pistol at me and rushed after it with a lifted knife.

I ducked, parried his lunge and countered with a thrust that bit deep into his ribs. He caught my wrist and I gripped his, and there we strained, breast to breast. His eyes were like a mad dog's in the starlight, his muscles like steel cords.

I ground my heel down on his bare foot, crushing the instep. He howled and lost balance, and I tore my knife hand free and stabbed him in the belly. Blood spurted and he dragged me down with him. I jerked loose and rose, just as he pulled himself up on his elbow and hurled his knife. It sang past my ear, and I stamped on his breast. His ribs caved in under my heel. In a red killing-haze I knelt, jerked back his head and cut his throat from ear to ear.

There was a pouch of dry powder in his belt. Before I moved further I reloaded my pistols. Then I went into the hut with a torch. And there I understood the doom the brown witch had meant for me. Tope Sorley lay moaning on a bunk. The transmutation that was to make him a mindless, soulless semi-human dweller in the water was not complete, but his mind was gone. Some of the physical changes had been made—by what godless sorcery out of Africa's black abyss I have no wish to know. His body was rounded and elongated, his legs dwarfed; his feet were flattened and broadened, his fingers horribly long, and webbed. His neck was inches longer than it should be. His features were not altered, but the expression was no more human than that of a great fish. And there, but for the loyalty of Jim Braxton, lay Kirby Buckner. I placed my pistol muzzle against Tope's head in grim mercy and pulled the trigger.

And so the nightmare closed, and I would not drag out the grisly narration. The white people of Canaan never found anything on the island except the bodies of Saul Stark and the brown woman. They think to this day that a swamp negro killed Jim Braxton, after he had killed the brown woman, and that I broke up the threatened uprising by killing Saul Stark. I let them think it. They will never know the shapes the black water of Tularoosa hides. That is a secret I share with the cowed and terror-haunted black people of Goshen and of it neither they nor I have ever spoken.

THE SILENT MAJORITY
Stephen Woodworth

Stephen Woodworth is a graduate of the Clarion West Writers Workshop and a First Place winner in the Writers of the Future Contest.

His Violet Series of paranormal suspense novels includes the *New York Times* bestsellers *Through Violet Eyes* and *With Red Hands*, as well as the most recent volumes, *In Golden Blood* and *From Black Rooms*.

Woodworth's short fiction has appeared in such publications as *The Magazine of Fantasy & Science Fiction*, *Year's Best Fantasy*, *Weird Tales*, *Aboriginal Science Fiction*, and *Realms of Fantasy*.

"Because I was born and raised in Orange County, California, Richard Nixon was an omnipresent figure in my youth," the author reveals. "His Birthplace and Library are in Yorba Linda, barely a fifteen-minute drive from where I still live. He attended college in Whittier, my wife's hometown, and La Casa Pacifica—the "Western White House"—still stands in San Clemente, where Nixon retired after his resignation.

"One of my clearest childhood memories is of the evening that Nixon gave his resignation speech on television. My parents, staunch Republicans, had set up a card table so that we could eat dinner while watching the address. Halfway through the speech, I left the living room in tears and finished eating my dinner in the kitchen.

I was only six years old and could not comprehend that a president might be guilty of a crime. To me, the U.S. presidents were like superheroes—defenders of Truth, Justice, and the American Way, and all I saw on the TV screen was a man who could easily have been my grandfather being forced out of his job.

"Later in life, I learned about the ways in which our 37th president had violated the Constitution and abused his power to persecute innocent people. Unlike a certain recent chief executive, however, Richard Nixon had real, historic accomplishments to his credit. Not enough to pardon his offenses, maybe, but perhaps enough to earn him a posthumous shot at redemption—if only as a zombie . . ."

And so tonight, to you—the great, silent majority of my
fellow Americans—I ask for your support.
—Richard M. Nixon, November 3, 1969

ON THE MORNING of the day the Apocalypse was due to commence, Richard Milhous Nixon, 37th President and late Commander-in-Chief of the United States of America, clawed his way out of his grave in the quaint formal gardens behind the memorial library that bore his name.

Although the darkness was absolute inside his casket, Nixon knew where he was, *what* he was, and what he had to do. He rammed his flattened palms against the coffin's satin-embossed roof—not from panic at the stifling confinement, which he had no reason to fear, but from a sense of urgent purpose, of a sacred duty he must perform.

Divine authority must have coursed through his embalmed flesh, for the hinged cover began to give, allowing dust to whisper into the upholstered interior. At the time of his death at age eighty-one, he could hardly have budged the casket's wooden lid, much less the hundreds of pounds of earth heaped upon it. He wondered whether the others would be as strong when they returned. If so, his mission was that much more crucial.

Clumps of sod tumbled in beside him as he forced the gap wider, until the trickle of soil became a flood. Nixon let it swamp him; he was counting on the dirt to prop the lid open enough for him to worm his way out of the coffin. The ground had settled and become hard-packed during the nearly three decades since his internment, and he had to rend and plow the loam with the hooks of his arthritic fingers as he swam upward through the solid earth. Dirt filled the flared nostrils of his pointed nose, smothering him with an odor of mold and earthworms, and he spluttered in disgust. If he were like Mao or Lenin, placed on public display for reverent followers to file past, he could simply have cast aside the glass case that enclosed him and stood up, immaculately preserved and attired and ready for business.

Never in his life had Dick Nixon so wished he'd been a Communist.

At last, he thrust a hand through a final foot of cold sod and felt warm, open air. Pulling himself up, he broke through a mat of grass and found himself blinded by the almost unbearable brightness of a Southern California springtime.

Almost as soon as he shut his eyes, however, he opened them again, savoring the wonder of vision. His eyes should have shriveled like raisins long ago, yet somehow they had been restored to him. He glanced down at his hands. They were gnarled with age, as they had been, the skin pallid and filthy, but they were neither desiccated nor skeletal. Though all the laws of Nature dictated the impossibility of the miracle, he had sight, he had strength, he had mind. Would the others—those who came after him—be as fortunate?

A phrase—a verse—returned to him from his Quaker childhood, one read to him by his sainted mother:

Behold, I shew you a mystery; We shall not all sleep, but we shall all be changed,
In a moment, in the twinkling of an eye, at the last trump: for the trumpet shall
sound, and the dead shall be raised incorruptible, and we shall be changed.

Incorruptible. Nixon wanted to laugh that such a word could apply to him, a man whose name had become synonymous with the Committee to Re-Elect the President and its dirty tricks, with enemies lists and wire-tapping, and ever and always, Watergate.

Yet he'd been granted a second chance to prove himself and he needed to make the most of it. If only his voice worked as well as the rest of him . . .

Nixon snorted dirt from his nose and surveyed the garden around him, redolent with the pleasant aroma of freshly mown grass. Somewhere, a war raged—there *had* to be a war involved, of that he was sure—and attendance at the Richard M. Nixon Library and Birthplace was sparse. Nevertheless, here in his hometown of Yorba Linda, in Orange County, the moribund heart of Republican conservatism, the disgraced President still counted some admirers, and at least one of them had come to pay her respects. A plump, silver-haired matron in a floral blouse and peacock-colored hat and skirt had propped herself on a walker outside the rectangle of foxgloves, roses, and shrubbery that bordered the burial plot. She'd frozen, aghast, as the lawn at her feet heaved and unfolded.

Still sunk up to his chest in soil, Nixon extended an arm toward her. Ripping open the threads that sewed his mouth shut, he spat grit and cleared his throat. "'Scuse me, ma'am, but would you mind giving me a hand here?"

The woman paled, the excess of rouge on her cheeks making her look if she'd been slapped. She shrieked and waddled away, practically vaulting over the walker in her haste.

Nixon grunted. If you wanted anything done right . . .

He dragged himself, hand-over-hand, free from the grave, stood, and brushed dust from his suit. Although he remembered this spot as well as if it were the Oval Office itself, he still took a moment to imbibe the memories it evoked. To his left, just over the low hedge of blooming flowers, was the refurbished white farmhouse where he'd been born, the equivalent of Abe Lincoln's log cabin in the personal mythology he'd constructed for himself. Around him blossomed the fastidiously-manicured flora of the First Lady's Garden, named for his darling Pat.

Finally, his gaze fell upon her grave marker, the one next to his. He did not know if his new eyes were capable of tears, but his throat tightened as he read the inscription, the way it had the last time he'd seen it, on the day of her funeral: EVEN WHEN PEOPLE CAN'T SPEAK YOUR LANGUAGE, THEY CAN TELL IF YOU HAVE LOVE IN YOUR HEART.

How he wanted to wait right there, until she, too, sprouted from the ground like the finest flower! He trembled as he imagined how he would drop to his knees in front of her to beg forgiveness for everything he'd put her through, to offer his unworthy thanks for loving him anyway.

But Pat, like the others that followed him, might not be . . . intact. Dick couldn't bear the thought of seeing her that way, and the image it conjured prodded him to get on with his mission. He had to get out of this place before its nostalgia buried him more completely than six feet of soil ever could.

Straightening his stained tie, Dick Nixon lurched away from the burial plot without daring to read his own headstone. For if there was one thing the 37th President feared even after death, it was how humanity had labeled him.

Climbing over the hedge, he stalked in the direction that the old lady with the walker had fled screaming: past the beds of roses, along the reflecting pool lined with palm trees, and into the Library's main gallery with its peaked roof of red tile. His wobbling gait improved as his stiff limbs got used to walking again, and he paused to regard his reflection in the glass door. He wanted to enter with some dignity, so he picked a few lumps of mud from his hair, smoothed his lapels, and stepped inside with his head held high.

The woman with the walker had plopped down on a padded bench in the lobby, where a bespectacled female docent attempted to calm her.

"I tell you, I know what I saw!" the old matron insisted.

"I'm sure you do," the docent said in soothing tones, "and I promise you, we'll investigate." She indicated the diminutive, baby-faced guard beside her, one of those short men with the pugilistic posture of a bantam rooster.

Nixon cut in. "Pardon me, ladies, but—"

The matron gaped at him and pointed, hyperventilating. "*That's him!* That's the man from the garden!"

She snatched up the walker again and made a break for the exit, leaving the startled docent to wonder whether to stop her or flee with her.

The guard whipped the pistol out of his side holster with a Dirty Harry flourish. "Hold it right there!"

Nixon brushed aside the command and advanced. "For God's sake, son, put that thing away! I need to see the President on a matter of national security, and I need you to take me to him."

"You mean *her*."

Nixon glowered at the docent, who slapped hands over her mouth to keep herself from speaking again.

Dick was a bit flummoxed. Things had changed more than he'd realized in his absence. "Yeah, well . . . whatever. The President. *Her*."

"You're not going anywhere." The guard still brandished his gun, but the brass had gone out of his words. "Stop or I'll shoot!"

"Watch it, young man. Can't you see who you're talking to?" Nixon's ill-fitting jacket bunched around his shoulders as he raised both arms to indicate the plethora of pictures that plastered the walls around them, photos from every phase of his storied career.

The guard's eyes flicked from Dick's face to the pictures and back again. Same widow's peak, same scowling brows, same bulldog jowls. Yet he refused to lower his weapon.

"I'm warning you! I'm not afraid to use this." His hand trembled as he said it, however, and Dick suspected that the gun subsequently went off by accident.

The shot slammed into Nixon's chest right above the heart, rocking him backward and nearly toppling him. *That's gonna leave a mark*, he thought.

The bullet did make a small hole in his dress shirt, but no blood came out. Fortunately, the guard hadn't had the presence of mind to shoot Dick in the head. He yelped as Nixon shrugged off the wound and kept coming.

"That's no way to treat a former Chief Executive!" Nixon closed the gap between them. The guard screeched and dropped the pistol as Dick grabbed his shirt.

"Now, listen to me, you little [expletive deleted]. You're going to take me to the [expletive deleted] President or I'm gonna kick your [expletive deleted] ass out of *my* Library!" Dick released the whimpering guard with a shove and looked down at his feet, which were shod only in a pair of bedraggled black dress socks. "And, for Christ's sake," he roared at the dumbstruck docent, "get me some [expletive deleted] *shoes!*"

. . . . .

Dick ultimately had to submit to a DNA test before anyone in Washington would entertain the idea that he was anything more than a hoax. The delay cost him precious hours, but at least it gave him time to procure a new navy-blue suit and a decent pair of Florsheims. He also washed his face and hands, although removing the grime only brought out the ghastly lividity of his complexion. There was still dirt under his fingernails, but that felt good to him, as if he'd done honest work.

A private jet flew him from Orange County to D.C., John Wayne to Ronald Reagan. A West Coast C.I.A. operative briefed him during the flight. There was, indeed, a war going on. As in the Yom Kippur War during Nixon's own administration, the Middle East had erupted into violence and ethnic hatred. As he had done, the present Commander-in-Chief had thrown U.S. support behind Israel, funneling American arms into the hands of Israeli troops to help repel Islamic forces from outside the country while purging Palestinian terrorists within. Tens of thousands of people—Muslims and Jews, military and civilians—had perished over the course of the three-year conflict. As Israel appeared to falter, the President had committed U.S. troops to the country's defense, leading to even heavier casualties.

And then, within the past five hours, an unknown party had detonated an atomic bomb in New York City, killing an estimated seven million American citizens.

The last trump had sounded.

Washington was in a state of siege, with Army and National Guard checkpoints hastily erected throughout the city and traffic into the Mall restricted to approved vehicles. As perversity would have it, they'd closed off the Arlington Memorial Bridge, so the black Lincoln limousine that conveyed Nixon to the White House had to detour via I-66 and the E Street Expressway, past the Kennedy Center.

The chauffeur glanced back at Nixon through the open window of the privacy partition. "Well, there it is!" he said with a big, dopey grin, as if Dick needed to be told.

"Yep. There it is." Nixon found his gaze drawn irresistibly toward the tiered, U-shaped building that glowed in the evening twilight outside the car's left-hand windows: the southern structure of the Watergate complex.

In the years since his resignation, he'd avoided coming anywhere near the place and had vainly hoped it might be demolished in the name of urban renewal. But it remained, decade upon decade, a monument to his failure, as damnably eternal as the Pyramids or nuclear waste.

Dick had only been playing politics the way he'd been taught: gloves off, bareknuckled and brutal. If you couldn't take it, you had no business in the ring. Had he demanded impeachment hearings when Daley's goddamn Chicago machine threw the '60 election to that bastard Kennedy? No, he'd conceded defeat rather than put the country through a contested election—but he wasn't going to let it happen again.

In retrospect, Dick realized that he needn't have bothered with dirty tricks in the '72 campaign. George McGovern was an idiot lib who'd have hung himself if Nixon had simply uncoiled enough rope for him. Instead, Dick had entrusted his career to morons like Hunt and Liddy, who hired even bigger imbeciles to bug the Democratic headquarters at the Watergate. He then compounded his error by covering up their incompetence instead of sending them all to the wall as he should have.

Yet was that mistake so horrible that it outweighed everything else he'd ever done—the opening of China, détente with the Soviets, the Clean Air Act, the Consumer Product Safety Commission, the Environmental Protection Agency—all of it? Nixon couldn't bear the thought that, to most people, he was nothing more than an easy punch line for stand-up comedians.

There was still time to change that, he told himself. Someone—some *thing*—knew that he was capable of more than that. A higher power had chosen him, made him whole again, for a reason. He dared not disappoint its faith in him.

When the limo arrived at the White House, Nixon let the sight of that glorious pediment with its Greco-Roman columns blot out all thoughts of the Watergate complex. As the chauffeur let him out of the car, the years since he'd flown away in that last helicopter ride following the resignation seemed to evaporate.

He was home.

The Oval Office had changed, of course. For one thing, a huge plasma-screen teleconferencing monitor curved along one wall, upon which a dozen displays broadcast news reports from around the world about the tense international situation in the wake of the nuclear attack. For another, a woman with iron-grey hair sat in the leather chair behind the desk, conferring with the cluster of dour-faced advisors that surrounded her. As soon as the Secret Service bodyguards led Nixon into the room, the muttered conversation ceased, and the woman got to her feet.

"My God . . . it really *is* you," she said.

He made a stiff bow. "Madame President."

Attired in a grey tweed suit, she seemed to be in her early seventies, which would have made her a teenager back in his administration. Dick prayed that he could reason with a hippie.

"How did you come back?" she asked.

He lifted an accusing finger. "*You* brought me back. If you retaliate to this terrorist act, it'll be the beginning of Armageddon." He quoted Revelation 20:13. "'*And the sea gave up the dead which were in it; and death and hell delivered up the dead which were in them.*' I'm only the first, but there will be billions more—more than all the people now alive. You *must* hold off the attack."

One of the advisors, an impudent whelp with slick black hair, shook his head. "I can't believe you're even listening to this guy. He's obviously a fraud sent here by the enemy. If we allow the New York atrocity to go unpunished, there's no telling which of our cities they'll obliterate next."

The President's expression hardened. "He's right. The people are screaming for blood. You of all people should know how that works: 'Death before dishonor,' and so on. They want me to nuke something, and right now, it's not a matter of *if*, it's a choice of which target."

"But you don't even know who was responsible!" Nixon protested.

"And we may never know. Hezbollah, Hamas, al Qaeda-does it really matter? A full investigation could take months, but the U.S. must demonstrate its force now."

"Even if it means doom for the whole human race?" Dick tried to stride across the floor's plush Presidential seal to confront her face-to-face, but the Secret Service agents caught hold of him. Although he could have flung them across the room like a couple of rag dolls, he relented.

"*Look* at me!" he beseeched the President. "You know who I am. Don't make the same mistake I did and let pride lead you into carrying on a war you can't win."

She stared at him, and Dick could tell that she needed no DNA test to prove his identity.

Then, with soul-deep weariness, she lowered herself back into her chair.

"Back in '71, I put flowers in my hair and marched in the streets of D.C. chanting 'Make Love, Not War' because you wouldn't get out of 'Nam. Now the kids are protesting *me*." She pleaded to Nixon with her eyes, the bags beneath them heavier than his own. "What should I do?"

"Negotiate."

The mousse-haired advisor exhaled disgust. "We don't negotiate with terrorists."

"Not with the terrorists, you jackass," Nixon said. "With the Israelis and the Muslims. *Use* this crisis to fashion a lasting peace."

The President raised her hands in exasperation. "But if Armageddon has already begun, what's the point?"

"It's not Armageddon until you make it Armageddon." Nixon shook off the grip of the bodyguards, who seemed inclined to let him go, and approached her desk. "Don't you see? The human race chooses the hour of its own destruction. Pull back from the brink before it's too late."

"Maybe it's already too late." The announcement came from a Hispanic female who would later introduce herself as the White House Press Secretary. During the debate, her attention had been drawn to the video monitors. "Madame President, I think you should see this."

Even before he looked, Nixon knew what he would find on the screen. There was only one story that could possibly distract the world's news media from coverage of the recent nuclear holocaust.

In footage from CNN, thousands of charred corpses from the ruin of New York—those that had not been vaporized by the initial blast—staggered out of the rubble to rip the limbs off relief workers in white radiation suits. On Fox News, a shaky cell-phone camera showed somnambulating bodies from a hospital morgue overwhelming a nurse, gouging strips of flesh from the victim with their hands and teeth. Similar scenes played out on channels from around the world as text crawls in Japanese, Arabic, and Russian scrolled superfluous explanations across the screens.

Dick saw his worst-case scenario confirmed. Unlike himself, these dead seemed to have lost all trace of humanity as they tore into the living with a blind wrath propelled by envy and vengeance. They had risen to scourge the world that had sent them to their graves.

Nixon imagined Pat reduced to a ravening, rotting animal, pictured her ravaging Tricia and Julie, the grandchildren and great-grandchildren. No . . . no, she would never—there had to be some way of reaching her, of reaching all of them . . .

"That's it, isn't it?" The President sounded more lifeless than the walking cadavers on the monitor. "We're finished."

"*No.*" Nixon leaned toward her, clenched his fist in sudden resolve. "This is precisely the motivating force you need to bring the Arabs and Israelis to the bargaining table. Nothing unites foes like a common enemy."

He flailed a hand toward one of the displays on the monitor, in which an Al Jazeera anchorman babbled beside shots of a burned-out Lebanese suburb where bombing victims walked side-by-side with dead G.I.s to mob the survivors of a recent battle.

"The Middle East will be overrun with corpses from the recent war. Offer both Israel and the Muslim countries U.S. military aid against the dead in exchange for concessions on a Palestinian homeland and official recognition of the Jewish state."

"Spoken like a true Machiavellian." The President's mouth twisted, as if she were washing the proposal over her tongue to see how it tasted. "But tell me, Dick . . . may I call you Dick?"

Nixon grimaced. "Everyone does."

"How am I supposed to offer military aid when I'm going to need every available soldier and weapon to defend *us*?"

"Let me talk to them."

"Who? The Arabs?"

"No. The dead."

The President darted a glance toward the mute malevolence of the massed corpses onscreen. "Can you *do* that?"

Nixon chuckled, a deep baritone gurgle. "Can't be any worse than dealing with Mao or Brezhnev."

The slick-haired advisor shook his head. "Madame President, you can't be serious—"

"Shut up." She didn't take her eyes off Nixon. "Tell me what you need," she said.

．　．　．　．　．

In truth, flying to China for the first time was easy compared to the task Nixon faced now. To make a rapprochement with any adversary, one had to meet him on his own turf. Therefore, as a gesture of good faith, Dick would have to go to the only place in the world he dreaded more the Watergate complex.

The Vietnam Veterans Memorial was situated on the Mall between the Lincoln Memorial and the Washington Monument, less than a mile from the White House, but the walk there seemed as long to Nixon as the road to Damascus. Although Dick had lived for more than a decade after the monument's completion in 1982, he had never dared to visit it. When he finally stood at the crux of that broad V of polished black stone, he could feel the weight of accusation that he'd avoided all those years. More than two hundred feet long and over ten feet high at its tallest point, the sheer wall of ebony granite appeared almost white with the density of text etched upon it.

Names. Thousands upon thousands of names. The monolith was a mammoth tombstone for an entire generation of American soldiers. At its base, the faithful had laid photos, flowers, Purple Hearts, and other offerings to show the dead that they had not been forgotten.

Dick gazed up at the columns of names that rose more than a yard above his head. So many. How much longer and higher had he made this wall by refusing to admit defeat until it became inevitable? He put out one quavering hand toward the reflective surface of the stone but couldn't bring himself to touch it.

"They're coming," the President announced from behind him, as if reading his mind. "Are you ready?"

Nixon nodded and turned to face out toward the moonlit reflecting pool of the Mall. He squinted at the painfully bright floodlights the satellite television crews had set up to illuminate the Memorial for the imminent broadcast. His speech would be transmitted live on all channels, on every radio station, and through every public address system in the nation. Special trucks equipped with loudspeakers would drive through every major city blaring his words.

In front of Nixon stood a single microphone on a stand. The solicitous White House Press Secretary asked him if he wanted a teleprompter or prepared speech, but Nixon refused. Tonight, he would be speaking from his heart, even if it wasn't beating.

Barely visible beyond the bright lights and cameras was a squad of National Guard soldiers armed with M-16s and grenade launchers—the last line of defense should anything go wrong. Secret Service bodyguards in flak helmets and bulletproof vests flocked around the President herself, who had insisted on remaining at Nixon's side over the vehement objections of her advisors. Together they stood, shoulder-to-shoulder, and waited for the others to arrive.

Across the Potomac, in the Arlington National Cemetery, row upon row of cement slabs, identical but for the names and dates chiseled upon them, shone stark white in the light of the gibbous moon overhead. In the darkness, the lush grass swelled like waves in a black sea. Miniature American flags left over from Memorial Day wobbled and fell over as the turf beneath them blistered, burst open. Even the Tomb of the Unknowns cracked and disgorged its anonymous remains. The creatures who shambled forth from the desecrated ground had become nearly as identical as their headstones, distinguishable only by the tatters of the dress uniforms that still clung to them. Their faces had withered to the bone, reduced to the death's-head that underlies every human visage. They represented every conflict since the Civil War—both World Wars, Korea, Desert Storm, Iraq, and, of course, Vietnam—but they now ranked themselves into a united force, speechlessly advancing, a legion of the silent yet unquiet dead.

Three hundred thousand strong, they marched in chaotic, stumbling cadence from their scattered graves to cluster at the two-lane entrance of the abandoned Arlington Memorial Bridge. Although security forces across the country had discovered that one could incapacitate the animate corpses with a direct hit to the head, the troops that blockaded the bridge earlier that day had long since withdrawn to defend the White House and the Vietnam Memorial. Unimpeded, the undead flowed *en masse* across the bridge to spill out onto the Mall, drawn onward by some sense more certain than the sight endowed to their eyeless sockets.

Nixon saw them swarm around the Lincoln Memorial, a black tide of silhouettes that surged forward as sinuously as a plague of rats. A few of the Guardsmen cast a contemptuous glance at the deceased Commander-in-Chief and raised their weapons, aimed into the onslaught.

Nixon raised a hand. "Hold your fire!"

When he failed to begin his speech, even the current President grew nervous.

"Dick?" She gaped at the coming horde. "You're *on*."

He stepped up to the microphone but waited a moment more, until that undifferentiated mass drew close enough for him to pick out individuals in the crowd, however decomposed and unrecognizable, to whom he could address his remarks.

"My fellow Americans." Nixon spread his arms as if to embrace them all. "For you *are* still Americans—every last one of you."

Loudspeakers echoed his words across the Mall; television and radio carried them across the continent. Yet they did nothing to slow the ghoulish army's advance. The National Guard soldiers fidgeted, fingers restive on triggers, but any resistance now would be token at best.

"Many of you have already made the ultimate sacrifice for this country we love. Tonight, I must ask you to make that sacrifice *again*."

Dick noted that one corpse missing a leg was able to hop forward by curling an arm around the shoulders of one of its comrades. If they could demonstrate that kind of altruism toward each other, he thought, perhaps they could still be made to care about the loved ones they left behind. It was his only chance.

"I know that many of you may feel that you died in vain, before your time, for a cause and a war you didn't believe in." He gestured to the wall of names behind him with one hand, spread the other on his chest. "Some of you are out there because I helped put you there. But *I* let you down—not your country."

Mere yards from the barricade the Guard unit had erected in front of the Memorial, the shuffling multitude halted, staring at Nixon with inscrutable impassivity. Had a flicker of comprehension flitted over their expressionless faces?

"Tonight, your country—your America—has resolved to leave behind its mistakes and misbegotten wars of the past." He indicated the President, who stepped free of her entourage to be recognized. "It has tried and failed to do so many times in its history and it may do so again.

"Does it deserve another chance? No, it does not, just as I did not. No one *deserves* another chance. Mercy cannot be earned; it is an act of grace.

"Therefore, I ask all of you, across this great nation of ours—those that died in battle and those that did not—to pardon whatever injustice you may have suffered; abandon your wrath, however righteous it may be; and return to your rest. Don't do it for me. Don't even do it for your country. Do it for those who still revere your memory." He swept a hand toward the Memorial with its heaped bouquets and mementos of bereavement. "Be the heroes—the Americans—you were and *are*."

His arm dropped to his side, and his final words were so soft that they were barely audible even when amplified. "Be *better* than I was."

Nixon still didn't know whether his new eyes were capable of tears, but they felt as if they were about to melt inside his skull and run down his nose. He closed them and bowed his head.

When the throng of dead soldiers did not storm over the barricade to maul the humans huddled in front of the Memorial, the President cautiously approached the edge of the monument's foundation and peered out at the spectral assembly before her. They hadn't moved since Nixon fell silent, merely gazed upon the scene with judicial gravity. They had been charged with the task of ending the human race and the decision was now theirs.

And one by one, they turned and walked away, until the last of them disappeared into the early morning mist that drifted in from the Potomac.

The President watched them depart, her mouth hanging open in wonder, until the Press Secretary waved to get her attention. "Ma'am! We're getting reports from across the country." The Latina cupped a hand over her ear-bud cell phone to hear better. "There're a few holdouts that security forces are cleaning up. But most are retreating voluntarily."

The President beamed. "You did it, Dick! You did it!"

But when the President wheeled around to flash a "V for Victory" sign at the elder statesman, she found only a mummified cadaver collapsed beside her, too withered to fill the new navy-blue suit that sagged around it. Of the familiar widow's peak on the scalp, only a few scraggly white hairs remained. The jowls had shrunk into starched, lumpy furrows, and the membranes of the eyelids now stretched like yellowed foolscap over vacant sockets. She could see that this was the same face, however, yet it had changed in a more profound way than the mere superficial disfigurement of decay. It bore a new expression of tranquility that death and time could not mar, of a sleep too restful to disturb.

Whatever power had brought Richard Nixon back to aid his nation evidently understood that his work was done.

. . . . .

Despite the hectic schedule of diplomatic negotiations she arranged in the days that followed, the President traveled to Southern California for the re-internment. She made sure that Richard Milhous Nixon, her predecessor and mentor, received a state burial befitting a former Chief Executive, complete with honor guard and twenty-one-gun salute. As he was lowered back into the small, flower-bordered plot situated between his Birthplace and his Library, she read the epitaph on Nixon's grave marker. It seemed more appropriate than ever:

THE GREATEST HONOR HISTORY CAN BESTOW
IS THE TITLE OF PEACEMAKER

SENSIBLE CITY
Harlan Ellison®

Harlan Ellison has been awarded the Hugo Award eight-and-a-half times, the Nebula Award three times, the Bram Stoker Award five times (including Lifetime Achievement), and the Edgar Award of the Mystery Writers of America twice.

He is also the recipient of the Silver Pen for Journalism by International PEN, the World Fantasy Award, the Georges Méliès Fantasy Film Award, an unprecedented four Writers Guild of America awards for Most Outstanding Teleplay, and the International Horror Guild's Living Legend Award. In 2006, he was made a Grand Master by the Science Fiction and Fantasy Writers of America (SFWA).

Born in Cleveland, Ohio, Ellison moved to New York in his early twenties to pursue a writing career. Over the next two years he published more than 100 stories and articles. Moving to California in 1962, he began selling to Hollywood, co-scripting the 1966 movie *The Oscar* and contributing two dozen scripts to such shows as *Star Trek*, *The Outer Limits*, *The Man from U.N.C.L.E.*, *The Alfred Hitchcock Hour*, *Cimarron Strip*, *Route 66*, *Burke's Law*, and *The Flying Nun*. His story "A Boy and His Dog" was filmed in 1975 starring Don Johnson, and Ellison was a creative consultant on the 1980s revival of *The Twilight Zone* TV series.

His more than seventy-five books include *Rumble* (a.k.a. *Web of the City*), *Rockabilly* (a.k.a. *Spider Kiss*), *All the Lies That Are My Life*, and *Mefisto in Onyx*, while some of his almost 2,000 short stories have been collected in *The Juvies* (a.k.a. *Children of the Street*), *Ellison Wonderland*, *Paingod and Other Delusions*, *I Have No Mouth and I Must Scream*, *Love Ain't Nothing but Sex Misspelled*, *The Beast That Shouted Love at the Heart of the World*, *Deathbird Stories*, *Strange Wine*, *Shatterday*, *Stalking the Nightmare*, *Angry Candy*, and *Slippage*.

Ellison also edited the influential science fiction anthology *Dangerous Visions* in 1967 and followed it with a sequel, *Again Dangerous Visions*, in 1972.

More recently, he was the subject of Erik Nelson's revelatory feature-length documentary *Dreams with Sharp Teeth* (2008), which was made over a period of twenty-seven years and chronicles the author's life and work.

"One of my pet shrieks in thriller movies—of outrage, not of terror—is when one idiot goes off alone to find out 'what's making that terrifying, strangulating, death-howl noise,'" explains Ellison, "and everyone knows that pro forma (as per 12,237 dopey movies back to Year One) he will very shortly be getting his head chain-sawed off, his chest pierced by a $19.95, TV-ad Mince-O-Matic, his eyeballs fried, or his nuts chewed off by rabid rarebits.

"Doesn't he hear that ominous music? Doesn't he know the name of this movie is *Don't Go into the Crypt When It Smells of Rotten Body Parts*—the point being, bad amateur horror-film directors (to whom a facial zit is as close as they'll ever get to menace and danger in *this* life), making your protagonist insensitive as a punk-rock aficionado and dense as a block of carbon-steel—is a shriek in a moviehouse. And I don't mean a shriek of horror.

"So, I decided to write a story in which the protagonist is *not* dumb and resists the Going into the Dark Room with all his might.

"As a side note, I wrote this story, in its entirety, while on the first and only cruise of my life. My wife, Susan, dragged me aboard this floating retirement home for the terminally hobbling, and I was bored, bored, *bo-ah-ord* outta my mind and spent my time sitting on deck, with my trusty Olympia manual typewriter, writing of horror while *on* an aquatic abattoir to Mexico. Turns out I am shit at shuffleboard."

DURING THE THIRD WEEK of the trial, sworn under oath, one of the Internal Affairs guys the D.A.'s office had planted undercover in Gropp's facility attempted to describe how terrifying Gropp's smile was. The IA guy stammered some; and there seemed to be a singular absence of color in his face; but he tried valiantly, not being a poet or one given to colorful speech. And after some prodding by the Prosecutor, he said:

"You ever, y'know, when you brush your teeth . . . how when you're done, and you've spit out the toothpaste and the water, and you pull back your lips to look at your teeth, to see if they're whiter, and like that . . . you know how you tighten up your jaws real good, and make that kind of death-grin smile that pulls your lips back, with your teeth lined up clenched in the front of your mouth . . . you know what I mean . . . well . . ."

Sequestered that night in a downtown hotel, each of the twelve jurors stared into a medicine cabinet mirror and skinned back a pair of lips, and tightened neck muscles till the cords stood out, and clenched teeth, and stared at a face grotesquely contorted. Twelve men and women then superimposed over the mirror reflection the face of the Defendant they'd been staring at for three weeks, and approximated the smile they had *not* seen on Gropp's face all that time.

And in that moment of phantom face over reflection face, Gropp was convicted.

Police Lieutenant W. R. Gropp. Rhymed with *crop*. The meat-man who ruled a civic smudge called the Internment Facility when it was listed on the City Council's budget every year. Internment Facility: dripping wet, cold iron, urine smell mixed with sour liquor sweated through dirty skin, men and women crying in the night. A stockade, a prison camp, stalag, ghetto, torture chamber, charnel house, abattoir, duchy, fiefdom, Army co-op mess hall ruled by a neckless thug.

The last of the thirty-seven inmate alumni who had been subpoenaed to testify recollected, "Gropp's favorite thing was to take some fool outta his cell, get him nekkid to the skin, then do this *rolling* thing t'him."

When pressed, the former tenant of Gropp's hostelry—not a felon, merely a steamfitter who had had a bit too much to drink and picked up for himself a ten-day Internment Facility residency for D&D—explained that this "rolling thing" entailed "Gropp wrappin' his big, hairy sausage arm aroun' the guy's neck, see, and then he'd *roll him* across the bars, real hard and fast. Bangin' the guy's head like a roulette ball around the wheel. Clank clank, like that. Usual, it'd knock the guy flat out cold, his head clankin' across the bars and spaces between, wham wham wham like that. See his eyes go up outta sight, all white; but Gropp, he'd hang on with that sausage aroun' the guy's neck, whammin' and bangin' him and takin' some goddam kinda pleasure mentionin' how much bigger this criminal bastard was than *he* was. Yeah, fer sure. That was Gropp's favorite part, that he always pulled out some poor nekkid sonofabitch was twice his size.

"That's how four of these guys he's accused of doin', that's how they croaked. With Gropp's sausage 'round the neck. I kept my mouth shut; I'm lucky to get outta there in one piece."

Frightening testimony, last of thirty-seven. But as superfluous as feathers on an eggplant. From the moment of superimposition of phantom face over reflection face, Police Lieutenant W. R. Gropp was on greased rails to spend his declining years for Brutality While Under Color of Service—a *serious* offense—in a maxi-galleria stuffed chockablock with felons whose spiritual brethren he had maimed, crushed, debased, blinded, butchered, and killed.

Similarly destined was Gropp's gigantic Magog, Deputy Sergeant Michael "Mickey" Rizzo, all three hundred and forty pounds of him; brainless malevolence stacked six feet four inches high in his steel-toed, highly-polished service boots. Mickey had only been indicted on seventy counts, as opposed to Gropp's eighty-four ironclad atrocities. But if he managed to avoid Sentence of Lethal Injection for having crushed men's heads underfoot, he would certainly go to the maxi-galleria mall of felonious behavior for the rest of his simian life.

Mickey had, after all, pulled a guy up against the inside of the bars and kept bouncing him till he ripped the left arm loose from its socket, ripped it off, and later dropped it on the mess hall steam table just before dinner assembly.

Squat, bulletheaded troll, Lieutenant W. R. Gropp, and the mindless killing machine, Mickey Rizzo. On greased rails.

So they jumped bail together, during the second hour of jury deliberation.

Why wait? Gropp could see which way it was going, even counting on Blue Loyalty. The city was putting the abyss between the Dept., and him and Mickey. So, why wait? Gropp was a sensible guy, very pragmatic, no bullshit. So they jumped bail together, having made arrangements weeks before, as any sensible felon keen to flee would have done.

Gropp knew a chop shop that owed him a favor. There was a throaty and hemi-speedy, immaculately registered, four-year-old Firebird just sitting in a bay on the fifth floor of a seemingly abandoned garment factory, two blocks from the courthouse.

And just to lock the barn door after the horse, or in this case the Pontiac, had been stolen, Gropp had Mickey toss the chop shop guy down the elevator shaft of the factory. It was the sensible thing to do. After all, the guy's neck *was* broken.

By the time the jury came in, later that night, Lieut. W. R. Gropp was out of the state and somewhere near Boise. Two days later, having taken circuitous routes, the Firebird was on the other side of both the Snake River and the Rockies, between Rock Springs and Laramie. Three days after that, having driven in large circles, having laid over in Cheyenne for dinner and a movie, Gropp and Mickey were in Nebraska.

Wheat ran to the sun, blue storms bellowed up from horizons, and heat trembled on the edge of each leaf. Crows stirred inside fields, lifted above shattered surfaces of grain and flapped into sky. That's what it looked like: the words came from a poem.

They were smack in the middle of the Plains state, above Grand Island, below Norfolk, somewhere out in the middle of nowhere, just tooling along, leaving no trail, deciding to go that way to Canada, or the other way to Mexico. Gropp had heard there were business opportunities in Mazatlán.

It was a week after the jury had been denied the pleasure of seeing Gropp's face as they said, "Stick the needle in the brutal sonofabitch. Fill the barrel with a very good brand of weed-killer, stick the needle in the brutal sonofabitch's chest, and slam home the plunger. Guilty, your honor, guilty on charges one through eighty-four. Give 'im the weed-killer and let's watch the fat scumbag do his dance!" A week of swift and leisurely driving here and there, doubling back and skimming along easily.

And somehow, earlier this evening, Mickey had missed a turnoff, and now they were on a stretch of superhighway that didn't seem to have any important exits.

There were little towns now and then, the lights twinkling off in the mid-distance, but if they were within miles of a major metropolis, the map didn't give them clues as to where they might be.

"You took a wrong turn."

"Yeah, huh?"

"Yeah, *exactly* huh. Keep your eyes on the road."

"I'm sorry, Looten'nt."

"No. Not Lieutenant. I told you."

"Oh, yeah, right. Sorry, Mr. Gropp."

"Not Gropp. Jensen. Mister *Jensen*. You're *also* Jensen; my kid brother. Your name is Daniel."

"I got it, I remember: Harold and Daniel Jensen is us. You know what I'd like?"

"No, what would you like?"

"A box'a Grape-Nuts. I could have 'em here in the car, and when I got a mite peckish I could just dip my hand in an' have a mouthful. I'd like that."

"Keep your eyes on the road."

"So whaddya think?"

"About what?"

"About maybe I swing off next time and we go into one'a these little towns and maybe a 7-Eleven'll be open, and I can get a box'a Grape-Nuts? We'll need some gas after a while, too. See the little arrow there?"

"I see it. We've still got half a tank. Keep driving."

Mickey pouted. Gropp paid no attention. There were drawbacks to forced traveling companionship. But there were many culs-de-sac and landfills between this stretch of dark turnpike and New Brunswick, Canada or Mazatlán, state of Sinaloa.

"What is this, the Southwest?" Gropp asked, looking out the side window into utter darkness. "The Midwest? What?"

Mickey looked around, too. "I dunno. Pretty out here, though. Real quiet and pretty."

"It's pitch dark."

"Yeah, huh?"

"Just drive, for godsake. Pretty. Jeezus!"

They rode in silence for another twenty-seven miles, then Mickey said, "I gotta go take a piss."

Gropp exhaled mightily. Where were the culs-de-sac, where were the landfills? "Okay. Next town of any size, we can take the exit and see if there's decent accommodations. You can get a box of Grape-Nuts, and use the toilet; I can have a cup of coffee and study the map in better light. Does that sound like a good idea, to you . . . Daniel?"

"Yes, Harold. See, I remembered."

"The world is a fine place."

They drove for another sixteen miles and came nowhere in sight of a thruway exit sign. But the green glow had begun to creep up from the horizon.

"What the hell is that?" Gropp asked, running down his power window. "Is that some kind of a forest fire, or something? What's that look like to you?"

"Like green in the sky."

"Have you ever thought how lucky you are that your mother abandoned you, Mickey?" Gropp said wearily. "Because if she hadn't, and if they hadn't brought you to the county jail for temporary housing till they could put you in a foster home, and I hadn't taken an interest in you, and hadn't arranged for you to live with the Rizzos, and hadn't let you work around the lockup, and hadn't made you my deputy, do you have any idea where you'd be today?" He paused for a moment, waiting for an answer, realized the entire thing was rhetorical—not to mention pointless—and said, "Yes, it's green in the sky, pal, but it's also something odd. Have you ever seen 'green in the sky' before? Anywhere? Any time?"

"No, I guess I haven't."

Gropp sighed, and closed his eyes.

They drove in silence another nineteen miles, and the green miasma in the air enveloped them. It hung above and around them like sea-fog, chill and with tiny droplets of moisture that Mickey fanned away with the windshield wipers. It made the landscape on either side of the superhighway faintly visible, cutting the impenetrable darkness, but it also induced a wavering, ghostly quality to the terrain.

Gropp turned on the map light in the dome of the Firebird, and studied the map of Nebraska. He murmured, "I haven't got a rat's-fang of any idea where the hell we *are!* There isn't even a freeway like this indicated here. You took some helluva wrong turn 'way back there, pal!" Dome light out.

"I'm sorry. Loo—Harold . . ."

A large reflective advisement marker, green and white, came up on their right. It said:

FOOD GAS LODGING

10 MILES

The next sign said:

EXIT

7 MILES

The next sign said:

OBEDIENCE
3 MILES

Gropp turned the map light on again. He studied the venue. "Obedience? What the hell kind of 'Obedience'? There's nothing like that *anywhere*. What is this, an old map? Where did you get this map?"

"Gas station."

"Where?"

"I dunno. Back a long ways. That place we stopped with the root beer stand next to it."

Gropp shook his head, bit his lip, murmured nothing in particular. "Obedience," he said. "Yeah, huh?"

They began to see the town off to their right before they hit the exit turnoff. Gropp swallowed hard and made a sound that caused Mickey to look over at him. Gropp's eyes were large, and Mickey could see the whites.

"What'sa matter, Loo . . . Harold?"

"You see that town out there?" His voice was trembling.

Mickey looked to his right. Yeah, he saw it. Horrible.

Many years ago, when Gropp was briefly a college student, he had taken a warm-body course in Art Appreciation. One oh one, it was; something basic and easy to ace, a snap, all you had to do was show up. Everything you wanted to know about Art from aboriginal cave drawings to Diego Rivera. One of the paintings that had been flashed on the big screen for the class, a sleepy 8:00 a.m. class, had been *The Nymph Echo* by Max Ernst. A green and smoldering painting of an ancient ruin overgrown with writhing plants that seemed to have eyes and purpose and a malevolently jolly life of their own, as they swarmed and slithered and overran the stone vaults and altars of the twisted, disturbingly resonant sepulcher. Like a sebaceous cyst, something corrupt lay beneath the emerald fronds and hungry black soil.

Mickey looked to his right at the town. Yeah, he saw it. Horrible.

Gropp saw bulging eyeballs. "*What?*" he demanded.

"I saw a place like that once!"

"What? What're you talking about?"

"I did, Harold; I swear to God, I did. Jus' like that out there!"

"Where? Where the hell could you've seen anything even *like* that?"

"It was a movie."

Gropp felt faint, his eyelids fluttered closed for an eternal moment with the crushing weight of years of Mickey kneeling on all fours on them. "A movie."

"Yeah. It was a *zombie movie*. It scared th'crap outta me!"

"*You* scare the crap outta me!" He pointed straight ahead: "Keep driving!" Gropp yelled, as his partner-in-flight started to slow for the exit ramp.

Mickey heard, but his reflexes were slow. They continued to drift to the right, toward the rising egress lane. Gropp reached across and jerked the wheel hard to the left. "I said: *keep driving!*"

The Firebird slewed, but Mickey got it back under control in a moment, and in another moment they were abaft the ramp, then past it, and speeding away from the nightmarish site beyond and slightly below the superhighway. Gropp stared mesmerized as they swept past. He could see buildings that leaned at obscene angles, the green fog that rolled through the haunted streets, the shadowy forms of misshapen things that skulked at every dark opening.

"That was a real scary-lookin' place, Looten . . . Harold. I don't think I'd of wanted to go down there even for the Grape-Nuts. But maybe if we'd've gone real fast . . ."

Gropp twisted in the seat toward Mickey as much as his muscle-fat body would permit. "Listen to me. There is this tradition, in horror movies, in mysteries, in TV shows, that people are always going into haunted houses, into graveyards, into battle zones, like assholes, like stone idiots! You know what I'm talking about here? Do you?"

"Yeah, sure, Lieuten . . . yeah, sure. The zombies."

"Zombies? Again with the zombies? Will you ferchrissakes can the zombie crap?"

"They really scare me, y'know."

"Lima*goddamBEANS* scare me, you jughead, but I don't run around screaming at them."

Mickey laughed lightly, "Aw, c'mon, Harold . . . that'd make no sense: lima beans can't hear you; but a zombie, hell, that's another thing entire; a zombie can hear ya okay. They're slow, maybe, but their ears is okay." He chuckled again.

"All right, let me give you an example. Remember we went to see that movie *Alien*? Remember how scared you were?"

Mickey bobbled his head rapidly, his eyes widened in frightened memory.

"Okay. So now, you remember that part where the guy who was a mechanic, the guy with the baseball cap, he goes off looking for a cat or somedamnthing? Remember? He left everyone else, and he wandered off by himself. And he went into that big cargo hold with the water dripping on him, and all those chains hanging down, and shadows everywhere . . . *do you recall that?*"

Mickey's eyes were chalky potholes. He remembered, oh yes; he remembered clutching Gropp's jacket sleeve till Gropp had been compelled to slap his hand away.

"And you remember what happened in the movie? In the theater? You remember everybody yelling, 'Don't go in there, you asshole! The thing's in there, you moron! Don't go in there!' But, remember, he *did*, and the thing came up behind him, all those teeth, and it bit his stupid head off! Remember that?"

Mickey hunched over the wheel, driving fast.

"Well, that's the way people are. They ain't sensible! They go into places like that, you can see are death places; and they get chewed up or the blood sucked outta their necks or used for kindling . . . but I'm no moron, I'm a sensible guy and I got the brains my mama gave me, and I don't go *near* places like that. So drive like a sonofabitch, and get us outta here, and we'll get your damned Grape-Nuts in Idaho or somewhere . . . if we ever get off this road . . ."

Mickey murmured, "I'm sorry, Lieuten'nt. I took a wrong turn or somethin'."

"Yeah, yeah. Just keep driv—" The car was slowing.

It was a frozen moment. Gropp exultant, no fool he, to avoid the cliché, to stay out of that haunted house, that ominous dark closet, that damned place. Let idiot others venture off the freeway, into the town that contained the basement entrance to Hell, or whatever. Not he, not Gropp!

He'd outsmarted the obvious.

In that frozen moment.

As the car slowed. Slowed, in the poisonous green mist.

And on their right, the obscenely frightening town of Obedience, that they had left in their dust five minutes before, was coming up again on the superhighway.

"Did you take another turnoff?"

"Uh . . . no, I . . . uh, I been just driving fast . . ."

The sign read:

NEXT RIGHT

50 YDS

OBEDIENCE

The car was slowing. Gropp craned his neckless neck to get a proper perspective on the fuel gauge. He was a pragmatic kind of a guy, no nonsense, and very practical; but they were out of gas.

The Firebird slowed and slowed and finally rolled to a stop.

In the rearview mirror Gropp saw the green fog rolling up thicker onto the roadway; and emerging over the berm, in a jostling, slavering horde, clacking and drooling, dropping decayed body parts and leaving glistening trails of worm ooze as they dragged their deformed pulpy bodies across the blacktop, their snake-slit eyes gleaming green and yellow in the mist, the residents of Obedience clawed and slithered and crimped toward the car.

"I drove inta zombies," Mickey whispered, all as one word.

"There's no such thing as zuh . . ." Lieutenant Gropp said, all as one word, no whisper, no breath.

"I don' wanna say so, Loo . . ." and all human sounds ceased. All sound, of many kinds, did not cease.

It was common sense any Better Business Bureau would have applauded: if the tourist trade won't come to your town, take your town to the tourists. Particularly if the freeway has forced commerce to pass you by. Particularly if your town needs fresh blood to prosper. Particularly if you have the civic need to share.

Green fog shrouded the Pontiac, and the peculiar sounds that came from within. Don't go into that dark room is a sensible attitude. Particularly if one is a sensible guy, in a sensible city.

GRANNY'S GRINNING
Robert Shearman

For years **Robert Shearman** wouldn't touch prose with a barge pole. The thought of punctuation and paragraphs stopped him cold. He enjoyed *reading* the stuff, of course, but he never thought it'd be the sort of writing he could even take a stab at.

Instead he became a playwright. In the early 1990s he was appointed resident dramatist at the Northcott Theatre in Exeter by the Arts Council in the U.K.—the youngest writer ever to be honored in such a way. Soon afterward he became a regular writer for Alan Ayckbourn at his theatre in Scarborough.

Most of his plays were comedies. Some of them even won prizes—*Easy Laughter* won the *Sunday Times* Playwriting Award; *Couplings* won the World Drama Trust Award; *Fool to Yourself* won the inaugural Sophie Winter Trust Award; and *Binary Dreamers* won the Guinness Award for Ingenuity in association with the Royal National Theatre.

His plays have been staged internationally—Francis Ford Coppola produced *Easy Laughter* in Los Angeles, and Shearman himself recently directed his play *Shaw Cornered* at the Old World Theatre Festival in Delhi, India.

He was one of the writers who worked on the first, BAFTA-winning, series of Russell T. Davies' revival of *Doctor Who* starring Christopher Eccleston. His episode, "Dalek," which reintroduced the Time Lord's greatest enemy to a new generation of ten-year-olds, was nominated for a Hugo Award.

Shearman's first collection of short stories, *Tiny Deaths*, won the World Fantasy Award in 2007. It was also short-listed for the Edge Hill Short Story Prize, and one of its stories has been made the international representative of the Read! Singapore campaign by the National Library of Singapore. His second collection, *Love Songs for the Shy and Cynical*, was recently published by Big Finish.

About this new story, especially written for this book, the author explains, "I tried the basic idea of this in one of my stage comedies once. But you could see on the audience's faces that they were revolted. No one seemed to get the joke. It made me laugh, though. Well, a bit."

Robert Shearman says he loves Christmas. But he never really gets what he wants.

SARAH DIDN'T WANT the zombie, and she didn't know anyone else who did. Apart from Graham, of course, but he was only four, he wanted *everything*; his Christmas list to Santa had run to so many sheets of paper that Daddy had said that Santa would need to take out a second mortgage on his igloo to get that lot, and everyone had laughed, even though Graham didn't know what an igloo was, and Sarah was pretty sure that Santa didn't live in an igloo anyway. Sarah had tried to point out to her little brother why the zombies were rubbish. "Look," she said, showing him the picture in the catalogue, "there's nothing to a zombie. They're just the same as us. Except the skin is a bit greener, maybe. And the eyes have whitened a bit." But Graham said that zombies were cool because zombies ate people when they were hungry, and when Sarah scoffed Graham burst into tears like always, and Mummy told Sarah to leave Graham alone, he was allowed to like zombies if he wanted to. Sarah thought that if it was all about eating people, she'd rather have a the vampire: they sucked your blood for a start, which was so much neater somehow than just chomping down on someone's flesh—and Sharon Weekes said that she'd tried out a friend's vampire, and it was great, it wasn't just the obvious stuff like the teeth growing, but your lips swelled up, they got redder and richer and plump, and if you closed your eyes and rubbed them together it felt just the same as if a boy were kissing you. As if Sharon Weekes would know, Sharon Weekes was covered in spots, and no boy had ever kissed her, if you even so much as touched Sharon her face would explode—but you know, whatever, the rubbing lips thing still sounded great. Sarah hadn't written down on her Christmas list like Graham had done, she'd simply told Santa that she'd like the vampire, please. Just the vampire, not the mummy, or the werewolf, or the demon. And definitely not the zombie.

. . . . .

Even before Granny had decided to stay, Sarah knew that this Christmas was going to be different. Mummy and Daddy said that if she and Graham wanted such expensive toys, then they'd have to put up with just one present this year. Once upon a time they'd have had tons of presents, and the carpet beneath the Christmas tree would have been strewn with brightly wrapped parcels of different shapes and sizes, it'd have taken hours to open the lot. But that was before Daddy left his job because he wanted to "go it alone," before the credit crunch, before those late night arguments in the kitchen that Sarah wasn't supposed to hear. Graham groused a little about only getting one present, but Daddy said something about a second mortgage, and this time he didn't mention igloos, and this time nobody laughed. Usually the kitchen arguments were about money, but one night they were about Granny, and Sarah actually bothered to listen. "I thought she was staying with Sonia!" said Mummy. Sonia was Daddy's sister, and she had a sad smile, and ever since Uncle Jim had left her for someone less ugly she had lived alone. "She says she's fallen out with Sonia," said Daddy, "she's coming to spend Christmas with us instead." "Oh, for Christ's sake, *for Christ's sake*," said Mummy, and there was a banging of drawers. "Come on," said Daddy, "she's my Mummy, what was I supposed to say?" And then he added, "It might even work in our favor," and Mummy had said it better bloody well should, and then Sarah couldn't hear any more, perhaps because they'd shut the kitchen door, perhaps because Mummy was crying again.

. . . . .

Most Christmases they'd spend on their own, just Sarah with Mummy and Daddy and Graham. And on Boxing Day they'd get into the car and drive down the motorway to see Granny and Granddad. Granny looked a little like Daddy, but older and slightly more feminine. And Granddad smelled of cigarettes even though he'd given up before Sarah was born. Granny and Granddad would give out presents, and Sarah and Graham would say thank you no matter what they got. And they'd have another Christmas meal, just like the day before, except this time the turkey would be drier, and there'd be brussels sprouts rather than sausages. There wouldn't be a Boxing Day like that again. Partly because on the way home last year Mummy had said she could never spend another Christmas like that, and it had taken all of Daddy's best efforts to calm her down in the Little Chef—but mostly, Sarah supposed, because Granddad was dead. That was bound to make a difference. They'd all been to the funeral, Sarah hadn't even missed school because it was during the summer holidays, and Graham had made a nuisance of himself during the service asking if Granddad was a ghost now and going to come back from the grave. And during the whole thing Granny had sat there on the pew, all by herself, she didn't want anyone sitting next to her, not even Aunt Sonia, and Aunt Sonia was her favorite. And she'd cried, tears were streaming down her face, and Sarah had never seen Granny like that before, her face was always set fast like granite, and now with all the tears it had become soft and fat and pulpy and just a little frightening.

. . . . .

Four days before Christmas Daddy brought home a tree. "One of Santa's elves coming through!" he laughed, as he lugged it into the sitting room. It was enormous, and Graham and Sarah loved it, its upper branches scraped against the ceiling, they couldn't have put the fairy on the top like usual, she'd have broken her spine. Graham and Sarah began to cover it with balls and tinsel and electric lights, and Mummy said, "How much did that cost? I thought the point was to be a bit more economical this year," and Daddy said he knew what he was doing, he knew how to play the situation. They were going to give Granny the best Christmas she'd ever had! And he asked everyone to listen carefully, and then told them that this was a very important Christmas, it was the first Granny would have without Granddad. And she was likely to be a bit sad, and maybe a bit grumpy, but they'd all have to make allowances. It was to be *her* Christmas this year, whatever she wanted, it was all about making Granny happy, Granny would get the biggest slice of turkey, Granny got to choose which James Bond film to watch in the afternoon, the one on BBC1 or the one on ITV. Could he count on Graham and Sarah for that? Could he count on them to play along? And they both said yes, and Daddy was so pleased, they were so good he'd put their presents under the tree right away. He fetched two parcels, the same size, the same shape, flat boxes, one wrapped in blue paper and the other in pink. "Now, no peeking until the big day!" he laughed, but Graham couldn't help it, he kept turning his present over and over, and shaking it, and wondering what was inside, was it a demon, was it a zombie? And Sarah had to get on with decorating the tree all by herself, but that was all right, Graham hadn't been much use, she did a better job with him out of the way.

· · · · ·

And that was just the start of the work! The next few days were frantic! Mummy insisted that Granny come into a house as spotless and tidy as could be, that this time she wouldn't be able to find a thing wrong with it. And she made Sarah and Graham clean even the rooms that Granny wouldn't be seeing in the first place! It was all for Granny, that's what they were told, all for Granny—and if Graham sulked about that (and he did a little), Daddy said that one day someone close to *him* would die, and then *he* could have a special Christmas where everyone would run around after *him*, and Graham cheered up at that. On Christmas Eve Daddy said he was very proud of his children, and that he had a treat for them both. Early the next morning he'd be picking Granny up from her home in the country—it was a four-and-a-half hour journey there and back, and that they'd been *so* good they were allowed to come along for the trip! Graham got very excited, and shouted a lot. And Mummy said that it was okay to take Graham, but she needed Sarah at home, there was still work for Sarah to do. And Sarah wasn't stupid, the idea of a long drive to Granny's didn't sound much like fun to her, but it had been offered as a treat, and it hurt her to be denied a treat. Daddy glared at Mummy, and Mummy glared right back, and for a thrilling moment Sarah thought they might have an argument—but they only *ever* did that in the kitchen, they still believed the kids didn't know—and then Daddy relaxed, and then laughed, and ruffled Graham's hair, and said it'd be a treat for the boys then, just the boys, and laughed once more. So that was all right.

. . . . .

First thing Christmas morning, still hours before sunrise, Daddy and Graham set off to fetch Granny. Graham was so sleepy he forgot to be excited. "Goodbye then!" said Daddy cheerily; "Goodbye," said Mummy, and then suddenly pulled him into a tight hug. "It'll all be all right," said Daddy. "Of course it will," said Mummy, "off you go!" She waved them off, and then turned to Sarah, who was waving along beside her. Mummy said, "We've only got a few hours to make everything perfect," and Sarah nodded, and went to the cupboard for the vacuum cleaner. "No, no," said Mummy, "to make *you* perfect. My perfect little girl." And Mummy took Sarah by the hand, and smiled at her kindly, and led her to her own bedroom. "We're going to make you such a pretty girl," said Mummy, "they'll all see how pretty you can be. You'll like that, won't you? You can wear your nice dress. You'd like your new dress. Won't you?" Sarah didn't like her new dress, it was hard to romp about playing a vampire in it, it was hard to play at *anything* in it, but Mummy was insistent. "And we'll give you some nice jewelry," she said. "This is a necklace of mine. It's pretty. It's gold. Do you like it? My Mummy gave it to me. Just as I'm now giving it to you. Do you remember my Mummy? Do you remember the Other Granny?" Sarah didn't, but said that she did, and Mummy smiled. "She had some earrings too, shall we try you out with those? Shall we see what that's like?" And the earrings were much heavier than the plain studs Sarah was used to, they stretched her lobes out like chewing gum, they seemed to Sarah to stretch out her entire face. "Isn't that pretty?" said Mummy, and when Sarah said they hurt a bit, Mummy said she'd get used to it. Then Mummy took Sarah by the chin, and gave her a dab of lipstick—and Sarah never wore make-up, not like the girls who sat on the back row of the school bus, not even like Sharon Weekes, Mummy had always said it made them cheap. Sarah reminded her of this, and Mummy didn't reply, and so Sarah then asked if this was all for Granny, and Mummy said, "Yes, it's all for Granny," and then corrected herself, "it's for *all* of them, let's remind them what a pretty girl you are, what a pretty woman you could grow up to be. Always remember that you could have been a pretty woman." And then she wanted to give Sarah some nail varnish, nothing too much, nothing too red, just something clear and sparkling. But Sarah had had enough, she looked in the mirror and she didn't recognize the person looking back at her, she looked so much older, and greasy, and plastic, she looked just like Mummy. And tears were in her eyes, and she looked behind her reflection at Mummy's reflection, and there were tears in Mummy's eyes too—and Mummy said she was sorry, and took off the earrings, and wiped away the lipstick with a tissue. "I'm sorry," she said again, and said that Sarah needn't dress up if she didn't want to, it was her Christmas too, not just Granny's. And Sarah felt bad, and although she didn't much like the necklace she asked if she could keep it on, she lied and said it made her look pretty—and Mummy beamed a smile so wide, and gave her a hug, and said of course she could wear the necklace, anything for her darling, anything she wanted.

. . . . .

The first thing Granny said was, "I haven't brought you any presents, so don't expect any." "Come on in," said Daddy, laughing, "and make yourself at home!" and Granny sniffed as if she found that prospect particularly unappealing. "Hello, Mrs. Forbes," said Mummy. "Hello, Granny," said Sarah, and she felt the most extraordinary urge to curtsey. Graham trailed behind, unusually quiet, obviously quelled by a greater force than his own. "Can I get you some tea, Mrs. Forbes?" said Mummy. "We've got you all sorts, Earl Grey, Lapsang Souchong, Ceylon . . ." "I'd like some tea, not an interrogation," said Granny. She went into the lounge, and when she sat down in Daddy's armchair she sent all the scatter cushions tumbling, she didn't notice how carefully they'd been arranged and plumped. "Do you like the tree, Mummy?" Daddy asked, and Granny studied it briefly, and said it was too big, and she hoped he'd bought it on discount. Daddy started to say something about how the tree was just to keep the children happy, as if it were really their fault, but then Mummy arrived with the tea; Granny took her cup, sipped at it, and winced. "Would you like your presents, Mummy? We've got you presents." And at the mention of presents, Graham perked up: "Presents!" he said, "presents!" "Not your presents yet, old chap," laughed Daddy amiably, "Granny first, remember?" And Granny sighed and said she had no interest in presents, she could see nothing to celebrate—but she didn't want to spoil anyone else's fun, obviously, and so if they had presents to give her now would be as good a time to put up with them as any. Daddy had bought a few gifts, and labeled a couple from Sarah and Graham. It turned out that they'd bought Granny some perfume, "your favorite, isn't it?" asked Daddy, and "with their very own pocket money too!" "What use have I got in perfume now that Arthur's dead?" said Granny curtly. And tilted her face forwards so that Sarah and Graham could kiss it, by way of a thank you.

. . . . .

Graham was delighted with his werewolf suit. "Werewolf!" he shouted, and waving the box above his head tore around the sitting room in excitement. "And if you settle down, old chap," laughed Daddy, "you can try it on for size!" They took the cellophane off the box, removed the lid, and took out the instructions for use. The recommended age was ten and above, but as Daddy said, it was just a recommendation, and besides, there were plenty of adults there to supervise. There was a furry werewolf mask, furry werewolf slippers, and an entire furry werewolf body suit. Granny looked disapproving. "In my day, little boys didn't want to be werewolves," she said. "They wanted to be soldiers and train drivers." Graham put the mask over his face, and almost immediately they could all see how the fur seemed to grow in response—not only outwards, what would be the fun in that?, but inwards too, each tiny hair follicle burying itself deep within Graham's face, so you could really believe that all this fur had naturally come out of a little boy. With a crack the jaw elongated too, into something like a snout—it wasn't a full wolf's snout, of course not, this was only a toy, and you could see that the red raw gums inside that slavering mouth were a bit too rubbery to be real, but it was still effective enough for Granny to be impressed. "Goodness," she said. But that was nothing. When Daddy fastened the buckle around the suit, straight away Graham's entire body contorted in a manner that could only be described as feral. The spine snapped and popped as Graham grew bigger, and then it twisted and curved over, as if in protest that a creature on four legs should be supporting itself on two—the now-warped spine bulged angrily under the fur. Graham gave a yelp. "Doesn't that hurt?" said Mummy, and Daddy said no, these toys were all the rage, all the kids loved them. Graham tried out his new body. He threw himself around the room, snarling in almost pantomime fashion, he got so carried away whipping his tail about he nearly knocked over the coffee table—and it didn't matter, everyone was laughing at the fun, even Sarah, even Granny. "He's a proper little beast, isn't he!" Granny said. "And you see, it's also educational," Daddy leapt in, "because Graham will learn so much more about animals this way, I bet this sends him straight to the library." Mummy said, "I wonder if he'll howl at the moon!" and Daddy said, "well, of course he'll howl at the moon," and Granny said, "all wolves howl at the moon, even I know that," and Mummy looked crestfallen. "Silly Mummy," growled Graham.

· · · · ·

From the first rip of the pink wrapping paper Sarah could see that she hadn't been given a vampire suit. But she hoped it wasn't a zombie, even when she could see the sickly green of the mask, the bloated liver spots, the word ZOMBIE! far too proudly emblazoned upon the box. She thought it must be a mistake. And was about to say something, but when she looked up at her parents she saw they were beaming at her, encouraging, urging her on, urging her to open the lid, urging her to become one of the walking dead. So she smiled back, and she remembered not to make a fuss, that it was Granny's day—and hoped they'd kept the receipt so she could swap it for a vampire later. Daddy asked if he could give her a hand, and Sarah said she could manage, but he was helping her already, he'd already got out the zombie mask, he was already enveloping her whole face within it. He helped her with the zombie slippers, thick slabs of feet with overgrown toenails and peeling skin. He helped her with the suit, snapped the buckle. Sarah felt cold all around her, as if she'd just been dipped into a swimming pool—but it was dry inside this pool, as dry as dust, and the cold dry dust was inside her. And the surprise of it made her want to retch, but she caught herself, she swallowed it down, though there was no saliva in that swallow. Her face slumped, and bulged out a bit, like a huge spot just ready to be burst—and she felt heavier, like a sack, sodden—but sodden with what, there was no water, was there, no wetness at all, so what could she be sodden with? "Turn around!" said Daddy, and laughed, and she heard him with dead ears, and so she turned around, she lurched, the feet wouldn't let her walk properly, the body felt weighed down in all the wrong areas. Daddy laughed again, they all laughed at that, and Sarah tried to laugh too. She stuck out her arms in comic zombie fashion. "Grr," she said. Daddy's face was shining, Mummy looked just a little afraid. Granny was staring, she couldn't take her eyes off her. "Incredible," she breathed. And then she smiled, no, it wasn't a smile, she *grinned*. "Incredible." Graham had got bored watching, and had gone back to doing whatever it was that werewolves do around Christmas trees.

. . . . .

"And after all that excitement, roast turkey, with all the trimmings!" said Mummy. Sarah's stomach growled, though she hadn't known she was hungry. "Come on, children, toys away." "I think Sarah should wear her suit to dinner," said Granny. "I agree," said Daddy, "she's only just put it on." "All right," said Mummy. "Have it your own way. But not you, Graham. I don't want a werewolf at the dining table. I want my little boy." "That's not fair!" screamed Graham. "But werewolves don't have good table manners, darling," said Mummy. "You'll get turkey everywhere." So Graham began to cry, and it came out as a particularly plaintive howl, and he wouldn't take his werewolf off, he *wouldn't*, he wanted to live in his werewolf forever, and Mummy gave him a slap, just a little one, and it only made him howl all the more. "For God's sake, does it matter?" said Daddy, "let him be a werewolf if he wants." "Fine," said Mummy, "they can be monsters then, let's *all* be monsters!" And then she smiled to show everyone she was happy really, she only sounded angry, really she was happy. Mummy scraped Graham's Christmas dinner into a bowl, and set it on to the floor. "Try and be careful, darling," she said, "remember how hard we worked to get this carpet clean? You'll sit at the table, won't you,

Sarah? I don't know much about zombies, do zombies eat at the table?" "Sarah's sitting next to me," said Granny, and she grinned again, and her whole face lit up, she really had quite a nice face after all. And everyone cheered up at that, and it was a happy dinner, even though Granny didn't think the turkey was the best cut, and that the vegetables had been overcooked. Sarah coated her turkey with gravy, and with cranberry sauce, she even crushed then smeared peas into it just to give the meat a bit more juice—it was light and buttery, she knew, it looked so good on the fork, but no sooner had it passed her lips than the food seemed stale and ashen. "Would you pull my cracker, Sarah?" asked Granny brightly, and Sarah didn't want to, it was hard enough to grip the cutlery with those flaking hands. "Come on, Sarah," laughed Daddy, and so Sarah put down her knife and fork, and fumbled for the end of Granny's cracker, and hoped that when she pulled nothing terrible would happen—she'd got it into her head that her arm was hanging by a thread, just one firm yank and it'd come off. But it didn't—*bang!* went the cracker, Granny had won, she liked that, and she read out the joke, and everyone said they found it funny, and she even put on her paper hat. "I feel like the belle of the ball!" she said. "Dear me, I *am* enjoying myself!"

. . . . .

After dinner Granny and Sarah settled down on the sofa to watch the Bond movie. Mummy said she'd do the washing up, and as she needed to clean the carpet too, she might be quite a while. And Daddy volunteered to help her, he said he'd seen this Bond already. Graham wanted to pee, so they'd let him out into the garden. So it was just Granny and Sarah sitting there, just the two of them, together. "I miss Arthur," Granny said during the title sequence. "Sonia tells me I need to get over it, but what does Sonia know about love?" Sarah had nothing to say to that. Sitting on the sofa was hard for her, she was top heavy and lolled to one side. She found though that she was able to reach for the buckle on her suit. She played with it, but her fingers were too thick, she couldn't get purchase. The first time Bond snogged a woman Granny reached for Sarah's hand. Sarah couldn't be sure whether it was Granny's hand or her own that felt so leathery. "Do you know how I met Arthur?" asked Granny. Sitting in her slumped position, Sarah could feel something metal jab into her, and realized it must be the necklace that Mummy had given her. It was buried somewhere underneath all this dead male flesh. "Arthur was already married. Did you know that? Does it shock you? But I just looked at him, and said to myself, I'm having that." And there was a funny smell too, thought Sarah, and she supposed that probably *was* her. James Bond got himself into some scrapes, and then got out of them again using quips and extreme violence. Granny hadn't let go of Sarah's hand. "You know what love is? It's being prepared to let go of who you are. To change yourself entirely. Just for someone else's pleasure." The necklace was really rather sharp, but Sarah didn't mind, it felt *real*, and she tried to shift her body so it would cut into her all the more. Perhaps it would cut through the layers of skin on top of it, perhaps it would come poking out, and show that Sarah was hiding underneath! "Before I met him, Arthur was a husband. And a father. For me, he became a nothing. A nothing." With her free hand Sarah tried at the buckle again, this time there was a panic to it, she dug in her nails but only succeeded in tearing a couple off altogether. And she knew what that smell was, Sarah had thought it had been rotting, but it wasn't, it was old cigarette smoke. Daddy came in from the kitchen. "You two lovebirds getting along?" he said. And maybe even winked. James Bond made a joke about re-entry, and at that Granny gripped Sarah's hand so tightly that she thought it'd leave an imprint for sure. "I usually get what I want," Granny breathed. Sarah stole a look out of the window. In the frosted garden Graham had clubbed down a bird, and was now playing with its body. He'd throw it up into the air and catch it between his teeth. But he looked undecided too, as if he were wondering whether eating it might be taking things too far.

. . . . .

Graham had tired of the werewolf suit before his bedtime. He'd undone the belt all by himself, and left the suit in a pile on the floor. "I want a vampire!" he said. "Or a zombie!" Mummy and Daddy told him that maybe he could have another monster next Christmas, or on his birthday maybe. That wasn't good enough, and it wasn't until they suggested there might be discounted monsters in the January sales that he cheered up. He could be patient, he was a big boy. After he'd gone to bed, Granny said she wanted to turn in as well—it had been such a long day. "And thank you," she said, and looked at Sarah. "It's remarkable." Daddy said that she'd now understand why he'd asked for all those photographs; to get the resemblance just right there had been lots of special modifications, it hadn't been cheap, but he hoped it was a nice present? "The best I've ever had," said Granny. "And here's a little something for both of you." And she took out a check, scribbled a few zeroes on to it, and handed it over. She hoped this might see them through the recession. "And merry Christmas!" she said gaily.

. . . . .

Granny stripped naked, and got into her nightie—but not so fast that Sarah wasn't able to take a good look at the full reality of her. She didn't think Granny's skin was very much different to the one she was wearing, the same lumps and bumps and peculiar crevasses, the same scratch marks and mottled specks. Hers was just slightly fresher. And as if Granny could read Sarah's mind, she told her to be a good boy and sit at the dressing table. "Just a little touch up," she said. "Nothing effeminate about it. Just to make you a little more you." She smeared a little rouge on to the cheeks, a dash of lipstick, mascara. "Can't do much with the eyeballs," Granny mused, "but I'll never know in the dark." And the preparations weren't just for Sarah. Granny sprayed behind both her ears from her new perfume bottle. "Just for you, darling," she said. "Your beautiful little gift." Sarah gestured towards the door, and Granny looked puzzled, then brightened. "Yes, you go and take a tinkle. I'll be waiting, my sweet." But Sarah had nothing to tinkle, had she, didn't Granny realize there was no liquid inside her, didn't she realize she was composed of dust? Sarah lurched past the toilet, and downstairs to the sitting room where her parents were watching the repeat of the Queen's speech. They started when she came in. Both looked a little guilty. Sarah tried to find the words she wanted, and then how to say them at all, her tongue lay cold in her mouth. "Why me?" she managed finally.

· · · · ·

Daddy said, "I loved him. He was a good man, he was a kind man." Mummy looked away altogether. Daddy went on, "You do see why it couldn't have been Graham, don't you? Why it had to be you?" And had Sarah been a werewolf like her brother, she might at that moment have torn out their throats, or clubbed them down with her paws. But she was a dead man, and a dead man who'd been good and kind. So she nodded briefly, then shuffled her way slowly back upstairs.

· · · · ·

"Hold me," said Granny. Sarah didn't know how to, didn't know where to put her arms or her legs. She tried her best, but it was all such a tangle. Granny and Sarah lay side by side for a long time in the dark. Sarah tried to feel the necklace under her skin, but she couldn't, it had gone. That little symbol of whatever femininity she'd had was gone. She wondered if Granny was asleep. But then Granny said, "If only it were real. But it's not real. You're not real." She stroked Sarah's face. "Oh, my love," she whispered. "Oh, my poor dead love."

· · · · ·

And something between Sarah's legs twitched. Something that had long rotted came to life, and slowly, weakly, struggled to attention. You're not real, Granny was still saying, and now she was crying, and Sarah thought of how Granny had looked that day at the funeral, her face all soggy and out of shape, and she felt a stab of pity for her—and that was *it*, the pity was the jolt it needed, there was something liquid in this body after all. "You're not real," Granny said. "I am real," he said, and he lent across, and kissed her on the lips. And the lips beneath his weren't dry, they were plump, they were moist, and now he was chewing at her face, and she was chewing right back, like they wanted to eat each other, like they were so hungry they could just eat each other alive. Sharon Weekes was wrong, it was a stray thought that flashed through his mind, Sharon Weekes didn't know the half of it. This is what it's like, this is like kissing, this is like kissing a boy.

Amerikanski Dead at the Moscow Morgue
or:
Children of Marx and Coca Cola

Kim Newman

Kim Newman is a novelist, critic and broadcaster. His books include *The Night Mayor*, *Bad Dreams*, *Jago*, the Anno Dracula novels, *The Quorum*, *The Original Dr. Shade and Other Stories*, *Famous Monsters*, *Seven Stars*, *Unforgivable Stories*, *Dead Travel Fast*, *Life's Lottery*, *Back in the USSA* (with Eugene Byrne), *Where the Bodies Are Buried*, *Doctor Who: Time and Relative*, *The Man From the Diogenes Club*, *Secret Files of the Diogenes Club*, and *Mysteries of the Diogenes Club* under his own name, and *The Vampire Genevieve* and *Orgy of the Blood Parasites* as Jack Yeovil.

Among his nonfiction works are *Nightmare Movies* (recently extensively revised), *Ghastly Beyond Belief* (with Neil Gaiman), *Horror: 100 Best Books* (with Stephen Jones), *Wild West Movies*, *The BFI Companion to Horror*, *Millennium Movies*, and BFI Classics studies of *Cat People* and *Doctor Who*.

He has written and broadcast widely on a range of topics, scripting radio documentaries about Val Lewton and role-playing games, and TV programs about movie heroes and Sherlock Holmes. His short story, "Week Woman," was adapted for the Showtime Network series *The Hunger*, and he has directed and written a tiny short film, *Missing Girl*.

Newman has won the Bram Stoker Award, the International Horror Critics Award, the British Science Fiction Award and the British Fantasy Award.

"Once, long ago and far away," recalls the author, "John Skipp and Craig Spector edited an anthology called *Book of the Dead* of mostly fine stories set more-or-less in the world of George A. Romero's Living Dead films. It was so well-received that the editors produced a further volume, *Still Dead*. Then, remembering that there were three Romero Dead movies, they set out to do a third volume, which may well have been called *Deader Than Ever* or *Deadest Yet*.

"Since, in my other life as a movie critic, I had written extensively about Romero in my book *Nightmare Movies*, I was pleased to be asked by John to come up with something for this third volume. I did a little rewriting at Craig's suggestion, got paid (as I remember it) and waited for the story to appear.

"Years passed. I'm not really privy to what happened, but various publishers and editors fell out with each other and, though the third Dead book nearly happened at least twice (I once received page proofs of the story) it never managed to stumble into print. If you've been picking up recent anthologies of original horror stories, you've already read quite a few ship-jumping tales from the collection (Douglas E. Winter's wonderful 'The Zombies of Madison County' is one). For a while, 'Amerikanski Dead' was due to come out as a chapbook—but that never quite happened either. Then, with the bogus millennium looming, I was asked by Al Sarrantonio if I had anything he might look at for what was then called *999: The Last Horror Anthology*, intended to be one of those genre-summing, *uber*-collection doorstops that the field needs every so often to stay alive. I dug out this, and it wound up as the lead-off story in the somewhat more modestly-titled *999: New Stories of Horror and Suspense*. For that appearance, the story lost its subtitle (a quote from Jean-Luc Godard) to keep the list of contents tidy, but I'm restoring it here.

"Though the rising of the dead is supposed to be a global phenomenon, Romero's original trilogy—*Night of the Living Dead* (1968), *Dawn of the Dead* (1979), and *Day of the Dead* (1984)—are all about America. One or two of the stories in the Dead collections are about foreign parts (Poppy Z. Brite's 'Calcutta, Lord of Nerves') and Clive Barker was connected with a comic book spin-off that had dead folks (including the Royal Family) in London. But Romero's films belong now to the era of the superpower face-off, and I thought it would be interesting to see what might be happening in the then–Soviet Union during the time between *Dawn* and *Day* and, more importantly, what it might *mean*. The title is a riff on *The Living Dead at the Manchester Morgue*, the British-release title of the Spanish-Italian movie *No profanar el sueño de los muertos* (1974)—known in America as *Don't Open the Window* or *Let Sleeping Corpses Lie* (rarely has one film had so many great titles).

"The business about reconstructing faces from skulls is mentioned in Martin Cruz Smith's *Gorky Park*, but I remembered it from a 1960s BBC science documentary (*Tomorrow's World*?) in which the skull of Ivan the Terrible was used as a template to recreate his head. For Rasputin details, I drew on Robert K. Massie's *Nicholas and Alexandra*, Sir David Napley's *Rasputin in Hollywood* and various unreliable movie and TV performances by whiskery scenery-chewers like Lionel Barrymore, Boris Karloff, Tom Baker and Christopher Lee."

AT THE RAILWAY STATION IN BORODINO, Yevgeny Chirkov was separated from his unit. As the locomotive slowed, he hopped from their carriage to the platform, under orders to secure, at any price, cigarettes and chocolate. Another unknown crisis intervened and the steam-driven antique never truly stopped. Tripping over his rifle, he was unable to reach the outstretched hands of his comrades. The rest of the unit, jammed half-way through windows or hanging out of doors, laughed and waved. A jet of steam from a train passing the other way put salt on his tail and he dodged, tripping again. Sergeant Trauberg found the pratfall hilarious, forgetting he had pressed a thousand roubles on the private. Chirkov ran and ran but the locomotive gained speed. When he emerged from the canopied platform, seconds after the last carriage, white sky poured down. Looking at the black-shingled track-bed, he saw a flattened outline in what had once been a uniform, wrists and ankles wired together, neck against a gleaming rail, head long gone under sharp wheels. The method, known as "making sleepers," was favored along railway lines. Away from stations, twenty or thirty were dealt with at one time. Without heads, Amerikans did no harm.

Legs boiled from steam, face and hands frozen from winter, he wandered through the station. The cavernous space was sub-divided by sandbags. Families huddled like pioneers expecting an attack by Red Indians, luggage drawn about in a circle, last bullets saved for women and children. Chirkov spat mentally; Amerika had invaded his imagination, just as his political officers warned. Some refugees were coming from Moscow, others fleeing to the city. There was no rule. A wall-sized poster of the New First Secretary was disfigured with a blotch, red gone to black. The splash of dried blood suggested something had been finished against the wall. There were Amerikans in Borodino. Seventy miles from Moscow, the station was a museum to resisted invasions. Plaques, statues and paintings honored the victories of 1812 and 1944. A poster listed those local officials executed after being implicated in the latest counter-revolution. The air was tangy with ash, a reminder of past scorched earth policies. There were big fires nearby. An army unit was on duty, but no one knew anything about a timetable. An officer told him to queue and wait. More trains were coming from Moscow than going to, which meant the capital would eventually have none left.

He ventured out of the station. The snow cleared from the forecourt was banked a dozen yards away. Sunlight glared off muddy white. It was colder and brighter than he was used to in the Ukraine. A trio of Chinese-featured soldiers, a continent away from home, offered to share cigarettes and tried to practice Russian on him. He understood they were from Amgu; from the highest point in that port, you could see Japan. He asked if they knew where he could find an official. As they chirruped among themselves in an alien tongue, Chirkov saw his first Amerikan. Emerging from between snowbanks and limping towards the guard-post, the dead man looked as if he might actually be an American. Barefoot, he waded spastically through slush, jeans-legs shredded over thin shins. His shirt was a bright picture of a parrot in a jungle. Sunglasses hung round his neck on a thin string. Chirkov made the Amerikan's presence known to the guards. Fascinated, he watched the dead man walk. With every step, the Amerikan crackled: there were deep, ice-threaded rifts in his skin. He was slow and brittle and blind, crystal eyes frozen open, arms stiff by his sides.

Cautiously, the Corporal circled round and rammed his rifle-butt into a knee. The guards were under orders not to waste ammunition; there was a shortage. Bone cracked and the Amerikan went down like a devotee before an icon. The Corporal prodded a colorful back with his boot-toe and pushed the Amerikan on to his face. As he wriggled, ice-shards worked through his flesh. Chirkov had assumed the dead would stink but this one was frozen and odorless. The skin was pink and unperished, the rips in it red and glittery. An arm reached out for the corporal and something snapped in the shoulder. The corporal's boot pinned the Amerikan to the concrete. One of his comrades produced a foot-long spike and worked the point into the back of the dead man's skull. Scalp flaked around the dimple. The other guard took an iron mallet from his belt and struck a professional blow.

It was important, apparently, that the spike should entirely transfix the skull and break ground, binding the dead to the earth, allowing the last of the spirit to leave the carcass. Not official knowledge: this was something every soldier was told at some point by a comrade. Always, the tale-teller was from Moldavia or had learned from someone who was. Moldavians claimed to be used to the dead. The Amerikan's head came apart like a rock split along fault lines. Five solid chunks rolled away from the spike. Diamond-sparkles of ice glinted in reddish-grey inner surfaces. The thing stopped moving at once. The hammerer began to unbutton the gaudy shirt and detach it from the sunken chest, careful as a butcher skinning a horse. The jeans were too deeply melded with meat to remove, which was a shame; with the ragged legs cut away, they would have made fine shorts for a pretty girl at the beach. The Corporal wanted Chirkov to have the sunglasses. One lens was gone or he might not have been so generous with a stranger. In the end, Chirkov accepted out of courtesy, resolving to throw away the trophy as soon as he was out of Borodino.

. . . . .

Three days later, when Chirkov reached Moscow, locating his unit was not possible. A dispatcher at the central station thought his comrades might have been reassigned to Orekhovo Zuyevo, but her superior was of the opinion the unit had been disbanded nine months earlier. Because the dispatcher was not disposed to contradict an eminent Party member, Chirkov was forced to accept the ruling that he was without a unit. As such, he was detailed to the Spa. They had in a permanent request for personnel and always took precedence. The posting involved light guard duties and manual labor; there was little fight left in Amerikans who ended up at the Spa. The dispatcher gave Chirkov a sheaf of papers the size of a Frenchman's sandwich and complicated travel directions. By then, the rest of the queue was getting testy and he was obliged to venture out on his own. He remembered to fix his mobility permit, a blue luggage-tag with a smudged stamp, on the outside of his uniform. Technically, failure to display the permit was punishable by summary execution.

Streetcars ran intermittently; after waiting an hour in the street outside central station, he decided to walk to the Spa. It was a question of negotiating dunes of uncleared snow and straggles of undisciplined queue. Teams of firemen dug methodically through depths of snow, side-by-side with teams of soldiers who were burning down buildings. Areas were cleared and raked, ground still warm enough to melt snow that drifted onto it. Everywhere, posters warned of the Amerikans. The Party line was still that the United States was responsible. It was air-carried biological warfare, the Ministry announced with authority, originated by a secret laboratory and disseminated in the Soviet Union by suicidal infectees posing as tourists. The germ galvanized the nervous systems of the recently-deceased, triggering the lizard stems of their brains, inculcating in the Amerikans a disgusting hunger for human meat. The "news" footage the Voice of America put out of their own dead was staged and doctored, footage from the sadistic motion pictures that were a symptom of the West's utter decadence. But everyone had a different line: it was . . . creeping radiation from Chernobyl . . . a judgement from a bitter and long-ignored God . . . a project Stalin abandoned during the Great Patriotic War . . . brought back from Novy Mir by cosmonauts . . . a plot by the fomenters of the Counter-Revolution . . . a curse the Moldavians had always known.

Fortunately, the Spa was off Red Square. Even a Ukrainian sapling like Yevgeny Chirkov had an idea how to get to Red Square. He had carried his rifle for so long that the strap had worn through his epaulette. He imagined the outline of the buckle was stamped into his collarbone. His single round of ammunition was in his inside breast pocket, wrapped in newspaper. They said Moscow was the most exciting city in the world, but it was not at its best under twin siege from winter and the Amerikans. Helicopters swooped overhead, broadcasting official warnings and announcements: comrades were advised to stay at their workplaces and continue with their duly-delegated tasks; victory in the struggle against the American octopus was inevitable; the crisis was nearly at an end and the master strategists would soon announce a devastating counter-attack; the dead were to be disabled and placed in the proper collection points; another exposed pocket of traitors would go on trial tomorrow.

In an onion-domed church, soldiers dealt with Amerikans. Brought in covered lorries, the shuffling dead were shifted inside in ragged coffles. As Chirkov passed, a dead woman, bear-like in a fur coat over forbidden undergarments, broke the line. Soldiers efficiently cornered her and stuck a bayonet into her head. The remains were hauled into the church. When the building was full, it would be burned: an offering. In Red Square, loudspeakers shouted martial music at the queues. John Reed at the Barricades. Lenin's tomb was no longer open for tourists. Sergeant Trauberg was fond of telling the story about what had happened in the tomb when the Amerikans started to rise. Everyone guessed it was true. The Spa was off the Square. Before the Revolution of 1918, it had been an exclusive health club for the Royal Family. Now it was a morgue.

. . . . .

He presented his papers to a thin officer he met on the broad steps of the Spa, and stood frozen in stiff-backed salute while the man looked over the wedge of documentation. He was told to wander inside smartly and look out Lyubachevsky. The officer proceeded, step by step, down to the square. Under the dusting of snow, the stone steps were gilded with ice: a natural defense. Chirkov understood Amerikans were forever slipping and falling on ice; many were so damaged they couldn't regain their footing, and were consequently easy to deal with. The doors of the Spa, three times a man's height, were pocked with bullet-holes new and old. Unlocked and unoiled, they creaked alarmingly as he pushed inside. The foyer boasted marble floors, and ceilings painted with classical scenes of romping nymphs and athletes. Busts of Marx and Lenin flanked the main staircase; a portrait of the New First Secretary, significantly less faded than neighboring pictures, was proudly displayed behind the main desk.

A civilian he took to be Lyubachevsky squatted by the desk reading a pamphlet. A half-empty vodka bottle was nestled like a baby in the crook of his arm. He looked up awkwardly at the new arrival and explained that last week all the chairs in the building had been taken away by the Health Committee. Chirkov presented papers and admitted he had been sent by the dispatcher at the railway station, which elicited a shrug. The civilian mused that the central station was always sending stray soldiers for an unknown reason. Lyubachevsky had three days' of stubble and mismatched eyes. He offered Chirkov a swallow of vodka—pure and strong, not diluted with melted snow like the rat poison he had been sold in Borodino—and opened up the lump of papers, searching for a particular signature. In the end, he decided it best Chirkov stay at the Spa. Unlocking a cabinet, he found a long white coat, muddied at the bottom. Chirkov was reluctant to exchange his heavy greatcoat for the flimsy garment but Lyubachevsky assured him there was very little pilferage from the Spa. People, even parasites, tended to avoid visiting the place unless there was a pressing reason for their presence. Before relinquishing his coat, Chirkov remembered to retain his mobility permit, pinning it to the breast of the laboratory coat. After taking Chirkov's rifle, complimenting him on its cleanliness and stowing it in the cabinet, Lyubachevsky issued him with a revolver. It was dusty and the metal was cold enough to stick to his skin. Breaking the gun open, Chirkov noted three cartridges. In Russian roulette, he would have an even chance. Without a holster, he dropped it into the pocket of his coat; the barrel poked out of a torn corner. He had to sign for the weapon.

Lyubachevsky told him to go down into the Pool and report to Director Kozintsev. Chirkov descended in a hand-cranked cage lift and stepped out into a ballroom-sized space. The Pool was what people who worked in the Spa called the basement where the dead were kept. It had been a swimming bath before the Revolution; there, weary generations of Romanovs had plunged through slow waters, the tides of history slowly pulling them under. Supposedly dry since 1916, the Pool was so cold that condensation on the marble floors turned to ice-patches. The outer walls were still decorated with gilted plaster friezes and his bootfalls echoed on the solid floors. He walked round the edge of the pit, looking down at the white-coated toilers and their unmoving clients. The Pool was divided into separate work cubicles and narrow corridors by flimsy wooden partitions that rose above the old water level. A girl caught his eye, blonde hair tightly gathered at the back of her neck. She had red lipstick and her coat sleeves were rolled up on slender arms as she probed the chest cavity of a corpse, a girl who might once have been her slightly older sister. The dead girl had a neat, round hole in her forehead and her hair was fanned over a sludgy discharge Chirkov took to be abandoned brains. He coughed to get the live girl's attention and inquired as to where he could find the Director. She told him to make his way to the Deep End and climb in, then penetrate the warren of partitions. He couldn't miss Kozintsev; the Director was dead center.

At the Deep End, he found a ladder into the pool. It was guarded by a soldier who sat cross-legged, a revolver in his lap, twanging on a jew's harp. He stopped and told Chirkov the tune was a traditional American folk song about a cowboy killed by a lawyer, "The Man Who Shot Liberty Valance." The guard introduced himself as Corporal Tulbeyev and asked if Chirkov was interested in purchasing tape cassettes of the music of Mr. Edward Cochran or Robert Dylan. Chirkov had no cassette player but Tulbeyev said that for five thousand roubles he could secure one. To be polite, Chirkov said he would consider the acquisition: evidently a great bargain. Tulbeyev further insinuated he could supply other requisites: contraceptive sheaths, chocolate bars, toothpaste, fresh socks, scented soap, suppressed reading matter. Every unit in the Soviet Union had a Tulbeyev, Chirkov knew. There was probably a secretary on the First Committee of the Communist Party who dealt disco records and mint-flavored chewing gum to the High and Mighty. After a decent period of mourning, Chirkov might consider spending some of Sergeant Trauberg's roubles on underwear and soap.

Having clambered into the Pool, Chirkov lost the perspective on the layout of the work-spaces he had from above. It was a labyrinth and he zigzagged between partitions, asking directions from the occasional absorbed forensic worker. Typically, a shrug would prompt him to a new pathway. Each of the specialists was absorbed in dissection, wielding whiny and smoky saws or sharp and shiny scalpels. He passed by the girl he had seen from above—her name-tag identified her as Technician Sverdlova, and she introduced herself as Valentina—and found she had entirely exposed the rib-cage of her corpse. She was the epitome of sophisticated Moscow girl, Chirkov thought: imperturbable and immaculate even with human remains streaked up to her elbows. A straggle of hair whisped across her face, and she blew it out of the way. She dictated notes into a wire recorder, commenting on certain physiological anomalies of the dead girl. There was a rubbery resilience in the undecayed muscle tissue. He would have liked to stay, but had to report to Kozintsev. Bidding her goodbye, he left her cubicle, thumping a boot against a tin bucket full of watches, wedding-rings and eyeglasses. She said he could take anything he wanted but he declined. Remembering, he found the bent and broken sunglasses in his trousers pocket and added them to the contents of the bucket. It was like throwing a kopeck into a wishing-well, so he made a wish. As if she were telepathic, Valentina giggled. Blushing, Chirkov continued.

. . . . .

He finally came to a makeshift door with a plaque that read V. A. KOZINTSEV, DIRECTOR. Chirkov knocked and, hearing a grunt from beyond, pushed through. It was as if he had left the morgue for a sculptor's studio. On one table were moist bags of variously colored clays, lined up next to a steaming samovar. In the center of the space, in the light cast by a chandelier that hung over the whole Pool, a man in a smock worked on a bust of a bald-headed man. Kozintsev had a neatly-trimmed beard and round spectacles. He was working one-handed; long fingers delicately pressing hollows into cheeks; a glass of tea in his other hand. He stood back, gulped tea and tutted, extremely dissatisfied with his efforts. Instantly accepting the newcomer, Kozintsev asked Chirkov for help in going back to the beginning. He set his glass down and rolled up his sleeves. They both put their hands in the soft face and pulled. Clays came away in self-contained lumps: some stranded like muscles, others bunched like pockets of fat. A bare skull, blotched with clay, was revealed. Glass eyes stared hypnotically, wedged into sockets with twists of newspaper. Chirkov realized he had heard of the Director: V. A. Kozintsev was one of leading reconstruction pathologists in the Soviet Union. He had, layering in musculature and covering the results with skin, worked on the skulls tentatively identified as those of the Former Royal Family. He had recreated the heads of Paleolithic men, murder victims and Ivan the Terrible.

Chirkov reported for duty and the Director told him to find something useful to do. Kozintsev was depressed to lose three days' work and explained in technical detail that the skull wasn't enough. There had to be some indication of the disposition of muscle and flesh. As he talked, he rolled a cigarette and stuck it in the corner of his mouth, patting his smock pockets for matches. Chirkov understood this was one of Kozintsev's historical projects: high profile work sanctioned by the Ministry of Culture, unconnected to the main purpose of the Spa—which, just now, was to determine the origins and capabilities of the Amerikans—but useful in attracting attention and funds. While the Director looked over charts of facial anatomy, puffing furiously on his cigarette, Chirkov picked up the discarded clays and piled them on the table. On a separate stand was a wigmaker's dummy head under a glass dome: it wore a long but neat black wig and facsimile wisps of eyebrows, moustache and beard. Once the skull was covered and painted to the correct skin tone, hair would be applied. He asked Kozintsev to whom the skull belonged, and, off-handedly, the Director told him it was Grigory Rasputin. There had been trouble getting glass eyes with the right quality. Contemporary memoirs described the originals as steely blue, with pupils that contracted to pinpoints when their owner was concentrating on exerting his influence. Chirkov looked again at the skull and couldn't see anything special. It was just bare bone.

. . . . .

Each evening at nine, the Director presided over meetings. Attendance was mandatory for the entire staff, down to Chirkov. He was billeted in the Spa itself, in a small room on the top floor where he slept on what had once been a masseur's table. Since food was provided (albeit irregularly) by a cafeteria, there was scarce reason to venture outside. At meetings, Chirkov learned who everyone was: the ranking officer was Captain Zharov, who would rather be out in the streets fighting but suffered from a gimpy knee; under Kozintsev, the chief coroner was Dr. Fyodor Dudnikov, a famous forensic scientist often consulted by the police in political murder cases but plainly out of his depth with the Spa's recent change of purpose. The Director affected a lofty disinterest in the current emergency, which left the morgue actually to be run by a conspiracy between Lyubachevsky, an administrator seconded from the Ministry of Agriculture, and Tulbeyev, who was far more capable than Captain Zharov of keeping greased the wheels of the military machine.

Chirkov's girl Valentina turned out to be very eminent for her years, a specialist in the study of Amerikans; at each meeting, she reported the findings of the day. Her discoveries were frankly incomprehensible, even to her colleagues, but she seemed to believe the Amerikans were not simple reanimated dead bodies. Her dissections and probings demonstrated that the Amerikans functioned in many ways like living beings; in particular, their musculature adapted slowly to their new state even as surplus flesh and skin sloughed off. Those portions of their bodies that rotted away were irrelevant to the functioning of the creatures. She likened the ungainly and stumbling dead creatures to a pupal stage, and expressed a belief that the Amerikans were becoming stronger. Her argument was that they should be categorized not as former human beings but as an entirely new species, with its own strengths and capabilities. At every meeting, Valentina complained she could only manage so much by examining doubly-dead bodies and that the best hope of making progress would be to secure "live" specimens and observe their natural progress. She had sketched her impressions of what the Amerikans would eventually evolve into: thickly-muscled skeletons like old anatomical drawings.

Valentina's leading rival, A. Tarkhanov, countered that her theories were a blind alley. In his opinion, the Spa should concentrate on the isolation of the bacteriological agent responsible for the reanimations, with a view to the development of a serum cure. Tarkhanov, a Party member, also insisted the phenomenon had been created artificially by American genetic engineers. He complained the monster-makers of the United States were so heavily financed by capitalist cartels that this state-backed bureaucracy could hardly compete. The one common ground Valentina held with Tarkhanov was that the Spa was desperately under-funded. Since everyone at the meetings had to sit on the floor, while Director Kozintsev was elevated cross-legged on a desk, the procurement of chairs was deemed a priority, though all the scientists also had long lists of medical supplies and instruments without which they could not continue their vital researches. Lyubachevsky always countered these complaints by detailing his repeated requests to appropriate departments, often with precise accounts of the elapsed time since the request had been submitted. At Chirkov's third meeting, there was much excitement when Lyubachevsky announced that the Spa had received from the Civil Defense Committee fifty-five child-sized blankets.

This was unrelated to any request that had been put in, but Tulbeyev offered to arrange a trade with the Children's Hospital, exchanging the blankets for either vegetables or medical instruments.

At the same meeting, Captain Zharov reported that his men had successfully dealt with an attempted invasion. Two Amerikans had been found at dawn, having negotiated the slippery steps, standing outside the main doors, apparently waiting. One stood exactly outside the doors, the other a step down. They might have been forming a primitive queue. Zharov personally disposed of them both, expending cartridges into their skulls, and arranged for the removal of the remains to a collection point, from which they might well be returned as specimens. Valentina moaned that it would have been better to capture and pen the Amerikans in a secure area—she specified the former steam bath—where they could be observed. Zharov cited standing orders. Kozintsev concluded with a lengthy lecture on Rasputin, elaborating his own theory that the late Tsarina's spiritual adviser was less mad than popularly supposed and that his influence with the Royal Family was ultimately instrumental in bringing about the Revolution. He spoke with especial interest and enthusiasm of the so-called Mad Monk's powers of healing, the famously ameliorative hands that could ease the symptoms of the Tsarevich's haemophilia. It was his contention that Rasputin had been possessed of a genuine paranormal talent. Even Chirkov thought this beside the point, especially when the Director wound down by admitting another failure in his reconstruction project.

. . . . . .

With Tulbeyev, he drew last guard of the night; on duty at 3:00 a.m., expected to remain at the post in the foyer until the nine o'clock relief. Captain Zharov and Lyubachevsky could not decide whether Chirkov counted as a soldier or an experimental assistant; so he found himself called on to fulfil both functions, occasionally simultaneously. As a soldier, he would be able to sleep away the morning after night duty, but as an experimental assistant, he was required to report to Director Kozintsev at nine sharp. Chirkov didn't mind overmuch; once you got used to corpses, the Spa was a cushy detail. At least corpses here *were* corpses. Although, for personal reasons, he always voted, along with two other scientists and a cook, in support of Technician Sverdlova's request to bring in Amerikans, he was privately grateful she always lost by a wide margin. No matter how secure the steam bath might be, Chirkov was not enthused by the idea of Amerikans inside the building. Tulbeyev, whose grandmother was Moldavian, told stories of *wurdalaks* and *vryolakas* and always had new anecdotes. In life, according to Tulbeyev, Amerikans had all been Party members: that was why so many had good clothes and consumer goods. The latest craze among the dead was for cassette players with attached headphones; not American manufacture, but Japanese. Tulbeyev had a collection of the contraptions, harvested from Amerikans whose heads were so messed up that soldiers were squeamish about borrowing from them. It was a shame, said Tulbeyev, that the dead were disinclined to cart video players on their backs. If they picked up that habit, everyone in the Spa would be a millionaire; not a rouble millionaire, a dollar millionaire. Many of the dead had foreign currency. Tarkhanov's pet theory was that the Americans impregnated money with a bacteriological agent, the condition spreading through contact with cash. Tulbeyev, who always wore gloves, did not seem unduly disturbed by the thought.

Just as Tulbeyev was elaborating upon the empire he could build with a plague of video-players, a knock came at the doors. Not a sustained pounding like someone petitioning for entry, but a thud as if something had accidentally been bumped against the other side of the oak. They both shut up and listened. One of Tulbeyev's tape machines was playing Creedence Clearwater Revival's "It Came Out of the Sky" at a variable speed; he turned off the tape, which scrunched inside the machine as the wheels ground, and swore. Cassettes were harder to come by than players. There was a four-thirty-in-the-morning Moscow quiet. Lots of little noises; wind whining round the slightly-warped door, someone having a coughing-fit many floors above, distant shots. Chirkov cocked his revolver, hoping there was a round under the hammer, further hoping the round wasn't a dud. There was another knock, like the first. Not purposeful, just a blunder. Tulbeyev ordered Chirkov to take a look through the spy-hole. The brass cap was stiff but he managed to work it aside and look through the glass lens.

A dead face was close to the spy-hole. For the first time, it occurred to Chirkov that Amerikans were scary. In the dark, this one had empty eye-sockets and a constantly-chewing mouth. Around its ragged neck were hung several cameras and a knotted scarf with a naked woman painted on it. Chirkov told Tulbeyev, who showed interest at the mention of photographic equipment and crammed around the spy-hole. He proposed that they open the doors and Chirkov put a bullet into the Amerikan's head. With cameras, Tulbeyev was certain he could secure chairs. With chairs, they would be the heroes of the Spa, entitled to untold privileges. Unsure of his courage, Chirkov agreed to the scheme and Tulbeyev struggled with the several bolts. Finally, the doors were loose, held shut only by Tulbeyev's fists on the handles. Chirkov nodded; his comrade pulled the doors open and stood back. Chirkov advanced, pistol held out and pointed at the Amerikan's forehead.

The dead man was not alone. Tulbeyev cursed and ran for his rifle. Chirkov did not fire, just looked from one dead face to the others. Four were lined in a crocodile, each on a different step. One wore an officer's uniform, complete with medals;

another, a woman, had a severe pinstripe suit and a rakish gangster hat; at the back of the queue was a dead child, a golden-haired, green-faced girl in a baseball cap, trailing a doll. None moved much. Tulbeyev returned, levering a cartridge into the breech, and skidded on the marble floor as he brought his rifle to bear. Taken aback by the apparently unthreatening dead, he didn't fire either. Cold wind wafted in, which explained Chirkov's chill. His understanding was that Amerikans always attacked; these stood as if dozing upright, swaying slightly. The little girl's eyes moved mechanically back and forth. Chirkov told Tulbeyev to fetch a scientist, preferably Valentina. As his comrade scurried upstairs, he remembered he had only three rounds to deal with four Amerikans. He retreated into the doorway, eyes fixed on the dead, and slammed shut the doors. With the heel of his fist, he rammed a couple of the bolts home. Looking through the spy-hole, he saw nothing had changed. The dead still queued.

Valentina wore a floor-length dressing-gown over cotton pajamas. Her bare feet must be frozen on the marble. Tulbeyev had explained about the night visitors and she was reminding him of Captain Zharov's report. These Amerikans repeated what the Captain had observed: the queuing behavior pattern. She brushed her hair out of the way and got an eye to the spy-hole. With an odd squeal of delight, she summoned Chirkov to take a look, telling him to angle his eye so he could look beyond the queue. A figure struggled out of the dark, feet flapping like beached fish. It went down on its face and crawled up the steps, then stood. It took a place behind the little girl. This one was naked, so rotted that even its sex was lost, a skeleton held together by strips of muscle that looked like wet leather. Valentina said she wanted that Amerikan for observation, but one of the others was necessary as well. She still thought of capturing and observing specimens. Tulbeyev reminded her of the strangeness of the situation and asked why the dead were just standing in line, stretching down the steps away from the Spa. She said something about residual instinct, the time a citizen must spend in queues, the dead's inbuilt need to mimic the living, to recreate from trace memories the lives they had once had. Tulbeyev agreed to help her capture the specimens but insisted they be careful not to damage the cameras. He told her they could all be millionaires.

Valentina held Tulbeyev's rifle as a soldier would, stock close to her cheek, barrel straight. She stood by the doorway covering them as they ventured out on her mission. Tulbeyev assigned himself to the first in the queue, the dead man with the cameras. That left Chirkov to deal with the walking skeleton, even if it was last in line and, in Moscow, queue-jumping was considered a worse crime than matricide. From somewhere, Tulbeyev had found a supply of canvas post-bags. The idea was to pop a bag over an Amerikan's head like a hood, then lead the dead thing indoors. Tulbeyev managed with one deft maneuver to drop his bag over the photographer's head, and whipped round behind the Amerikan, unraveling twine from a ball. As Tulbeyev bound dead wrists together, the twine cut through grey skin and greenish-red fluid leaked over his gloves. The rest of the queue stood impassive, ignoring the treatment the photographer was getting. When Tulbeyev had wrestled his catch inside and trussed him like a pig, Chirkov was ready to go for the skeleton.

He stepped lightly down to the skeleton's level, post-bag open as if he were a poacher after rabbit. The Amerikans all swiveled their eyes as he passed and, with a testicles-retracting spasm of panic, he missed his footing. His boot slipped on icy stone and he fell badly, his hip slamming a hard edge. He sledged down the steps, yelping as he went. A shot cracked and the little girl, who had stepped out of the queue and scrambled towards him, became a limp doll, a chunk of her head dryly gone. Tulbeyev had got her. At the bottom of the steps, Chirkov stood. Hot pain spilled from his hip and his side was numb. His lungs hurt from the frozen air, and he coughed steam. He still held his bag and gun; luckily, the revolver had not discharged. He looked around: there were human shapes in the square, shambling towards the Spa. Darting up the steps, unmindful of the dangers of ice, he made for the light of the doorway. He paused to grab the skeleton by the elbow and haul it to the entrance. It didn't resist him. The muscles felt like snakes stretched over a bony frame. He shoved the skeleton into the foyer and Tulbeyev was there with his ball of twine. Chirkov turned as Valentina shut the doors. More Amerikans had come: the skeleton's place was taken and the little girl's, and two or three more steps were occupied. Before bolting the doors, Valentina opened them a crack and considered the queue. Again, the dead were still, unexcited. Then, like a drill team, they all moved up a step. The photographer's place was taken by the officer, and the rest of the line similarly advanced. Valentina pushed the doors together and Chirkov shut the bolts. Without pausing for breath, she ordered the specimens to be taken to the steam baths.

. . . . .

Breakfast was a half-turnip, surprisingly fresh if riddled with ice-chips. Chirkov took it away from the cafeteria to chew and descended to the Pool to report to the Director. He assumed Valentina would make mention at the evening meeting of her unauthorized acquisition of specimens. It was not his place to spread gossip. Arriving at the cubicle before the Director, his first duty was to get the samovar going: Kozintsev survived on constant infusions of smoky tea. As Chirkov lit the charcoal, he heard a click, like saluting heels. He looked around the cubicle and saw no-one. All was as usual: clays, wig, shaping-tools, skull, samovar, boxes piled to make a stool. There was another click. He looked up at the chandelier and saw nothing unusual. The tea began to bubble and he chewed a mouthful of cold turnip, trying not to think about sleep, or Amerikans.

Kozintsev had begun again on the reconstruction. The skull of Grigory Yefimovich Rasputin was almost buried in clay strips. It looked very much like the head of the Amerikan Chirkov had secured for Valentina: flattened reddish ropes bound the jaws together, winding up into the cavities under the cheek-bones; enamel chips replaced the many missing teeth, standing out white against grey-yellow; delicate filaments swarmed round the glass eyes. It was an intriguing process and Chirkov had come to enjoy watching the Director at work. There was a sheaf of photographs of the monk on one stand but Kozintsev disliked consulting them. His process depended on extrapolating from the contours of the bone, not modeling from likenesses. Rasputin's potato-like peasant nose was a knotty problem. The cartilage was long-gone, and Kozintsev obsessively built and abandoned noses. Several were trodden flat into the sloping tile floor. After the Revolution, the faith healer had been exhumed by zealots from his tomb in the Imperial Park and, reportedly, burned; there was doubt, fiercely resisted by the Director, as to the provenance of the skull.

As Chirkov looked, Rasputin's jaw sagged, clay muscles stretching; then, suddenly, it clamped shut, teeth clicking. Chirkov jumped, and spat out a shocked laugh. Kozintsev arrived, performing a dozen actions at once, removing his frock-coat and reaching for his smock, bidding a good morning and calling for his tea. Chirkov was bemused and afraid, questioning what he had seen. The skull bit once more. Kozintsev saw the movement at once, and asked again for tea. Chirkov, snapping out of it, provided a cupful and took one for himself. Kozintsev did not comment on the appropriation. He was very interested and peered close at the barely animated skull. The jaw moved slowly from side to side, as if masticating. Chirkov wondered if Grigory Yefimovich were imitating him and stopped chewing his turnip. Kozintsev pointed out that the eyes were trying to move, but the clay hadn't the strength of real muscle. He wondered aloud if he should work in strands of string to simulate the texture of human tissue. It might not be cosmetically correct. Rasputin's mouth gaped open, as if in a silent scream. The Director prodded the air near the skull's mouth with his finger and withdrew sharply as the jaws snapped shut. He laughed merrily, and called the monk a cunning fellow.

. . . . .

The queue was still on the steps. Everyone had taken turns at the spy-hole. Now the line stretched down into the square and along the pavement, curving around the building. Tulbeyev had hourly updates on the riches borne by the Amerikans. He was sure one of the queue harbored a precious video-player: Tulbeyev had cassettes of *One Hundred & One Dalmatians* and *New Wave Hookers* but no way of playing them. Captain Zharov favoured dealing harshly with the dead, but Kozintsev, still excited by the skull activity, would issue no orders and the officer was not about to take action without a direct instruction, preferably in writing. As an experiment, he went out and, half-way down the steps, selected an Amerikan at random. He shot it in the head and the finally dead bag of bones tumbled out of the queue. Zharov kicked the remains, and, coming apart, they rolled down the steps into a snowdrift. After a pause, all the dead behind Zharov's kill took a step up. Valentina was in the steam baths with her specimens: news of her acquisitions had spread through the Spa, inciting vigorous debate. Tarkhanov complained to the Director about his colleague's usurpation of authority, but was brushed off with an invitation to examine the miraculous skull. Dr. Dudnikov placed several phone calls to the Kremlin, relaying matters of interest to a junior functionary, who promised imminent decisions. It was Dudnikov's hope that the developments could be used as a lever to unloose vital supplies from other institutions. As ever, the rallying cry was *Chairs for the Spa!*

In the afternoon, Chirkov napped standing up as he watched Kozintsev at work. Although the jaw continually made small movements, the skull was co-operative and did not try to nip the Director. He had requisitioned Tulbeyev's jew's harp and was implanting it among thick neck muscles, hoping it would function as a crude voicebox. To Chirkov's disgust, Rasputin was becoming expert in the movement of its unseeing eyes. He could suck the glass orbs so the painted pupils disappeared in the tops of the sockets, showing only milky white marbles. This was a man who had been hard to kill: his murderers gave him poison enough to fell an elephant, shot him in the back and chest with revolvers, kicked him in the head, battered him with a club and lowered him into the River Neva, bound in a curtain, through a hole in the ice. The skull bore an indentation which Kozintsev traced to an aristocrat's boot. In the end, men hadn't killed the seer; the cause of his death was drowning. As he worked, the Director hummed cheerful snatches of Prokofiev. To give the mouth something to do, Kozintsev stuck a cigarette between the teeth. He promised Grigory Yefimovich lips would come soon, but there was nothing yet he could do about lungs. His secret dream, which he shared with the skull (and, perforce, Chirkov), was to apply his process to a complete skeleton. Regrettably, and as he had himself predicted while alive, most of the monk had been scattered on the wind.

Lyubachevsky barged into the cubicle, bearing a telephone whose cord unreeled through the maze of the Pool like Ariadne's thread. There was a call from the Kremlin, which Kozintsev was required to take. While Chirkov and Lyubachevsky stood, unconsciously at attention, the Director chatted with the New First Secretary.

Either Dr. Dudnikov had tapped into the proper channels or Tarkhanov was the spy everyone took him for and had reported on the sly to his KGB superior. The First Secretary was briefed about what was going on at the Spa. He handed out a commendation to Kozintsev and insisted extra resources would be channeled to the morgue. Chirkov got the impression the First Secretary was mixing up the projects: Kozintsev was being praised for Valentina's studies. The Director would be only too delighted to employ any funds or supplies in furthering his work with the skull.

Following the telephone call, the Director was in excellent spirits. He told the skull a breakthrough was at hand, and insisted to Lyubachevsky that he could hear a faint twang from the jew's harp. Grigory Yefimovich was trying to communicate, the Director claimed. He asked if he remembered eating the poisoned chocolates? After the jaw first moved, Kozintsev had constructed rudimentary clay ears, exaggerated cartoon curls which stuck out ridiculously. Having abandoned any attempt to simulate the appearance in life of the monk, he was attempting instead to provide working features. Since Rasputin's brains must have rotted or burned years ago, it was hard to imagine what the Director aspired to communicate with. Then, over the loudspeaker, Dr. Dudnikov reported that there were soldiers outside the Spa, setting up explosives and declaring an intention to dynamite the building. Grigory Yefimovich's glass eyes rolled again.

. . . . .

Engineers were packing charges around the foyer. Entering the Spa through the kitchens, they had avoided the Amerikan-infested steps. It appeared a second queue was forming, stretching off in a different direction, still leading to the front doors. The officer in command, a fat man with a facial birthmark that made him look like a spaniel, introduced himself as Major Andrey Kobylinsky. He strode about, inspecting the work, expressing pride in his unit's ability to demolish a building with the minimum of explosive matter. As he surveyed, Kobylinsky noted points at which surplus charges should be placed. To Chirkov's unschooled eye, the Major appeared to contradict himself: his men were plastering the walls with semtex. Kozintsev and Captain Zharov were absorbed in a reading of a twelve-page document which authorized the demolition of the Spa. Dr. Dudnikov protested that the First Secretary himself had, within the last minute, commended the Spa and that important work to do with the Amerikan invasion was being carried out in the Pool, but Kobylinsky was far more interested in which pillars should be knocked out to bring down the decadent painted roof. As they worked, the engineers whistled "Girls Just Want to Have Fun."

Satisfied that the charges were laid correctly, Major Kobylinsky could not resist the temptation to lecture the assembled company on the progress and achievements of his campaign. A three-yard square map of Moscow was unfolded on the floor. It was marked with patches of red as if it were a chessboard pulled out of shape. The red areas signified buildings and constructions Kobylinsky had blown up. Chirkov understood the Major would not be happy until the entire map was shaded in red; then, Kobylinsky believed the crisis would be at an end. He proclaimed that this should have been done immediately the crisis begun, and that the Amerikans were to be thanked for prompting such a visionary enterprise. As the Major lectured, Chirkov noticed Tulbeyev at the main desk with Lyubachevsky, apparently trying to find a pen that worked. They sorted through a pot of pencils and chalks and markers, drawing streaks on a piece of blotting paper. Under the desk were packages wired to detonators. Kobylinsky checked his watch and mused that he was ahead of his schedule; the demolition would take place in one half an hour. Lyubachevsky raised a hand and ventured the opinion that the explosives placed under the main staircase were insufficient for the task of bringing down such a solidly-constructed structure. Barking disagreement, Kobylinsky strutted over and examined the charges in question, finally agreeing that safe was better than sorry and ordering the application of more explosives.

While Kobylinsky was distracted, Tulbeyev crept to the map and knelt over Red Square, scribbling furiously with a precious red felt-tip. He blotched over the Spa, extending an area of devastation to cover half the Square. When Kobylinsky revisited his map, Tulbeyev was unsuspiciously on the other side of the room. One of the engineers, a new set of headphones slung round his neck, piped up with an observation of a cartographical anomaly. Kobylinsky applied his concentration to the map and gurgled to himself. According to this chart, the Spa had already been dealt with by his unit: it was not a building but a raked-over patch of rubble. Another engineer, a baseball cap in his back pocket, volunteered a convincing memory of the destruction, three days ago, of the Spa. Kobylinsky looked again at the map, getting down on his hands and knees and crawling along the most famous thoroughfares of the city. He scratched his head and blinked in his birthmark. Director Kozintsev, arms folded and head high, said that so far as he was concerned the matter was at an end; he requested the engineers to remove their infernal devices from the premises. Kobylinsky had authorization to destroy the Spa but once, and had demonstrably already acted on that authorization. The operation could not be repeated without further orders, and, if further orders were requested, questions would be asked as to whether the engineers were as efficient as Kobylinsky would like to claim: most units needed to destroy a building only once for it to remain destroyed. Almost in tears, the bewildered Major finally commanded the removal of the explosives and, with parental tenderness, folded up his map into its case. With no apologies, the engineers withdrew.

. . . . .

That night, Valentina's Amerikans got out of the steam bath and everyone spent a merry three hours hunting them down. Chirkov and Tulbeyev drew the Pool. The power had failed again and they had to fall back on oil lamps, which made the business all the more unnerving. Irregular and active shadows were all around, whispering in Moldavian of hungry, unquiet creatures. Their progress was a slow spiral; first, they circled the Pool from above, casting light over the complex, but that left too many darks unprobed; then they went in at the Deep End and moved methodically through the labyrinth, weaving between the partitions, stumbling against dissected bodies, ready to shoot hatstands in the brain. Under his breath, Tulbeyev recited a litany he claimed was a Japanese prayer against the dead: *sanyo, sony, seiko, mitsubishi, panasonic, toshiba . . .*

They had to penetrate the dead center of the Pool. The Amerikans were in Kozintsev's cubicle: staring at the bone-and-clay head as if it were a color television set. Rasputin was on his stand under a black protective cloth which hung like long hair. Chirkov found the combination of the Amerikans and Rasputin unnerving and, almost as a reflex, shot the skeleton in the skull. The report was loud and echoing. The skeleton came apart on the floor and, before Chirkov's ears stopped hurting, others had come to investigate. Director Kozintsev was concerned for his precious monk and probed urgently under the cloth for damage. Valentina was annoyed by the loss of her specimen but kept her tongue still, especially when her surviving Amerikan turned nasty. The dead man barged out of the cubicle, shouldering partitions apart, wading through gurneys and tables, roaring and slavering. Tarkhanov, incongruous in a silk dressing gown, got in the way and sustained a nasty bite. Tulbeyev dealt with the Amerikan, tripping him with an axe-handle, then straddling his chest and pounding a chisel into the bridge of his nose. He had not done anything to prove Valentina's theories; after a spell in captivity, he simply seemed more decayed, not evolved. Valentina claimed the thing Chirkov had finished had been a model of biological efficiency, stripped down to essentials, potentially immortal. Now, it looked like a stack of bones.

. . . . .

Even Kozintsev, occupied in the construction of a set of wooden arms for his reanimated favorite, was alarmed by the size of the queue. There were four distinct lines. The Amerikans shuffled constantly, stamping nerveless feet as if to keep warm. Captain Zharov set up a machine-gun emplacement in the foyer, covering the now-barred front doors, although it was strictly for show until he could be supplied with ammunition of the same gauge as the gun. Chirkov and Tulbeyev watched the Amerikans from the balcony. The queue was orderly; when, as occasionally happened, a too-far-gone Amerikan collapsed, it was trampled under by the great moving-up as those behind advanced. Tulbeyev sighted on individual dead with binoculars and listed the treasures he could distinguish. Mobile telephones, digital watches, blue jeans, leather jackets, gold bracelets, gold teeth, ball-point pens. The Square was a paradise for pickpockets. As night fell, it was notable that no lights burned even in the Kremlin.

When the power came back, the emergency radio frequencies broadcast only soothing music. The meeting was more sparsely attended than usual, and Chirkov realized faces had been disappearing steadily, lost to desertion or wastage. Dr. Dudnikov announced that he had been unable to reach anyone on the telephone. Lyubachevsky reported that the threat of demolition had been lifted from the Spa and was unlikely to recur, though there might now prove to be unfortunate official side effects if the institution was formally believed to be a stretch of warm rubble. The kitchens had received a delivery of fresh fish, which was cause for celebration, though the head cook noted as strange the fact that many of the shipment were still flapping and even decapitation seemed not to still them. Valentina, for the hundredth time, requested specimens be secured for study and, after a vote—closer than usual, but still decisive—was disappointed. Tarkhanov's suicide was entered into the record and the scientists paid tribute to the colleague they fervently believed had repeatedly informed on them, reciting his achievements and honors. Tulbeyev suggested a raiding party to relieve the queuing Amerikans of those goods which could be used for barter, but no one was willing to second the proposal, which sent him into a notable sulk. Finally, as was expected, Kozintsev gave an account of his day's progress with Grigory Yefimovich. He had achieved a certain success with the arms: constructing elementary shoulder joints and nailing them to Rasputin's stand, then layering rope-and-clay muscles which interleaved with the neck he had fashioned. The head was able to control its arms to the extent of stretching out and bunching up muscle strands in the wrists as if clenching fists which did not, as yet, exist. The Director was also pleased to report that the head almost constantly made sounds with the jew's harp, approximating either speech or music. As if to demonstrate the monk's healing powers, Kozintsev's sinus trouble had cleared up almost entirely.

· · · · ·

Two days later, Tulbeyev let the Amerikans in. Chirkov did not know where the Corporal got the idea; he just got up from the gun emplacement, walked across the foyer, and unbarred the doors. Chirkov did not try to stop him, distracted by efforts to jam the wrong type of belt into the machine gun. When all the bolts were loose, Tulbeyev flung the doors back and stood aside. At the front of the queue, ever since the night they had brought in Valentina's specimens, was the officer. As he waited, his face had run, flesh slipping from his cheeks to form jowly bags around his jaw. He stepped forwards smartly, entering the foyer. Lyubachevsky woke up from his cot behind the desk and wondered aloud what was going on. Tulbeyev took a fistful of medals from the officer, and tossed them to the floor after a shrewd assessment. The officer walked purposefully, with a broken-ankled limp, towards the lifts. Next in was the woman in the pinstripe suit. Tulbeyev took her hat and perched it on his head. From the next few, the Corporal harvested a silver chain identity bracelet, a woven leather belt, a pocket calculator, an old brooch. He piled the tokens behind him. Amerikans filled the foyer, wedging through the doorway in a triangle behind the officer.

Chirkov assumed the dead would eat him and wished he had seriously tried to go to bed with Technician Sverdlova. He still had two rounds left in his revolver, which meant he could deal with an Amerikan before ensuring his own everlasting peace. There were so many to choose from and none seemed interested in him. The lift was descending and those who couldn't get into it discovered the stairs. They were all drawn to the basement, to the Pool. Tulbeyev chortled and gasped at each new treasure, sometimes clapping the dead on the shoulders as they yielded their riches, hugging one or two of the more harmless creatures. Lyubachevsky was appalled, but did nothing. Finally, the administrator got together the gumption to issue an order: he told Chirkov to inform the Director of this development. Chirkov assumed that since Kozintsev was, as ever, working in the Pool, he would very soon be extremely aware of this development, but he snapped to and barged through the crowd anyway, choking back the instinct to apologize. The Amerikans mainly got out of his way, and he pushed to the front of the wave shuffling down the basement steps. He broke out of the pack and clattered into the Pool, yelling that the Amerikans were coming. Researchers looked up—he saw Valentina's eyes flashing annoyance and wondered if it was not too late to ask her for sex—and the crowd edged behind Chirkov, approaching the lip of the Pool.

He vaulted in and sloshed through the mess towards Kozintsev's cubicle. Many partitions were down already and there was a clear path to the Director's work-space. Valentina pouted at him, then her eyes widened as she saw the assembled legs surrounding the Pool. The Amerikans began to topple in, crushing furniture and corpses beneath them, many unable to stand once they had fallen. The hardiest of them kept on walking, swarming round and overwhelming the technicians. Cries were strangled and blood ran on the bed of the Pool. Chirkov fired wildly, winging an ear off a bearded dead man in a shabby suit, and pushed on towards Kozintsev. When he reached the center, his first thought was that the cubicle was empty, then he saw what the Director had managed. Combining himself with his work, V. A.

Kozintsev had constructed a wooden half-skeleton which fitted over his shoulders, making his own head the heart of the new body he had fashioned for Grigory Yefimovich Rasputin. The head, built out to giant size with exaggerated clay and rubber muscles, wore its black wig and beard, and even had lips and patches of sprayed-on skin. The upper body was wooden and intricate, the torso of a colossus with arms to match, but sticking out at the bottom were the Director's stick-insect legs. Chirkov thought the body would not be able to support itself but, as he looked, the assemblage stood. He looked up at the caricature of Rasputin's face. Blue eyes shone, not glass but living.

Valentina was by his side, gasping. He put an arm round her and vowed to himself that if it were necessary she would have the bullet he had saved for himself. He smelled her perfumed hair. Together, they looked up at the holy maniac who had controlled a woman and, through her, an empire, ultimately destroying both. Rasputin looked down on them, then turned away to look at the Amerikans. They crowded round in an orderly fashion, limping pilgrims approaching a shrine. A terrible smile disfigured the crude face. An arm extended, the paddle-sized hand stretching out fingers constructed from surgical implements. The hand fell onto the forehead of the first of the Amerikans, the officer. It covered the dead face completely, fingers curling round the head. Grigory Yefimovich seemed powerful enough to crush the Amerikan's skull, but instead he just held firm. His eyes rolled up to the chandelier, and a twanging came from inside the wood-and-clay neck, a vibrating monotone that might have been a hymn. As the noise resounded, the gripped Amerikan shook, slabs of putrid meat falling away like layers of onionskin. At last, Rasputin pushed the creature away. The uniform gone with its flesh, it was like Valentina's skeleton, but leaner, moister, stronger. It stood up and stretched, its infirmities gone, its ankle whole. It clenched and unclenched teeth in a joke-shop grin and leaped away, eager for meat. The next Amerikan took its place under Rasputin's hand, and was healed too. And the next.

TELL ME LIKE YOU DONE BEFORE

Scott Edelman

Scott Edelman has published more than seventy-five short stories in magazines such as *PostScripts*, *The Twilight Zone*, *Absolute Magnitude*, *The Journal of Pulse-Pounding Narratives*, *Science Fiction Review*, and *Fantasy Book*, and in numerous anthologies, including *The Mammoth Book of Best New Horror*, *The Solaris Book of New Science Fiction: Volume Three*, *Crossroads: Southern Tales of the Fantastic*, *Men Writing SF as Women*, *MetaHorror*, *Once Upon a Galaxy*, *Moon Shots*, *Mars Probes*, *Forbidden Planets*, *Summer Chills*, and *The Mammoth Book of Monsters*.

A collection of his horror fiction, *These Words Are Haunted*, was published by Wildside Press in 2001, and a stand-alone novella, *The Hunger of Empty Vessels*, appeared from Bad Moon Books in early 2009. Upcoming stories will appear in *PostScripts*, *Talebones*, and *Space & Time*. A collection of his zombie fiction will also be appearing from PS Publishing in early 2010. He has been a Bram Stoker Award finalist four times, in the categories for both Short Story and Long Fiction.

Additionally, Edelman currently works for the Syfy Network as the Features Editor for *SCI FI Wire*, an online site of news, reviews and interviews. He was the founding editor of *Science Fiction Age*, which he edited during its entire eight-year run, after which he edited *Science Fiction Weekly* for eight years. He also edited *SCI FI* magazine, previously known as *Sci-Fi Entertainment*, for over a decade, as well as two other science fiction media magazines, *Sci-Fi Universe* and *Sci-Fi Flix*. He has been a four-time Hugo Award finalist for Best Editor.

"I knew I wanted to write 'Tell Me Like You Done Before' at least a decade before I wrote the first sentence or figured out the details of the plot," the author reveals. "I carried the seed around in the folds of my brain, waiting for the right catalyst to begin. Then came the 2009 Stoker Awards weekend in Burbank and a conversation with the editor of this anthology. I returned home, energized as I so often am from such gatherings, and wrote the first draft of this story so quickly that it was almost as if I was transcribing it, rather than composing it for the first time.

"That was a gift from my subconscious, which—unbeknownst to me—had been working on the story all along, and had been awaiting my call.

"This story's creation reminds me of the apocryphal tale of an auto mechanic who stops to help a man whose car had broken down on a country road. It takes the mechanic five minutes to fix the problem, and then he charges the stranded driver $50 for the service. The man is outraged.

"'Fifty dollars for five minutes work!' he protests.

"'No,' says the mechanic. 'The $50 was for thirty years of experience. I tossed in the five minutes for free.'

"So think of this as a story which took ten years and two weeks to complete. This kind of thing doesn't happen often, but when it does, this writer knows enough to be grateful."

AS THE STAR-SPECKLED BLACK of the sky gave way to an unbroken dark blue canvas that promised a dawn, a thin man, his shoulders slumped as if he had been carrying the world upon them, rose from where he had been hiding amidst the brush.

He slapped at the dry earth that clung to the folds of his well-worn clothing. The grim expression on his sharp features softened slightly as he was swallowed by the resulting cloud of dust.

He stared down into the valley to where he knew a ranch was nestled several miles away, miles he'd had no remaining juice to cover the night before. Even though a new day was on the verge of being born, he still could make it out by but a few pinpoints of campfire.

He smiled then, a change in expression so slight that it would have been perceptible only to someone who had known him for many years.

But there was only one friend like that who still walked God's green Earth. And he was many miles away, the miles growing greater each day. Or so this weary man hoped.

Besides, that friend was dead.

Death was supposed to have stopped him.

It hadn't.

The man had made it to the start of another day, something which he'd been wise enough not to count on. He wished he could have made it to the ranch the night before, where surrounded by others he might have been lulled into a false sense of security that would have let him get some rest, instead of a broken sleep which left him as exhausted now as before he lay down, but fatigue had overtaken him there among the sycamores, and that was that.

He heard a scraping at his feet, and looked down to see a small rabbit, its bones bent, its eyes glowing, dragging itself toward him through the brown grass. Before he could react, it leapt at him, though because its frame was crippled, it could only propel itself to the top of his left boot, and no further. The wretched thing drove its incisors into the thick leather at the man's calf.

He shrieked, and struggled to kick at it with the heel of his other boot, but his angle was all wrong, and so he struck it with only glancing blows. He fell, even as he was doing so telling himself how stupid he'd been to let his throat get within the creature's reach. The rabbit dropped its jaws, a noxious liquid spilling forth, and as it readied itself for another leap, one which would end this terrifying dance, the man's scrabbling fingers chanced on a medium-sized rock. He scooped it up and slammed it hard against the thing's skull.

The cony dropped to the man's side, still wriggling, preparing for another attack, and so he quickly rolled to his knees, bashing at it again with the rock. But it kept coming, not giving up until he caught its skull directly. He brought the rock down once, twice, again, so many times he lost count.

Only then did it lay still.

The man fell back, gasping for breath, shuddering not only from the close call, but also from the memories which had haunted him ever since the night he'd pulled that trigger and killed his best friend, embers which the violent encounter had stirred into a raging fire. He'd been haunted even before that dreadful dusk, but he'd thought that with his ultimate action, once the bullet had flown, it would surely be over.

Turned out all he'd done was trade one kind of haunting for another.

He lay on his back until the sky had turned a bright cloudless blue, a color that told him he was free of any further such encounters, at least until night began to fall once more. He stood then, looked down at the ranch the morning had revealed. He'd hoped that might be the place to rest for a spell, but he now saw that he still needed to put a few more miles on his boots.

He sighed. That had been much too close. He couldn't afford to linger.

There would be other ranches.

There would have to be.

He listened for a moment to the rumble in his belly, and then moved on.

．　．　．　．　．

During the day, as he picked his way through the willows that lined the banks of the Salinas, hoping that it would cover his tracks and knowing at the same time that hope was pointless, he hunted for food. During the days, he could. That was when the things, and most importantly, the thing (though it hurt to call him that), which hunted him could not.

He was hungry, but even so, he hesitated when he saw his first rabbit that morning. Daylight or no, the flood of the reanimated had taught him to be wary. And there'd been so many of them killed by his friend over the years. Lenny had been clumsy that way. Who knew how long they would keep coming, his personal parade of the damned? So the first live one of the day got away. But then, spurred on by the increasing volume of the rumbling in his gut, he shook off his close call at dawn and was able to bring himself to bring one down.

And he needed to. He had to keep up his strength, and the cans of beans he'd "borrowed"—he preferred to call it that rather than use the word "stolen"—had only lasted so far. He'd thought events had taken a bad turn in Weed, but on the night when he'd had to make that horrible choice, to do that terrible thing to the friend who'd trusted him more than anybody else in the world, they'd gotten worse. As worse as he thought it was possible for a life to get.

He'd been wrong. He'd been wrong about a lot.

He worried that, warm meat settling in his belly or no, he could only go on so far.

But he would have to try.

.   .   .   .   .

He reached the next ranch in the late afternoon, when almost all of the men were still out in the fields. He'd done that sort of thing before, shown up too late for work and gotten a meal without having to toil for it, but in the old days, that action had been a choice, and he hadn't been alone.

Of course, however it seemed, he really wasn't alone now. That's why he had to keep moving. But he'd grown wearier than usual these past few days, and had to take the risk. At least briefly.

He entered the bunkhouse and found one lone ranch hand begrudgingly sweeping the stained floor. The hand paused, leaning against his broom, and eyed the intruder warily.

"Well, aren't you the special cuss," he said. "Waltzing in here like this with the day's work just about done."

"No, I ain't nobody special. Name's George. George Milton."

George held out a hand, but the man refused to take it, keeping his fingers wrapped around the broom handle.

"Sorry," he continued. "Hitched a ride, and meant to be here early, but I got dropped off one ranch over. Had to hoof it from there. Mighty impressive spreads in these parts. Took a mess of hiking to get me here."

"You're damned lucky we're down a few hands, otherwise the boss would send you on your way like that." He snapped his fingers, and that action somehow broke his resolve. His grimace blossomed into a smile, and he held out a hand. "Name's Willie."

"Pleased to meet ya, Willie," said George, as the two men shook.

"So how come you're short?" asked George, after the pleasantries were done. "Times like these, no one just walks away from a job without a good reason."

"You'd think so," said Willie, his brow wrinkling. "Only, that's what done happened. Three guys just took off in the middle of the night during the last week alone, one at a time, without even the decency to say why or goodbye. Lucky for you, they didn't take any of their stuff, so since it don't look like you're carrying much in the way of supplies, you're welcome to their leftovers."

Normally, George would be grateful for that spot of good luck. There was only so much he could carry, so he'd had to leave a lot behind. But he didn't like the sound of this. Turning your back on three squares and a cot was crazy, with what the you-ess-of-ay was going through in the '30s, with the Dust Bowl swallowing up farmland, and both food and work so scarce. Just wasn't done. Not by anyone. And certainly not by three from the same ranch, so close together.

But he didn't have time to think much further on the puzzle, because that's when the men returned from their long day in the fields.

They were glad to see him, or made a show of being so anyway, because being down a few men, their routine had become even more brutal than usual. And he was glad to see them, too, because in those few minutes of exchanging names and slapping backs, in the midst of a dozen or so men laughing, cursing, spitting, he felt almost normal. By the time the introductions were over, he had trouble remembering most of the names, but it didn't matter that he couldn't keep them straight, because he knew their types well.

Maybe they'd been bucking barley. Maybe they were just back from haying. It didn't really matter. Guys like that were the same all over.

Here was the joe who blamed the world for all of his problems, there the silent one who might be stupid or might not, but since he rarely opened his mouth, few could tell for sure (George quickly moved on from that one for fear of remembering his friend too fully once more), here the one with the tripwire temper who was quick to anger, there the lazy bastard who hoped no one would notice but knew everyone did . . .

There the calm and steady one, the one George could tell people listened to. That last one's name he'd make sure to remember. Jackson. He was the rarest type of all, the peacemaker, a sort not always found in the muddle of men on ranches and farms. And he might come in handy.

Then the dinner bell rang and George met the boss around a long table as plates of tough meat and tougher rolls were passed around, and the men gobbled them down like candy. The meat tasted like horse—it was a sign of the times that he could identify the flavor, for once he'd never have been able to do that—but he was glad of any meal he didn't have to kill for himself.

The boss, a barrel-shaped man named Dix, didn't question him much, so George didn't have to explain what had happened to drive them out of Weed, or the reason he'd had to do what he'd done not so very much later a few miles south of Soledad. George wasn't a very good liar, so he wasn't sure how well he would have been able to hide the truth, but the boss seemed too needy to go hunting after possible distressing facts anyway.

After the meal, the guys pitched a few horseshoes, and smoked a few cigarettes, but they were all too worn out for much more fun than that, the men from their work, George from his long hike and close escape. Only after he'd crawled into bed did he remember that he'd intended to ask about the men who'd vanished, find out what kind of people they were, if there was a simple reason why so many workers would have gotten skittish enough to bolt so close together.

He knew that a hunger for room and board wasn't the only reason men stayed anchored to any job they were lucky enough to find these days, regardless of working conditions. It just wasn't safe to hit the road or ride the rails any more, not with all those whispers of others like his friend who wouldn't stay underground where they was put.

He'd come to realize that Lenny hadn't been the first. Just his first. And with what he'd been hearing lately, not even George would have been on the move unless he was being tracked. Being hunted.

Those men had to have had a damn good reason to leave, too. He wondered what it could be . . .

But then sleep overcame him, and he was off in dream, telling the same old story again, the story his friend had always begged for and yet always treated as new, the one about the little house they'd get on a couple of acres, with a vegetable garden, and the rabbits.

Always the rabbits.

.   .   .   .   .

George jerked awake at dawn, when the sun's first rays crept into the room. He had learned what that first light meant. He'd survived another night, and nothing could get at him until another one fell. The work to come that he would normally have cursed as backbreaking would instead be a relief, because it would tell him that he was alive. Even a poorly cooked breakfast, with bits of shell mixed into the scrambled eggs, didn't dampen his mood, and when he leapt with the other men into the wagon and headed out for the barley, he was filled with as much happiness as his present life could muster.

As he worked that day, watching the sun track across the sky, he found himself wishing it would move more slowly. Ever since he'd done what he'd done, there was no end of things out there looking for him.

The big lummox had snuffed out so many of them. Only they hadn't stayed snuffed out. He couldn't even get that right.

But George must have made a mess of it big time as well. He'd shot Lenny, seen him fall. He'd shot him in the sweet spot, right where he was supposed to, supposed to so that the long troubled journey of his friend's life would all be over.

Only it wasn't.

When he got back to the bunk-house at the end of the day, he discovered that a rope had been stretched between two trees out front, a sheet tossed over it to hang limply.

"What do you suppose that's about?" asked George.

"I don't rightly know," said Jackson. George had attached himself to the man, hoping to borrow some of his calm. "Been here a piece but never seen it done before."

They shrugged and passed the set-up by, heading in for another overcooked meal. When they pushed back from their plates, Dix stood up, and leaned forward with his palms flat on the table.

"I have a treat for you fellers tonight," he said. "As soon as it's fully dark, we're going to have ourselves a picture show."

The men chattered excitedly as they rushed outside.

"What do you think it's gonna be?" said one.

"I hope it's a dancing picture," said the quiet one, who surprised them by speaking up at such length. "I like them dancing pictures."

"Don't matter to me much," said George. "As long as it takes me away from here."

"Oh, it ain't so bad here," said Jackson. "We got food, a place to lay our heads. And sure, Dix can be tough at times, but believe me, I've seen worse. Who could want anything more than that?"

George could, and he wasn't the only one. He could think of a few others, others like Candy and Crooks, who would want more as well, and he knew exactly what it was they'd want. How he was the one who'd made them want it, made them want to join the two friends who looked like they might actually pull off that dream of a couple of acres of their own, and living off the fat of the land . . . And how he had gone ahead and ruined it for them all.

You couldn't blame the big lummox. He didn't know what he was doing. But George . . . he was supposed to know better. All that came after. That was his own damn fault.

Dix directed the men to set up rows of crates in the wide space between the bunkhouse and the stables, and then they sat there, working at their toothpicks, spitting in the dust, waiting for the purple sky to turn black. George didn't like being exposed out in the open like that, but he couldn't figure any way around it. He pressed himself into the center of the men. The boss carried out a projector and fussed with it, not letting any of the others help him with the delicate machine. That didn't stop him from cursing at Willie as the hand played out a length of cable that ran from the small generator which usually kept the boss' house lit.

"Settle down, men," shouted Dix. "I don't exactly know what we got ourselves here, but from what they tell me, it's supposed to be a doozy."

George shifted uncomfortably on his crate, and was relieved when the utter darkness was broken by a beam of light. One of the guys nearest the screen laughed and jumped up, throwing his silhouette on the sheet, but a shout from Dix returned him to his crate. Soon the night was pierced by a beating of drums, and the words WHITE ZOMBIE stretched before them.

"Hey, look," someone shouted, as Bela Lugosi's name appeared, "it's got that vampire guy in it!"

George didn't know what the hell he was talking about. He wasn't much for picture shows, at least not lately, not when he'd had more important plans for his money. But not just with his money . . .

Best not to think of it. Best not to think of any of it, the missed picture shows, the skipped visits to fine parlors, all sacrificed in pursuit of—

Forget it. Forget it all.

Maybe this movie, whatever it was, would take his mind elsewhere. But based on how it began, it served only to refocus him more fully on his problem. Off in a country not really so distant and yet as far away to him as the moon, dead men walked, dead men who were at the same time somehow undead.

"Haiti is full of nonsense and superstition," said one character to another, but to be either of those, a thing had to be untrue, didn't it? George understood all too well the truth of his situation, that there could be life after death, though not much of one, and as the movie went on, his skin prickled with recognition. And when, about fifteen minutes in, the camera closed in tight on a huge bull of a man, his eyes wide, his soul gone, looking as if he could crush you with one hand, it all became too much. He leapt up from the center of the men, almost knocking a few of them over, ignoring the boss when he shouted at him to stay.

He fled, circling to the opposite side of the bunkhouse, cursing. He crouched down there, leaned his back against the wall, and with shaking hands rolled himself a cigarette. He could barely steady his fingers to bring match to tip, and it wasn't until he'd smoked it halfway down that his trembling stopped.

Jackson was suddenly there with him.

"Mind if I join you?" he asked.

George shook his head, and waved with his free hand at the patch of ground beside him.

They sat there quietly for a while. George wanted to say something, anything, to cover the sound of the movie that whispered at them around the corners of the bunkhouse, but he couldn't think of a damn thing.

"So what was that all about?" Jackson finally asked.

George had half a mind to tell him everything. He remembered another man like him, one who took George under his wing after the deed was done. He got George stinking drunk, and made him think that life could go on after what he'd had to do.

Life went on all right, but not the way either of them had thought. Now Slim was dead, George was on the run, and there was something after him, which though no longer capable of running, seemed pretty much unstoppable. But how to begin to tell something like that?

Before George could speak, a shuffling sound came from out of the desert, one that could barely be heard over the movie's buzz on the other side of the bunkhouse. George noticed it first, his senses having been made more alert to such things due to his recent situation.

Jackson noticed him squinting, and followed his gaze.

"What are you looking at?" he asked. "I don't see anythi—why, would you look at that!"

A small dog crawled toward them in the darkness, one of its front legs broken. Even so, it managed to close the gap between them quickly. George pressed his back more forcefully against the wall of the bunkhouse, unable to move any further, even as Jackson stood up and took a step toward it.

"Jackson, no!" George shouted.

But before Jackson could heed George's warning, he was on his knees beside the thing, reaching out to stroke it. It responded by biting hard into the meaty part of the man's thumb. Jackson yanked back his hand, but the animal wouldn't let go, and so was pulled into the air as he jumped up. He leapt around in pain, flinging his hand about, snapping the animal this way and that to no avail. It clung to him with the hunger of another world.

Jackson's yelps finally propelled George to action. He slid his work gloves from where they were tucked into his belt, and grabbed the thing by its hind legs, angry memories flooding back. He knew who had broken that one leg. He knew who had killed it. And yet not even those injuries, sudden, foolish, and fatal, had been enough to stop its vicious hunt. It had still kept coming, tracking him, sensing him out, and if George didn't act quickly, it would turn the man who'd come between them into another victim of his unwise choices.

He pinched at the hinge of its jaw, forcing it to release its grip, and hurled it to the ground. He brought down his heel, catching it in the midsection as it made to escape, flattening it as surely as if it had been run over by a wagon wheel, but though it burst, intestines spilling out, that wasn't enough to stop it. It still struggled for them. He slammed down his heel again and caught it near one ear, while Jackson continued to yowl in pain, cradling his arm, unable to help. George could hear a crunch of bone, but because of his angle he didn't think that had been enough to take care of it.

Though its lower jaw now hung at an ugly angle, he could see that he hadn't yet finished it. It moved away from the two men, more quickly than George thought would have been possible, and he had a choice. He'd always had choices. Wasn't that what had brought him here? Too many had died because of him, and so he knelt beside Jackson, held him as the creature vanished into the night.

"What the hell was that thing?" said Jackson, puking. He slumped against George. "Oh, I don't feel so good."

George helped Jackson to his feet, and saw that they were still alone. Good. The fact that they were still by themselves meant that thanks to the sounds from the movie and the whoops of the men, no one had heard anything. There was still time, time to save Jackson and time to keep his secret.

But not much. Jackson's eyes were dilated. His tongue lolled in his mouth.

"Do you want to live?" asked George. Jackson jerked his head, but George couldn't tell whether the man was nodding or shaking it. "Jackson, listen to me. You want to live, don't you?"

Jackson was beyond answering, so George answered for him. He dragged him into the bunkhouse through the back door, and lay him down on his cot. He got a knife, a candle, and a bottle of whiskey, and then took a brief furtive look out the front door.

The men were still mesmerized, not giving a damn that two of their comrades were gone. George pulled back from the door, avoiding even the slightest glance at the screen. That would be too much, even now. White Zombie be damned.

George lit the candle, and held the blade of the knife over the flame. He poured the whiskey, first on the heated knife, then down Jackson's throat. The man hardly had the power to swallow, and barely even had the power to choke. George crushed one corner of the bed sheet and jammed it into Jackson's mouth.

George held the knife against the base of Jackson's thumb, which by then was almost black, and oozing a foul pus. He held the knife an inch below the bite marks, pressed it against the part of flesh where the skin was already turning from pink to grey.

"There's no other way," said George. "I wish there was, but there ain't."

He took a deep breath and sliced as cleanly as he knew how, while Jackson howled through the cloth, which thankfully dampened the sound of it, and then fainted. George poured another slug of whiskey onto the wound, then wrapped the hand tightly with scraps from a shirt that had been abandoned by one of the men who had vanished.

Having just encountered the undead cur, he now was pretty certain where they had gone.

He'd answer Jackson's question when he woke, tell him exactly what that was all about. He swore he would. Because though he may have decided he'd just have to get used to being one of the loneliest guys in the world, something which he never thought he'd have to be, there was no way out of this life alone.

Tonight proved that.

.   .   .   .   .

The men never saw how the movie played out, whether or not the fancy pants hero managed to save the day against "that vampire guy." George ended it all when he came running out of the bunkhouse, screaming, his eyes wild. He sprinted up to the boss, shouting hysterically, grabbing his collar, calling out Jackson's name. They all followed him back inside and found Jackson stretched out there, his hand a ball of bloody cloth.

George tried to explain what had happened, what he wanted them to think had happened, but couldn't be heard over the chaotic questions from the men. Dix had to fire a shot into the ceiling to shut them up. With the room silent, George was barely coherent, or at least tried his best to be, and Willie insisted he down some whiskey, which helped in his pretense, especially considering he'd already taken a few shots on his own before sprinting outside.

He explained how a coyote had attacked them as they'd been talking there quietly in the dark, and how they'd fought it off, but not before Jackson had lost a thumb. One of the men, who'd almost finished high school, and had done some book reading, peeled back the sodden makeshift bandages. George could see that the blood ran red, thank god, and so what he'd done had been worth the funny look the man then gave him. George looked away as the man did his best to sew up Jackson's hand, though he heard him explain that he wouldn't be able to return to work for at least weeks. George then saw the guy whispering to Dix, who walked over to him angrily.

"Are you sure you're telling us what really happened?" he barked.

George protested that he had, and Dix seemed to take his word for it. At least at first, for he did glare back at him suspiciously after he returned to stand over Jackson.

George hoped that once he woke, the man would be able to keep his story straight. George's life, George's plan, depended on it.

George's life? Hah!

One way or another, it would have to end.

. . . . .

George spent the next day toiling in the field while wondering how Jackson was doing, what he was saying, and how everything could have gone so wrong. Nobody was in the mood to talk much, and the men kept their distance from him, so he had plenty of time in which to wonder.

He'd sworn, though his intentions then were not what they were now, that his aim had been true. He'd pressed the barrel of that gun right where Lenny's spine and skull joined, but he must have closed his eyes, or looked away at the last moment, or done something to stop the shot from firing straight. How else to explain it? It was love that had caused him to do what had to be done, but he guessed that it was also love that had left space for the mistake that had allowed his friend to come back.

The day passed quickly, because even though he pressed himself to work like a dog, harder than he ever had before, in an attempt to forget, he wasn't really there, since that attempt was a failure. He was instead off in that clearing in the brush where it had all gone down—had it truly been only a few weeks before? That seemed impossible—but also lost in the night before, when in the instant Jackson was attacked he had made a decision. So he was in those two places, not out under the hot sun. He had no way to undo either of those events, but he could damn well make sure that there would be no other such events in the future. If only Jackson could remember what George had whispered to him through his delirium.

By the look Dix gave him when the crew returned at the end of the day, it seemed as if he had. George nodded at his boss, and the man nodded back without judgment. As the rest of the men ran to the dining table, George slipped away to sit himself down next to Jackson's cot. Jackson, propped up by a pile of sweat-soaked pillows, was clear-eyed, and appeared fully himself again.

"I'm sorry," said George, his voice cracking.

Jackson studied George, taking his measure of him, and then nodded.

Then George told him everything.

He told him all about Lenny, big as an ox and just as dumb, and how Aunt Clara had asked him to watch out for the poor bastard, and all the promises he had made, and livin' off the fat of the land, and what happened to drive him and Lenny out of Weed, and about how Curley had picked on Lenny, and come out on the wrong end of things, and how Curley's wife, damn her roving eye, had toppled the house of cards by inviting Lenny to stroke her hair, strokes which had killed her, even though the big lug had meant none of it, really, he hadn't, he was just too damn stupid to know what it was he was doing, and it all tumbled out breathlessly, right up until that horrible night in the clearing near the brush by the river.

And through it all, Jackson kept nodding, his expression revealing nothing. So the tale he never thought he'd tell anyone kept pouring out of him, those impossible things that came after, how Lenny, and the things he had killed, had started to come back. Back for him.

Finally, there was nothing more left to tell. Nothing. Except—

"I need your help," said George.

Jackson held up his crippled hand.

"Help?" he said, snorting. "What can I do? What good would I be?"

"More good than what all of the others could possibly be put together," said George. "After what you seen, you'll believe."

Then George told him of his plan.

"Will you do it?" said George. "As far as I can figure, that's the only way to make it stop."

Jackson whistled.

"You're a crazy bastard, you know that?" he said. "Crazy as a wedge."

"Maybe. But that don't mean it won't work. Will you help me?"

This time, Jackson didn't hesitate.

"From the sound of it, you saved my life," he said. "Wouldn't seem right not to."

George reached out to shake Jackson's hand, then frowned, letting his own undamaged hand fall back into his lap.

. . . . .

By the time George finished laying out what the two of them would do next and got to the dinner table, most all of the food was gone, but it didn't really bother him. His hunger had been dampened by his plans. He mopped up some gravy with a heel of bread and mulled them over. That would have to be enough for now.

Once the meal was done, and the men poured outside to unwind with jawing and horseshoes, with one an excuse for the other, and it was never clear which the excuse and which the thing that had brought them there, he snuck back in and made his way to the deserted kitchen. He packed a bindle with half a loaf of bread, a rind of cheese, and a couple of cans of beans. Such a theft had become far too familiar to him, and he hated that, but depending on how things went, one way or another, this would be the last time he did this.

He returned to his bunk, hid the supplies under his covers, and pretended to sleep. When the snores of the other hands began to echo through the room, he slipped to his feet, tucked his boots under one arm, and made his way over to Jackson. He nudged the man, who snapped awake.

"It's time," he whispered.

George grabbed Jackson's things so that he wouldn't have to use his bum hand to fumble with them, and led him out the door, feeling crazy for doing so as the darkness swallowed them.

.   .   .   .   .

They hadn't been on the road for more than a couple of hours before they came upon Curley's wife shambling toward them in the moonlight.

Seeing her make her way unerringly in his direction through the bramble, each step clumsy yet determined, George realized that if they hadn't left when they did, this encounter might have occurred at the ranch, and then he would have been responsible for even more wreckage than he'd spread so far. Three men whom he did not know were already dead. He wouldn't have been able to bear the burden of more.

Her right leg was twisted in a way a leg shouldn't be able to go and still function, while her left shoulder seemed dislocated, the arm that hung straight down from it dangling limply.

"Damn you," screamed George. "You done this! If not for you, we still coulda been back there, still hoping, still dreaming, still pulling together our stake. But you had to go and mess things up, didn't you, you had to—"

Jackson dropped his good hand on George's shoulder.

"She can't hear you, George," he said. "There ain't nothing left inside of her to hear."

"Maybe you're right," said George. "Considering what we gotta do to that woman, I sure hope so."

George pulled out the pistol he had taken, a theft for which he hoped Dix would forgive him, but Jackson tapped his wrist with cold metal of his own and shook his head. George could see that he was grasping his baling hook.

"Save your bullets," said Jackson. "From what you been telling me, we're going to need them."

The two men separated, moving in wide circles to take up positions on opposite sides of the woman, their hands filled with curved steel. That she moved toward George without hesitation, whether from conscious thought or just some primal animal instinct that remained, ignoring Jackson as if he was nothing more than part of the landscape, told him, as if he needed any more convincing, that all his running had been pointless. He could never run far enough that she, or something like her, would not have been able to follow him.

As George looked at her then, her once shining sausage curls now dull as they hung from a grizzled flap of scalp, the splotch of red smeared across her mouth no longer lipstick but rather fresh blood, the hatred he'd been carrying around for her suddenly vanished. Whether that was going to make what was about to occur easier or more difficult he could not reckon.

He didn't have much time to figure that out, either, because he could see Jackson coming up behind her, beginning to make his move, and so he dashed in and dropped to his knees, swinging wildly to slash at the tendons in her calves. Unable to die or not, that would at least slow her down. As she bent toward him, he rolled to one side, and as he hacked at her again, Jackson joining him, she toppled like a downed oak.

With her face in the earth, Jackson leapt upon her, pressing both knees into the small of her back. He plunged his hook into the base of her neck, tearing through the grey flesh. George was right there with him, alternating his blows so that they only slashed her, and not each other, their hooks occasionally getting stuck in her skull and needing to be pulled free. The ichor flew like ribbons in the wind each time they raised their fists to the sky, and they did not halt their attack until what had once been Curley's wife stopped wriggling beneath them on the ground. Then they fell back, gasping for breath, dropping their weapons into the dry earth.

George poked at her with the toe of his boot. He felt the bile rise in his throat, felt as if he was about to retch, but he somehow managed to hold himself back.

He'd only known the woman for a little while, and still it had been difficult. But Lenny . . . Lenny was like a brother. He couldn't imagine how much more painful that would be.

He looked across her broken body at Jackson.

"The next one won't be so easy," said George.

Jackson looked at the blood seeping through his bandages, and nodded. He glanced down at Curley's wife, and suddenly grew solemn.

"She deserves a decent burial after all she's been through, don't you think," he said.

"She's already had one," said George. "And one is more than most of us ever get. Besides, we just don't have the time."

So they piled stones on her until she could no longer be seen, though George doubted that any animal would be drawn in by what was left of her and be tempted to feast. He said a short prayer to keep Jackson happy, even though he believed in God less now than ever.

They stood silently for a moment, until George could bear no more, and then they continued on.

. . . . .

As George led Jackson back, back to where this final chapter had begun, the journey made him feel as if they were traveling not just in space but in time. If only that were possible, if only he could have undone it all with different choices, instead of what was coming. But that was wishful thinking, and he had no more wishes left.

He did not follow a path which would lead them there directly, because he did not want them to meet head-on the one who followed, but rather force this to be ended where it seemed right that it should be ended. So they circled back around the far side of the valley, made their way as far up the foothills of the Galiban mountains as they had the energy to spare.

George wanted no possibility that they would meet at some random mid-point. Rather, he wanted to draw his friend back, back to that place in the brush by the sandy banks of the Salinas River.

Lenny would remember that place, even with all that had occurred, even with what he had become. George had made sure to drum that hiding place into his feeble brain until it stuck like tar. If all else was burned away, that would remain. George was sure of that.

It took them several days to reach the spot, and several further encounters with pets that Lenny, when living, had not been able to help but kill, and by the time they arrived, night had already fallen. George could barely see the outlines of the place, but in his bones, he knew. This was where his friend had been reborn.

"What do we do now?" asked Jackson.

"We wait," said George. "It shouldn't be long now until he returns, until it's over."

He knelt, ran his fingers through the soil on the patch of ground where his friend had fallen.

"I don't know that I'll be able to sleep," he continued. "But I have to at least try. Why don't you take the first watch?"

George threw himself down under a sycamore tree, and closed his eyes, but even though he was exhausted, his eyelids a-twitch with fatigue, sleep would not come. Somehow beyond conscious thought he must have sensed that he should be aware of that stretch of final moments before he did what he had to do, and not pass through them unconscious. He looked at the branches above him, and then closed his eyes to think about his next step, and when he opened them, he found that he must have fallen asleep anyway, for Lenny was there, crouched beside him.

George quickly glanced over to where Jackson was supposed to be keeping watch. The fool was slumped over, having fallen asleep, instead of preparing to do to Lenny what they had done to Curley's wife. He cursed, not at Jackson, but at himself. It was too much to have asked of him, after he'd already undergone so much.

George looked back at Lenny, who sat there as if frozen. He could have been a statue in the moonlight, rather than a man—a dead man—but still a man. George could make out a wound at the base of his throat, the bullet hole not where he would have imagined it to be. He hadn't been able to look before, but now he knew for certain he must have pointed the gun down at the last instant, missing the brain completely. It had been enough to kill him. It just wasn't enough to keep him killed.

They sat there, unmoving, and in George's mind it was almost like the old days, a night like any other in a long string of nights, and he was being asked to tell him like he done before, asked this time not with words, but with silence. And he knew that he would answer that request, as he always had.

"Guys like us are the loneliest guys in the world," said George in a whisper, not because that's what he intended, but because that's all that would come out at first. "They got no family, nothing to look ahead to. But not us. No, not us. Because I got you to look after me, and you got me to look after you!"

George looked over at Jackson, his sleep unbroken by the bizarre conversation occurring so close beside him. George raised his voice, hoping to rouse the man.

"We're gonna get the jack together and get a little place," he continued. "We're gonna live off the fat of the land."

That's when Lenny would normally have punctuated the speech by clapping his hands together. George hesitated, leaving a space for the old familiar answer. He waited, looked for any movement, however imperceptible, from his old friend, but none came.

"We'll have chickens, and a vegetable patch—and rabbits. Rabbits, Lenny. Rabbits!"

George was shouting now, but no matter how loud the words came, Jackson would not move. He could see then in the moonlight that the man wasn't sleeping after all.

Arrayed around him were dozens of undead mice in various stages of decomposition, and all the other animals Lenny had in his clumsiness put down. Every watchful eye was aglow. The puppy they'd encountered earlier sat curled in Jackson's lap, its intestines draped over the man's legs like ribbons.

His neck was bent and broken, and what George had earlier taken to be a shadow from the brim of the hat pulled low over his eyes had actually once been a waterfall of blood, a waterfall now stilled. George looked back at Lenny to see a matching patch of color smeared across his face.

George stood slowly.

"I guess I'm not going to get to tell you about the rabbits no more, am I?" he said.

Lenny answered by also getting to his feet, and once he started rising, he kept on rising. George tilted his head back to look him in the face, the way he'd had to for years. He was surprised that even though it hadn't been that long, he'd already forgotten how amazingly tall Lenny had been. His friend stepped closer, but George did not retreat. There would have been no point.

And besides, all was as it should be.

He'd made a promise to Lenny's Aunt Clara, a promise to watch over him, to make sure no harm came to her addled nephew.

He'd failed. Failed them all.

Failed Lenny, and Clara . . . and Candy and Crooks, too, who'd hoped to join George and Lenny in that dream none of them would ever live to see.

And now Jackson.

And himself. Most of all, himself.

He'd made endless promises, and he failed to deliver on any of them, and whatever happened next in the remaining moments of his short, hardscrabble life, he deserved it.

Everybody in the whole damn world was scared of each other.

But George wasn't scared no more.

Not even when Lenny's teeth ripped through his stomach to what lay beneath.

George had always told Lenny that someday his friend would be living off the fat of the land.

As his life seeped from him, as he began to lose consciousness, he managed in his last moments to be strangely comforted by the sudden awareness that even though the alfalfa and chickens and rabbits would now be forever out of reach, even though he had fulfilled no other promise on this Earth, he had at least fulfilled that one.

HOME DELIVERY
Stephen King

Stephen King is the world's most famous and successful horror writer. The winner of numerous awards—including both the Horror Writers Association and World Fantasy Convention Lifetime Achievement Awards and a Medal for Distinguished Contribution to American Letters from the National Book Foundation—he lives with his wife, novelist Tabitha King, in a reputedly haunted house in Bangor, Maine.

His first novel, *Carrie*, appeared in 1974. Since then he has published a phenomenal string of bestsellers, including *Salem's Lot*, *The Shining*, *The Stand*, *Dead Zone*, *Firestarter*, *Cujo*, *Pet Sematary*, *Christine*, *It*, *Misery*, *The Dark Half*, *Needful Things*, *Rose Madder*, *The Green Mile*, *Bag of Bones*, *The Colorado Kid*, *Lisey's Story*, and *Duma Key*, to name only a few.

The author's short fiction and novellas have been collected in *Night Shift*, *Different Seasons*, *Skeleton Crew*, *Four Past Midnight*, *Nightmares and Dreamscapes*, *Hearts in Atlantis*, *Everything's Eventual*, *The Secretary of Dreams* (two volumes), *Just After Sunset: Stories*, and *Stephen King Goes to the Movies*.

King has written the nonfiction volumes *Danse Macabre*, *Nightmares in the Sky: Gargoyles and Grotesques* (with photographs by f-stop Fitzgerald), and *On Writing: A Memoir of the Craft*. He also contributes the occasional "The Pop of King" column to *Entertainment Weekly*, and in 2007 he guest-edited a volume of *The Best American Short Stories*.

Many of Stephen King's books and stories have been adapted for movies and television, most recently *1408*, *The Mist*, *Dolan's Cadillac* and *Everything's Eventual*, while his 2006 zombie novel *Cell* is being developed into a four-hour miniseries for television.

"Home Delivery" was originally published in John Skipp and Craig Spector's seminal 1989 zombie anthology *Book of the Dead*, yet, despite his prolific output, King has written surprisingly little about the walking dead during his career.

"There is an absurd element to zombies," the author claimed in a recent interview, "especially when you see a rotting corpse in a movie wearing a stewardess uniform or something. Zombies are a connection between what's funny and what's horrible, and that's potent stuff."

There's certainly nothing absurd about the powerful story that follows. But it's definitely potent stuff.

CONSIDERING THAT IT was probably the end of the world, Maddie Pace thought she was doing a good job. *Hell* of a good job. She thought, in fact, that she just might be coping with the End of Everything better than anyone else on earth. And she was *positive* she was coping better than any other *pregnant* woman on earth.

Coping.

Maddie Pace, of all people.

Maddie Pace, who sometimes couldn't sleep if, after a visit from Reverend Johnson, she spied a single speck of dust under the dining-room table. Maddie Pace, who, as Maddie Sullivan, used to drive her fiancé, Jack, crazy when she froze over a menu, debating entrees sometimes for as long as half an hour.

"Maddie, why don't you just flip a coin?" he'd asked her once after she had managed to narrow it down to a choice between the braised veal and the lamb chops, and then could get no further. "I've had five bottles of this goddam German beer already, and if you don't make up y'mind pretty damn quick, there's gonna be a drunk lobsterman *under* the table before we ever get any food *on* it!"

So she had smiled nervously, ordered the braised veal, and spent most of the ride home wondering if the chops might not have been tastier, and therefore a better bargain despite their slightly higher price.

She'd had no trouble coping with Jack's proposal of marriage, however; she'd accepted it—and him—quickly, and with tremendous relief. Following the death of her father, Maddie and her mother had lived an aimless, cloudy sort of life on Little Tall Island, off the coast of Maine. "If I wasn't around to tell them women where to squat and lean against the wheel," George Sullivan had been fond of saying while in his cups and among his friends at Fudgy's Tavern or in the back room of Prout's Barber Shop, "I don't know what'n hell they'd do."

When her father died of a massive coronary, Maddie was nineteen and minding the town library weekday evenings at a salary of $41.50 a week. Her mother minded the house—or did, that was, when George reminded her (sometimes with a good hard shot to the ear) that she had a house which needed minding.

When news of his death came, the two women had looked at each other with silent, panicky dismay, two pairs of eyes asking the same question: *What do we do now?*

Neither of them knew, but they both felt—felt strongly—that he had been right in his assessment of them: they needed him. They were just women, and they needed him to tell them not just what to do, but how to do it, as well. They didn't speak of it because it embarrassed them, but there it was—they hadn't the slightest clue as to what came next, and the idea that they were prisoners of George Sullivan's narrow ideas and expectations did not so much as cross their minds. They were not stupid women, either of them, but they *were* island women.

Money wasn't the problem; George had believed passionately in insurance, and when he dropped down dead during the tiebreaker frame of the League Bowl-Offs at Big Duke's Big Ten in Machias, his wife had come into better than a hundred thousand dollars. And island life was cheap, if you owned your place and kept your garden tended and knew how to put by your own vegetables come fall. The *problem* was having nothing to focus on. The *problem* was how the center seemed to have dropped out of their lives when George went facedown in his Island Amoco bowling shirt just over the foul line of lane nineteen (and goddam if he hadn't picked up the spare his team had needed to win, too). With George gone their lives had become an eerie sort of blur.

It's like being lost in a heavy fog, Maddie thought sometimes. *Only instead of looking for the road, or a house, or the village, or just some landmark like that lightning-struck pine out on the point, I am looking for the wheel. If I can ever find it, maybe I can tell myself to squat and lean my shoulder to it.*

At last she found her wheel: it turned out to be Jack Pace. Women marry their fathers and men their mothers, some say, and while such a broad statement can hardly be true all of the time, it was close enough for government work in Maddie's case. Her father had been looked upon by his peers with fear and admiration—"Don't fool with George Sullivan, dear," they'd say. "He'll knock the nose off your face if you so much as look at him wrong."

It was true at home, too. He'd been domineering and sometimes physically abusive, but he'd also known things to want and work for, like the Ford pick-up, the chainsaw, or those two acres that bounded their place to the south. Pop Cook's land. George Sullivan had been known to refer to Pop Cook as one armpit-stinky old bastid, but the old man's aroma didn't change the fact that there was quite a lot of good hardwood left on those two acres. Pop didn't know it because he had gone to living across the reach in 1987, when his arthritis really went to town on him, and George let it known on Little Tall that what that bastid Pop Cook didn't know wouldn't hurt him none, and furthermore, he would disjoint the man or woman that let light into the darkness of Pop's ignorance. No one did, and eventually the Sullivans got the land, and the hardwood on it. Of course the good wood was all logged off inside of three years, but George said that didn't matter a tinker's damn;

land always paid for itself in the end. That was what George said and they believed him, believed *in* him, and they worked, all three of them. He said: You got to put your shoulder to this wheel and *push* the bitch, you got to push ha'ad because she don't move easy. So that was what they did.

In those days Maddie's mother had kept a produce stand on the road from East Head, and there were always plenty of tourists who bought the vegetables she grew (which were the ones George *told* her to grow, of course), and even though they were never exactly what her mother called "the Gotrocks family," they made out. Even in years when lobstering was bad and they had to stretch their finances even further in order to keep paying off what they owed the bank on Pop Cook's two acres, they made out.

Jack Pace was a sweeter-tempered man than George Sullivan had ever thought of being, but his sweet temper only stretched so far, even so. Maddie suspected that he might get around to what was sometimes called home correction—the twisted arm when supper was cold, the occasional slap or downright paddling—in time; when the bloom was off the rose, so as to speak. There was even a part of her that seemed to expect and look forward to that. The women's magazines said marriages where the man ruled the roost were a thing of the past, and that a man who put a hard hand on a woman should be arrested for assault, even if the man in question was the woman in question's lawful wedded husband. Maddie sometimes read articles of this sort down at the beauty shop, but doubted if the women who wrote them had the slightest idea that places like the outer islands even existed. Little Tall *had* produced one writer, as a matter of fact—Selena St. George—but she wrote mostly about politics and hadn't been back to the island, except for a single Thanksgiving dinner, in years.

"I'm not going to be a lobsterman all my life, Maddie," Jack told her the week before they were married, and she believed him. A year before, when he had asked her out for the first time (she'd said yes almost before all the words could get out of his mouth, and she had blushed to the roots of her hair at the sound of her own naked eagerness), he would have said, "I *ain't* going to be a lobsterman all my life." A small change . . . but all the difference in the world. He had been going to night school three evenings a week, taking the old *Island Princess* over and back. He would be dog-tired after a day of pulling pots, but off he'd go just the same, pausing only long enough to shower off the powerful smells of lobster and brine and to gulp two No Doz with hot coffee. After a while, when she saw he really meant to stick to it, Maddie began putting up hot soup for him to drink on the ferry-ride over. Otherwise he would have had nothing but one of those nasty red hot-dogs they sold in the *Princess's* snack-bar.

She remembered agonizing over the canned soups in the store—there were so *many!* Would he want tomato? Some people didn't like tomato soup. In fact, some people *hated* tomato soup, even if you made it with milk instead of water. Vegetable soup? Turkey? Cream of chicken? Her helpless eyes roved the shelf display for nearly ten minutes before Charlene Nedeau asked if she could help her with something—only Charlene said it in a sarcastic way, and Maddie guessed she would tell all her friends at high school tomorrow, and they would giggle about it in the girls' room, knowing exactly what was wrong with her—poor mousy little Maddie Sullivan, unable to make up her mind over so simple a thing as a can *of soup.* How she had ever been able to decide to accept Jack Pace's proposal was a wonder and a marvel to all of them . . . but of course they didn't know about the wheel you had to find, and about how, once you found it, you had to have someone to tell you when to stoop and where exactly to push the damned thing.

Maddie had left the store with no soup and a throbbing headache.

When she worked up nerve enough to ask Jack what his favorite soup was, he had said: "Chicken noodle. Kind that comes in the can."

Were there any others he specially liked?

The answer was no, just chicken noodle—the kind that came in the can. That was all the soup Jack Pace needed in his life, and all the answer (on that particular subject, at least) that Maddie needed in hers. Light of step and cheerful of heart, Maddie climbed the warped wooden steps of the store the next day and bought the four cans of chicken noodle soup that were on the shelf. When she asked Bob Nedeau if he had anymore, he said he had a whole damn *case* of the stuff out back.

She bought the entire case and left him so flabbergasted that he actually carried the carton out to the truck for her and forgot all about asking why she wanted so *much*—a lapse for which his long-nosed wife and daughter took him sharply to task that evening.

"You just better believe it and never forget," Jack had said that time not long before they tied the knot (she *had* believed it, and had never forgotten). "More than a lobsterman. My dad says I'm full of shit. He says if draggin' pots was good enough for his old man, and his old man's old man and all the way back to the friggin' Garden of Eden to hear *him* tell it, it ought to be good enough for me. But it ain't—*isn't,* I mean—and I'm going to do better." His eye fell on her, and it was a stern eye, full of resolve, but it was a loving eye, full of hope and confidence, too. "More than a lobsterman is what I mean to be, and more than a lobsterman's wife is what I intend for you to be. You're going to have a house on the mainland."

"Yes, Jack."

"And I'm not going to have any friggin' Chevrolet." He drew in a deep breath and took her hands in his. "I'm going to have an *Oldsmobile.*"

He looked her dead in the eye, as if daring her to scoff at this wildly upscale ambition. She did no such thing, of course; she said yes, Jack, for the third or fourth time that evening. She had said it to him thousands of times over the year they had spent courting, and she confidently expected to say it a million times before death ended their marriage by taking one of them—or, better, both of them together. *Yes, Jack;* had there ever in the history of the world been two words which made such beautiful music when laid side by side?

"More than a friggin' lobsterman, no matter what my old man thinks or how much he laughs." He pronounced this last word in the deeply downeast way: *luffs.* "I'm going to do it, and do you know who's going to help me?"

"Yes," Maddie had responded calmly. "*I* am."

He had laughed and swept her into his arms. "You're damned tooting, my little sweetheart," he'd told her.

And so they were wed, as the fairytales usually put it, and for Maddie those first few months—months when they were greeted almost everywhere with jovial cries of "Here's the newlyweds!"—*were* a fairytale. She had Jack to lean on, Jack to help her make decisions, and that was the best of it. The most difficult household choice thrust upon her that first year was which curtains would look best in the living room—there were so *many* in the catalogue to choose from, and her mother was certainly no help. Maddie's mother had a hard time deciding between different brands of toilet paper.

Otherwise, that year consisted mostly of joy and security—the joy of loving Jack in their deep bed while the winter wind scraped over the island like the blade of a knife across a breadboard, the security of having Jack to tell her what it was they wanted, and how they were going to get it. The loving was good—so good that sometimes when she thought of him during the days her knees would feel weak and her stomach fluttery— but his way of knowing things and her growing trust in his instincts were even better. So for awhile it *was* a fairytale, yes.

Then Jack died and things started getting weird. Not just for Maddie, either.

For everybody.

. . . . .

Just before the world slid into its incomprehensible nightmare, Maddie discovered she was what her mother had always called "preg," a curt word that was like the sound you made when you had to rasp up a throatful of snot (that, at least, was how it had always sounded to Maddie). By then she and Jack had moved next to the Pulsifers on Gennesault Island, which was known simply as Jenny by its residents and those of nearby Little Tall.

She'd had one other agonizing interior debates when she missed her second period, and after four sleepless nights she made an appointment with Dr. McElwain on the mainland. Looking back, she was glad. If she'd waited to see if she was going to miss a third period, Jack would not have had even one month of joy and she would have missed the concerns and little kindnesses he had showered upon her.

Looking back—now that she was *coping*—her indecision seemed ludicrous, but her deeper heart knew that going to have the test had taken tremendous courage. She had wanted to be more convincingly sick in the mornings so she could be surer; she had longed for nausea to drag her from her dreams. She made the appointment when Jack was out at work, and she went while he was out, but there was no such thing as *sneaking* over to the mainland on the ferry; too many people from both islands saw you. Someone would mention casually to Jack that he or she had seen his wife on the *Princess* t'other day, and then Jack would want to know what it was all about, and if she'd made a mistake, he would look at her like she was a goose.

But it hadn't been a mistake; she was with child (and never mind that word sounded like someone with a bad cold trying to clear his throat), and Jack Pace had had exactly twenty-seven days to look forward to his first child before a bad swell had caught him and knocked him over the side of *My Lady-Love*, the lobster boat he had inherited from his Uncle Mike. Jack could swim, and he had popped to the surface like a cork, Dave Eamons had told her miserably, but just as he did, another heavy swell came, slewing the boat directly into him, and although Dave would say no more, Maddie had been born and brought up an island girl, and she knew: could, in fact, *hear* the hollow thud as the boat with its treacherous name smashed its way into her husband's head, letting out blood and hair and bone and perhaps the part of his brain that had made him say her name over and over again in the dark of night, when he came into her.

Dressed in a heavy hooded parka and down-filled pants and boots, Jack Pace had sunk like a stone. They had buried an empty casket in the little cemetery at the north end of Jenny Island, and the Reverend Johnson (on Jenny and Little Tall you had your choice when it came to religion: you could be a Methodist, or if that didn't suit you, you could be a lapsed Methodist) had presided over this empty coffin as he had so many others. The service ended, and at the age of twenty-two Maddie had found herself a widow with a bun in the oven and no one to tell her where the wheel was, let alone when to put her shoulder to it or how far to push it.

She thought at first she'd go back to Little Tall, back to her mother, to wait her time, but a year with Jack had given her a little perspective and she knew her mother was as lost—maybe even *more* lost—than she was herself, and that made her wonder if going back would be the right thing to do.

"Maddie," Jack told her again and again (he was dead in the world but not, it seemed, inside her head; inside her head he was as lively as any dead man could possibly get . . . or so she had thought *then)*, "the only thing you can ever decide on is not to decide."

Nor was her mother any better. They talked on the phone and Maddie waited and hoped for her mother to just *tell* her to come back home, but Mrs. Sullivan could tell no one over the age of ten anything. "Maybe you ought to come on back over here," she had said once in a tentative way, and Maddie couldn't tell if that meant *please come home* or *please don't take me up on an offer which was really just made for form's sake.* She spent long, sleepless nights trying to decide which it had been and succeeded only in confusing herself more.

Then the weirdness started, and the greatest mercy was that there was only the one small graveyard on Jenny (and so many of the graves filled with those empty coffins—a thing which had once seemed pitiful to her now seemed another blessing, a grace). There were two on Little Tall, both fairly large, and so it began to seem so much safer to stay on Jenny and wait.

She would wait and see if the world lived or died.

If it lived, she would wait for the baby.

.   .   .   .   .

And now she was, after a life of passive obedience and vague resolves that usually passed like dreams an hour or two after she got out of bed, finally *coping*. She knew that part of this was nothing more than the effect of being slammed with one massive shock after another, beginning with the death of her husband and ending with one of the last broadcasts the Pulsifers' high-tech satellite dish had picked up: a horrified young boy who had been pressed into service as a CNN reporter saying that it seemed certain that the President of the United States, the first lady, the Secretary of State, the honorable senior senator from Oregon, and the emir of Kuwait had been eaten alive in the White House East Room by zombies.

"I want to repeat this," the accidental reporter had said, the firespots of his acne standing out on his forehead and chin like stigmata. His mouth and cheeks had begun to twitch; his hands shook spastically. "I want to repeat that a bunch of corpses have just lunched up on the President and his wife and a whole lot of other political hotshots who were at the White House to eat poached salmon and cherries jubilee." Then the kid had begun to laugh maniacally and to scream *Go, Yale! Boola-boola!* at the top of his voice. At last he bolted out of the frame, leaving a CNN news-desk untenanted for the first time in Maddie's memory. She and the Pulsifers sat in dismayed silence as the news-desk disappeared and an ad for Boxcar Willie records—not available in any store, you could get this amazing collection only by dialing the 800 number currently appearing on the bottom of your screen—came on. One of little Cheyne Pulsifer's crayons was on the end table beside the chair Maddie was sitting in, and for some crazy reason she picked it up and wrote the number down on a sheet of scrap paper before Mr. Pulsifer got up and turned off the TV without a single word.

Maddie told them good night and thanked them for sharing their TV and their Jiffy Pop.

"Are you sure you're all right, Maddie dear?" Candi Pulsifer asked her for the fifth time that night, and Maddie said she was fine for the fifth time that night, that she was *coping,* and Candi said she *knew* she was, but she was welcome to the upstairs bedroom that used to be Brian's anytime she wanted. Maddie hugged Candi, kissed her cheek, declined with the most graceful thanks she could find, and was at last allowed to escape. She had walked the windy half mile back to her own house and was in her own kitchen before she realized that she still had the scrap of paper on which she had jotted the 800 number. She had dialed it, and there was nothing. No recorded voice telling her all circuits were currently busy or that the number was out of service; no wailing siren sound that indicated a line interruption; no boops or beeps or clicks or clacks. Just smooth silence. That was when Maddie knew for sure that the end had either come or was coming. When you could no longer call the 800 number and order the Boxcar Willie records that were not available in any store, when there were for the first time in her living memory no Operators Standing By, the end of the world was a foregone conclusion.

She felt her rounding stomach as she stood there by the phone on the wall in the kitchen and said it out loud for the first time, unaware that she had spoken: "It will have to be a home delivery. But that's all right, as long as you get ready and stay ready, kiddo. You have to remember that there just isn't any other way. It *has* to be a home delivery."

She waited for fear and none came.

"I can cope with this just fine," she said, and this time she heard herself and was comforted by the sureness of her own words.

A baby.

When the baby came, the end of the world would itself end.

"Eden," she said, and smiled. Her smile was sweet, the smile of a Madonna. It didn't matter how many rotting dead people (maybe Boxcar Willie among them, for all she knew) were shambling around the face of the earth.

She would have a baby, she would accomplish her home delivery, and the possibility of Eden would remain.

. . . . .

The first reports came from an Australian hamlet on the edge of the outback, a place with the memorable name of Fiddle Dee. The name of the first American town where the walking dead were reported was perhaps even more memorable: Thumper, Florida. The first story appeared in America's favorite supermarket tabloid, *Inside View*.

DEAD COME TO LIFE IN SMALL FLORIDA TOWN! the headline screamed. The story began with a recap of a film called *Night of the Living Dead*, which Maddie had never seen, and went on to mention another—*Macumba Love*—which she had also never seen. The article was accompanied by three photos. One was a still from *Night of the Living Dead*, showing what appeared to be a bunch of escapees from a loonybin standing outside an isolated farmhouse at night. One was from *Macumba Love*, showing a blonde whose bikini top appeared to be holding breasts the size of prize-winning gourds. The blonde was holding up her hands and screaming in horror at what could have been a black man in a mask. The third purported to be a picture taken in Thumper, Florida. It was a blurred, grainy shot of a person of indeterminate sex standing in front of a video arcade. The article described the figure as being "wrapped in the cerements of the grave," but it could have been someone in a dirty sheet.

No big deal. BIGFOOT RAPES CHOIR BOY last week, dead people coming back to life this week, the dwarf mass murderer next week.

No big deal, at least, until they started to come out in other places, as well. No big deal until the first news film ("You may want to ask your children to leave the room," Tom Brokaw introduced gravely) showed up on network TV, decayed monsters with naked bone showing through their dried skin, traffic accident victims, the morticians' concealing make-up sloughed away so that the ripped faces and bashed-in skulls showed, women with their hair teased into dirt-clogged beehives where worms and beetles still squirmed and crawled, their faces alternately vacuous and informed with a kind of calculating, idiotic intelligence. No big deal until the first horrible stills in an issue of *People* magazine that had been sealed in shrink-wrap and sold with an orange sticker that read NOT FOR SALE TO MINORS!

Then it was a big deal.

When you saw a decaying man still dressed in the mud-streaked remnants of the Brooks Brothers suit in which he had been buried tearing at the throat of a screaming woman in a T-shirt that read PROPERTY OF THE HOUSTON OILERS, you suddenly realized it might be a very big deal indeed.

That was when the accusations and saber rattling had started, and for three weeks the entire world had been diverted from the creatures escaping their graves like grotesque moths escaping diseased cocoons by the spectacle of the two great nuclear powers on what appeared to be an undivertible collision course.

There were no zombies in the United States, Communist Chinese television commentators declared; this was a self-serving lie to camouflage an unforgivable act of chemical warfare against the People's Republic of China, a more horrible (and deliberate) version of what had happened in Bhopal, India. Reprisals would follow if the dead comrades coming out of their graves did not fall down decently dead within ten days. All U.S. diplomatic people were expelled from the mother country and there were several incidents of American tourists being beaten to death.

The President (who would not long after become a Zombie Blue Plate Special himself) responded by becoming a pot (which he had come to resemble, having put on at least fifty pounds since his second-term election) calling a kettle black. The U.S. government, he told the American people, had incontrovertible evidence that the only walking-dead people in China had been set loose deliberately, and while the Head Panda might stand there with his slanty-eyed face hanging out, claiming there were over eight thousand lively corpses striding around in search of the ultimate collectivism, *we* had definite proof that there were less than forty. It was the *Chinese* who had committed an act—a *heinous* act—of chemical warfare, bringing loyal Americans back to life with no urge to consume anything but other loyal Americans, and if these Americans—some of whom had been good Democrats—did not lie down decently dead within the next *five* days, Red China was going to be one large slag pit.

NORAD was at DEFCON-2 when a British astronomer named Humphrey Dagbolt spotted the satellite. Or the spaceship. Or the creature. Or whatever in hell's name it was. Dagbolt was not even a professional astronomer but only an amateur star-gazer from the west of England—no one in particular, you would have said—and yet he almost certainly saved the world from some sort of thermonuclear exchange, if not flat-out atomic war. All in all not a bad week's work for a man with a deviated septum and a bad case of psoriasis.

At first it seemed that the two nose-to-nose political systems did not *want* to believe in what Dagbolt had found, even after the Royal Observatory in London had pronounced his photographs and data authentic. Finally, however, the missile silos closed and telescopes all over the world homed in, almost grudgingly, on Star Wormwood.

The joint American/Chinese space mission to investigate the unwelcome newcomer lifted off from the Lanzhou Heights less than three weeks after the first photographs had appeared in the *Guardian,* and everyone's favorite amateur astronomer was aboard, deviated septum and all. In truth, it would have been hard to have kept Dagbolt off the mission—he had become a worldwide hero, the most renowned Briton since Winston Churchill. When asked by a reporter on the day before lift-off if he was frightened, Dagbolt had brayed his oddly endearing Robert Morley laugh, rubbed the side of his truly enormous nose, and exclaimed, "Petrified, dear boy! Utterly pet-trified!"

As it turned out, he had every reason to be petrified.

They all did.

. . . . .

The final sixty-one seconds of received transmission from the *Xiaoping/Truman* were considered too horrible for release by all three governments involved, and so no formal communiqué was ever issued. It didn't matter, of course; nearly twenty thousand ham operators had been monitoring the craft, and it seemed that at least nineteen thousand of them had been rolling tape when the craft had been—well, was there really any other word for it?—invaded.

Chinese voice: Worms! It appears to be a massive ball of—

American voice: Christ! Look out! It's coming for us!

Dagbolt: Some sort of extrusion is occurring. The portside window is—

Chinese voice: Breach! Breach! To your suits, my friends! (Indecipherable gabble.)

American voice: —and appears to be eating its way in—

Female Chinese voice (Ching-Ling Soong): Oh stop it stop the eyes—

(Sound of an explosion.)

Dagbolt: Explosive decompression has occurred. I see three—er, four—dead, and there are worms . . . everywhere there are worms—

American voice: Faceplate! Faceplate! *Faceplate!*

(Screaming.)

Chinese voice: Where is my mamma? Oh dear, where is my mamma?

(Screams. Sounds like a toothless old man sucking up mashed potatoes.)

Dagbolt: The cabin is full of worms—what appear to be worms, at any rate—which is to say that they really *are* worms, one realizes—that have apparently extruded themselves from the main satellite—what we took to be—which is to say one means—the cabin is full of floating body parts. These space-worms apparently excrete some sort of acid—

(Booster rockets fired at this point; duration of the burn is 7.2 seconds. This may have been an attempt to escape or possibly to ram the central object. In either case, the maneuver did not work. It seems likely that the blast-chambers themselves were clogged with worms and Captain Lin Yang—or whichever officer was then in charge—believed an explosion of the fuel tanks themselves to be imminent as a result of the clog. Hence the shutdown.)

American voice: Oh my Christ they're in my head, *they're eating my fuckin' br*—

(Static.)

Dagbolt: I believe that prudence dictates a strategic retreat to the aft storage compartment; the rest of the crew is dead. No question about that. Pity. Brave bunch. Even that fat American who kept rooting around in his nose. But in another sense I don't think—

(Static.)

Dagbolt: —dead after all because Ching-Ling Soong—or rather, Ching-Ling Soong's severed head, one means to say—just floated past me, and her eyes were open and blinking. She appeared to recognize me, and to—

(Static.)

Dagbolt: —keep you—

(Explosion. Static.)

Dagbolt: —around me. I repeat, all around me. Squirming things. They—I say, does anyone know if—

(Dagbolt, screaming and cursing, then just screaming. Sound of toothless old man again.)

(Transmission ends.)

The *Xiaoping/Truman* exploded three seconds later. The extrusion from the rough ball nicknamed Star Wormwood had been observed from better than three hundred telescopes earth-side during the short and rather pitiful conflict. As the final sixty-one seconds of transmission began, the craft began to be obscured by something that certainly *looked* like worms. By the end of the final transmission, the craft itself could not be seen at all—only the squirming mass of things that had attached themselves to it. Moments after the final explosion, a weather satellite snapped a single picture of floating debris, some of which was almost certainly chunks of the worm-things. A severed human leg clad in a Chinese space suit floating among them was a good deal easier to identify.

And in a way, none of it even mattered. The scientists and political leaders of both countries knew exactly where Star Wormwood was located: above the expanding hole in earth's ozone layer. It was sending something down from there, and it was not Flowers by Wire.

Missiles came next. Star Wormwood jigged easily out of their way and then returned to its place over the hole.

On the Pulsifers' satellite-assisted TV, more dead people got up and walked, but now there was a crucial change. In the beginning the zombies had only bitten living people who got too close, but in the weeks before the Pulsifers' high-tech Sony started showing only broad bands of snow, the dead folks started *trying* to get close to the living folks.

They had, it seemed, decided they *liked* what they were biting.

The final effort to destroy the thing was made by the United States. The President approved an attempt to destroy Star Wormwood with a number of orbiting nukes, stalwartly ignoring his previous statements that America had never put atomic SDI weapons in orbit and never would. Everyone else ignored them, as well. Perhaps they were too busy praying for success.

It was a good idea, but not, unfortunately, a workable one. Not a single missile from a single SDI orbiter fired. This was a total of twenty-four flat-out failures.

So much for modern technology.

. . . . .

And then, after all these shocks on earth and in heaven, there was the business of the one little graveyard right here on Jenny. But even that didn't seem to count much for Maddie because, after all, she had not been there. With the end of civilization now clearly at hand and the island cut off—*thankfully* cut off, in the opinion of the residents—from the rest of the world, old ways had reasserted themselves with unspoken but inarguable force. By then they all knew what was going to happen; it was only a question of when. That, and being ready when it did.

Women were excluded.

. . . . .

It was Bob Daggett, of course, who drew up the watch roster. That was only right, since Bob had been head selectman on Jenny for about a thousand years. The day after the death of the President (the thought of him and the first lady wandering witlessly through the streets of Washington, D.C., gnawing on human arms and legs like people eating chicken legs at a picnic was not mentioned; it was a little much to bear, even if the bastid and his blonde wife *were* Democrats), Bob Daggett called the first men-only Town Meeting on Jenny since sometime before the Civil War. Maddie wasn't there, but she heard. Dave Eamons told her all she needed to know.

"You men all know the situation," Bob said. He looked as yellow as a man with jaundice, and people remembered his daughter, the one still living at home on the island, was only one of four. The other three were other places . . . which was to say, on the mainland.

But hell, if it came down to that, they *all* had folks on the mainland.

"We got one boneyard here on Jenny," Bob continued, "and nothin' ain't happened there yet, but that don't mean nothin' *will*. Nothin' ain't happened yet lots of places . . . but it seems like once it starts, nothin' turns to somethin' pretty goddam quick."

There was a rumble of assent from the men gathered in the grammar-school gymnasium, which was the only place big enough to hold them. There were about seventy of them in all, ranging in age from Johnny Crane, who had just turned eighteen, to Bob's great-uncle Frank, who was eighty, had a glass eye, and chewed tobacco. There was no spittoon in the gym, of course, so Frank Daggett had brought an empty mayonnaise jar to spit his juice into. He did so now.

"Git down to where the cheese binds, Bobby," he said. "You ain't got no office to run for, and time's a-wastin'."

There was another rumble of agreement, and Bob Daggett flushed. Somehow his great-uncle always managed to make him look like an ineffectual fool, and if there was anything in the world he hated worse than looking like an ineffectual fool, it was being called Bobby. He owned property, for Chrissake! And he *supported* the old fart—bought him his goddam chew!

But these were not things he could say; old Frank's eyes were like pieces of flint.

"Okay," Bob said curtly. "Here it is. We want twelve men to watch. I'm gonna set a roster in just a couple minutes. Four-hour shifts."

"I can stand watch a helluva lot longer'n four hours!" Matt Arsenault spoke up, and Davey told Maddie that Bob said after the meeting that no welfare-slacker like Matt Arsenault would have had the nerve to speak up like that in a meeting of his betters if that old man hadn't called him Bobby, like he was a kid instead of a man three months shy of his fiftieth birthday, in front of all the island men.

"Maybe you can 'n' maybe you can't," Bob said, "but we got plenty of warm bodies, and nobody's gonna fall asleep on sentry duty."

"I ain't gonna—"

"I didn't say *you,*" Bob said, but the way his eyes rested on Matt Arsenault suggested that he might have *meant* him. "This is no kid's game. Sit down and shut up."

Matt Arsenault opened his mouth to say something more, then looked around at the other men—including old Frank Daggett—and wisely held his peace.

"If you got a rifle, bring it when it's your trick," Bob continued. He felt a little better with Arsenault more or less back in his place. "Unless it's a twenty-two, that is. If you ain't got somethin' bigger'n that, come 'n' get one here."

"I didn't know the school kep a supply of 'em handy," Cal Partridge said, and there was a ripple of laughter.

"It don't now, but it will," Bob said, "because every man jack of you with more than one rifle bigger than a twenty-two is gonna bring it here." He looked at John Wirley, the school principal. "Okay if we keep em in your office, John?"

Wirley nodded. Beside him, Reverend Johnson was dry-washing his hands in a distraught way.

"Shit on that," Orrin Campbell said. "I got a wife and two kids at home. Am I s'posed to leave 'em with nothin' to defend themselves with if a bunch of cawpses come for an early Thanksgiving dinner while I'm on watch?"

"If we do our job at the boneyard, none will," Bob replied stonily. "Some of you got handguns. We don't want none of those. Figure out which women can shoot and which can't and give 'em the pistols. We'll put 'em together in bunches."

"They can play Beano," old Frank cackled, and Bob smiled, too. That was more like it, by the Christ.

"Nights, we're gonna want trucks posted around so we got plenty of light." He looked over at Sonny Dotson, who ran Island Amoco, the only gas station on Jenny. Sonny's main business wasn't gassing cars and trucks—shit, there was no place much on the island to drive, and you could get your go ten cents cheaper on the mainland—but filling up lobster boats and the motorboats he ran out of his jackleg marina in the summer. "You gonna supply the gas, Sonny?"

"Am I gonna get cash slips?"

"You're gonna get your ass saved," Bob said. "When things get back to normal— if they ever do—I guess you'll get what you got coming."

Sonny looked around, saw only hard eyes, and shrugged. He looked a bit sullen, but in truth he looked more confused than anything, Davey told Maddie the next day.

"Ain't got n'more'n four hunnert gallons of gas," he said. "Mostly diesel."

"There's five generators on the island," Burt Dorfman said (when Burt spoke everyone listened; as the only Jew on the island, he was regarded as a creature both quixotic and fearsome, like an oracle that works about half the time). "They all run on diesel. I can rig lights if I have to."

Low murmurs. If Burt said he could do it, he could. He was a Jewish electrician, and there was a feeling on the outer islands, unarticulated but powerful, that that was the best kind.

"We're gonna light that graveyard up like a friggin' stage," Bob said.

Andy Kingsbury stood up. "I heard on the news that sometimes you can shoot one of them things in the head and it'll stay down, and sometimes it won't."

"We've got chainsaws," Bob said stonily, "and what won't stay dead . . . why, we can make sure it won't move too far alive."

And, except for making out the duty roster, that was pretty much that.

. . . . .

Six days and nights passed and the sentries posted around the little graveyard on Jenny were starting to feel a wee bit silly ("I dunno if I'm standin' guard or pullin' my pud," Orrin Campbell said one afternoon as a dozen men stood around the cemetery gate, playing Liars' Poker) when it happened . . . and when it happened, it happened fast.

Dave told Maddie that he heard a sound like the wind wailing in the chimney on a gusty night, and then the gravestone marking the final resting place of Mr. and Mrs. Fournier's boy Michael, who had died of leukemia at seventeen (bad go, that had been, him being their only child and them being such nice people and all), fell over. A moment later a shredded hand with a moss-caked Yarmouth Academy class ring on one finger rose out of the ground, shoving through the tough grass. The third finger had been torn off in the process.

The ground heaved like (like the belly of a pregnant woman getting ready to drop her load, Dave almost said, and hastily reconsidered) a big wave rolling into a close cove, and then the boy himself sat up, only he wasn't anything you could really recognize, not after almost two years in the ground. There were little splinters of wood sticking out of what was left of his face, Davey said, and pieces of shiny blue cloth in the draggles of his hair. "That was coffin-linin'," Davey told her, looking down at his restlessly twining hands. "I know that as well's I know m'own name." He paused, then added: "Thank Christ Mike's dad din't have that trick."

Maddie had nodded.

The men on guard, bullshit-scared as well as revolted, opened fire on the reanimated corpse of the former high-school chess champion and All-Star second baseman, tearing him to shreds. Other shots, fired in wild panic, blew chips off his marble gravestone, and it was just luck that the armed men had been loosely grouped together when the festivities commenced; if they had been divided up into two wings, as Bob Daggett had originally intended, they would very likely have slaughtered each other. As it was, not a single islander was hurt, although Bud Meechum found a rather suspicious-looking hole torn in the sleeve of his shirt the next day.

"Prob'ly wa'ant nothin' but a blackberry thorn, just the same," he said. "There's an almighty lot of 'em out at that end of the island, you know." No one would dispute that, but the black smudges around the hole made his frightened wife think that his shirt had been torn by a thorn with a pretty large caliber.

The Fournier kid fell back, most of him lying still, other parts of him still twitching . . . but by then the whole graveyard seemed to be rippling, as if an earthquake were going on there—but *only* there, no place else.

Just about an hour before dusk, this had happened.

Burt Dorfman had rigged up a siren to a tractor battery, and Bob Daggett flipped the switch. Within twenty minutes, most of the men in town were at the island cemetery.

Goddam good thing, too, Dave Eamons said, because a few of the deaders almost got away. Old Frank Daggett, still two hours from the heart attack that would carry him off just as the excitement was dying down, organized the new men so they wouldn't shoot each other, either, and for the final ten minutes the Jenny boneyard sounded like Bull Run. By the end of the festivities, the powder smoke was so thick that some men choked on it. The sour smell of vomit was almost heavier than the smell of gunsmoke . . . it was sharper, too, and lingered longer.

. . . . .

And still some of them wriggled and squirmed like snakes with broken backs—the fresher ones, for the most part.

"Burt," Frank Daggett said. "You got them chainsaws?"

"I got 'em," Burt said, and then a long, buzzing sound came out of his mouth, a sound like a cicada burrowing its way into tree bark, as he dry-heaved. He could not take his eyes from the squirming corpses, the overturned gravestones, the yawning pits from which the dead had come. "In the truck."

"Gassed up?" Blue veins stood out on Frank's ancient, hairless skull.

"Yeah." Burt's hand was over his mouth. "I'm sorry."

"Work y'fuckin' gut all you want," Frank said briskly, "but toddle off 'n' get them saws while you do. And you . . . you . . . you . . . you . . ."

The last "you" was his grandnephew Bob.

"I can't, Uncle Frank," Bob said sickly. He looked around and saw five or six of his friends and neighbors lying crumpled in the tall grass. They had not died; they had swooned. Most of them had seen their own relatives rise out of the ground. Buck Harkness over there lying by an aspen tree had been part of the crossfire that had cut his late wife to ribbons; he had fainted after observing her decayed, worm-riddled brains exploding from the back of her head in a grisly grey splash. "I can't. I c—"

Frank's hand, twisted with arthritis but as hard as stone, cracked across his face.

"You can and you will, chummy," he said.

Bob went with the rest of the men.

Frank Daggett watched them grimly and rubbed his chest, which had begun to send cramped throbs of pain all the way down his left arm to the elbow. He was old but he wasn't stupid, and he had a pretty good idea what those pains were, and what they meant.

. . . . .

"He told me he thought he was gonna have a blow-out, and he tapped his chest when he said it," Dave went on, and placed his hand on the swell of muscle over his own left nipple to demonstrate.

Maddie nodded to show she understood.

"He said, 'If anything happens to me before this mess is cleaned up, Davey, you and Burt and Orrin take over. Bobby's a good boy, but I think he may have lost his guts for at least a little while . . . and you know, sometimes when a man loses his guts, they don't come back.'"

Maddie nodded again, thinking how grateful she was—how very, very grateful—

that she was not a man.

"So then we did it," Dave said. "We cleaned up the mess."

Maddie nodded a third time, but this time she must have made some sound, because Dave told her he would stop if she couldn't bear it; he would gladly stop.

"I can bear it," she said quietly. "You might be surprised how much I can bear, Davey." He looked at her quickly, curiously, when she said that, but Maddie had averted her eyes before he could see the secret in them.

. . . . .

Dave didn't know the secret because no one on Jenny knew. That was the way Maddie wanted it, and the way she intended to keep it. There had been a time when she had, perhaps, in the blue darkness of her shock, pretended to be coping. And then something happened that *made* her cope. Four days before the island cemetery vomited up its corpses, Maddie Pace was faced with a simple choice: cope or die.

She had been sitting in the living room, drinking a glass of the blueberry wine she and Jack had put up during August of the previous year—a time that now seemed impossibly distant—and doing something so trite it was laughable. She was Knitting Little Things. Booties, in fact. But what else *was* there to do? It seemed that no one would be going across the reach to the Wee Folks store at the Ellsworth Mall for quite some time.

Something had thumped against the window.

A bat, she thought, looking up. Her needles paused in her hands, though. It seemed that something bigger had moved jerkily out there in the windy dark. The oil lamp was turned up high and kicking too much reflection off the panes for her to be sure. She reached to turn it down and the thump came again. The panes shivered. She heard a little pattering of dried putty falling on the sash. Jack had been planning to re-glaze all the windows this fall, she remembered, and then thought, *Maybe that's what he came back for.* That was crazy, he was on the bottom of the ocean, but . . .

She sat with her head cocked to one side, her knitting now motionless in her hands. A little pink bootie. She had already made a blue set. All of a sudden it seemed she could hear so *much.* The wind. The faint thunder of surf on Cricket Ledge. The house making little groaning sounds, like an elderly woman making herself comfortable in bed. The tick of the clock in the hallway.

"Jack?" she asked the silent night that was now no longer silent. "Is it you, dear?" Then the living-room window burst inward and what came through was not really Jack but a skeleton with a few moldering strings of flesh hanging from it.

His compass was still around his neck. It had grown a beard of moss.

. . . . .

The wind flapped the curtains in a cloud above him as he sprawled, then got up on his hands and knees and looked at her from black sockets in which barnacles had grown.

He made grunting sounds. His fleshless mouth opened and the teeth chomped down. He was hungry . . . but this time chicken noodle soup would not serve. Not even the kind that came in the can.

Grey stuff hung and swung beyond those dark barnacle-encrusted holes, and she realized she was looking at whatever remained of Jack's brain. She sat where she was, frozen, as he got up and came toward her, leaving black kelpy tracks on the carpet, fingers reaching. He stank of salt and fathoms. His hands stretched. His teeth chomped mechanically up and down. Maddie saw he was wearing the remains of the black-and-red-checked shirt she had bought him at L. L. Bean's last Christmas. It had cost the earth, but he had said again and again how warm it was, and look how well it had lasted, how much of it was left even after being under water all this time.

The cold cobwebs of bone which were all that remained of his fingers touched her throat before the baby kicked in her stomach—for the first time—and her shocked horror, which she had believed to be calmness, fled, and she drove one of the knitting needles into the thing's eye.

Making horrid thick choking noises that sounded like the suck of a swill pump, he staggered backward, clawing at the needle, while the half-made pink bootie swung in front of the cavity where his nose had been. She watched as a sea slug squirmed from that nasal cavity and onto the bootie, leaving a trail of slime behind it.

Jack fell over the end table she'd gotten at a yard sale just after they had been married—she hadn't been able to make her mind up about it, had been in agonies about it, until Jack finally said either she was going to buy it for their living room or he was going to give the biddy running the sale twice what she was asking for the goddam thing and then bust it up into firewood with—

—with the—

He struck the floor and there was a brittle, cracking sound as his febrile, fragile form broke in two. The right hand tore the knitting needle, slimed with decaying brain tissue, from his eye-socket and tossed it aside. His top half crawled toward her. His teeth gnashed steadily together.

She thought he was trying to grin, and then the baby kicked again and she remembered how uncharacteristically tired and out of sorts he'd sounded at Mabel Henratty's yard-sale that day: *Buy it, Maddie, for Chrissake! I'm tired! Want to go home and get m'dinner! If you don't get a move on, I'll give the old bat twice what she wants and bust it up for firewood with my—*

Cold, dank hand clutching her ankle; polluted teeth poised to bite. To kill her and kill the baby. She tore loose, leaving him with only her slipper, which he chewed on and then spat out.

When she came back from the entry, he was crawling mindlessly into the kitchen—at least the top half of him was—with the compass dragging on the tiles. He looked up at the sound of her, and there seemed to be some idiot question in those black eye-sockets before she brought the axe whistling down, cleaving his skull as he had threatened to cleave the end table.

His head fell in two pieces, brains dribbling across the tile like spoiled oatmeal, brains that squirmed with slugs and gelatinous sea worms, brains that smelled like a woodchuck exploded with gassy decay in a high-summer meadow.

Still his hands clashed and clittered on the kitchen tiles, making a sound like beetles.

She chopped . . . chopped . . . chopped.

At last there was no more movement.

A sharp pain rippled across her midsection and for a moment she was gripped by terrible panic: *Is it a miscarriage? Am I going to have a miscarriage?* But the pain left and the baby kicked again, more strongly than before.

She went back into the living room, carrying an axe that now smelled like tripe.

His legs had somehow managed to stand.

"Jack, I loved you so much," she said, "but this isn't you." She brought the axe down in a whistling arc that split him at the pelvis, sliced the carpet, and drove deep into the solid oak floor beneath.

The legs separated, trembled wildly for almost five minutes, and then began to grow quiet. At last even the toes stopped twitching.

She carried him down to the cellar piece by piece, wearing her oven gloves and wrapping each piece with the insulating blankets Jack had kept in the shed and which she had never thrown away—he and the crew threw them over the pots on cold days so the lobsters wouldn't freeze.

Once a severed hand closed upon her wrist. She stood still and waited, her heart drumming heavily in her chest, and at last it loosened again. And that was the end of it. The end of *him.*

There was an unused cistern, polluted, below the house—Jack had been meaning to fill it in. Maddie slid the heavy concrete cover aside so that its shadow lay on the earthen floor like a partial eclipse and then threw the pieces of him down, listening to the splashes. When everything was gone, she worked the heavy cover back into place.

"Rest in peace," she whispered, and an interior voice whispered back that her husband was resting in *pieces,* and then she began to cry, and her cries turned to hysterical shrieks, and she pulled at her hair and tore at her breasts until they were bloody, and she thought, *I am insane, this is what it's like to be insa—*

But before the thought could be completed, she had fallen down in a faint, and the faint became a deep sleep, and the next morning she felt all right.

She would never tell, though.

Never.

. . . . .

"I can bear it," she told Dave Eamons again, thrusting aside the image of the knitting needle with the bootie swinging from the end of it jutting out of the kelp-slimed eye-socket of the thing which had once been her husband, and co-creator of the child in her womb. "Really."

So he told her, perhaps because he had to tell someone or go mad, but he glossed over the worst parts. He told her that they had chainsawed the corpses that absolutely refused to return to the land of the dead, but he did not tell her that some parts had continued to squirm—hands with no arms attached to them clutching mindlessly, feet divorced from their legs digging at the bullet-chewed earth of the graveyard as if trying to run away—and that these parts had been doused with diesel fuel and set afire. Maddie did not have to be told this part. She had seen the pyre from the house.

Later, Gennesault Island's one firetruck had turned its hose on the dying blaze, although there wasn't much chance of the fire spreading, with a brisk easterly blowing the sparks off Jenny's seaward edge. When there was nothing left but a stinking, tallowy lump (and still there were occasional bulges in this mass, like twitches in a tired muscle), Matt Arsenault fired up his old D-9 Caterpillar—above the nicked steel blade and under his faded pillowtick engineer's cap, Matt's face had been as white as cottage cheese—and plowed the whole hellacious mess under.

. . . . .

The moon was coming up when Frank took Bob Daggett, Dave Eamons, and Carl Partridge aside. It was Dave he spoke to.

"I knew it was coming, and here it is," he said.

"What are you talking about, Unc?" Bob asked.

"My heart," Frank said. "Goddam thing has thrown a rod."

"Now, Uncle Frank—"

"Never mind Uncle Frank this n Uncle Frank that," the old man said. "I ain't got time to listen to you play fiddlyfuck on the mouth-organ. Seen half my friends go the same way. It ain't no day at the races, but it could be worse; beats hell out of getting whacked with the cancer-stick.

"But now there's this other sorry business to mind, and all I got to say on that subject is, when I go down I intend to *stay* down. Cal, stick that rifle of yours in my left ear. Dave, when I raise my left arm, you sock yours into my armpit. And Bobby, you put yours right over my heart. I'm gonna say the Lord's Prayer, and when I hit amen, you three fellows are gonna pull your triggers at the same time."

"Uncle Frank—" Bob managed. He was reeling on his heels.

"I told you not to start in on that," Frank said. "And don't you *dare* faint on me, you friggin' pantywaist. Now get your country butt over here."

Bob did.

Frank looked around at the three men, their faces as white as Matt Arsenault's had been when he drove the 'dozer over men and women he had known since he was a kid in short pants and Buster Browns.

"Don't you boys frig this up," Frank said. He was speaking to all of them, but his eye might have been particularly trained on his grandnephew. "If you feel like maybe you're gonna backslide, just remember I'd'a done the same for any of you."

"Quit with the speech," Bob said hoarsely. "I love you, Uncle Frank."

"You ain't the man your father was, Bobby Daggett, but I love you, too," Frank said calmly, and then, with a cry of pain, he threw his left hand up over his head like a guy in New York who has to have a cab in a rip of a hurry, and started in with his last prayer. "Our Father who art in Heaven—*Christ*, that hurts!—hallow'd be Thy name—oh, son of a *gun!*—Thy kingdom come, Thy will be done, on earth as it . . . as it . . ."

Frank's upraised left arm was wavering wildly now. Dave Eamons, with his rifle socked into the old geezer's armpit, watched it as carefully as a logger would watch a big tree that looked like it meant to do evil and fall the wrong way. Every man on the island was watching now. Big beads of sweat had formed on the old man's pallid face. His lips had pulled back from the even, yellowy-white of his Roebuckers, and Dave had been able to smell the Polident on his breath.

". . . as it is in Heaven!" the old man jerked out. "Lead us not into temptation butdeliverusfromeviloshitonitforeverandeverAMEN!"

All three of them fired, and both Cal Partridge and Bob Daggett fainted, but Frank never did try to get up and walk.

Frank Daggett had meant to *stay* dead, and that was just what he did.

· · · · ·

Once Dave started that story he had to go on with it, and so he cursed himself for ever starting. He'd been right the first time; it was no story for a pregnant woman.

But Maddie had kissed him and told him she thought he had done wonderfully, and that Frank Daggett had done wonderfully, too. Dave went out feeling a little dazed, as if he had just been kissed on the cheek by a woman he had never met before.

In a very real sense, that was true.

She watched him go down the path to the dirt track that was one of Jenny's two roads and turn left. He was weaving a little in the moonlight, weaving with tiredness, she thought, but reeling with shock, as well. Her heart went out to him . . . to all of them. She had wanted to tell Dave she loved him and kiss him squarely on the mouth instead of just skimming his cheek with her lips, but he might have taken the wrong meaning from something like that, even though he was bone-weary and she was almost five months pregnant.

But she *did* love him, loved *all* of them, because they had gone through hell in order to make this little lick of land forty miles out in the Atlantic safe for her.

And safe for her baby.

"It will be a home delivery," she said softly as Dave went out of sight behind the dark hulk of the Pulsifers' satellite dish. Her eyes rose to the moon. "It will be a home delivery . . . and it will be fine."

ABOUT THE EDITOR

Stephen Jones

Stephen Jones is the winner of three World Fantasy Awards, four Horror Writers Association Bram Stoker Awards, and three International Horror Guild Awards, and is an eighteen-time recipient of the British Fantasy Award and a Hugo Award nominee. A former television producer/director and genre movie publicist and consultant (including the first three Hellraiser movies, *Night Life*, *Nightbreed*, *Split Second*, *Mind Ripper*, and *Last Gasp*, among others), he is the co-editor of *Horror: 100 Best Books*, *Horror: Another 100 Best Books*, *The Best Horror from Fantasy Tales*, *Gaslight & Ghosts*, *Now We Are Sick*, *H. P. Lovecraft's Book of Horror*, *The Anthology of Fantasy & the Supernatural*, *Secret City: Strange Tales of London*, *Great Ghost Stories*, *Tales to Freeze the Blood: More Great Ghost Stories*, and the Dark Terrors, Dark Voices, and Fantasy Tales series. He has written *Coraline: A Visual Companion*, *Stardust: The Visual Companion*, *Creepshows: The Illustrated Stephen King Movie Guide*, *The Essential Monster Movie Guide*, *The Illustrated Vampire Movie Guide*, *The Illustrated Dinosaur Movie Guide*, *The Illustrated Frankenstein Movie Guide*, and *The Illustrated Werewolf Movie Guide*, and has compiled The Mammoth Book of Best New Horror series, *The Mammoth Book of Terror*, *The Mammoth Book of Vampires*, *The Mammoth Book of Zombies*, *The Mammoth Book of Werewolves*, *The Mammoth Book of Frankenstein*, *The Mammoth Book of Dracula*, *The Mammoth Book of Vampire Stories by Women*, *The Mammoth Book of New Terror*, *The Mammoth Book of Monsters*, *Shadows Over Innsmouth*, *Weird Shadows Over Innsmouth*, *Dark Detectives*, *Dancing with the Dark*, *Dark of the Night*, *White of the Moon*, *Keep Out the Night*, *By Moonlight Only*, *Don't Turn Out the Light*, *H. P. Lovecraft's Book of the Supernatural*, *Travellers in Darkness*, *Summer Chills*, *Exorcisms and Ecstasies* by Karl Edward Wagner, *The Vampire Stories of R. Chetwynd-Hayes*, *Phantoms and Fiends* and *Frights and Fancies* by R. Chetwynd-Hayes, *James Herbert: By Horror Haunted*, *Basil Copper: A Life in Books*, *Necronomicon: The Best Weird Tales of H. P. Lovecraft*, *The Complete Chronicles of Conan* and *Conan's Brethren* by Robert E. Howard, *The Emperor of Dreams: The Lost Worlds of Clark Ashton Smith*, *Sea-Kings of Mars and Otherworldly Stories* by Leigh Brackett, *The Mark of the Beast and Other Fantastical Tales* by Rudyard Kipling, *Clive Barker's A-Z of Horror*, *Clive Barker's Shadows in Eden*, *Clive Barker's The Nightbreed Chronicles*, and the *Hellraiser Chronicles*. A Guest of Honor at the 2002 World

Fantasy Convention in Minneapolis, Minnesota, and the 2004 World Horror Convention in Phoenix, Arizona, he has been a guest lecturer at UCLA, London's Kingston University and St. Mary's University College. You can visit his web site at www.stephenjoneseditor. com. He lives in London, England.